Matteo stayed behind her, following her from roo...

"Phoebe… Ms. Ga... ... ... the job?"

She could hardly sp... ... ... inter room, there were so many thoughts clambering in her brain about how gorgeous she could make this place that she could hardly form words. Her dream job. The job that could change her whole career. A chance to pay off her mother's medical bills. A chance to move forward. A chance to pull herself out of the fog that had hung around her for the last few years.

"Phoebe." His voice grew sharp and he gave her arm a pull, tugging her around to face him. Her hands rested on his upper arms. She couldn't help herself. She almost wanted to give him a kiss on the cheek. She let out a laugh.

"Do I want the job? Absolutely. Now I've seen it, this place is mine. Matteo, I'm going to do such a good job, you're never going to want to let me go."

It was the briefest of seconds. A wash of sadness seemed to sweep his face. A whole host of something she really didn't understand. But as soon as it had appeared, the shutters came down in his eyes again. Matteo Bianchi had the perfect mask. The perfect face for business.

The edges of his lips curved upward. For the first time since she'd met him, the tension in his shoulders actually looked as if it disappeared a little. "Phoebe, a quarter of a million dollars for four weeks' work, and I *will* let you go."

THE ITALIAN BILLIONAIRE'S NEW YEAR BRIDE

BY
SCARLET WILSON

First Published in Great Britain 2018
By Mills & Boon, an imprint of HarperCollins*Publishers*
1 London Bridge Street, London, SE1 9GF

© 2018 Scarlet Wilson

ISBN: 978-0-263-93633-9

23-0118

MIX
Paper from
responsible sources
FSC™ C007454
FSC
www.fsc.org

paper to ensure

Scarlet Wilson writes for both Mills & Boon Cherish and Medical Romance. She lives on the west coast of Scotland with her fiancé and their two sons. She loves to hear from readers and can be reached via her website, www.scarlet-wilson.com.

This book is dedicated to my mom and dad, Joanne and John Wilson, for their continued support of all my writing endeavors and all the help they give me with my boys, Elliott and Rhys.

CHAPTER ONE

THE SHRILL RING of the phone invaded her dream just as she was about to save the world with Hugh Jackman. Phoebe stuck her hand out from under the snuggly white duvet and blindly felt around the bedside table as her brain tried to orientate her to time and day. She'd just been about to remove Hugh's shirt...all in the name of saving the world, of course.

After a few fumbles, she finally found the phone and pulled it under the duvet next to her ear. "Phoebe Gates." She winced. The phone was cold, much like the air outside her duvet. New York had spent the last few days covered in a snowstorm and her boiler was behaving like a temperamental teenager.

"Ms. Gates, how would you like to earn a quarter of a million dollars?"

The voice was smooth. Italian. Rich and deep with a timbre she didn't recognize. It was like being smothered in melted chocolate.

"Wh...what?" She snuggled further down under the duvet. Maybe she was still sleeping. Maybe this was all just part of the dream.

"I said how would you like to earn a quarter of a million dollars?"

Phoebe frowned and rolled onto her back. "That would be wonderful."

"Are you free?"

"Excuse me?"

"Are you free for the next month?"

Her brain started to shift gear. "Hey, wait a minute. You're one of those creepy callers, aren't you? Well, you picked the wrong girl. There's no way—"

"Ms. Gates," the voice interrupted her with a hint of impatience but Phoebe had finally started to wake up.

"Well, if you're not a creepy caller you're one of those scam artists. Don't tell me—you just need the details of my checking account and you'll get the money right to me."

She pushed herself up in the bed, wincing at the bright white light everywhere. Snow just seemed to reflect snow. "Do you know what day it is?" She turned to her clock, "And what *time* it is?" She ran her fingers through her thick tangled curls. Thank goodness there was no mirror around. She was definitely the "before" of some kind of wonder conditioner commercial. "It's Boxing Day. It's eight a.m. Haven't you heard of the word *Christmas*?"

There was a loud impatient sigh at the other end of the phone. "Ms. Gates, are you available in the next few weeks or not?"

She was definitely waking up now. Arrogant. He'd invaded the best dream in the world, ruined her lazy morning and he thought he could be snarky?

"That depends entirely who I'm talking to and what you're talking about. You haven't seemed to introduce yourself. In my world, we call those bad manners."

Silence at the end of the phone. Good. Maybe Hugh Jackman was still waiting for her.

"Apologies, Ms. Gates. You're right. My grand-mother is currently spinning in her grave and slapping the back of my head."

This time there was almost an edge of humor in his voice.

"Matteo Bianchi. I have a house—two houses in fact—that I need some work done on. I need them dressed and ready to sell in a few weeks."

Work. This really was work. But she couldn't help herself. "And you had to phone me at eight a.m. on Boxing Day morning?"

"Christmas Day is over. I don't like to waste time. Are you available, or not?"

He was getting snarky again. Phoebe shifted position in her bed and looked out at the falling snow. She'd planned on going to the sales. But braving the snow, as well as the chaos of the crowded shops, was slipping further down her list of priorities.

"Where are the houses?" she asked.

"The first is in the Hamptons," he said quickly. "Southampton, to be exact."

She felt her heart rate quicken. The Hamptons. Million-dollar houses with million-dollar budgets. The two things she'd always dreamed of. Particularly as her mother's medical costs mounted.

She tried to stop her voice squeaking. "And the second?" How much had he offered to pay?

"Rome." Her heart plummeted. Rome. An airplane ride away. Probably more than one airplane. Her skin prickled instantly and it wasn't the cold.

"Oh." It was the best response she could do.

"I'd need you to start straight away. I'll make sure you have a company credit card to pay for any work or items that you need."

She hadn't found her voice yet. Her heart was clamouring against her chest wall. Rome. How could she go to Rome?

"Ms. Gates? Are you still there?"

"Yes. The Hamptons is fine. I can look at the house whenever suits. As for the house in Rome—that might be more of an issue."

"Why do you need to see the house?" It didn't matter she hadn't met Mr. Bianchi yet, she could almost picture him frowning.

"I always look over any house before I agree to dress it for sale." He didn't mention the Rome comment.

There was another sigh.

Her curiosity was sparked. She'd never heard of Matteo Bianchi and, with an accent like that, if she'd met him before, she could guarantee she'd remember.

"Fine. I'll pick you up in an hour."

"What?" She sat bolt upright in the bed.

"You want to see the house? I'll pick you up in an hour and you can see the house."

She was stunned. One minute she was in the middle of a blissful dream—next she was working on Boxing Day.

Something pricked in her brain. "Mr. Bianchi, where did you hear about me?"

"I saw the apartment you dressed near Central Park." He paused for a second as her brain caught up. "I liked it."

She couldn't help but smile. "In Madison Court?" She'd loved that job. The apartment belonged to an old sea captain. Other interior designers had suggested ripping the apartment bare, painting all the walls white and tiling all the floors. She'd been the only designer to suggest embracing the whole essence of Captain

Monaghan's life. She'd scaled back some of the clutter and enhanced the whole seafaring lifestyle by focusing on a few key pieces. A ship's wheel. A handcrafted lighthouse. A small-scale model of one of the ships he'd captained. The apartment had sold for well over the asking price—with a key request to keep the design aspects.

A warm feeling spread through her belly. The fact that Matteo had seen her work and liked it made her smile. Madison Court had been her biggest job yet. She hadn't told anyone she'd met the old sea captain when he was getting chemotherapy in the same hospital as her mother. It was funny where some of the turning points in your life could be.

She rested back against the pillows.

"Yes," came the rich smooth voice. "Madison Court was…unusual. So, are you available for the next few weeks?"

A quarter of a million dollars. That was what he'd offered her.

She and her mom had some savings. But not enough to cover what the medical insurance didn't. This could be the answer to their prayers. This could stop the shadows that were currently residing under her mother's eyes.

The words came out before she could think about it any longer. "I'll see you in an hour."

"Looking forward to it, Ms. Gates."

She glanced at the clock again. Something still didn't sit quite right with her. The apartment at Central Park was gorgeous. But in New York there were dozens of interior designers—competition was tough. She'd never been near a house in the Hamptons before. If that was where Matteo Bianchi owned property he must have a whole range of other contacts.

She smiled. "Mr. Bianchi?"

"Yes, Ms. Gates?"

"How many other interior designers did you call this morning before me?"

There was the briefest hesitation. "Seven."

She let out a laugh. "See you in an hour," she said as she replaced the phone.

Matteo glanced at his watch for the fifth time as he tried not to curse under his breath. It seemed that limousines and New York snowstorms didn't work in partnership together. The car had edged along an inch at a time. Finally, they pulled up outside an apartment. Two seconds later a round figure emerged from the building. She was covered in so many layers he couldn't even see her face. The driver opened the door and Phoebe Gates practically rolled into the car alongside him.

She pushed back her numerous hoods, fixing him with the darkest brown eyes he'd ever seen. She was younger than he'd expected—prettier than he'd expected too, with smooth coffee-colored skin and curls poking out around her face.

She gave him a wide smile as she started unzipping all her jackets. "I think I might have overdone it. I took one look at the snow and put on just about everything I owned."

"I can see that." He couldn't help but smile as she started to emerge from underneath all the layers.

He shook his head as she stripped off a raincoat, a black parka, a zip-up hoody and pushed her mass of curls back from her face. She gave her head a shake. "Wow. It's hot in here."

He kept watching as she folded her arms across her

chest and hitched one knee a little on the seat so she turned to face him. "So, I was number eight, huh?"

He shrugged. "Apparently I picked the wrong time of year to look for an interior designer."

He liked the fact she wasn't afraid to say what she thought. A straight talker. She laughed. "No, I just think you picked the wrong day."

She stared at the snow-covered streets. "So what's the big rush anyhow?"

He settled back into the plush leather seats. "The time is just right."

She wrinkled her nose. It looked as if she might be about to say something when she gave a yell. "Stop the car!"

The driver screeched to a halt, throwing them both forward. "What is it? Did we hit someone?"

She shook her head and shot him a huge grin as she opened the car door. "No. It's my favorite coffee cart. What can I get you?"

Matteo tried not to say the expletives that were circling around his head. "You what? You stopped us like that for *coffee*?"

She stared at him for a second with those big brown eyes, narrowing them for a millisecond as if she were surprised at his reaction. She touched the driver on the shoulder. "You're a macchiato, aren't you?"

The driver blinked in surprise and nodded. She glanced over at the cart. "And a chocolate donut?" He nodded again. She got out of the car and gave her order to the vendor then ducked her head back in and turned to Matteo. She put one finger next to her mouth. "Hmm."

"What?" He was getting annoyed now. New York was starting to get busy with shoppers. It would take around ninety minutes to reach the house and he wanted to get moving as soon as possible.

She gave a half-smile. "I'm trying to work out whether you're a double espresso or an Americano kind of guy."

She ducked back out and spoke quietly to the vendor, who laughed and filled her order. Two minutes later she was in the car and settled back in her seat, handing him a hot paper cup and something in a bag.

She shrugged as he continued to frown. "I get cranky if I don't have coffee in the morning." She shook her head. "And believe me, you won't like me when I'm cranky."

A caramel aroma was drifting over toward him and he watched as she pulled out a raspberry-covered donut, taking a large bite. "Best donuts in New York. Nowhere else comes close."

She nudged him. "Go on. Try yours."

Phoebe Gates was nothing like he'd expected. The last time he'd dealt with an interior designer she'd been all business suits, stiletto heels and clipboards. Her assistant had hung on her every word, constantly taking notes. She'd been abrupt, professional and aloof.

He stared down at the Americano in his hand. Just the way he liked it. And in the paper bag? A regular sugar donut. He hated icing and sprinkles nearly as much as he hated filled donuts.

He frowned. "How did you know?" he asked.

She swallowed her donut and took a sip of her coffee. "How did I know what?"

He held up his Americano and paper bag. "This. How did you know this?"

He was suspicious. People didn't generally surprise him. It wasn't as if she could have done an Internet search to find out what kind of coffee and donut he preferred.

She shrugged again and smiled. "I just know these things." She grinned and tapped her nose. "Interior design. It's all based on observation skills."

Matteo narrowed his gaze. Maybe he'd made a mistake this morning, but by the time he'd reached call number eight he was reaching the desperate stage. In amongst the family feuds of Christmas, the one thing that his overextended Italian family had agreed on was that it was time to get rid of some of the family property. Matteo had agreed to take charge and he intended to get this over with as quickly as possible. He'd thought with the price tag he was offering any interior designer would snap his hand off for the job. Turned out he was wrong. Four of the designers he'd called were on holiday with only an answer-phone message saying calls wouldn't be returning until the new year. Two had answered but refused due to family commitments. One was currently working in Washington. By the time he'd reached Phoebe he just wanted someone to say yes. But then she'd surprised him.

Matteo was used to doing business. He paid a price and a job got done. End of story. So he'd been a little surprised that Phoebe had insisted on seeing the property instead of just agreeing to the job straight away. This was time he really didn't have to spare.

And it wasn't that she seemed unprofessional—that was too harsh. It was just, she seemed so…relaxed.

He'd be paying her a quarter of a million dollars. Was it wrong to expect a little more deference? His insides cringed at the thought. Was he being archaic—or sexist even? In this day and age, neither would be acceptable and both could earn him a slap around the back of the head from his very feisty sister.

She nudged him. "Eat up, or I'll start to think my instincts are off. Now, we've got a bit of time. Give me some history about the house."

Matteo finally took a sip of the coffee. Surprisingly good for a street vendor. He opened his mouth to speak just as his phone rang. He glanced at the caller. Vittore. His brother. Doubtless this would be another fight.

The interruption clarified things in his mind. He turned to Phoebe. "I'm not going to give you any background information on the house." He tried not to look amused. "Let's just see what your instincts tell you." He settled back against the seat as he pressed the phone to his ear.

"Vittore?"

She'd spent the last hour staring out the window at the passing view, desperately wanting to talk. But Mr. Bianchi appeared to conduct most of his business on his phone. Something she'd find depressing on a good day.

Right now, she could be in the middle of Macy's searching for the best bargains.

Maybe the purple coat her mother had admired would be half-price. She could have bought that as a "getting better" present. She'd like to get her mom something to put a smile back on her face. It certainly would be better than spending an hour in forced silence.

The city view had changed rapidly to an even more snow-covered landscape. There was a reason the Hamptons was famous. The popular seaside resort was a historical summer colony on the south fork of Long Island. It featured some of the most luxurious and expensive

real estate in all of New York and was regularly featured on TV shows and films.

Phoebe had visited here as a child and a teenager.
She'd even spent a semester at the university campus
out here and seen exactly how the other half could live.
It was almost as if the whole atmosphere changed the
further away from the city you got.

She loved New York. She loved the hustle and bus-
tle, she loved the people and she definitely loved living
in the city that never slept. But she'd also always loved
the Hamptons. Sure, she might not have a billion-dollar
bank account. But there was something about this place
that made her heartbeat quicken as they passed through
one village and hamlet after another. The space. The
air. The views. And the houses.

The houses here were *to die for.*

Her stomach gave a little flip-flop as the road
stretched ahead of them and they passed one palatial
mansion after another. Each one was individual, styled
a little differently from its neighbor. Some had been up
for more than a hundred years. A few had appeared in
the late eighties with a completely modern design that
already looked dated.

Mansion spotting was a popular pastime in the
Hamptons. A few house builders had obviously decided
not to take part in the game and set their homes far back
from the road. Phoebe wrinkled her nose. Those people
had no sense of fun. What was the point in house spotting if you couldn't even see it?

The car slowed a little and her eyes widened. She was
familiar with the surroundings. Anyone who watched
TV would be familiar with the surroundings. One of the
streets around here was nicknamed Billionaires' Row.
Some of the most expensive homes in the US were here.

Phoebe leaned back in the seat and tried to catch her breath. Any minute now they would turn another corner in another direction. She shot a sideways glance at Matteo. He'd told her his home was in Southampton. But she hadn't really thought he'd meant this street. Did people *actually* live here?

The car moved toward the oceanfront, glided through a set of wrought-iron gates, then snaked its way down a long driveway. Sitting in prime position on the oceanfront was one of the biggest houses Phoebe had ever seen.

She couldn't breathe. She actually couldn't breathe. By some miracle Matteo had managed to finish a call and put his phone away.

Please don't let him expect me to be able to talk right now.

He seemed unfazed. He glanced upwards—a look of indifference.

To a house like this? Really?

She tried to swallow as there was a little glint of yellow from the top of the house. A curve, covered in snow. Was that an atrium?

The question started to form on her lips then she glimpsed a flash of something else from Matteo. Distaste. Or dislike. She wasn't quite sure which. Really? To a place like this?

Play it cool. The words kept repeating over and over in her head. She hadn't been joking when she'd said she liked to see a property before deciding if she would take on a job. But she also liked a chance to meet the client. Interior designers sometimes worked alone. Getting a feel for a job and a client had given her a "Get out of Jail Free" card on a few occasions. Safety always came first and on the odd occasion something just didn't feel right. It had been okay when Jason had been around. He'd always had her back. Clients had taken one look at the strapping ex-Navy pilot and any erroneous thoughts had vanished from their minds. At least that was the way it had always seemed.

But three years ago life had changed in the blink of an eye. Or, more accurately, the stall of two plane engines—something that apparently never happened.

Except to her fiancé. And life would never be the same again.

She'd had to get used to working with no backup plan and part of today had been making sure she felt safe to work for Matteo Bianchi. She shot him a sideways glance. For the most part he seemed like a workaholic typical New York billionaire businessman. An exceptionally *handsome* Italian workaholic businessman.

And that was interesting. Handsome wasn't something she'd noticed in the last three years. Matteo Bianchi had all the traditional attributes of every Italian movie star she'd ever seen on screen. Thick dark hair, deep green eyes, sallow smooth skin and straight white teeth. The only thing that marred his good looks was that permanent frown on his forehead.

She got the distinct impression that he really didn't have time for her. In fact, she got the distinct impression that Matteo Bianchi didn't have time for much of anything.

The car pulled up outside the huge cream-colored mansion and Matteo opened the door straight away. Phoebe fumbled around, trying to select one of her many jackets, finally settling on a red one. She stepped out of the car and looked up at the outside of the house.

The grounds were pristine. She could imagine how manicured the lawns were in summer, even though they were covered in snow right now. The façade was elegant, if a little faded. The double front door was arched and the front of the house lined with mahogany windows covered by internal shutters. Why was a place as beautiful as this all closed up?

If she closed her eyes for a second she could imagine how beautiful this house could be at Christmas. Lights. Trees. Decorations. Instead, it was all closed up like an unwanted present.

Phoebe tilted her head to the side. "Do you only use the house in the summer?"

Matteo shook his head. "We've never really used this house."

"What?" Phoebe spun around and looked at him. "What do you mean, you've never used this house?"

Matteo shook his head and stuck his hands in his pockets. "It's been in the family for a while. But...we've never really stayed here." There was something odd about the way he said that.

Phoebe couldn't help but shake her head. She couldn't get past the fact that this beautiful house was sitting empty—and had done for years.

"Who takes care of it?"

Matteo gave the briefest shake of his head. "I have a caretaker. They come in a few times a year to clean up and maintain the place. Over the years, the electrics, heating and plumbing have all been kept up to date but..." he paused for a second "... I imagine there will be lots of areas in the house that need updating."

Phoebe wrinkled her nose for a second as she stared up at the three-story building with its shuttered windows. "It looks around a hundred years old. Please tell me it's been updated since then."

Matteo gave a nod. "Of course it has. Just not recently."

He pulled a large key from his pocket, along with his phone. As they approached the thick double entrance door he lifted his phone to a panel at the door side. There was a short beep before he turned the key. "Alarm," he said simply before pushing the door open.

Phoebe smiled as she watched him pull the key from the lock. "You put in a digital alarm but didn't put in digital locks?"

He shrugged. There was something so juvenile about it. Like a naughty teenager. "Who says I didn't? I might just be trying to fool you."

It was the first time she'd seen a spark of something. A glimpse of something other than the very busy businessman. A hint of what might lie beneath the surface.

Matteo stood back and she stepped inside the wide entranceway and sucked in a breath.

The air was still all around her. Silent.

But there was something else. Something almost magical.

She held out her hands and spun around. Light flooded in from the open door, allowing her to see the huge curved staircase with intricate iron railing that spiraled up through three floors of the house. Every step she took on the tiled floor echoed upwards to the yellowed glass dome at the top of the house. By the time she stopped spinning and brought her gaze back down to the current floor she finally got a feel for the place. The entranceway was huge.

Matteo was looking at her curiously. There was something odd. He looked uncomfortable. She gave a little stagger and laughed as she put out her hand, grasping onto his sleeve to try and stop her head spinning.

Now she could see all the rooms off the entranceway. Most of them had glass-paneled doors, hinting at what lay beyond. Her heart gave a little flutter.

She'd dreamed of getting the chance to do a house in the Hamptons. It had always been an ambition that she'd hoped to achieve. She just thought it was still at least a few years away. Her fingers were itching to touch this house. To run through every room. To suck in the atmosphere. Trying to appear cool, calm and collected was rapidly slipping from her grasp. Even though Matteo Bianchi was staring her down with that disapproving glare.

She looked to the side again. The room directly to her right was practically calling out to her. "May I?" She gestured with her head.

Matteo stopped glaring and glanced toward the room. A furrow lined his brow. "Actually, I want you to let me know what your instincts tell you."

It was the way he said it. The tone. And the way the glare in his eyes had been replaced by a kind of mischievous twinkle. He was testing her. Or teasing her.

She tilted her chin upwards. Matteo Bianchi had no idea who he was dealing with. She met his green gaze straight on. "You know you're being unfair—but that's fine." She held up her hands. "I've already told you I think the house is around a hundred years old." She wrinkled her nose. "About twenty thousand square meters? Maybe around eight or nine bedrooms? Probably four or five bathrooms or half-baths. I expect two or three formal rooms. I expect a dining room, a large kitchen, laundry, study and a basement and wine cellar." She put her hand on her chest. "And I'm hoping there are *exceptional* views over Mecox Bay from the rear of the property. Am I getting close? Can I actually get in to see the main sitting room?"

Matteo gave a nod toward the door. Phoebe didn't wait another second; she was through that door in a flash.

It was like a moment out of time. She blinked as a memory of a movie she'd watched flooded through her senses. The hero and heroine had flitted back and forth between modern day and fifty years before. Phoebe felt as if she were currently standing by their side.

She couldn't help but touch. Tiny slivers of bright light tried to edge their way around the shutters. Phoebe didn't wait, she walked over to the nearest set and gave them a tug.

Nothing happened.

She tried again. This time there was a creak. A squeak. She slid her hand up the side, checking for any extra latches or bolts. Once she was sure there were none, she pulled with all her might.

Two seconds later she was flat on her back on the carpet as the winter's day light filled the room. She laughed as Matteo moved above her, holding his hand out toward her. "Are you okay?"

She kept laughing and stayed on the floor, shaking her head. "I'm still dreaming, aren't I? Because this dream just seems to get kookier by the minute."

He frowned, staring at his outstretched hand, as if he were trying to figure out what was wrong with it. "I have no idea what you mean."

"Oh, come on." She leaned up on her hand, still staying on the carpet as her gaze swept across the room. "You phoned me this morning and offered me a quarter of a million dollars for a few weeks' work, dressing a home in the Hamptons. Every designer's dream. Then you bring me here. The house to end *all* houses." She was shaking her head again now. "Then, we come in, and it's a time warp. A perfect time warp." She held up her hand as her eyes tried not to goggle in amazement at the contents of the room.

"I still don't know what you mean."

She pushed herself up onto her bottom. "This place. This furniture."

Matteo shook his head. "I know. I know. Everything will need replacing it's all so out of date. Don't worry. I'll give you a credit card with no limit. You can buy whatever you need to dress the house." He waved his hand. "As long as you keep receipts, of course."

"Are you crazy?" She couldn't believe what he was saying. She reached out and touched the chair next to her. "This stuff is pristine. Perfect. People would pay an absolute fortune for things like this. And I won't need to. Because it's all here. Matteo, don't you realize how fantastic this place already is?"

He was looking at her as if she were out of her mind.

She grabbed his hand and pulled herself up as she paced quickly around the room. "This—this is why I think I'm still dreaming. See this? This nineteen-fifties chair? I paid over a thousand dollars for one of these last time I dressed a home. You've got six." She touched the L-shaped sofa in the corner. "I might get this reupholstered but the style and shape is just fabulous."

Her heart skittered across her chest as she took in all the fixtures and fittings. The lamps, the shades, the telephone, the vases. She shook her head again as she murmured, "It's like interior design heaven. That's why this must be a dream. Things like this don't happen to me."

She spun around and gasped. Matteo had walked right up behind her. He was closer than expected and was watching her with the most curious expression on his face. Her dream from earlier had been filled by Hugh Jackman. If she were still dreaming, wouldn't Hugh be the man that had brought her to this house instead of Matteo Bianchi?

"Pinch me," she said firmly.

"What?"

"Pinch me. I have to know this isn't a dream."

He was right in front of her. Staring her down with those green eyes. Part of him looked amused, part of him looked annoyed. Or maybe she was just misreading him. The hint of aftershave was distracting her. It was subtle. She'd never smelt it before. Amber, musk and oak moss. People didn't realize that interior designers knew that scent was everything. Half of all homes sold on scent alone.

"Go on," she urged. "Just do it."

He pulled an exasperated face then lifted his hand to her arm.

"Yeowwww!" She jumped backwards, rubbing her wrist. "Okay, then. Turns out I'm definitely awake." She shot him a suspicious glance. "You've got sisters, haven't you? Or *a* sister."

"How on earth do you know that?"

"Believe me." She kept rubbing her smarting wrist. "A girl can tell."

He stared at her curiously for a second. "And for the record, I have one sister. One is enough."

She took a deep breath. This was it. This was where she found out if this really was the dream job. "Tell me, is every room as good as this one?"

Matteo raised his eyebrows. "You mean, is every room in the same kind of time warp as this one? Oh, I can guarantee that, Phoebe." He was looking at her as if he couldn't quite understand why she thought this was a good thing. But Phoebe was off. Tearing through the next few rooms of the house to check them out. A dining room. A huge kitchen. A laundry room. Another sitting room. A study. Two bathrooms—they might need a little work. And a phenomenal room at the back of the house with windows and glass doors that looked out over Mecox Bay.

Matteo stayed behind her, following her from room to room. "Phoebe... Ms. Gates. Does this mean you'll take the job?"

She could hardly speak. Room after room, there were so many thoughts clambering in her brain about how gorgeous she could make this place that she could hardly form words. Her dream job. The job that could change her whole career. A chance to pay off her mother's medical bills. A chance to move forward. A chance to pull herself out of the fog that had hung around her for the last few years.

"Phoebe." His voice grew sharp and he gave her arm a pull, tugging her around to face him. Her hands rested on his upper arms. She couldn't help herself. She almost wanted to give him a kiss on the cheek. She let out a laugh.

"Do I want the job? Hell, yes. Now I've seen it, this place is mine. Matteo, I'm going to do such a good job, you're never going to want to let me go."

It was the briefest of seconds. A wash of sadness seemed to sweep his face. A whole host of something she really didn't understand. But as soon as it had appeared, the shutters came down in his eyes again. Matteo Bianchi had the perfect mask. The perfect face for business.

The edges of his lips curved upwards. For the first

time since she'd met him, the tension in his shoulders
actually looked as if it disappeared a little. "Phoebe,
quarter of a million dollars for four weeks' work, and
I *will* let you go."

CHAPTER TWO

FOR THE FIRST time in years Phoebe actually felt lucky. It was a strange concept. Unfamiliar.

Lucky had been something she'd taken for granted for so long. Then Jason, her fiancé, had been killed in a freak flying accident. They'd only just got engaged and started to make plans for the future. All of those things wiped out in the blink of an eye—or the failure of two engines at once. She still couldn't even think about it. But Phoebe hadn't needed therapy. She was strong. Or so she'd thought. She'd been devastated to lose her fiancé, but she'd picked herself up and continued to go through the motions.

Then her mother had got sick. Cancer. Surgery. Chemotherapy. Radiotherapy. And a million scans. Phoebe had been determined to take her to every appointment, every treatment. And she had. Running herself into the ground while she did it. Forgetting to eat. Forgetting to sleep. And eventually having to hit therapy. Because she *did* need it. She just hadn't wanted to acknowledge it.

It was just lately that she'd felt as if she was starting to come out the tunnel she'd been hiding in. Her mom was doing better. They only had to settle the medical bills now. But work had picked up. The apartment near Central Park had been a real coup for her. But this?

This was the icing on the cake. Better than that. This was the sugar on the sprinkles, on the chocolate, on the icing on the cake.

She wasn't the slightest bit perturbed by Matteo telling her he'd let her go. She'd been on a high. She still was. He was somewhere behind her as she rushed from room to room, throwing open shutters and taking photo after photo with her phone. Occasionally she stopped to make a few notes. But only for a second. The essence of this house was invading her senses. The myriad of bedrooms. The bathrooms that could do with a little updating. The totally and completely gorgeous central yellow glass dome. And the kitchen. She could do so much with the kitchen that she almost wanted to start this very second.

Matteo's mood seemed a little odd. Almost sedated if that made sense. She got the distinct impression he didn't want to be here at all. It was almost as if he didn't even like the place.

By the time she returned to the main room Matteo was back on his phone. She should probably be paying some kind of deference to him since he was going to be paying her enormous salary, but she was far too excited for all that.

She walked straight over to him. "I still hurt from where you pinched me."

He was mid conversation and raised one eyebrow at her. After the briefest of pauses he pulled the phone away from his ear. "I'm in the middle of something."

"So am I. And you spent all the time in the car on the phone." There was something about this guy. He was obviously far too wealthy for words. He was clearly a workaholic. But there was just something in his eyes. He liked someone to challenge him. He was amused by her. And somehow she already knew she wanted to earn his respect. If that meant demanding his attention, then she could do that.

He glanced at his phone, but didn't continue with that conversation. The edges of his lips curved again. "You asked me to pinch you. I only did what you asked." There was a cheeky hint in his tone.

"When do I get to meet your sister? I can already tell that I'll be bruised from that pinch and I want to compare notes with her."

He paused and disconnected the call. "The very *last* person I'm introducing you to is my sister. Brianna is even crazier than you are. You'd be a lethal combination."

Phoebe folded her arms across her chest. "Brianna. I like the sound of her." She nodded her head. "You don't need to worry. I'll meet her. And I promise to be on my best behavior." She held up her hands. "Now, the house. I have so many ideas. So many plans. Let's walk through and I'll talk you through them. I can draw up something more formal in a few days. I'll need to check if any of the people I regularly use are free to help out." She raised her eyebrows. "For some people, this is the holiday season."

Matteo frowned and shook his head. "No, no. I'll leave all that to you. I don't need to see plans. I don't need to know your thoughts. I can give you contacts for teams to assist."

Phoebe stood back a little and looked at him incredulously. "You are joking, right?"

He gave her a stern stare. "Why would I be joking?"

She couldn't believe what she was hearing. "Mr. Bianchi, usually clients want consulted on the plans, the overall look for their home. Often they want consulted on any major purchases." She couldn't help but frown. "People are generally passionate about how their homes are marketed—what they look like. They usually want to be involved to ensure they get the best price possible."

Matteo gave an ironic smile. "I take it you're used to clients who generally care about their homes—and the price they achieve. I care about neither. I just want this place off my hands." As he finished his phone started ringing again and he strode out of the room, pressing it to his ear, leaving Phoebe wondering whether to laugh or cry. It was clear the conversation was over.

He'd picked a crazy woman. At one point he'd thought Phoebe Gates would start cartwheeling around the place. She was barely managing to keep her excitement simmering beneath the surface. Her joy at having this job seemed to emanate from every pore in her body.

That actually made a tiny little part of him happy. There was something nice about her enthusiasm and straightforwardness. In his line of business he was used to fake smiles and poker faces; somehow he didn't think Phoebe Gates would know how to do either one.

But Phoebe obviously had very different ideas from him. She'd thrown open shutters and flooded this dusty old house with light, her face brightening as she'd practically run from room to room. He was surprised that she loved the ancient furniture and fittings. He'd been sure any interior designer would just skip the contents of the house and redecorate the place from top to bottom. Phoebe had obviously decided to take a different tack.

He'd reached the kitchen by now and let out a long sigh. The sooner he got out of here, the better. He only had one association with this house. And it was one he had no intention of revisiting.

He stared around the kitchen for a few seconds as something flashed through his brain. A long-forgotten memory. His mother. Those memories were so fleeting. So scant.

Her dark hair and bright eyes. Dressed in a swirling red dress. She'd been excited. Just the way that Phoebe was. Full of ideas and plans for what she could do to the house. The house they'd just bought that was stuck in a time warp. It had been owned by an elderly actress who had died a few months earlier. His mother could hardly wait to bring it up to modern-day living.

He remembered his father leaning against the double sink and folding his arms, smiling and watching Matteo's mother the way he'd always watched her—with love and adoration in his eyes.

When Matteo blinked, the memory was gone. He inhaled deeply and leaned back against the sink—just the way his father had. Was the memory even real? He would only have been around five when they stayed here for a few weeks. Brianna was only a few weeks old and Vittore around three.

But everything changed. The house was boarded up and they moved with their father back to Rome, flitting between the capital and an apartment in New York City, then London for a while. The house in the Hamptons was never mentioned. Ignored.

Too many painful memories. It was only now, thirty years later, the family had decided it was time to sell.

Phoebe floated into the kitchen. Literally, floated. Her smile spread from ear to ear, showing off her straight white teeth and enhancing her glowing coffee-colored skin. Her hair bounced as she walked, tight corkscrew curls resting on her shoulders. There was something about her. An aura. She made him want to smile. He couldn't even remember the last time he'd felt like that. For a few seconds she'd even made him forget where he actually was. But the truth was, he just couldn't shake the sense of this place. The dark memories. The secrets he'd learned to keep. The ones that kept him locked away.

Phoebe moved in front of him. She'd shed more layers. Now he could see the way her green fine-knit jumper and fitted black trousers clung to her curves. Many of the women Matteo came across in New York were skeletally thin. It was a look he'd never appreciated. Italian men much preferred women with curves—and Phoebe wore them well.

Her perfume drifted up around him as she fixed her chocolate-brown eyes on him. She paused for a second, with an amused expression on her face. It was clear she was contemplating how to phrase her words.

"Ms. Gates?" he prompted.

She gave a nod. "How about we settle on Phoebe and Matteo? I think that might make things a bit easier. After all, we will be seeing a lot of each other."

There was a sparkle in her eyes.

He slid his hand into his pocket and pulled out a credit card. "I'm not sure that will be necessary. But I'm happy to call you Phoebe if that's what you prefer."

She took the credit card without a glance, merely sliding it into the back pocket of her trousers.

"We need to talk about this place, Matteo. We need to discuss my plans." It was clear that persistence was one of her traits.

He was curt. "No. We don't."

He turned on his heel and walked out of the kitchen, heading in the direction of the front door. In the space of few seconds it almost felt as if the walls were closing in around him.

The cool air almost bit into his skin as he stepped outside and he blinked at the brightness. He hadn't realized quite how blinkered the house had been.

His phone started ringing. He pulled it from his pocket—Brianna. He might have guessed. They were closer than some families. He spoke to both his brother and sister a few times a day. A few female companions in the past had commented on it—finding it strange. But Matteo had never cared for other people's opinions on his family. They hadn't lived his life, they didn't know that he and his siblings were the glue that held their splintered family together.

"Did you get one?" Brianna was speaking rapidly in Italian. She was probably doing ten things at once.

"I did."

"And? Are they good?"

Was Phoebe Gates good? He didn't really know. He'd called her both on a whim and out of desperation. Captain Monaghan had been one of the most interesting men Matteo had ever had the pleasure of meeting. But his apartment had been a cluttered, claustrophobic mess. Rudy Monaghan was clearly a hoarder. He'd sailed the seven seas and collected just about everything he'd ever seen.

Matteo had never met Phoebe, but Rudy had been full of praise for the beautiful, enthusiastic and, most importantly, respectful interior designer that he'd hired. The crew she'd hired to assist her had been given very clear instructions. Carefully pack up everything without a yellow sticker. Walls had been painted, windows shined, pictures moved and rehung. She'd stripped the place bare but kept its heart and essence.

No, she'd kept Rudy Monaghan's heart and essence.

Matteo had dropped in one evening just before he knew Rudy was due to move out and been struck by the enormity of the changes. Rudy had been sitting in his wooden rocking chair, his genuine ancient ship's wheel still next to him, bathed in the orange setting sun, watching the view of Central Park. That sight would stay with Matteo forever.

He took a deep breath. Now he remembered the transformation he almost wished he'd called Phoebe first. He couldn't help but smile. He could just imagine how she'd have been if he'd called her at seven instead of eight. "They're not good, Brianna," he said deliberately.

"What?" she shrieked from somewhere in New York.

"They're great. *She's* great."

There was silence for a few seconds. He waited for the tirade of abuse from his sister for momentarily teasing her but it didn't come.

"Matteo, who is *she*?"

There was something about his sister's tone. Her curiosity. He instantly felt a prickle down his spine. Brianna was nosey. Brianna was beyond nosey. He probably shouldn't have said anything at all.

He kept his voice brisk. "She's Phoebe Gates. Remember Rudy's apartment at Central Park? She did that one. She'll do a good job for us."

He could almost hear the cogs and whirrs of Brianna's brain. "Yeah, I remember the apartment at Central Park. It ended up as part of a bidding war, didn't it?"

"Well, if that's what you heard, it must be true."

"So, we know Ms. Gates can dress an apartment—but can she dress a Hampton house?"

She hadn't said the words out loud but the implication was clear. An apartment at Central Park was big. A house in the Hamptons was in a whole other league.

"Have a little faith in your brother, Brianna."

There was a loud sigh at the end of the phone. "I have a lot of faith in my brother. Both my brothers." There was a pause for a second. Matteo had kept walking. The fresh air was calling to him, along with the spectacularly white snow. The tone of her voice softened. "How are you?"

He didn't answer. Cold air was filling his lungs, letting his heart race a little quicker and letting him shake off the cobwebs.

It was hard to explain. The only other people to have walked in his shoes were Vittore and Brianna. No one else would ever understand. He wouldn't expect them to. He wouldn't want them to. And the truth was, Vittore and Brianna didn't understand entirely either— because he didn't want them to. He was oldest. It was his job to guard his younger brother and sister.

"Matteo?" Her voice was soft, almost a whisper.

Matteo closed his eyes. "I'm fine, Brianna. Of course, I'm fine. It's just this place. You know that. I'm going to leave everything in Phoebe's hands. She doesn't see this place the way we do. She loves it. She thinks it's great. She…she has the ability to dress it and make it sell. That's all that we need."

He could almost hear the shake in her voice. "Is it?"

It was as if the cold air penetrated every part of him. He wouldn't go there. He wouldn't have the conversation that his sister sometimes pushed him toward. He'd learned how to deal with it over the years. It was as if he owned his own set of black shutters. Push him so far and he would just slam them shut. "Goodbye, Brianna," he said smartly as he finished the call.

* * *

Phoebe was sitting on the curved staircase. Her feet had actually started to follow him out of the kitchen, then her instincts had kicked in and told her not to. Told her to give him a little space.

Mr. Bianchi was more than a little temperamental. Was this an Italian trait?

She sighed and closed her eyes, trying to breathe in the essence of this beautiful home. Her brain instantly took her to the place she wanted to be. Right now she was recreating her own favorite musical and was tap dancing up and down these stairs in a bouffant yellow dress. She just hadn't decided who her imaginary leading man was yet. A twinge of guilt set in.

For the first year after Jason's death he'd been the main feature of every dream she'd had. But for the last year, several movie stars had started to creep in and take over. In a way, it had been a relief to stop waking up with her heart in her throat. That horrible little millisecond of time—the briefest of moments—where she thought everything was just the same, Jason was still here, her mom wasn't sick yet and then, she remembered.

And that overwhelming colossal black wave swamped back on top of her, every morning, making her relive every moment and making her want to be sick all over her bed. It took months for that to fade. Months to wake up to the reality that was her life.

But every time she felt relief that didn't happen anymore, guilt pricked at her conscience.

She took a deep breath and pressed her hands on the cool marble stairs, letting her eyes flicker open. She could imagine the beautiful women and men who'd walked these steps. The hopes, dreams and fantasy life-styles. Things that were all so far out of her reach.

She shook her head and smiled. Jealousy had never been a Phoebe trait. She loved that this place had history. She loved that it had been captured in time. She would probably never get a chance like this again. She just had to know what to keep to help capture the story, and know what to replace to make this home still seem appealing to a modern-day buyer.

The color palette here was unreal. She'd found an avocado bathroom. That would definitely have to be dealt with. But so much else just needed tweaks. She pulled out her phone and flicked through her contacts as she breathed in deeply. There was a bit of an odor. A tang that frequently featured in houses that hadn't really been lived in for a number of years.

Smell was so much. But she could deal with that. Carpets, drapes and upholstery could all be replaced. But she wasn't sure she would change the style. So much of it was perfect.

She pressed a familiar number of her phone. It answered on the second ring.

"Hello, baby girl."

"Hi, Momma. I've got news."

"Are you at the sales? What did you buy?"

Phoebe laughed. "No, Momma. I'm in a whole different place." She looked around as her heart gave a little jump. "I just want you to know that in a few weeks, the medical bills won't be a problem."

There was a sharp intake of breath. Her mother's voice was panicked. "Baby girl, what have you done?"

It didn't matter she was twenty-seven. It didn't matter that she had her own place and her own life. She would always be her mother's baby.

She laughed. "I haven't done anything, Momma. I just got the job of my dreams. And it pays more than I could ever have hoped for."

Her mother's tone hadn't changed from panic. "Phoebe, what kind of job is this?"

Phoebe shook her head. "It's exactly the kind of job I do every day. But this house…" she pressed one hand to her chest and breathed in, as if saying it made everything real "…it's in the Hamptons."

"What?" Her mother's voice came out as a squeak.

"Yes," Phoebe said quickly. "I got a call this morning." She lowered her voice to a whisper. "A quarter of a million dollars if I can work over the next four weeks and redress this house."

"How much?" This time it wasn't a squeak. This time it was more like a shriek.

But Phoebe didn't get a chance to answer. "Who is this person with a house in the Hamptons? Are they a criminal? Who have you got mixed up with? How did they find out about you?"

Phoebe shook her head. "Calm down, Mom. They know Rudy. That's how they know about me. They liked the work I did on his apartment. That's how I got this job. I came out to see the house this morning and…" she tried to steady her thoughts "…it's a dream come true. It's like walking into a fifties TV show. The whole place, it's just…epic." She laughed at using such a juvenile word, but nothing else seemed to come close.

Her mother cut straight to the chase. "Are you safe? Have you met these folks? Are they good people?"

"They're an Italian family."

Her mother's voice lowered to a hushed tone. "Are they part of the mob?"

Phoebe choked. "What? No? Don't be ridiculous.

They've had this house for a while. It's just time to sell it." But something prickled. Matteo hadn't been exactly straight with her. The timing did seem a little off. Exactly how old was he? "And yes. I'm safe. Matteo is a bit buttoned up. He's a businessman. One of those high-flyer types. But he seems sincere. And I think I'm going to love doing this job. This could be it. This could be the one. It will pay off the bills and maybe put me on the map."

There was a few seconds' silence. "Then go nail it. I love you, baby girl."

Phoebe smiled as she pushed her phone back in her pocket and stood up again. The front door was wide open to the world, letting in an icy blast. Matteo must have gone outside.

She'd left her jacket somewhere she couldn't entirely remember, so she crossed her hands over her body as she walked outside.

Matteo had that strange, dark expression on his face again. The one where he didn't really answer any questions. But Phoebe was determined. She might have the credit card, but she wanted to do the best job in the world. Her career could depend on it. Her bank balance certainly did. And for that, she needed a bit more information.

"Matteo?" He spun around, frowning. It seemed to be his default expression.

She walked up to him, close enough to let his body block out the swirling wind coming from Mecox Bay. "You haven't been entirely straight with me."

The furrow on his brow deepened. "What do you mean?"

She gave a gentle smile. "Unless, of course, you're a modern-day Peter Pan."

Now he just looked confused. "What?"

She inched a little closer. Probably more than she meant to. Her hair was getting caught by the wind, blowing her springy curls in front of her eyes. "The timing doesn't fit," she said quietly. "I'm trying to work out why you lived in a nineteen-fifties-style house." She tilted her head to the side as she studied him a little harder. "Don't get me wrong—I love it. But you don't look in your sixties. Maybe you've discovered some secret cream the rest of the world just needs to find?"

She could almost see the penny drop. She expected him to smile. But he didn't. Instead she could almost feel the wave of sadness. His voice was quiet. "We bought the house in the late eighties when I was a child. It belonged to some ageing starlet who had moved into it in the nineteen-fifties and not redecorated since. My parents had plans to redecorate the whole house. But... things changed. We only stayed here a few weeks. My father's business meant we had to go to Rome, then London for a while. When we came back to New York, we had a few other properties that were ready to move into as a family."

He said the words as if something were squirming in his chest, and his bright green eyes only met her gaze for the most fleeting of seconds.

It wasn't a lie. But it didn't feel like the truth. *Trust your instincts,* the voice in her head said. She wasn't getting the fight-or-flight feeling. There was more to this. But whatever it was—it wasn't enough to walk away from her dream job. A chance to pay the medical bills and possibly make her mark on the Hamptons.

"You've moved around a lot. The family business— what kind of business are you in?"

The fleeting mob reference from her mother was momentarily playing on her mind.

"I'm Italian." He raised his eyebrows. "We're in the wine business."

"You own vineyards?"

Matteo gave a tight smile "We own seventeen vineyards in Italy. Sixteen in Spain, fourteen in California, and several in Portugal."

"Wow. That's a lot of wine." She rolled her eyes. "I guess I don't need to worry about stocking the cellar, then."

He gave a brief shake of his head. "Let me deal with that."

She nodded. "Are you in a hurry to leave? I'd like to stay. I'd like to spend as much time as I can here, to get a feel for the place. I need to go over every room in detail, and I need to call contacts to check availability, and see what I can achieve over the next four weeks."

She wanted him to know she was serious. She wanted him to know that this was important to her.

He glanced toward the limousine then shook his head. "Keep the car, it's fine. I can arrange another form of transport." His gaze actually met hers. This time there was something else. Something that made her heart swell a little. Respect?

She turned to go back to the house but his voice carried on the wind toward her.

"Ms. Gates? I trust you. I know you'll do a good job."

Her footsteps froze, but by the time she turned back around he already had the phone pressed against his ear again.

Had she imagined it?

CHAPTER THREE

THE PHOTOGRAPHS OF how the house looked right now were printed. She'd spent the last two days sketching her new vision for the house. The avocado bathroom was already gone. Some things didn't need to wait. She'd learned very quickly that Matteo really didn't want to take her calls.

He'd given her a credit card that she hadn't used yet. But working with contractors was different. She'd had to agree the price for a few jobs—and at this time of year—and for a house in the Hamptons—some of the prices quoted had been exorbitant. Any good interior designer would run those past her employer and that was all Phoebe was doing. Though Matteo wasn't really interested in contractor prices. So far, he'd said yes to anything without so much as a blink.

Her biggest expense for the house was going to be fabric. She wanted new drapes for just about every room, and lots of the signature pieces reupholstered. And good quality fabric was *not* cheap. Which was why she standing in one of the most prestigious, well-stocked warehouses on the outskirts of New York.

But this place didn't like to waste time. The assistant assigned to her held out her hand. "We'll just put your credit card on file to ease things along."

She got it. She did. The assistant didn't want to spend the next four hours helping Phoebe find everything she wanted, only to have the credit card declined at the end.

Phoebe slipped the black card from her purse and handed it over. She had a long list of fabrics she wanted to find. A color palette already existed in her head, but would she find a match in this warehouse? That was always the danger of getting too carried away with one idea. Sometimes color trends and seasons just didn't match. So, she'd prepared some sketches with one set of colors, and prepared some more as a backup plan.

The assistant walked back over and held out the credit card as if it had the plague. "I'm sorry. Your credit line doesn't seem to be approved. Do you have another card you can use?"

Phoebe felt her cheeks flush. She did have another credit card. Unfortunately it was maxed out with her mother's medical expenses, and the amount of money she'd likely spend in here today could never be covered by the small amount of money in her current account.

She'd had a bad start already this morning, tangling herself up in her sheets when the alarm had gone off, falling out of bed and catching the side of her cheek on the bedside cabinet. She was just hoping it wouldn't bruise.

"Give me a minute," she said, trying not to seem embarrassed. She pulled her phone from her pocket and dialed Matteo's number. *Please answer.* She didn't want to have to walk out of here after presenting a dud card. She'd never be able to show her face again, and this place was every interior designer's dream. She couldn't afford to have a bad rep in here.

"Matteo Bianchi." His reply was curt. But he couldn't hide that wonderful Italian accent that sent tingles down to her toes. Every time she called she forgot about it and spent the first few seconds of their conversation lost in a little fog.

Right now she didn't have time for a fog. She cut to the chase. "Matteo, the credit card you gave me isn't working."

It took a few seconds for a reply. She could almost picture him staring at the name on the phone. How many people did he give credit cards to? "Phoebe?"

"Of course, Phoebe. Who else would it be?"

"Where are you?"

"I'm at a warehouse on the outskirts of New York. I need to buy fabrics, leathers—a whole host of things for the house." She lowered her voice as the assistant glared at her, obviously labeling her as a time waster. "This place is expensive and you've given me a limited amount of time."

"Let me speak to them."

Phoebe sighed and handed over the phone to the assistant, pacing at the side while Matteo obviously had a curt conversation with her.

"No, Mr. Bianchi. Your personal guarantee is not good enough."

Phoebe tried not to smile at the thought of Matteo's response.

"You'll need to speak to your credit card provider."

The assistant rolled her eyes and held the phone a little away from her ear. Phoebe walked over to some large rolls of fabric and started to study them closely.

"The only way around things is for you to come down yourself and bring your alternative credit card. No, we can't just take the number over the phone. We need to see the card, along with your signature." The woman let out a sigh. "Yes. That's the only way."

She replaced the receiver and gave Phoebe a fake smile. "Mr...Bianchi will be with you shortly."

"Great," Phoebe muttered as every little hair on her arm stood on end. Just what she needed, an angry Matteo.

This day was getting better and better.

Matteo tried not to curse at his driver as they took another wrong turn. It seemed the sat-nav had decided not to work properly and this industrial estate had dozens of identical giant warehouses, along with no map at the entrance to the site.

He was annoyed at himself. He was sure he'd activated that card. But in amongst the family discussions at Christmas it was possible he might have forgotten. And he should have kept a copy of Phoebe's signature on record so it could be verified, but visiting the house in the Hamptons again had scrambled his normally precise brain.

He hadn't expected to be hit by the wave of emotions. How much could a five-year-old really remember? But being back in that environment had swamped him in a way he hadn't expected. And having the unconventional Ms. Gates with him had probably been a blessing. She'd distracted him from too much melancholy. Too much emotion. Too many flashbacks he hadn't counted on.

And now? Now, more than ever he just wanted to finalize the sale of the house. In his head this was the only way to push all these feelings back into the box where they belonged.

"It's this one," said the driver as they pulled up.

Matteo gave a nod and stepped outside onto the frost-covered ground. This shouldn't take long. He had work to do.

The warehouse was massive, cavernous with an echo that seemed to reverberate all around him. But the first thing that struck him was how methodical everything seemed. The fabrics were stored by color, stacked for what seemed like miles. Large trolleys were pushed around by assistants, who guided customers around the warehouse.

He could pick Phoebe out easily. She was wearing a bright pink coat with matching furry hat and leather gloves. She gave him a rueful smile as he approached. "You might have checked the card worked before you gave it to me."

He tried to hide his annoyance as he pulled his own from his wallet. He glanced around him. "What do you need me to pay for?"

Phoebe wrinkled her nose. "Nothing…yet. They wouldn't let me start shopping until I had a credit line."

"You mean you haven't even started shopping?" His voice echoed louder than expected.

Phoebe pulled back a little and gave him a frown. "No. I haven't started."

Matteo strode over to the counter and thrust his card in front of one of the assistants. "Here's my card. Can you take the details, so I can leave?"

The assistant gave him an icy stare. It was clear she didn't like being treated so dismissively. She gave him a haughty smile. "I can take your details now—but you have to produce your card and match the signature to complete your purchases." She gestured to the side. "You can always get yourself a coffee while your wife shops."

Matteo started. She thought Phoebe was his wife? He stared at the boutique-style coffee shop housed inside the warehouse. While the smell of coffee was tempting, the waste of his time was not.

He turned to face Phoebe, who was standing open-mouthed. She must have heard the comment too. "How long will this take?"

Phoebe cringed. It was clear she didn't want to give the true answer.

He flung up his hands. "How long does it take to buy some fabric and some vases?"

Phoebe's face became pinched. She strode over to the nearest large trolley and turned to one of the assistants. "Are we ready to get started?"

Matteo tried not to let his mouth bounce off the floor. She'd just completely ignored him. Part of him was amused, part of him was annoyed. She had a huge sketch pad balanced on top of the trolley. She tossed her hair over her shoulder and pointed to her first sketch. "This is the color palette I'm interested in. Can we go in that direction please?"

Matteo's curiosity was piqued. Didn't every interior designer just paint houses in white or shades of cream?

The assistant looked positively excited. "Oh, that's so unusual." She leaned over the sketch. "And I love this color palette. I'm sure we can find you some perfect fabrics that will suit."

The assistant started pushing the trolley in one direction. Matteo glanced at the coffee shop. He could sit there. But as he glanced at his phone he could see the signal here wasn't great—probably why the sat-nav hadn't functioned. How much work would he really get done?

Before he could think again, his feet started to follow the trolley and Phoebe and the assistant. They moved past the white and cream rolls of fabrics, away from

the brighter reds and oranges and toward the back of
the warehouse. Whatever color she'd chosen it clearly
wasn't the most popular. His stomach gave a little twist.
Maybe he should be showing more interest?

He walked quickly, catching up with them and leaning directly over Phoebe's shoulder. He blinked. Then
nearly stumbled, reaching out and catching onto the
handle of the trolley.

"Yellow?" he asked Phoebe.

She gave him a firm stare. "Oh, you've joined us."
Her tone reminded him of a headmistress.

His eyes couldn't move from the sketch. It was more
than good. A hand drawing that had captured the whole
breadth of the main room, gently shaded with coloring
pencils in shades of gray, yellow, pale blue and cream.

It was beautiful. Exquisite even. But yellow was a
color he'd never really seen at any other houses for sale.
It did seem unusual.

Phoebe pointed to the sketch. "I always like to choose
a color palette—a theme—for any house that I dress."
She pressed her lips together for a second. "While it
makes sense to use a neutral background color, I always
have to pick some secondary colors to highlight parts
of the interior." She turned to face Matteo. "In your
case, what other color could I choose? The yellow dome
above the atrium is really the focal point of the house.
It bathes the whole house in that magical yellow light.
Yellow seems the natural color to pick out. I've teamed
it with some shades of pale blue, gray and cream." She
flicked the first page to show him a sketch of one of the
bathrooms, followed by one of the bedrooms, then the
back room that looked out over Mecox Bay.

The attention to detail was extraordinary. The main
room still had the same nineteen-fifties sofa, but this

time it was covered in what looked like pale blue leather. The drapes were striped in shades of pale yellow and gray. There was a sleek gray rug on the large wooden floor. All of this was dressed with bursts of bright yellow. A sunflower portrait on the wall. A few cushions, and a bright yellow table lamp. "You did all these in the last few days?"

Phoebe nodded. "Of course, I did. This is what I do." She looked at him hesitantly. "I did do an alternative color scheme if you'd prefer." She flicked to the back of the sketch pad where she had the same room sketches, but this time with white, beige and splashes of orange. It was more abstract, but more traditional. The kind of thing he was used to seeing in other houses. He gave a little shudder. Even though the yellow was a surprise, it was clear the more stark colors wouldn't complement the house as much. The yellow gave the house a warmth that made it much more welcoming.

"What do you think?" She sounded a little nervous.

He nodded. "I think it's good. You're right about the yellow." He glanced around. "I just hope you can find what you need—and quickly," he added with a murmur.

They turned a corner in the warehouse and Matteo stopped walking. The shades of yellow were overwhelming. And it seemed this warehouse didn't just keep the same color fabrics together. No, across wide display units there were rugs, bedding, vases, lamps and ornaments all in complementary shades.

Phoebe let out a little gasp and walked away, running her hand over a large dark gray rug, with pale yellow circles. "This is perfect," she said, nodding to the assistant. "We'll take it." She moved without drawing breath over to a wooden cabinet with upright rolls of fabric. She pointed to a pale gray and yellow stripe. "I'll have this one. And the one next to it with duck-egg blue and yellow." She turned to face the wooden cabinets behind them. "I also want the pale yellow and cream pattern over there. It will be perfect for the master bedroom."

Her bright pink coat swirled around her as she picked up bedding, ornaments, vases and lamp shades in a whole variety of shades of gray, blue and yellow. When she'd finished loading the trolley she waved Matteo over to another part of the warehouse. "Let's pick some prints," she said as she started flicking through a sheaf of prints held behind plastic frames.

The colors stood out, but it was clear that Matteo didn't have Phoebe's designer eye. She let out a little squeal as she found a yellow sunflower similar to the one she'd sketched in her designs. She flicked on and found a gold *broderie anglaise* design, some pale blue cornflowers, and a beautiful beach scene with a turquoise sea.

By now, it seemed that she'd forgotten her apparent bad mood with Matteo. Every single time she found another item she couldn't stop talking. "This is perfect for the back room." She was holding a swirling glass ornament in shades of pale blue. "I can see it sitting on a table with a view of Mecox Bay in the background." She turned and pointed at a pale blue patterned fabric. "And this will frame the windows in the kitchen perfectly. It's just the right shade of blue. And look at these ceramic jugs in blue and cream. They'll be perfect to dress the kitchen." She turned to face him. "Did I tell you I'm getting the sink replaced? There's going to be dual sinks, deep white Belfast sinks, with a thick dark wood countertop. That, along with some replacement handles, will set the kitchen off perfectly. Oh, and I've ordered some new appliances." She glanced in her diary. "They arrive tomorrow. We'll need to have a chat about access."

Matteo nodded. She was like a firecracker. Once she started, she just couldn't stop. The enthusiasm just brimmed out of her. Part of him wished he'd met Phoebe Gates somewhere else. Anywhere but the house. She had a warmth about her. A glow. And an honesty about her that was sometimes missing in the people he normally came across.

But this was business. This was family business. He couldn't let it be anything else. The family had decided it was time to get rid of all reminders. And that was what Phoebe would be now, because he would forever associate her with the Hamptons house.

He dug into his pocket and pulled out a set of keys.

"Here, I got these cut for you. I'd be grateful if you could make arrangements between yourself and the caretaker to give all the trade personnel the access that they need."

She held out her hand then paused. "What about the alarm?"

Of course. He'd forgotten about that. "Give me your phone."

"What?"

She looked surprised. He smiled as he pressed the keys into her outstretched hand. "It's a digital alarm, remember? I'll put the app and the code into your phone."

She gave him a nod and fumbled in her pocket for her phone, her fingers brushing against his as she handed it over. He ignored the tingle—that little acknowledgement of warmth as skin contacted with skin. For the second time in as many minutes he reminded himself this was a business arrangement and focused on the phone.

It was more outdated than he would have expected.

Most business people he worked with had the latest version of everything. After a few seconds he frowned. "No signal. We'll need to go someplace else so I can input the code."

He paused for a second as he looked at the loaded trolley. There really was no room for anything else. "Are you done?"

She bit her lip and shook her head. "I just need to pick some leather." She counted down on her list. "There are seven sofas to be recovered, and twenty chairs."

"How many?" His brain was beginning to throb. It was clear that even though he could manage multiple dealings in his company, across different time zones and continents—the minutiae of dealing with preparing a house for sale were beyond him.

She gave a smile and arched one eyebrow. "But hey? How long does it take to buy some fabric and some vases?" There was a twinkle in her eyes that he knew he deserved.

He couldn't help but smile. In the last two days she'd literally sketched designs for every room in two color palettes, organized refitting of the kitchen and some of the bathrooms, decided what pieces to keep and which to refurbish, all without any help. He held up his hands. "Okay, you got me. I didn't really know what it was that you did."

"But you hired me for a quarter of a million dollars anyway?"

He didn't quite know how to respond to that, but Phoebe was already off again, talking to the assistant. "Is this the way to the leather?"

An hour later Matteo had seen, touched and smelt more varieties of leather than he'd ever really known existed and, even though he had no experience, it felt as if Phoebe had chosen well. She was still talking though. "I have a van parked outside. Can I get everything transferred into that?" she asked the assistant.

Matteo interrupted. "You brought a van? You're not getting everything delivered?"

She shook her head. "Why would I do that? I want to take everything back to the house myself. I want to check I'm happy with the fabrics before I get the drapes and furnishings made up. The leather will be delivered direct to the upholsterer, and tomorrow the chairs and sofas will be taken to his workshop so his team can get started."

Matteo pulled his credit card from his pocket and settled the bill. Yes, it was large. But no more than he'd really expected. The whole inside of the house needed a facelift, and he knew it.

Phoebe was still chattering away. She was very self-effacing but also extremely efficient. She had a way of getting things done. And she'd certainly moved with speed.

Something inside him was twisting around. It had to be the house. It had been so long since he'd actually been there, that it was only natural returning would be unsettling. But that didn't explain why he couldn't seem to take his eyes away from the girl in the bright pink coat, with the mad curls and coffee-tinted skin.

She bent down and talked to a toddler in a stroller while the mother was paying for her purchases, tracing her finger around the little one's palm as she sang "Ring-a-Ring o' Roses."

All of the women he'd been involved with spent their lives dressed in suits and formal dresses. Phoebe was wearing jeans, boots and a pale blue jumper under her coat. He liked her like that.

Like. A word he hadn't contemplated in a while. He could almost hear the roaring in his ears. When was the last time he'd actually liked someone?

He pushed the thoughts from his mind. His phone signal was still poor, and he still had to put the alarm code into Phoebe's phone. He had work to do. Being around Phoebe seemed to permanently distract him.

"Phoebe, do you want to grab some lunch? We need to find a place with a better signal so I can put the alarm code into your phone."

Phoebe looked surprised. "Well, sure. But don't you need to go back into the city? Because I was going to head down to the Hamptons."

Why was he doing this? His head wasn't entirely sure. The logical part of his brain was telling him this made perfect sense, it was all about an alarm code. If Phoebe had her own set of keys and the alarm code, then there was no reason for her to bother him again.

But even the rational part of his brain could sense this was a smoke screen. Whether he wanted to admit it, or not.

Phoebe licked her lips. They were painted pink today to match her coat, but the truth was she didn't need any makeup. Her natural beauty shone through. From the glow in her cheeks, to the shine on her springy curls and the sparkle in her eyes.

Matteo nodded. "Let's head toward the Hamptons. I'll get the driver to follow you. We can pull in at the first café we see in Westhampton."

Phoebe gave a nod. "You'll need to give me time to get the van loaded."

More time. There was only one thing for it.

He gave a nod of his head and held out his hands. "What am I here for?"

* * *

She wasn't quite sure what was going on. Matteo Bianchi was still as confusing as ever. One second he was a pleasant guy with a spark in his eye and a sense of humor, next second he was a grump, with dark shadows sweeping across his face. She wasn't sure whether he really found her a hindrance or a help.

She'd tried her best not to laugh as his suit had got wrinkled and smudged as he'd helped load up the van. She imagined that Matteo spent most of his life looking immaculate. Much like the people around him. Why did she get the feeling she'd never fit in?

Her stomach gave a growl as she arrived in Westhampton and signaled to pull into the parking lot. There were numerous cafés around and she was sure they would find something good to eat in most of them.

Matteo's driver was close behind her and by the time she'd locked up the van, Matteo was standing on the sidewalk waiting for her. He gestured toward the Rose Bakery Café, adorned with yellow cladding and with red and white awning flickering in the strong winds. "Want to try in here?"

There was a smell of cinnamon wafting from the front door. "Absolutely." She smiled.

They walked up the steps and he held the door open for her. The waitress quickly showed them to a table, gave them some menus and took their order for drinks.

Phoebe let out a laugh as her stomach gave an obligatory growl. "What do you want to eat?" Matteo asked.

Phoebe closed her eyes for a second and breathed in deeply. "There's far too many delicious smells in here. I can smell omelets, cinnamon buns, raspberry croissants and some delicious soups."

He leaned across the table toward her. It was the first

time she'd had a chance to notice the shadow along his jaw. Or the lines around his eyes. She rested her elbows on the table. It was so easy to lean forward too. "Are you okay, Matteo? Did you sleep last night?"

He blinked but didn't pull back. He just tipped his head a little to the side. "I hate that you do that sometimes."

"What?" He might be saying he hated her, but the expression on his face was telling her a whole other story.

He sighed as the waitress appeared with their drinks. "Blindside me." He stared down at his Americano and laughed. He gave his head a shake. "Not many people in this life can do that."

She licked her lips and smiled as the waitress stood poised with her order pad. "What'll it be, folks?"

Phoebe looked at the waitress with hopeful eyes. "What kind of soup do you have?"

The waitress checked her pad. "Today we have potato chowder, lentil and bacon, and chicken and rice."

"I'll have the potato chowder, please."

Matteo nodded. "I'll have the omelet, please, with mushrooms and cheese."

The waitress raised her eyebrows. "With salad or fries?"

"Salad, thanks." The waitress gave a nod and waved her hand at the glass cabinet behind her. "Just remember, we have some great desserts too."

Phoebe watched her saunter away then smiled at Matteo. "Do you think our order wasn't big enough for her?"

He shrugged. "Hey, she's right. They do have some great desserts. Maybe we'll have some pie."

Phoebe leaned her head on one hand as she stirred

her caramel latte. "You don't strike me as a pie kind of guy."

He raised his eyebrows. "I don't? What kind of guy do I strike you as?"

She kept stirring her coffee as she contemplated her answer. "I think you might be a bit of a traditionalist. I'm surprised you didn't try and steer us toward an Italian restaurant instead of a bakery."

He gave a slow nod of his head. "Any other insights you want to share about me?"

This time his voice had the slightest edge. As if he were silently putting up walls between them.

She couldn't help herself. She just started speaking. "You haven't shaved. Last time I saw you, you were immaculate. And you look tired today. I'm sorry if I offended you. Because I didn't mean to. I was just worried about you, because you looked so tired. You offered to help load the van and came out of your way to have lunch with me."

"Do you always worry about people you hardly know?"

His steady green eyes were fixed on hers. She held her breath. She should take it as a compliment, but he hadn't quite phrased it that way. He'd phrased it more as if she were just far too nosey.

She remembered talking to Captain Monaghan in the hospital. He'd been exhausted—and very sick. When she'd gone to get some light refreshments for her mother, she'd offered to get some for Rudy too. In fact, she'd ended up getting food and drinks for most of the other patients. It was her nature. Her way. She couldn't and wouldn't change it because Matteo Bianchi found her intrusive.

She shrugged and smiled. "Some people say I have a kind heart. I can live with that."

As she looked up Matteo was studying her hard. A frown creased his brow and he leaned closer and lifted his fingers to her cheek. The contact made her flinch.

"Phoebe, did someone hurt you? Is that a bruise?"

She shook her head as she lifted her own hand to her cheek. "Don't panic. It's me." She lowered her gaze, almost embarrassed to answer. "In my excitement to get started this morning I fell out of bed. I hit my face on my bedside cabinet."

Matteo didn't speak. He just kept staring. Then he glanced down at her hand. She could see the tension across his shoulders and the tic at the side of his jaw. "Is there someone in your life, Phoebe?"

She jerked and sat back in her seat, her mouth instantly dry. Everything about this felt wrong. He'd more or less just accused her of being too nosey, but now she could feel the intensity of his gaze. She could see both the sympathy and revulsion in his eyes. He'd jumped to a conclusion that was entirely wrong. She didn't doubt for a second what Matteo Bianchi would do to a man who was abusing his wife.

Tears pooled in her eyes. But for none of the reasons that Matteo was obviously assuming. She opened her mouth to speak but the words stuck in her throat. Why were they so hard to say?

"There…there's…no one in my life, just me." She shook her head as the tears threatened to fall. "Can't blame anyone else for my clumsiness."

His shoulders fell a little but the crease in his brow remained.

The waitress appeared at that second, gave them a

peculiar glance and put their plates on the table. "Anything else?"

Phoebe shook her head quickly. "We're fine," replied Matteo.

They sat in silence for a few seconds. Phoebe staring at her potato chowder. The smell that had seemed so delicious earlier, now just seemed to make her stomach do uncomfortable flip-flops.

Matteo lifted his fork and picked at his omelet. After a few seconds he let out a sigh and put his fork back down, sliding his hand over the table and letting it cover hers.

"Is there anything you need to tell me?"

She shook her head as one tear finally slid down her cheek. The lump in her throat had grown to epic proportions. Her other hand was still automatically stirring her soup.

Matteo pressed his lips together for a moment. His hand was warm against hers. Her fingers had never felt quite so cold. Up until a few moments ago she'd felt fine. Now, she just felt so…empty.

Why? Jason had died three years ago. She'd had to tell friends and family about the terrible accident. But she'd simply never found herself in a circumstance like this.

Matteo was only showing concern over something he'd misinterpreted. It should be no big deal. She should just have waved her hand and laughed it off.

But when he'd stared at her with those big green eyes and asked her if there was someone in her life it was the first time in three years she actually felt *something*.

And that terrified her.

She shook her head and stared down at her soup. She could tell him why she was tearful. She could tell him that her fiancé had died a few years before. Then, he would know that there was no hint of trouble in her life.

But somehow she couldn't find the words.

She'd tried dating. Once or twice. But her heart just wasn't in it. Jason had held every part of her heart. She'd loved him. Totally. He'd been her soul mate. And when he'd died? She'd tried so hard to soldier on.

But the hurt was inexplicable. Something she could never, ever forget. And it had made her learn to build walls, put up barriers, to keep herself safe. It was the only way. She couldn't—*wouldn't*—ever allow herself to feel like that again.

Which was why being around Matteo and feeling something again—no matter how small and unexplained—was unsettling her beyond words.

But then he did something unexpected. His hand was already sitting over hers. He gave it a squeeze and gestured down to their plates. "I think maybe our waitress was right. I think we should move straight on to desserts. Why waste time when we both know we want an explosion of sweetness?" He stood up and took her hand in his, pulling her up toward him and giving the waitress a wave. Phoebe's legs were shaking. What on earth was wrong with her?

But Matteo did his best to put her at ease by throwing a relaxed arm behind her waist and moving her a little closer to the glass counter. The waitress gestured toward the cakes. "What'll it be?"

Matteo nudged Phoebe. "What's your favorite?"

There was a mountain of choice. Chocolate cake, cheesecake, carrot cake, apple pie, cherry pie, strawberry shortcake, cupcakes and cookies. Too much choice. She couldn't even pick. Matteo waved his hand. "Just give us one of everything. We'll share."

The words seem to bring her back to her senses. "Matteo? We'll never be able to eat all that."

He smiled. "No. But we can take a bite of each. Can't you remember as a kid always wanting to do something like that? Let's relive a bit of our childhoods."

It was the most relaxed she'd seen him. They sat back down at their table and the waitress brought over a large tray with every dessert on a separate plate and lots of cutlery. She topped up their drinks, cleared away their other plates, then left them to it.

Phoebe picked up her fork as Matteo raised his eyebrows. "How do you want to do this? A bite each?"

Phoebe put her fork against her lips. "That sounds fair. But who gets to go first?"

He smiled. "Well, that's easy. My grandmother trained me well. Ladies first."

Phoebe took a deep breath. The tension was finally starting to leave her muscles. She grinned and reached over, digging her fork into the carrot cake with frosting. It was delicious.

She took a sip of her coffee and sat back in the seat. Matteo grinned back and didn't hesitate, heading straight for the cherry pie. "You thought I wasn't really a pie kind of guy? Well, watch and learn. Apple, peach, plum, cherry, I'm not fussy. I'll take them all."

"Does anyone else get to try the cherry pie?" She snagged a little from the side. "Hmm. Lovely."

She gave another smile. "So, I take it the sugar burst is helping with the tiredness?"

His eyes widened in surprise. He'd just gotten a forkful of chocolate cake. He stared at it for a second then nodded. "Actually it is. Do I really look that bad?"

She shook her head. "Of course not. Just tired. Were

you working late? I imagine it's hard coordinating things on different continents."

He pressed his lips together for a second. "Sometimes." He lowered his eyes as he ate the piece of chocolate cake.

Phoebe tried the strawberry shortcake. "Oh, wow, this is delicious. It's my favorite."

Matteo looked up. "Why don't you just finish it? Go on."

She shook her head and put her fork down. "No, honestly, I couldn't. But—you were right—just being able to take a bite out of each is fabulous." She put both hands on the table. "Thank you for this, Matteo. I'm so looking forward to getting this job started. The house is just wonderful. And I promise, once I'm sure about the fabrics, I'll get the order for the drapes placed. The painters start tomorrow and I've already agreed on the colors for every room. The only other major thing I need to see about is replacing some of the carpets." She was starting to babble again. She couldn't help it. Interior design was the area she was comfortable with. She couldn't wait to get started on the job.

But instead of being enthused by her response it was almost as if Matteo switched off. The warmth that had been in his eyes seemed to dissipate.

She kept talking. "Do you want to look at some more of my sketches? Is there anything you'd like to discuss about them? I am open to any changes."

Matteo shook his head and held out his hand. "Give me your phone and I'll put the alarm code in for you."

She handed the phone over and he programmed it in a few seconds.

His phone buzzed and he stood up. "Like I said, I'm happy for you to carry on with the changes. You've told me about most of them, and I've seen some of the sketches. That's enough. I don't need to know the details. I'll contact the bank and make sure your card is activated. You can let me know when you're done. At that point, we can discuss the house in Rome."

She could almost feel all the blood being sucked from her body. Rome. A few plane rides away. They hadn't really mentioned it.

She'd had a chance. She'd had a chance to tell Matteo the truth about her life, and the fact a plane ride might not be so easy for her.

But when the chance had arisen, she just couldn't find the words. Pathetic really.

It wasn't as if it were a state secret. But saying the words herself was different.

And saying the words to a man she barely knew, who was confusing her in a dozen different ways, wasn't exactly easy.

She took back her phone when he offered it and turned it over in her hand. It looked easy enough. She just had to bring up the barcode and show it to the reader on the alarm.

"This will be fine, thanks."

Matteo nodded and picked up the check. The sparkle from his eyes had vanished. The façade was back in place. What was it with this man?

She watched as he settled the check and then headed to the door. He paused, as if his manners were telling him he should wait for her, but she shook her head. "Go ahead." She glanced down at the table. "I'm going to pack some of these up. The tradesmen that are coming to do some of the jobs will be grateful."

She lifted her chin as she tried to calm her jangling nerves.

It was amazing. One minute he was cold and distant, the next, care and compassion seemed to shine from those dark eyes. But nothing seemed to meet in the middle. She felt like Belle in *Beauty and the Beast*, torn between two people.

If this was how it was going to be, how on earth would she survive the next four weeks?

CHAPTER FOUR

THREE DAYS. THAT was how long she'd been here. Phoebe always worked long hours on the job once she got started and this house was no different.

With the avocado bathroom gone, the walls were now smooth and ready for retiling. The plumbing and electrics had been checked and any problems fixed. The ancient chimneys had been swept. The whole house smelled of paint, and there was a perpetual thin layer of dust wherever she went.

It wasn't that the clean-up crew weren't doing their job. They were. It was just they were having to do their job over and over again as the endless stream of trades-men came and went from the house.

Today there was a joiner oiling and re-hanging some of the shutters. They really were gorgeous and they'd all been repainted a brilliant white. The kitchen ap-pliances had been delivered, but not connected. The Belfast sinks were still to be fitted along with the new countertop. Phoebe had a spreadsheet with all times, dates and phone numbers for everyone responsible.

She walked up the curved stairs humming to herself with a pile of bedding and towels in her arms. Two of the bedrooms and half-baths were ready for her inspec-tion. The drapes for the bedrooms wouldn't be here for another week. But there was no reason she couldn't start to look at some of the finishing touches.

The porcelain sink and toilet gleamed bright white, along with the tiles. The clean-up crew had guaranteed they could restore the pieces to their former glory and they'd been as good as their word. She smiled as she put the pale yellow towels on the floor. She'd bought some cute ottomans for the bathrooms. She'd need to find them.

She glanced out the window toward Lake Mecox. Snow was starting to fall heavily again. She had hours of work still to do. She didn't want to start the journey back home because of the bad weather—even more so, she didn't want any of the tradesmen to leave early.

She'd ordered new mattresses for all the beds. So she spent a few minutes making up the bed in one set of bedclothes, then five minutes later in another. The pale yellow had seemed a little washed out in this room. The duck-egg blue was much better. Most people didn't understand how much light played in dressing a house. One of the first things she considered was whether a room was south, east, north or west facing. It could make all the difference.

She looked at the pile of bedclothes she still had to go through. There was no reason why she couldn't start looking at the other rooms. She had cushions, new lights, new lamp shades. There was a world of work she could do right now. Enthusiasm sparked inside her. Now, where had she put those prints she'd bought the other day?

"You look like crap."

Brianna had never been one to hold back.

Matteo waved his hand and shook his head while he

finished his call. Brianna swept through the door and strode across his office. She was wearing a bright blue designer coat that she took off and practically dumped in his lap.

Patience had never been his sister's greatest virtue.

She sighed, then tapped the desk, before finally perching on the edge of it. Matteo finished his call then leant back in his chair. "What do you want?"

He knew not to ignore her. Any man who ignored Brianna Bianchi was a fool, and soon learned the consequences of their actions.

"I'm ready to meet her."

"Ready to meet who?"

She waved her hand nonchalantly. "That girl that you won't really talk about. Makes me suspicious. I definitely have to meet her."

Matteo shook his head as he stared at the laptop on his desk. There was a problem at one of the vineyards in Portugal. He really needed to call. Soon.

Brianna licked her glossy lips. As usual, his sister looked impeccable. And very much like their mother.

Brianna always liked to be reminded of that. She'd only been a few weeks old when their mother had died, so didn't have any memories of her at all—only a few family photographs. But for Matteo it was harder. He had lots of memories.

Brianna had the same shiny dark hair and eyes, the same skin tone and frame. It was uncanny, and sometimes she even did little movements similar to their mother. There was no way it could be learned behavior. It could only be genetics. And sometimes that terrified Matteo. Especially now.

He'd always been close to his brother and sister. How would they feel about him if he ever told them the truth about their mother? Would they hate him, resent him for keeping quiet? He couldn't bear the thought of not being this close to them. His insides twisted again. For now, it was best that he continued to keep his secret. He could watch Brianna. Keep close to her. That way, he'd know if there was anything to worry about. He wasn't a child anymore. He was an adult. An informed adult.

Brianna rested her hands on her swollen abdomen. "What's she like anyway? I looked her up. She's pretty." She gave Matteo a sideways glance. "Very pretty, actually. And she wasn't wearing a ring in the picture that I found. Is she attached?"

Matteo couldn't even hide his surprise at his sister's brazenness. "Why on earth would that matter?"

Brianna arched her back then stood up and walked around the desk, all the while her eyes carefully focused on her brother. "Well, of course, it doesn't. I'm just curious. How soon will she be finished?"

Matteo kept his voice steady. "Just a few weeks, I expect. Phoebe seems super-organized. She's running the place like an army colonel."

Brianna's eyes gleamed and she leaned across the desk toward him. "So, it's Phoebe already, and not Ms. Gates?"

He met her gaze square on. "Stop it, Brianna. You being pregnant won't prevent me from throwing you out of my office."

She threw back her head and laughed. "As if." Then her face fell a little. "I'm twitchy. I feel as if I'm going stir crazy. I'd love to be at the house in Rome. I'd love to help with the renovations." She rested her hands on her stomach. "But *some people* have decided I shouldn't fly."

He couldn't help but smile. "The whole world thinks you shouldn't fly right now."

Brianna bit her bottom lip and gave him *that* look. The one she always used when she wanted something.

"What? What is it?"

"I wondered if you would mind having a look for something for me."

Matteo frowned. "What do you mean?"

Brianna averted her gaze. "I've been looking for some photographs. Dad told me about them. But he could never find them."

Matteo felt a chill across his skin. "What photographs?"

Brianna licked her lips. He could tell she'd been practicing this conversation in her head. "Their wedding photographs. Dad thought he might have left them in the house. He said that they might have been left in one of the cupboards. They're in a red photograph album."

Matteo could feel every little hair on the back of his neck stand on end. "Dad told you this when?"

Brianna lifted her darkened eyelids. "Just before he died. He told me he wanted me to see their wedding pictures. So I would always remember just how happy they'd been." Her voice shook a little. And that for Brianna was big. She hardly ever let her emotions betray her. "It was just after I told him I was pregnant."

"And you just mention this now?" Brianna flinched at his snappiness.

He cringed. He couldn't help it.

Brianna waved her hand angrily. "There's never been a good time. Dad was sick, then he died. Then we had to sort out the business. Then it was Christmas and we had to agree about the house sales. Now *is* the time to talk about this. Before we sell the house at the Hamptons."

She blew part of her fringe off her face. "If this is such a bother for you, Matteo, I'll do it myself. I thought, since you'd already spent some time down there, it might be something you could do." She lifted her chin and stared off into the corner. "I could always ask Vittore."

She knew just what buttons to press. Always had. Always would. The gift of being a sister.

"Which cupboard? Where?"

She shrugged. "He wasn't specific. He just said that they'd cleared things out quickly and maybe the photographs had been left behind."

Matteo sucked in a deep breath in an effort to keep calm. He didn't want Brianna to know how difficult he was finding this. He didn't want to give any indication of how many memories being back at the house had stirred up. He was head of the family now. He had to show strength. Resilience. And he had that in spades. It just felt as if he'd had to keep reminding himself of that in the last few days.

His eyes rested on his sister's stomach. Especially now. How could he say no? He stood up quickly. "Of course I'll look for the album. If it's there—I'll find it."

He walked across the room and dropped a kiss on her cheek. "I'll let you know how I get on."

Brianna gave a nod of her head. "I knew I could count on you."

"Phoebe? Do you realize what time it is?"

Phoebe jerked up from where she'd been contemplating how to redress the gorgeous library. She'd missed this room on her first visit to the house. It seemed that when the Bianchis had first moved in they hadn't gotten around to clearing out the masses of books that the former actress had owned. Some of the subject matter almost made Phoebe blush. It seemed there had been much more to the demure actress than met the eye.

She turned to the door where Al, one of the joiners, was standing. His tool chest was in his hand and he was already wearing his jacket. She looked at her watch.

"Seven o'clock? Really? I had no idea. Al, I'm sorry. It's New Year's Eve. You should have gone home an hour ago."

Al shrugged. "I was in the middle of things, but I'm going to head off now. Family party. The snow is getting worse. Where do you live? I'm in Hoboken. Can I drop you somewhere?"

Phoebe shook her head swiftly. "No, of course not. I'm fine. I have my car."

Al raised his eyebrows. "Be careful out there. I'm not sure your car is designed for roads covered in snow. And it already looks as if some of the New Year revelers are out."

She gave a smile and nodded. "No problems."

Al disappeared and thirty minutes later Phoebe had finally decided on a plan for the library. She'd never been a fan of New Years. Her mom had let her know well in advance that she was having a glass of wine with a neighbor, then going home to bed. Phoebe had no reason to rush back into the city and experience the Times Square madness. She walked through to the kitchen with her sketch pad in her hands. The window ledge of the kitchen was stacked with snow. Phoebe wrinkled her brow and sat the pad down on the large kitchen table. Maybe she *should* head home—that snow was deeper than she'd expected.

She grabbed her bag and jacket and headed to the front door. The sky was already black and the snow was swirling around. Her Mini was coated in a thick layer of it. She smiled. Most New Yorkers saw no need for a car. Transport in the city was good. But Phoebe's interior design job meant she frequently needed to travel further afield.

She'd watched a movie years ago that featured three of these cars and had dreamed of one ever since. When she'd found a second-hand one—that came from the UK—a few months ago, she'd had to buy it.

The driveway was thick with ice and Phoebe practically skidded as she headed to the car. She jumped inside and started the engine. The car was always reliable and turned over first time. But as she moved the car into first gear—she'd finally got used to the stick shift—the wheels spun in the snow. She tried again, and again, but the car didn't move.

Somewhere in the distance fireworks exploded in the dark sky. It seemed that the Hampton parties had started already. People weren't waiting for the stroke of midnight for the fun to start. She could only imagine the chaos around Times Square right now with people crushing in, waiting to see the famous ball drop. Did she really want to head back there?

She sighed and leaned back in her seat as the thick flakes of snow continued to fall. She stared back at the house. Just as well she loved the place—looked as if she'd have to stay.

Phoebe scrambled back out of the car and into the house. Now the work crew had all left it was amazing how much her footsteps echoed through the house. She pulled out her phone and searched for the nearest pizza place—thank goodness it was still open. Two minutes later she'd ordered, warning their delivery driver about the driveway.

She glanced at her phone and sent a quick text to

her mother. It would be so easy to sit down and spend all night on social media, but it wasn't really what she wanted to do. None of the TVs in the house was currently working. The satellite company wasn't scheduled to arrive until next week.

She smiled. Of course. The library. The perfect place to spend a snow-filled evening. It was stacked with multiple shelves of books, accessible by an old-style set of moving steps. In a way, it was the perfect place for her to see in the New Year.

She grabbed the bag she carried with her. Unlike some interior designers she always had a change of clothes so she could do as much physical work as possible. It only took ten minutes to head upstairs and shower and change into the gray sweatpants and long-sleeved pink top she had with her. Comfort first. The bed that she'd made up earlier looked good. Only thing was, the room was a little cold. The heating system was something she'd have to look at the next day. It might be a bit chilly, but staying here wouldn't be such a hardship.

She headed back down the stairs and spent fifteen minutes trying to light the fire in the library. Eventually she conceded defeat and did an Internet search and watched a video that showed her how to do it. Five minutes later she finally had the flicker of flames, followed by the arrival of her pizza. The delivery guy gave her a wry smile. "Just as well we have a four-by-four. Your driveway doesn't take any prisoners. And I'm heading home now."

Phoebe nodded and smiled as she paid him and gave him a big tip. "Thanks so much for this. Happy New Year. Drive safely."

Your driveway. The guy was assuming she actually owned the house. Maybe in some wild dream or fantasy she would actually own a house in the Hamptons. Phoebe couldn't stop smiling as she closed the door.

The pizza was lukewarm. But it didn't matter. She hadn't realized she was quite so hungry. She carried it through to the library and looked around. Even though the fire was lit she still felt a little cold. She hesitated for only a few seconds before she ran back up the stairs and pulled the new bedclothes from the bed. There was no point in being cold.

Two slices of pizza later, she'd found a book that could make her hair curl even tighter and she settled down on the rug in front of the fire. This could be interesting.

Matteo let out another curse as his car skidded and he struggled to stop the back end fishtailing. Although the roads from the city had been glistening with snow, the gritters had been out and main highways were clear. The roads through the hamlets and villages of the Hamptons were a little different. He'd had the choice of any car in the garage and had chosen the one he'd thought most practical. The large four-by-four had initially made the journey easy, but the hardest part of the journey was now his own driveway. It currently resembled some kind of ice rink.

He frowned as he finally pulled up outside the house. He'd never intended to be this late, but a conference call had gone on much longer than expected. So by the time he'd started the journey to the Hamptons it was already dark. There was another car sitting in front of the house—one he didn't recognize.

It was New Year's Eve. Who on earth would still be here? Chances were it was nobody. Maybe one of the workers had decided to take a ride home with someone else—perhaps to join in some New Year's celebrations.

Matteo had tactfully given apologies to three potential party invitations, and the last place on earth he wanted to be right now was in the heart of New York at Times Square. The streets had been crammed as he'd left the city and they'd be worse by now.

He stepped outside of the car and promptly landed on his butt. He got up quicker than he'd gone down, groaning and rubbing his backside, flicking his head from side to side. Of course no one had seen him—no one was here. But his reactions were just automatic. He pulled his phone from his pocket praying the screen wasn't smashed.

The spider's web across the glass told him otherwise.

He held it up to the alarm scanner. Nothing. Nothing happened. He tried again, then frowned as he turned the key in the lock. A couple of seconds and a few careful steps later he was inside the house.

As soon as he was in the entrance hall he knew something wasn't right.

There was...something.

A noise. A smell.

He turned in that direction and started walking. At the end of the corridor there was a glow. None of the lights were on in this part of the house. He could easily flick the switches. But he was far too stubborn minded to slow down. He shook his head as he kept walking. For the first time since he'd been a teenager, every bad horror movie he'd ever watched suddenly made sense. He'd always shouted at the screen before—*why haven't you put on the lights? Why are you walking toward the trouble?* But here he was, doing exactly the same.

That car still bothered him. But it could easily belong

to one of the clean-up crew who didn't want to drive a small car home in the snow and had traveled home with someone else. The door had been locked, but the alarm hadn't been on.

Could this be an intruder? Someone who'd heard the house was being renovated and had decided there might be something worth stealing?

His hands clenched into fists. Matteo didn't need any kind of weapon. He was more than a match for any intruder.

As he strode down the corridor he realized where the light was coming from. The library? Why on earth would any intruder go to the library? It was a place he'd never spent much time in; he hadn't even remembered to direct Phoebe here when she was looking around the house.

There was something strange about the light. And the smell. Was something burning?

His heart rate quickened as he swung the door open—to the most peaceful scene.

Phoebe was lying curled up on the floor, covered in blankets in front of a flickering fire.

A fire. Of course. Although the house had multiple fireplaces, Matteo had never seen any of the fires lit in this house. They'd only stayed here for a few weeks one fateful summer. It hadn't even occurred to him that the light might be coming from one of the fireplaces.

Phoebe's curls were fanned out all around her, her head on a cushion that must have come from one of the high-back chairs. On the floor in front of her was a pizza box, with only a few slices missing.

For a few moments he didn't move. Just watched the rise and fall of her chest. Her skin glowed in the orange flickering flames. Her lips full and pink.

Something clenched inside him and he turned away. She was an employee. A business associate. Even if it was for only a few weeks. He had to push any other kind of thoughts away. He had too much else to deal with—too much else to worry about. He couldn't afford any distractions.

"Matteo?"

He turned around. Phoebe was pushing herself up, moving her hair away from her tired eyes. "When did you get here?" She looked confused. "What time is it?"

Matteo straightened up. "It's after ten. Phoebe, what are you doing here? It's New Year's Eve. Are you staying here?"

She gave a weak smile. "I kind of got snowed in. My Mini wouldn't move. The wheels just kept spinning in the snow. They couldn't get any grip."

She looked down at the bedding around her, and pulled a face as if she realized how inappropriate it might look. "I'm sorry about this. I came down here because I was cold. We'll need to check the boilers. Once I'd lit the fire and had something to eat, I just closed my eyes for a second and…" Her voice tailed off, then she let out a little laugh and pulled her knees up to her chest. "But isn't this the perfect place to spend New Year's?"

The heat from the room reached out toward Matteo. The fire was inviting. But the sleepy-eyed woman seemed even more so. It was the expression on her face when she said those words. Any other woman that Matteo had been involved with would have made a song and dance about New Year's Eve and parties. More than once he'd ended up spending New Year's dressed in a tuxedo and celebrating with people he barely knew, as the woman on his arm complained about her shoes and drank more champagne. He wasn't at all sorry not to be in that situation this year.

Phoebe, in her casual clothes, with pizza and a bed in front of the fire, was like a revelation.

He stepped inside. Phoebe gave a rueful smile and held up the pizza box. "Can I offer you some cold pizza? The delivery guy managed to get here, so pizza—" she looked around "—and soda is all I can offer you."

Matteo shook his head. "I didn't come here for food."

"Oh, what did you come for?"

The question was innocent. He knew that. But it sent up all his defenses. "Just something for the family."

Phoebe looked at him curiously as she pushed herself to her feet. "Can I help you?"

She moved over toward him, obviously feeling self-conscious as she tugged at her clothes. "Not the most professional-looking—I know. But, sometimes dressing homes isn't as glamorous as it sounds. Sometimes I just get down on my hands and knees and scrub floors."

Something flared in his mind. A few years ago he'd sold another property. The interior designer hired then had swanned around in a suit and heels with her hair swept up in a bun, a scarf around her neck and a clipboard permanently in her hand. Ms. Dragon, as he'd nicknamed her, wouldn't ever dream of getting her hands dirty. She was too busy ordering her minions about. There was something reassuring about knowing how committed to the job Phoebe was.

Phoebe tilted her head to the side and a waft of roses seemed to reach out toward him. It took him a few seconds to realize the scent was coming from her. Had she just showered? "It's late. Couldn't what you need wait until morning?" Phoebe turned and walked to the window, pulling back the shutters and looking at the white landscape outside. "If you're not careful, you'll end up just as stranded as me."

Matteo walked up behind her, standing a little closer than he should. The scent of roses was definitely coming from her. Fresh and light, it was almost intoxicating. Maybe it was the heat from the fire? Or maybe it was just his lack of sleep catching up with him. But something was sending all his senses into overload.

"What brought you to the library?" Matteo looked around the room. It was darker than the rest of the house, mainly because of the polished mahogany lining the shelves and walls. The only splash of color came from the wingback chairs covered in deep red velvet and the thick red rug in front of the fire. The shelves were lined with a myriad hardback books in a variety of shades that Matteo had never even looked at.

Phoebe held up her hands, her eyes sparkling. "It's the most beautiful room in the house. I love it." She walked over to the old-style moving steps. "Have you any idea how excited I was when I saw these? It's like every bookworm's dream. All these books. And these stairs? I could spend all day, every day in this room." She held up her hands in front of her chest. "I mean, imagine having a library in your house?" Her enthusiasm practically emanated from every pore.

Matteo leaned back against the wall. He'd never really thought about the library at all. He hadn't had any interest in it as a five-year-old—he'd been much more excited by the tennis court and swimming pool in the grounds of the house. But the enthusiasm brimming from Phoebe was almost infectious. He walked over and ran his hand across the spines of some of the books. The library had that old-world sort of smell. The kind you either loved—or hated.

Most of the books looked like encyclopedia-style volumes. He gave a smile. "Remember the world before the Internet, when you actually had to go to a library and search in a book when you wanted to find out something?"

Phoebe nodded. She was staring at the books in front of her. "Two seconds, that's how long it takes now to search for something. Think of the hours you had to spend before."

She was still smiling as she pulled one of the books from the shelf. "Some of these books look demure. But looks can be deceiving." There was a glint in her eye as she let the book fall open in her hands.

Matteo was curious and walked toward her. The heat in the room was building and he shrugged off his jacket. His eyes widened as he looked at the illustrations in the book and choked with laughter. He leaned closer and frowned. "Can people even get in that position?"

Phoebe met his gaze with a glint in her eye. "Only if you're a contortionist. I'm assuming these books belonged to the previous owner?"

Matteo nodded his head. He couldn't help but smile. "Melinda Mulrooney had a reputation for being demure. Seems like there was much more to her than met the eye."

Phoebe smiled as she closed the book and slid it back into place. She turned back toward Matteo and bit her lip. "I'm sorry that I'm here. Obviously, I didn't mean to be."

Matteo shrugged. "It's fine." He glanced at the heap of bedclothes on the floor. "But don't you want to sleep in a bed?"

"I would have—but it was a little cold upstairs. And what with the fire down here and—" she held out her hands "—all these wonderful books. I kind of decided that this was all the entertainment a girl could need."

The sentence was light-hearted but their gazes connected as she said the last few words. It seemed to hang in the air between them. Against the crackle of the fire in the background he could almost hear the sizzle in the air. His skin buzzed and blood rushed to parts at the rate of a Grand Prix driver racing around Le Mans. He was holding his breath without even realizing it, and as Phoebe's tongue slipped from her mouth and slid along her bottom lip it glistened in the dim light. There was a roaring in his ears. What on earth was happening between them? After the longest pause, Phoebe pulled her eyes away from his. It was excruciating.

"I've made up a few of the rooms. If you need to stay too—it should be comfortable." She pulled a face. "It just might not be too warm."

Matteo looked out of the window, trying not to let his brain go to the place it wanted to right now. Stay here? With Phoebe? The snow was falling even heavier now. The very last thing he wanted was to be stranded in this house. It didn't matter that this room was warm and inviting. It didn't matter that the house was solid, that there was food and there were beds. It was this place. For him, the heat level was irrelevant; he would always feel a chill just being here.

Phoebe reached up and touched his arm. Her warm fingertips sent a jolt through him. "Hey, you came to find something. Want some help?"

"No."

The word came out before he had time to think and Phoebe jerked backwards.

"Sorry," he said quickly as he ran his hand through his hair. He was being ridiculous. Even he knew that.

He was looking for an album he'd never seen, in a house with dozens of rooms and a million cupboards. It would be like looking for a needle in a haystack. And help should be gratefully received.

His stomach growled loudly. Phoebe pressed her lips together. "Unless you went grocery shopping, it's cold pizza, or cold pizza."

He nodded and sighed. "I guess it's cold pizza, then." He walked over and sat down on the rug in front of the fire. The snow had started to pile against the window. His stomach gave a flip as he realized there was no way he was getting out of here.

He looked down at the pizza. "What is this?"

Phoebe gave him a challenging look. "It's a mega meat feast with spicy hot sauce." She raised her eyebrows. "Why did you think I needed the soda?"

He nodded and licked his lips. "Okay then. I took you for a Hawaiian kind of girl."

"Ouch. Hawaiian is for wimps."

Matteo took a bite of the pizza. Within a few seconds the hot sauce hit his taste buds and his eyes started to water. "Wow." It came out kind of high pitched and he followed it with a deep, hearty laugh and a cough.

Phoebe laughed too and slapped his back. "Too much for you?"

He met her gaze straight on. "Not a chance." He eyed the pizza again. "I can do this. Hot sauce is nothing. I eat this kind of thing for breakfast."

"Well, don't eat it all," said Phoebe quickly. "We'll need to have it for breakfast too."

He hadn't even said the words out loud, but clearly she knew there was no way he was getting out of here tonight. Trying to travel in that thick snow would be stupid. And it was New Year's. Last thing he wanted to do was get stranded somewhere and have to call on any emergency services. Traveling now would be stupid and selfish. Matteo was neither.

He held his hand out for the soda that Phoebe passed with a laugh. "Should I have got you Hawaiian?"

He shook his head as the soda finally cooled the explosions in his taste buds.

Phoebe had pulled her knees up in front of her and leaned her head on her elbow. "So, it might be a little late, but I'm not that tired. You might not know this, but the TVs aren't working yet, and the wi-fi doesn't get fitted until next week. So, it's books or nothing."

Matteo leaned back on his hands and stretched his legs out in front of him. He might have taken his jacket off, but he was still wearing the suit he'd been dressed in all day. After sixteen hours his handmade leather shoes were starting to pinch. Phoebe looked much more comfortable than he did. "I'd kill for those sweatpants," he murmured.

Phoebe nodded and pulled at the stretchy material. "There's a reason I always have fall-back clothes." She held up her hands. "And this, is it."

Matteo shook his head. "How often do you get stranded or snowed in at work?"

Phoebe grinned. "You'd be surprised. Quite often I'm working at a place that is a bit out of the way. Or, is in the midst of renovations that means the water is turned off, or the electricity." She lifted her hands higher. "So, this is really a palace in comparison to some of the other places."

Phoebe was just so easy to be around. She was relaxed—comfortable in her own skin, and much more beautiful than she clearly realized.

But it was her manner that came over most. She had

a good heart. Five minutes in her company virtually told you everything you'd ever need to know. She'd never be the person who was thoughtless or insincere. Business had made him hard. He was used to ruthlessness and backstabbing. It was refreshing to be in different company.

The only light in the room was the flickering flames and right now they were reflecting off Phoebe's dark brown eyes. The noise from the fire—and the occasional spark—was actually very peaceful. For a few seconds he was sorely tempted just to sit here.

But Phoebe had already said she wasn't tired—clearly, because she'd already slept. But how to spend the next few hours?

He took a deep breath. He only had one reason for being here. And the truth was, he didn't even know where to start looking. Would it really be so hard for him to actually ask for a little help? He met Phoebe's gaze again. "How about we play a game of hide and seek?"

She gave herself a shake. Had she just heard him correctly? It was possible she was hallucinating. In fact, it was possible she'd gone back to that dream state she'd thought she was in last week when she'd first met Italian stallion, Matteo Bianchi.

She tried not to smile at the nickname her brain had automatically conjured up for him.

Chances were, she was still sleeping in front of that crackling fire after getting snowed in. Matteo Bianchi wasn't really sitting by her side, with his shirtsleeves pushed up and his dark hair flopping over his mesmerizing eyes. That would just be too good to be true. Really.

His hand closed over hers. Warmth. Heat. "What do you say?"

Nope. She wasn't sleeping. She was definitely awake. A dream wouldn't be making her heart beat so fast she couldn't breathe.

"Hide and seek?" Her brain couldn't really compute. He wanted to play a childhood game with her?

He nodded and changed position so he was kneeling next to her. "I told you that I came here to find something. Truth is, I'm not even sure where to look."

She frowned. "What do you mean?"

His voice was steady. "I'm looking for an old photo album. There's no guarantee it's even here, but my family think it could be in a cupboard somewhere."

The frown on her forehead deepened. Her head flicked from side to side. "In a cupboard, in here?"

In a place this size, how would they ever find it?

But Phoebe managed to shake off the enormity of the task quickly. Matteo had come all this way on New Year's Eve to find a family heirloom. The least she could do was be helpful. "Any clues? Do you know any more about it?"

He hesitated. "I know it's red. And it's their wedding album."

"Whose wedding album?"

He sucked in a deep breath. "My parents'."

"They lost their wedding album?" She didn't mean for it to come out like that—as if she almost couldn't believe someone would lose something so precious.

She watched him swallow as he waved his hand. "There was a lot going on the last time we were here. My mother was—ill. My father just recently died and my sister would really like to find the album."

There it was again. That little feeling she sometimes got around Matteo. He was telling her something—but not everything. Not that it was any of her business. She had no right to pry and ask questions. But she couldn't pretend she wasn't curious.

She pushed herself up onto her knees, mirroring his position. "Okay, so we're looking for a red wedding album somewhere in this house. Do you have any idea at all where it might be?"

He shook his head. Phoebe put her hand on her chin and thought hard. "Okay, so I've been in some of the cupboards in the bedrooms and bathrooms—and I've definitely been in every one of the kitchen cupboards, and each of them were empty. There might have been some old cleaning products, or dishcloths, but I haven't found anything personal at all. In fact—" she leaned a bit and looked around the room "—this place, these books, are the most personal things that I've found. But these didn't belong to your family."

Matteo's face fell a little. "Maybe this is all a wild goose chase."

She hated that. She hated seeing him look defeated. She grabbed his hand. "Get up. Let's think about this." Matteo stood next to her, as she started to walk around. She smiled at him and followed his example from earlier. "Let's play hide and seek. So, we don't think it's deliberately hidden somewhere?"

He shook his head.

"Okay, then, if you'd just moved in somewhere new—" she glanced at Matteo again "—and you had young kids—and you had plans to pretty much renovate the whole house—where would you put something precious? Where would someplace safe be?"

Matteo looked around too, as if he were trying to follow her train of thought. He gave her a hopeful smile. "Let's find out."

Almost two hours later they sagged back into the library. Even though the clean-up crew had been through the entire house more than once, it turned out that poking around the back of cupboards could still leave your hair and clothes covered in dust.

He was tired. He was definitely cranky. And even the woman who'd already had some sleep seemed to be flagging. He was ready to give up. The snow was still thick and heavy outside and it looked as if the gritters hadn't made it onto the roads yet. He'd definitely be spending the rest of the night here.

Phoebe flopped down for a few minutes onto the bedclothes that were still strewn across the rug, putting her hands on her belly. She almost drummed a tune on her flat stomach as she spoke to herself.

"What makes sense? The bedroom cupboards are all empty. You wouldn't put something as fragile as a photo album in the kitchen or any of the bathrooms. The main dining room and living room cupboards are empty. And I nearly broke my back trying to scramble up into the attic space."

Matteo couldn't help himself. He started to laugh. Maybe it was being overtired. Maybe it was just frustration that he couldn't get away from the one place he didn't want to be. Or maybe it was the sight of Phoebe's legs hanging from the attic and doing her best impression of a spider trying to cling to any surface.

She opened her eyes and stared up at him. "Matteo Bianchi, are you laughing at me?"

Before he had a chance to answer she sat bolt upright

again and smacked her hand off her forehead. "Oh, my goodness. We're idiots. Complete idiots."

Matteo shook his head. "What? What is it?"

Phoebe spread her arms wide. "What was the one place you know your family didn't have any immediate plans for?"

Matteo shook his head again. He was still tired. He'd been tempted to lie down on one of the beds that Phoebe had already dressed upstairs, regardless of whether it would ruin the look of the room or not.

Phoebe jumped up. Literally, jumped up onto her feet, a wide smile across her face. "We're dummies," she declared before spinning around. "Here, Matteo. *Here*. The library. The place that was going to remain undisturbed. The place that children probably wouldn't play, and the renovations wouldn't touch." She ran over and flicked the main light switch, flooding the room with light.

It was like being hit by a thunderbolt. Of course. *Of course.*

Phoebe had already made her way over to the shelves. She wagged her finger at him. "It's time for us to stop sniggering like naughty school kids at the ancient sex manuals and look for the real prize. A red album. It has to be here."

Phoebe climbed up the shaky rolling steps and started to look at the top shelves. She pointed downwards. "Let's be methodical about this. You look at the shelves underneath me."

Matteo nodded. His eyes swept along the shelves. A lot of the books were far too thick to be a photo album. Most of them were the wrong color. He pulled out a few, checking they really were books, then pushing them back onto the shelves.

"Right," came Phoebe's authoritative voice from above him. "Push me along a bit."

He looked up and pulled a face at her.

"What? There's no point in me climbing up and down, when you can just push me along."

"I think you're enjoying this a little too much."

She shrugged and gave him a little smile. "Maybe. But push me along anyhow."

The ladder squeaked and shook as he wheeled her along. "Don't get used to this," he murmured.

She laughed above him and his stomach gave a little flip. The horrible dread and associations he'd always had about this place didn't seem quite so bad when Phoebe was around. Five minutes later—after she'd got used to ordering him around—Phoebe let out a squeal.

"I think I've got it!"

Matteo jumped back, stopping at the bottom of the steps. Phoebe spun around above him, clutching a red album in one hand. Excitement seemed to bubble from her. He lifted his arms up toward her. It just seemed so natural. So easy. And Phoebe didn't hesitate—she let him lift her down the steps.

The album was in her hands. It looked old. She flicked open the front page then stopped and stared at him. "Oh, I'm sorry. Do you want to do this yourself?"

He hesitated. Part of him absolutely did.

But part of him absolutely didn't.

All of a sudden the lights in the library seemed too bright.

"Give me a second." He walked over and flipped them off. Somehow it seemed safer to be in the flickering firelight. "Let's sit down," he said.

Phoebe nodded and walked back over, sitting down in front of the fireplace with the album on her lap. She waited until he joined her, then opened the first page again.

There was no photo. Instead his parents' names were written in calligraphy.

15th June 1980
Roberto Matteo Bianchi and Lucianna Maria Aquino

His mouth suddenly felt dry and he was conscious of Phoebe's eyes on him. He couldn't remember ever looking at his parents' wedding album before. He was sure he'd seen one wedding picture. His father had kept one in a frame, hidden away in his study for years. But the rest? Matteo had never seen them.

He flicked over the next page and caught his breath. His mother. So young. She was twenty-two when she got married. She was sitting in her wedding dress in front of her dressing table looking suitably nervous for a young bride.

Her dress was an Italian lace overlay over a white bodice. It was simple. Round necked and short sleeved. It cinched in at the waist, with the skirt flaring out. Her dark brown curls cascaded over one shoulder and clutched in her hand a bunch of white lilies surrounded by baby's breath. His mother had always loved those. They'd decorated the house frequently.

Phoebe touched the plastic covering the photo. "Her dress is beautiful," she murmured. Matteo licked his lips. He'd always known that Brianna was the spitting image of their mother, but never had it been so apparent. They could almost be the same person. That thought was enough to send a cold chill down his spine.

Phoebe flicked the page. The wedding album was filled with all the usual pictures. Matteo's mother with her own father, looking suitably proud. A gaggle of bridesmaids, all dressed in wide pale pink dresses. A whole host of relatives that even Matteo wasn't entirely sure of.

But then Phoebe flicked the page again and there was his father. His eyes full of joy and life. It was like a fist closing around Matteo's heart.

It wasn't that his father had spent the rest of his life miserable. There had been the odd glimmer of spark and happiness. But the truth was, those moments had been few and far between. After the death of his mother, his father had focused all his energy and attention on business. He'd been ruthless. Sometimes heartless about the decisions he'd made.

He'd never been a bad father. He'd never ignored his children. He'd just been a little...vacant.

Seeing this picture of him so full of life and joy almost wrenched the heart from Matteo's chest. Phoebe was oblivious. She had a dreamy smile on her face as she flicked the pages. The next showed his mother and father clasping hands at the altar and exchanging vows. The love and devotion was painted on their faces for all the world to see.

Phoebe let out a little wistful sigh. "How gorgeous," she whispered.

The twisting sensation in his chest stopped. He looked at the picture again with new eyes. It *was* gorgeous. It was a moment in time—a moment to remember. He lifted his fingers to the page. "I think I'd quite like to copy that photograph," he said, his voice heavy with emotion.

"You've lost them both now, haven't you?"

The emotions were bubbling up inside him. He'd been feeling anger—despair. Everything about this place overwhelmed him with sadness. But just that single comment. And just the chance to sit down and look through these photos was helping him to take stock.

His parents on their wedding day. So much happiness. So much hope. They'd lived a good life together. His father's business had flourished. His mother had always been adventurous. She'd relished the move to the United States. She'd loved New York and been happy to plan to bring her children up here.

She'd been happy. She'd adored her husband, and looked forward to a lifetime together. Matteo's stomach gave a little twist. But fate and misfortune had cut that short. He lowered his head. If he'd raised the alarm... if he'd realized she wasn't sleeping...

Phoebe turned toward him, her rose scent drifting up around him. Her face was only inches away from his. Their bodies were so close. His arm was resting on the floor, but placed between her arm and her body. Just by looking at the album they'd practically found themselves intertwined. Was this fate? Or was this fortune?

It was almost as if all his instincts about Phoebe fell into place at once. She lifted her head, her nose brushing against his chin, and reached up and touched his cheek.

It was the smallest of movements, with a whole lot of heart.

"I think it would be beautiful as a black and white canvas," she whispered. "Something to look at, and remember." She paused for a second then added, "We all should remember the things that are precious to us."

He looked up and met her gaze. In the flickering firelight it was possible he'd never seen a woman look quite so beautiful. Phoebe might be dressed in the most casual of clothes, her hair might show remnants of dust, but her light brown skin glowed, and her dark eyes pulled him in.

There was something there. Something he'd never experienced before. A connection. A feeling. A sincerity.

The timing might be wrong. The circumstances might be less than ideal. But he couldn't help his instincts. As the world burst into life outside and fireworks filled the air to celebrate the New Year, Matteo bent his head and met her soft lips.

There was no shock. No disdain. Phoebe's lips were as sweet and inviting as he could have hoped for. The kiss was gentle—sweet. She returned it, her lips parting ever so slightly, encouraging him.

His hand reached up and tangled in her curls, pulling her head closer to his. She let out a little sigh and it was almost his undoing. It would be so easy to continue. So easy to let this progress. They were already on the floor. The bedclothes were scattered around them. He could just pull her on top of him, or slip his hand under the pink top. He could see her gentle curves, and the temptation to touch them was overwhelming.

But, for the first time in his life, Matteo didn't let his natural instincts set the pace. Instead, he swallowed, and reluctantly let his lips part from hers. He could still taste her, and he'd never felt so hungry for more. Every part of his body urged him to continue.

But he took a deep breath and rested his forehead against hers, his hand still tangled in her hair. Phoebe's breathing was labored and heavy, just like his. But she didn't push for anything else. She seemed happy to take a moment too. Her chest was rising and falling in his eye line as they stayed for a few minutes with their heads together.

Everything felt too new. Too raw. Did he even know what he was doing here?

"Happy New Year," he said softly. "At least I'm guessing that's why we can still hear fireworks."

"There are fireworks outside? I thought they were inside." Her sparkling dark eyes met his gaze and she smiled. "Wow," she said huskily.

He let out a laugh. "Wow," he repeated.

Her hand was hesitant, reaching up, then stopping, then reaching up again. She finally rested it against his chest, the fingertips pausing on one of the buttons of his shirt.

His mind was willing her to unfasten it. But she just let it sit there. The warmth of her fingertips permeating through his designer shirt. He could sense she wanted to say something, and it made him want to stumble and fill the silence.

For the first time in his life, Matteo Bianchi was out of his depth. It was a completely alien feeling for him. In matters of the opposite sex he was always in charge, always the one to initiate things, or, more likely, finish them. He'd never been unsure of himself, never uncomfortable.

But from the minute he'd met this woman with a warm smile and thoughtful heart, he just hadn't known how to deal with her. She had a way of looking at him as he answered a question that let him know his blasé, offhand remarks didn't wash with her. She didn't push. She didn't need to. He was quite sure that, if she wanted to, Phoebe Gates would take no prisoners. But the overwhelming aura from Phoebe was one of warmth, of kindness and sincerity. And it was making his heart beat quicker every minute.

She pulled back and blew out a long breath, watching him with her steady eyes. She glanced down at her watch. "Yup—two minutes past. I guess we missed the big countdown."

It would be so easy. So easy to make a mistake here. So easy to do everything wrong, just because it might feel a little right. "I don't think we did," he said softly.

For a few seconds they just sat and breathed. Her fingers intertwined with his. His sallow skin with her light coffee skin. They seemed to match perfectly.

"Give me a minute," he said as he jumped to his feet. She looked a little surprised but didn't speak. There was almost a roaring in his ears as he raced first up the stairs to grab some pillows and another set of blankets, then he grabbed his car keys to head out to the car.

He shook his head as he glanced at the icy driveway, taking careful steps to find what he was looking for from the glove box of the car. A few minutes later he was back in the library.

Phoebe looked a little self-conscious now, tugging at her sleeves and biting her bottom lip. Her eyes widened at the pillows. But Matteo knew exactly what he was doing. He kept things easy. He kept things relaxed as he threw the pillows on the floor. "It's late. I figured we're both tired by now. Here, I thought the cushions might be a little uncomfortable. You're right, the rest of the house is just too cold. So, we'll camp down here tonight and sort things out tomorrow. I even have a surprise." He couldn't help but smile as a frown creased Phoebe's brow.

"What surprise?"

He pulled the candy bars from behind his back and tossed them toward her. "Don't let it be said that I don't have any vices. I keep a secret stash in my glove box. Don't you remember as a child all the best movies had kids having midnight feasts? Think of this as our own version."

The tension in Phoebe's shoulders dissipated a little. She stared at the four candy bars scattered on the bedclothes in front of her and looked up and gave him a little smile. "Do I get first pick?"

"Always," he said as he plumped down beside her. "I'm a gentleman, didn't you know that?"

There was a pause. A second where their gazes meshed. An understanding. There was no pressure here. There were no uncomfortable thoughts. He wasn't going to pursue something. He had too much respect for her for that.

He wanted things to be on her terms. Strictly speaking, Phoebe was an employee. It didn't matter if it was only for a few weeks.

Then, there was the fact they were currently stranded here. Above all he wanted Phoebe to feel safe around him. He might hate the fact he was going to have to spend the night in this house—but Phoebe being here made everything a whole lot easier.

The truth was, he probably wouldn't have found the album without her. And if she hadn't been here he would certainly have made the foolhardy decision to try and travel back on the icy roads rather than stay here alone.

That simple statement seemed to have done the trick. Phoebe grabbed one of the pillows and put it next to her. It seemed that bunking down in front of the fire wasn't so scary after all. She gave a slow nod and held her hand over one bar, then another. "Decisions, decisions," she teased. "I'd hate to make the wrong choice."

"I'm not sure you ever make the wrong choice." The words were out before he had time to think about them. "Look what you've done with the house so far," he added quickly. Trying to keep things simple.

Phoebe's eyebrows were raised, but she lowered them again and closed her hand over the chocolate and caramel bar.

"Thank goodness," he sighed as he whipped the raspberry and dark chocolate from under her nose.

Phoebe held up her bar. "If only we had coffee to go with these."

He held up his hands. "I'm good, but I'm not that good."

Phoebe took a bite of her chocolate bar, then settled her blankets out. She gave him a cute smile. "Who says you're good?"

CHAPTER FIVE

SHE FELT FUGGY. Was that even a real word?

"Ms. Gates? Ms. Gates, are you here?"

Her mouth was dry and uncomfortable and her back ached. But something was warm. Something felt cozy. It was a sensation she hadn't felt in a long time.

That ease of someone close behind, their body next to hers, a relaxed arm resting over her stomach, and warm breath near her neck.

"Ms. Gates, are you here?" There was a creak. A noise.

Phoebe sat bolt upright. Oh, no. Oh…what?

The joiner was standing at the door of the library. "Oops, excuse me. I saw your car outside and just thought I'd check you were safe." His eyes fixed behind her, his cheeks flamed and he shook his head and backed out the door. "Sorry."

"No, Al." Phoebe jumped to her feet and ran to the door. "I'm sorry. We got stranded here last night with the roads. I couldn't get the car to move." She frowned. "Wait a minute. How did you get here? How did you get in?"

Al shrugged. "The gritters have been out since three a.m. Most of the roads are passable now. The caretaker met me outside. Turned out he'd some rock salt and put it on the driveway this morning." Al glanced at his watch. "I take it the others will be here any minute."

"They will?" Phoebe turned on her heel and dashed back into the library. Matteo was already on his feet, tugging at his completely wrinkled shirt and trousers. Thank goodness they were both fully dressed.

Her mind did a bit of a backspin. Things could have totally gone in another direction last night. Part of her was glad it hadn't, and part of her was secretly disappointed. How would she have felt this morning if things had progressed?

She'd kissed him. She'd kissed Matteo Bianchi. *Her boss.*

And he'd kissed her back.

It was the first time she'd kissed someone since Jason had died. And the wash of guilt was overwhelming.

What was worse—she hadn't felt it last night. It hadn't even crossed her mind last night. What kind of person did that make her? To forget her dead fiancé after three years at the glint of an Italian man's eyes? Her body started to tremble.

She'd never felt ready. Never felt ready to move on. To take the first step. Her few dates had been disasters. But this had been unexpected—unplanned. What was she thinking?

Matteo looked confused as she walked back in. "You have people working on New Year's Day?"

She tried to gather her thoughts. Matteo seemed a bit uncomfortable. Maybe he was having regrets too. But this was business. This was work. She replied quickly. "Actually, *you* do. And you're paying them a big bonus for doing it. This is a rush job—remember?"

He didn't look particularly happy. He tied his shoes and stared disdainfully at the crumpled bedclothes on the floor. Phoebe winced. Yesterday, they had been smooth and pristine on the beds upstairs. In the cold light of day, it looked as if the adults in the room had been romping all night.

She bent down and scooped them up into her arms. Last thing she wanted was the rest of the people working in the house to see this. It made her feel like some kind of naughty school kid—even though nothing had really happened.

"Let me take care of these," she said quickly to Matteo as she disappeared back out of the door.

It only took a second to realize her mistake. A waft of his aftershave floated up from the blankets and her footsteps faltered. That kiss. How could she forget that kiss? The one that made her float toward the ceiling and never come back down. Just that memory made her heart rate quicken all over again. She kept walking to the kitchen, trying not to rethink things, ignoring the way that all the little hairs on her arms had just stood on end.

Jason. She should be thinking about Jason. Her breathing stuttered along with her footsteps. For the last year, the memories that used to be so vivid had started to fade a little. But right now, that just made her feel a million times worse. Was she going to forget about him completely? Her brain was so muddled. First her mother being sick and needing treatment, then the hospital bills, followed by the dream job, and the mysterious Italian. It was no wonder she couldn't think straight.

By the time she reached the kitchen she realized she was crazy. The washer wasn't plumbed in yet. She couldn't do the laundry and wash his smell out the bedclothes. She sighed. She didn't want to leave them in the kitchen where they could get even dirtier as the kitchen refit continued, so she turned back to head to the stairs.

Matteo was striding toward her, the album under his arm. He almost tripped when he saw her—it was clear he'd been planning on heading straight out of the door.

She swallowed again and felt a little surge of anger. The rattling kind that meant she really needed her morning dose of caffeine. That was it. The first thing she was doing today was going out to buy a coffeepot somewhere. He opened his mouth to speak, but nothing came out.

She gave him her best smile. "Let me know if there's anything specific you want me to do in the house."

Bland. Idiotic. It was the best she could do. She felt like the high school girl who the Prom King had kissed by mistake. Not exactly the best feeling in the world.

He licked his lips as that floppy brown hair of his fell over his eyes. If she had a razor right now, she would shave it clean off.

He glanced around. What was he looking at? He was surrounded by cream-colored walls. "You seem to have everything under control here. Maybe next week we should talk about plans for Rome?"

Her tongue glued itself to the top of her mouth. Rome. No. No. No.

That was a plane ride away. Probably more than one.

It was clear that he took her silence as agreement. He walked past. "Drop me an email when the house is ready and I'll contact the realtor."

She pressed her lips together as the surge of anger flooded her veins. Would it be wrong to push her employer straight out of the front door? She let her feet stay rooted to the spot, with her arms tightly clutching the bedclothes until she heard the door close behind him.

Nothing. No, *Thanks for last night.* No, *That was nice.* No, *Will I call you?* And definitely no, *I'm sorry.*

It was like being dismissed. Being ignored.

She stamped up the curving stairs, every step a little more forceful. Was this what Matteo did with women? Kiss them mercilessly, then just walk away?

Tears burned in her eyes. She was overreacting. She knew she was. But she couldn't fight the wave of hurt that burned through her.

He wasn't to know that it was her first kiss since her fiancé had died. He wasn't to know that even though she'd tried to get back out in the dating game, her heart just hadn't been in it.

He wasn't to know that last night, for the first time in three years, she'd actually *felt* something again. A spark. A glimmer of hope.

It was as if the cloud that had settled on her shoulders had finally started to lift. It was as if a stream of sunlight was starting to poke through.

Before, she'd always felt guilty. Guilty she was on a date. Guilty she was out again. It had never felt quite right. She had never felt quite ready.

So why did now have to be the time for her to feel ready? Why did the first guy who sent tingles down her spine and kissed her as she'd never been kissed before have to be her boss?

Matteo had lit a flame that had been tempered for so long.

Last night had felt so right. Why was he acting as if it were so wrong?

Maybe she was crazy—a whole world of crazy. How could she possibly even consider putting her heart out there again? It had been broken in the worst kind of way.

There was no way she could consider letting herself be hurt like that again.

She dumped the bedclothes in the corner of one of the rooms. She didn't care how messy they were. They could stay like that until the washer was finally plumbed in.

She pressed her lips together and put her hands on her hips. Right now she was so mad it was easy to push the other stuff out of her head. The Rome stuff. She would find an excuse. A reason not to be able to go.

He would still pay her for her work here. That would surely be enough to put a dent in the bill for her mother's medical care. The very last thing she wanted to do was spend any more time in an enclosed space with Matteo Bianchi—the guy who could kiss her, then treat her as if she'd never existed.

She looked around and lifted her chin. He wanted this house dressed?

Then, boy, he could have it.

"Mr. Bianchi?" Constance, his new, efficient, but very nervous PA was hovering by the door. She had a habit of shifting from foot to foot. At first he'd thought the stilettos that she favored were either too high, or too uncomfortable. But he'd quickly realized it was just a nervous habit.

He barely looked up. "Yes?"

There was silence. So he did look up—just in time to see her bite her bottom lip.

"What is it?"

She took a few tentative steps into the room, a piece of paper in her hand. She held it out rather shakily. "I just thought you should know that, in the last few days, there's been…extensive billing to the business account."

He frowned, not quite sure what she meant. "What?" He took the piece of paper and studied it.

His eyes just about popped out of their sockets as he stood up so quickly his chair fell to the floor behind him with a crash. Constance was out the room in a flash; apparently she could move quicker than a speeding bullet—even in stilettos.

Matteo started walking toward the door but was blocked by a figure in the doorway. Brianna's eyebrows were raised and her arms folded across her chest. It seemed as if her belly got bigger every single day. "Well, somebody's in a good mood."

"Leave it, Brianna. I have to go." He sighed, as he had to stop walking. "Any chance of letting me past?"

Brianna shook her head. She was dressed more casually than normal, her dark hair tied up in a ponytail. "Not until I know what's going on."

He held up the printout for her to see. "What's going on is that my interior designer has just gone stir crazy!"

Brianna screwed up her eyes and looked at the figure at the bottom of the page. "Wow," she said as a smile spread from ear to ear.

"That's all you can say—wow?"

She shook her head. "Actually, I can say a whole lot more." She gave Matteo her special gaze. The one that clearly meant he was in trouble. "I don't care what she spends. We've agreed we want to sell the house— and the house is decades out of date. As far as I'm concerned, as long as it sells, the interior design bill doesn't matter." She shook her head and stepped closer to her brother. "Oh, no. What I'm interested in, is what *you've* done."

"What's that supposed to mean?"

Brianna tapped him on the chest. "You think I'm stupid? First week you went shopping with her at the ware-house. She bought a whole host of things—but nothing outrageous." Brianna scanned the piece of paper again. "But this list? *These* purchases?" She started to laugh. "This is the sign of a woman scorned." She shook her head again. "I so want to meet this woman. Look how wound up you are—I haven't seen you like this in…" She frowned and met his gaze. "In forever."

Her voice softened. "What happened, Matteo?"

Matteo paused. He'd spent the last four days cring-ing inside and out. He'd handled things badly. He'd ac-tually spent a beautiful night with a gorgeous, sensitive woman, then acted like the town fool the next morning. Matteo had never been the tongue-tied adolescent be-fore, so finding himself turned into one that morning had been a completely alien experience.

It was obvious he'd hurt her feelings—even though that had never been his intention. And it was clear that now she was just letting him know.

He stepped backwards. Every day Brianna looked more like their mother. And every day it reminded him of exactly what had happened. It seemed as if his stom-ach had been in a permanent knot since Brianna had announced her pregnancy. He couldn't tell her just how worried he was. She'd already had a few little hiccups. Borderline blood pressure and a little bleeding in the early stages. For a single man, he'd quickly learned more about pregnancy than he'd ever wanted to.

Her gaze narrowed. It was almost as if she could partly read his mind. "Matteo, did you find it—did you find the album?"

He gave a nod and walked back to the desk, sliding open one of the drawers and pulling out the red album. He hesitated. "Phoebe helped me find it."

Brianna walked swiftly around the desk, righting Matteo's chair and sitting down with the album in front of her. She rested her hands on the album tentatively. "Have you looked at this?"

He pressed his lips together, then walked back to the door, picking up something behind it. It was a canvas. He'd listened to Phoebe. He spun it around and Brianna let out a little whimper. She was on her feet instantly. "Oh, my goodness." She reached her hands out to gently touch the canvas. "This is beautiful. They look so happy. It's just so, so…" Tears brimmed in her eyes. "How on earth?" Her voice tailed off.

Matteo's heart was heavy in his chest. "It's one of the photos in the album. Phoebe suggested getting it made into a black and white canvas." He gave a nod of acknowledgement. "She has a good eye."

Tears started to flow down Brianna's cheeks. "Oh, she *so* does." She looked over her shoulder. "It's one from the album?"

He nodded and she walked back over and sat down, spending the next five minutes flicking slowly through the pictures. He couldn't speak—only watch as his sister went through the same experience that he had. When she reached the last page she closed the album and held it close to her chest. She stayed that way for a few seconds then stood up and walked over, wrapping her arms around his neck.

"Thank you," she whispered. "Thank you for going back to the house and finding this for me."

Her swollen stomach was pressed against him and her baby decided to give a little kick. He jumped back in surprise as Brianna smiled and put her hand on her stomach.

"My little one is grateful too. Now, he or she gets

to see pictures of their past. Pictures of the people we love."

Matteo gave a slow nod. He knew she was right. But everything just seemed so raw right now. Brianna stepped forward again. "Are you going to tell me what happened?"

He felt a chill all over his body. Of course Brianna wasn't talking about their mother. She couldn't possibly know. His brain tried to rationalize. "About the album?"

She reached down and picked up the piece of paper. "About this? What did you do to her, Matteo? What did you do to upset the girl who has finally put a little sparkle in your eyes?"

He blinked. "What?"

"You heard me. You like her. I know you do. You've been different these past few weeks."

He threw up his hands in frustration. "I'm different because I have things to deal with. We have two houses to sell."

Brianna gave a nod of acknowledgement. "We have. And I thought you might find this stressful. You were the oldest. You saw much more than Vittore or I did. But..." she looked up at him "...you've been better than I thought." She took the crumpled paper from his hand. "And I think it's because of this. I think it's because of her." She glanced at the figure at the bottom again and smiled and shook her head. "And it looks like you better start apologizing soon. Otherwise it will be a *very* long flight to Rome."

Phoebe looked around. She'd thrown herself into finishing this place, bringing down some clothes from her apartment and even spending the last few nights here.

She'd hired extra staff and yet another cleaning crew to achieve everything she wanted.

The last person had left half an hour ago. So, she'd taken some time to shower and change out of her grubby clothes into something bright, something fresh, and probably far too cold for a winter's day. But Phoebe didn't care. There was a paycheck on the horizon. Her bright yellow dress was a signal of triumph.

The drapes were hung, the light fittings all changed, the beds remade. The recovered chairs and sofas were exquisite. The leather was soft and tactile, the muted shades suited the rooms perfectly. All the finishing touches were in place. The lamps, the vases, cushions and throws. New prints and mirrors hung on freshly painted walls and light streamed in every window.

She walked from room to room, lighting candles along the way. Orange and lemon in the main rooms, clean linen candles in the bedrooms, and lavender and rose in the newly finished kitchen. She wiped a cloth across the deep white Belfast sinks. They were gorgeous. Just perfect in the old-style kitchen.

There was an aura about this place. Something special. She'd felt it the moment she'd arrived. And now, finally, she was finished.

She pulled her phone from her pocket and stared at it a few seconds. The realtor had already visited this morning, measuring rooms and taking hundreds of photos. Her over-eagerness at the possibility of a sale was palpable. Phoebe looked around. How much would a place like this be worth? It had to be over fifty million dollars. It *had* to be.

Everyone had left now. She was entirely alone. The scented candles started to gently fill the air around her.

She drifted back down the corridor to the main entrance and that gorgeous atrium and curved staircase.

Images floated into her mind of her favorite childhood cartoon movie. She started to hum one of the tunes and dance a little around the bottom of the stairs. All she needed was a yellow ball gown. Her yellow dress only reached her knees, but it was floaty enough. She lifted her hands as if she had a magical partner and started to waltz around as the humming changed to singing. Phoebe had never really been a singer, but who could hear? Right now, this was her palace. In here, her mother had never been sick. There were no bills. Jason had never died.

She started to dance up the stairs. That was the favorite part of the movie for her. She didn't need a partner. It was much easier if it was all just in her head. She'd probably never get the chance to do something like this again. She was going to just enjoy every minute.

She couldn't help but smile. Hopefully whoever bought his place would appreciate it as much as she did.

"Is this what you always do when left alone?"

The voice cut through her thoughts and made her stumble. Her foot slid on the stairs and she fell—straight into a strong pair of arms.

Instantly, she was defensive. His skin was next to hers. The smell of his aftershave enveloped her. She pushed back. Heat rushing to her face. She'd been dancing around like a five-year-old. *Singing.* And he'd seen her. He'd caught her in the act.

There was a glimmer of a smile on his face. But she couldn't return it. She was still angry at the way he'd treated her so indifferently.

She'd played on those few seconds over and over. What she *should* have said. What she *should* have done.

So many different scenarios that all added up to the same thing.

She needed to get away from Matteo Bianchi as soon as possible.

Matteo must have noticed her expression because he didn't even wait for a response to his previous question. "We need to talk."

There was something in his tone. Something that sent a little shiver down her spine.

She tilted her chin up toward him and held out her hands. "What about? Haven't you seen—I'm done here. The house is finished. The realtor's been. All that happens now is that you pay me."

She was being bold. She'd never been so forward with a client before. But then again, a client had never kissed her before. Or was it she that had kissed him?

Her insides turned over. *Who had kissed who?*

Something flickered in his eyes. Almost as if he were assessing the situation. Or assessing *her*. Something was off. Almost as if...was it hurt? A wave of pain? Why on earth would Matteo feel like that? What was it with this guy? Trying to figure him out was driving her crazy.

Matteo looked around. "Let's take a walk through. Show me what you've done." There was a waver in his voice.

She blinked. He hadn't even reacted to her almost cheeky remarks. She spun around. "Absolutely, let's start in the kitchen."

It didn't matter that her blood was currently racing through her veins. It didn't matter that she really wanted to limp on the stumbled ankle. She was proud of her work. She'd done a good job—she knew she had.

She could do a walk-through. Then she could see about getting paid.

* * *

Matteo's heart was somewhere between his mouth and the pit of his stomach. She couldn't know. She just couldn't.

But when he'd seen Phoebe twirling on the stairs he'd had a complete flashback to his mother. It didn't matter that they looked entirely different. Matteo's mother's long dark hair and sallow skin was entirely different from Phoebe's springy curls and pale coffee complexion. But it was the essence of them that seemed the same, that sent that surge of familiar emotions sweeping through his body. The life that was in them. Or used to be.

Phoebe's bright yellow dress was beautiful. A little unusual for this time of year. Maybe she had plans? Maybe she had somewhere else to go today? His stomach gave another flip as he followed her into the kitchen. Could she have a date?

Why was the coffee he'd drunk an hour ago suddenly gurgling around inside him?

It was amazing how a few subtle changes could transform a place. The large Belfast sinks were definitely the focal point. Phoebe gave him a minute to look around. "You'll see the sinks are now finished, the cream kitchen units have been revamped, some have been moved around. The walls are now a pale yellow to add a hint of color." She ran her hand along the new countertop. "And the dark wooden countertop is just the perfect finish, don't you agree?"

The way she phrased her words was almost as if she was challenging him to disagree. But he couldn't. The kitchen looked impressive. As did the laundry room, and the storage room.

Phoebe led him through to the main room. "You

can see how the color palette worked out," she said. The drapes at the window were striped, the sofas and chairs covered in soft gray leather, with a large gray and yellow rug dressing the light oak floor. Most other houses he'd visited over the years were almost bland. Everything either white or cream.

But Phoebe had a good understanding of color. The room was light enough to still enhance its size, but the color added something else—a sense of life. A sense of harmony. With a citrus scent in the air.

He pressed his lips together as she led him through to the sitting room at the back of the house. This room had glass doors that opened out to Mecox Bay. Here, the drapes were minimal, tied back to let the choppy waters of the bay be the focal point. The colors in here were slightly different. More pale blue than gray. It was almost as if, instead of dressing the house, Phoebe had been dressing the bay. She understood even more than he'd given her credit for.

She flicked on a small lamp in the corner. He sucked in a breath. "Is that a Tiffany?"

She laughed. "Of course not. I didn't spend *that* much money. It's a reproduction. But I thought it helped. There's very little color in this room, just cream and pale blue. Can you imagine, at night, sitting here, staring out over the dark bay, and flicking on this lamp, having the reflections of the blue, yellow and red glass across the walls? It would be almost magical."

For a few seconds, Matteo held his breath. He could almost picture it in his head. The trouble was that picture seemed homely. Warm. Inviting. Things he just couldn't associate with this house anymore.

He kept his voice steady. "Interesting. I think you've done a good job in the house, so far."

Phoebe made the tiniest movement. Did she flinch? Her face appeared a bit pinched. He'd thought he'd just complimented her work, but maybe not.

She swept past him and kept going. "Let's move up to the second floor."

They moved back out to the staircase, and Phoebe practically ran up it—obviously trying to shake the memories of being caught dancing on it earlier.

The bedrooms were all finished to a high standard, each with a few unique or quirky items just to personalize the rooms. The bathrooms were similar. Sparkling white, with some yellow or pale blue accessories.

Phoebe walked at speed, moving from room to room and talking constantly. Her work was impeccable. He'd already had a call from the realtor, who had gushed and complimented him so much he'd actually wondered at one stage if she was going to offer to have his baby. The realtor loved the house and had hinted that she predicted a sale would be quick.

"This is obviously the master bedroom so it's been dressed a little more demurely than the others. Again, since the view is a pivotal part of this room I've kept the color palette sedated."

She was tugging at a little bit of hair at the nape of her neck. *She's nervous.* Of course she was. The last time he'd seen her they'd been kissing.

His fingers crackled the paper in his pocket. He'd come here to question her about the expenses. But, as he walked from room to room, he could see exactly where every single cent had been spent. The house wasn't completely transformed. But it *was* different.

It felt different. Even to him. There was no question he was still haunted by the memories of his mother. But at least now he could start to dissociate himself from this place. Phoebe had made everything look new. It even smelled different.

Phoebe was still talking. Still tugging at her hair. "So, there's only a few other rooms. But I don't think you need to see them." She turned to face him.

"As you can see, my job here is complete." She gave him a bright smile that seemed forced. "Maybe we should talk about my payment?"

He raised his eyebrows. "Maybe we should talk about Rome? That is our agreement. Complete both houses, not just one. I can arrange plane tickets for tomorrow. Once I've shown you the house, and introduced you to the staff, I can leave."

Phoebe visibly blanched but Matteo continued, his hands in his pockets as he walked around the room. "You've done an excellent job. The look of the house is much improved." He gave a little smile. "Even though you might have broke the bank this last week." He moved over to the window and stared out at the bay. Even in the middle of winter, the choppy sea was a mixture of blues and grays. There were a few boats out on the bay. The view was entirely spectacular and would probably be the selling point of this house. "I think it's time to move forward."

He turned back around to face Phoebe. She was staring at the floor, fumbling with her hands. "I think that Rome might not work. It would make more sense for you to deal with an Italian interior designer who has a good idea of the best selling points for the Italian market. And the best tradesmen to work with. I have absolutely no grasp of the Italian language. I think I'd be far more of a hindrance than a help."

Matteo frowned and stepped forward. "But we had an agreement. I asked you to do both houses for me."

He dug his hands a little deeper in his pockets. "And wouldn't a house in Rome be good for your CV? As well as the house in the Hamptons?" Matteo wasn't stupid. He knew exactly how much kudos doing this house would give her. He couldn't understand why she wouldn't want to also have an international mansion on her portfolio.

Phoebe still refused to meet his gaze. She was shaking her head the whole time. Did she even realize she was doing it?

He pulled his phone from his jacket pocket. "Let me book the flights. When you see the house, you'll love it." He started flicking through the contacts in his phone.

"No." The word was almost a whisper.

His head jerked back up. "What?"

"No." The word was now a little less shaky. She lifted her head and finally met his gaze again. It was almost as if she were struggling to get her breath.

"What are you talking about?" He moved even closer. He was starting to get annoyed. "I employed you to dress both houses, the one here and the one in Rome."

"I know that…" she started, "but…"

"But what?" He threw up his hands. "Why on earth are you stalling? We had an agreement."

"I… I… I…"

There was something about the way she was stuck for words. That didn't seem normal for Phoebe. Her eyes filled with tears as he watched her.

He stepped over and touched her bare arm. "What on earth is wrong?"

She glanced down at his hand on her arm and he frowned. Something shot through his head and he was flooded with panic. "Is this about us? Is this about this kiss?"

Darn it. He knew he'd handled things badly—probably closest to a hormonal teenager. It was ridiculous. He was a grown man with a world of experience in kissing women.

But he'd never kissed a girl like Phoebe. He'd never kissed a girl who'd made him feel as if the fireworks going off outside were actually part of him. He'd never wanted to continue a kiss more than he'd wanted to that night. But it had been an impulsive thing. A lapse of judgement.

So why couldn't he get it out of his head?

Phoebe met his gaze again. "It's nothing to do with the kiss." She sounded exasperated, and a little bit sad. "It's just a whole other part of my life that I'm just not ready to deal with."

Matteo pulled back a little. "Phoebe, what is going on? Is something wrong?" The mark on her face the other day? Was this something to do with that? It was amazing how instantly protective he still felt about her.

She took a deep breath and he let his hand fall from her arm. Physical contact between them wasn't a good idea. "No, it's nothing like that."

He was getting impatient. "Then I'll see you at JFK airport tomorrow. The flight takes around eight and a half hours and it's a red eye. Dress comfortably."

"It's just…"

"Phoebe, I don't have time for this." He couldn't hide his frustration. Timing was everything. February was a crucial time for his business. He couldn't be distracted. He needed to deal with the house in Rome now. "I was clear. I offered you a quarter of a million dollars to dress two houses for me. One in the Hamptons. One in Rome. You agreed." He shrugged. "I don't take kindly to people who renege on business agreements. There are…consequences."

She blinked and he could see her brain trying to interpret those words. "You mean if I don't come to Rome, you won't pay me?" The shock on her face was clear.

"We had a deal, Phoebe. You keep your end of the bargain. I keep mine. I like to deal with professionals. I thought that's what you were." His eyes swept up and down her. Taking in the yellow dress and nude heels. "Maybe I was wrong."

Her words were strained. Her jaw clenched. "I am a professional. My job here proves it. This house will sell easily."

He walked straight over to her. Closer than he intended. He could see every inch of her smooth clear skin. The mascara outlining her long dark lashes. The hint of red on her lips. Her very kissable lips. "Your professionalism is proved once you complete the job."

He met her dark gaze. He couldn't read what was going on in those strong brown eyes. Phoebe's eyes had always flashed a multitude of emotions. Today? It was almost as if a set of shutters had closed across them. They were angry. Detached.

She tilted her chin up toward him. He could see the tiny pulse at the base of her throat. "What time do you need me?"

"I'll have a car pick you up at six p.m."

"Fine." She turned on her heel, her yellow dress swirling around her knees, as she walked out of the room.

CHAPTER SIX

SHE HADN'T EVEN met his gaze since she'd climbed in the car.

Pride and terror wouldn't let her. But as the car had got closer and closer to the airport she could almost hear the tattoo of her heartbeat against her chest.

The worst thing had been her mother. When she'd told her she was going to Rome to do a job, her mother's eyes had filled with tears and she'd cupped Phoebe's face and told her how proud she was of her. And how it was time.

All the words of fear and anxiety that had been ready to spill out of her mouth had halted instantly. Her mother was feeling well. Her treatments were finished and she was under instruction to rest for the next month. Phoebe couldn't use her mother's illness as an excuse not to go. Her mother would never forgive her.

Matteo's secretary had contacted Phoebe for her passport number and checked them both in online. As soon as they'd stepped out of the car the noise of the airport had overwhelmed her. The constant whoosh of planes taking off and landing. The chatter of people arriving or leaving. The thumping of cases. The toot of taxis.

It was like a roaring in her ears.

Matteo, of course, seemed oblivious. He steered her

to the priority security line and then in the direction of the first-class lounge. First class. They were flying first class. Of course they were.

She'd never been in a first-class lounge before. It was luxurious and open, but bright and friendly with decadent décor and dramatic lighting. The seats were comfortable and the service impeccable.

But the lounge had a mezzanine level with views across the airport. If she was sitting down, the bottom half of the glass was smoked. But when she stood up... she could see all the planes sitting at their gates, with others taxiing to and from the runways.

Which was why her heart was currently in her mouth. She took another gulp of the champagne that was sitting next to her.

It was ridiculous. It was irrational. And she knew all that.

Over the course of her life she'd been on dozens of flights. But ever since Jason had died, just the glimpse of a plane made her uncomfortable.

Right now, her skin was itching, her breath catching somewhere in her throat and her heart racing inside her chest.

She stood up and made a grab for her bag. "Excuse me."

With her head fixed firmly on the wall adorned with bright prints she made her way to the ladies' room.

The bright lights and white tiles were a relief. Phoebe splashed some water on her face and took some deep breaths. They'd be due to board any minute now. She fumbled in her bag.

Phoebe stared at the pills in her hand. She'd never taken anything like this before.

Never had to. Never wanted to.

But, after verging on a panic attack at the thought of boarding a plane, she'd gone to see her doctor first thing in the morning. She'd been sympathetic, and talked Phoebe through all the irrational fears she had. She'd wanted to try other methods, other therapies, but Phoebe had told her the urgency of the trip and how much depended on it.

So, she'd given her some breathing exercises. A few methods of control, and, as a last resort, the chance to take something that could reduce her anxiety.

There was nothing shameful in taking a few tablets. Lots of people had problems flying. Once the flight had taken off, she could try and sleep. And once they were due to land again, she could take another.

It was a temporary measure. She looked at her own reflection in the mirror. Life with Jason had been easy, relaxed. He'd been her best friend.

But New Year's Eve with Matteo had been entirely different. The fireworks hadn't just been exploding outside the room. And that connection had been terrifying. Not least, because there seemed to be so much that Matteo was hiding.

She splashed more water. Three years. Three years since Jason was gone. He wouldn't recognize the wide-eyed, terrified girl in the mirror right now. Her hand went to her throat as she held back a sob. And he would hate the fact that she was now petrified of the thing that he loved. The thing that had practically flowed through his veins.

She took a deep breath and shoved the tablets back in her bag. She tried a few of the breathing exercises her doctor had shown her. She could do this. She could do it. She could get on this plane and land in Rome. Yesterday had been key. She'd gone home to the final bill for her mother's medical expenses. She needed this money. She needed to be paid. This job would lift a huge weight off the shoulders of both herself and her mother. The last thing she wanted was for her mother to be stressed about paying for her treatment. Stress could impede her full recovery and Phoebe would never let that happen.

She walked outside. Matteo was pacing outside the door impatiently. "Are you ready? It's time to board."

Phoebe gulped. The sooner this was over—the better.

What was wrong with her? She'd checked her seat belt a dozen times and had her eyes fixed firmly on the screen in front of her. Her endless fidgeting was driving him nuts. Phoebe had never struck him as a fidget.

"Miss? Can I get you a drink prior to departure?" The stewardess had a trolley filled with fine wines, champagnes and spirits. Phoebe glanced in the direction of the trolley for a few seconds, then shook her head. "No. No, thank you."

Her hands twisted in her lap again as the stewardess moved away and a few minutes later the plane started taxiing. Phoebe leaned back in her seat and closed her eyes, her hands gripping the seat rests so tightly her knuckles were white.

A strange feeling washed over Matteo. She'd objected quite strongly to the trip to Rome. "Phoebe, are you scared of flying? Haven't you ever flown before?"

She didn't even open her eyes, or release her grip. There was a tic at the side of her jaw as she spoke through clenched teeth. "I've flown lots of times. Just not recently."

"And are you always like this when you fly?"

He was astonished. She generally seemed quite relaxed and happy. This was a whole other side of her.

The plane started to pick up speed for take-off. As the nose lifted her hand stopped gripping the seat rest and grabbed his hand, squeezing so tightly he lost all feeling in his fingers.

Matteo leaned back in his seat and said nothing. It seemed Phoebe's grip was stronger than expected. After a few minutes he put his other hand over hers. "Phoebe, you okay? Want to talk?"

Now he was feeling guilty. He'd given her an ultimatum. He'd forced her to come on this trip. He'd been so blindsided by getting the houses finished and on the market that he hadn't really considered anything else.

Phoebe started doing some breathing exercises. In. Out. In. Out. He felt himself breathe along with her. Now he knew why she'd been so tetchy. He should have considered something like this.

"Take it easy, Phoebe. We're up. Safe take-off. You can relax."

She opened her eyes, and he was surprised to see they were wet with tears. "I won't relax until we're back on the ground."

"You're *that* scared of flying? Why didn't you say?"

She pressed her lips together and shook her head. "I couldn't. It's new. Well, not that new."

He rubbed her hand again. "At some point I'm going to have to regain the feeling in my fingers. I might need them." He gave her a gentle smile. "What happened that you feel like this?" He knew he was prying. He knew this was none of his business. But he hated seeing Phoebe like this.

Her grip loosened just a little on his hand, but she didn't pull it away. "Sorry," she breathed, then stayed quiet for a few minutes. After a bit she licked her lips and met his gaze. "I had a fiancé. Jason. He was a pilot. He died in a flying accident three years ago."

It was like being punched in the guts. A fiancé?

"I'm sorry, Phoebe. I had no idea." He couldn't help the next words. "What happened?"

She blinked. Her voice was a little shaky. "Engine failure. Double engine failure. Something that shouldn't happen. Jason tried to land the plane. He had to divert it away from a built-up area and ended up crashing in woods." She gave her head a shake. "I've just had a thing about flying since then." She took a deep breath. "I had a funeral to go to last year—an old school friend. I'd bought a plane ticket but just couldn't do it. I ended up driving the four and a half hours to Washington instead of taking the hour-long flight."

"Is this the first flight you've been on?"

She bit her lip and nodded. Matteo hadn't let go of her hand yet. He gave it another squeeze. "You should have told me."

She raised her eyebrows. "I tried to say no. You didn't like that."

He sighed. "I thought you were just reneging on the deal. I didn't know there was something else going on. If you'd told me, I would have acted differently."

"Would you?"

"Of course I would." He waited a few seconds then added, "But I'm really glad you're here. Just wait. It will be worth it. The first time you do anything again is always the hardest."

She frowned as she looked at him, almost as if she were connecting the words with something else, then she gave him a soft smile and nodded. "You could be right."

He leaned over and whispered in her ear. "I promise you, you'll love Rome, and you'll love the house."

"I hope so," she said, as she leaned back in her chair and finally pulled her hand away.

Matteo stared down at his hand.

All of a sudden it surprised him how empty his hand felt.

He glanced sideways. Phoebe had been engaged. She'd had a fiancé.

He couldn't help but be curious about the man that had captured Phoebe Gates's heart.

He just couldn't figure out why it made him so uncomfortable.

The plane gave a jolt and Phoebe felt a tear escape down her cheek. She couldn't breathe. Was it engine failure? What if she never saw her mother again?

Matteo's hand closed over hers again. "Grip as hard as you like. It's just a little bit of turbulence. I can take it." He gave her a reassuring smile. "I'm here with you, Phoebe. We'll get through this."

His green eyes were warm and sincere. She couldn't help the second tear that slid down her cheek. Matteo reached up with his free hand and gently brushed it away. "Tell me about Jason," he said. "Tell me what he was like."

The breath that was caught in the back of her throat came out steadily. "He...he was good," she murmured. "He was great." It was odd to talk about Jason with someone that had never known him. Her brain tried to sort out her jumbled thoughts. "He was a couple of years older than me. We met in Central Park when I was nineteen. He was already in the navy, training as a pilot." She nodded. "He loved his job, completely loved it. Flying was a huge part of his life."

"And you?"

Matteo's finger started tracing soothing circles on the back of her hand. "Oh, he loved me too. Just as much as I loved him." Her voice stuttered a little as a memory swamped her. But it was a good memory, something that made her happy. "He used to make me laugh. He used to make me laugh so hard my sides hurt." She shook her head. "And he shared my sci-fi addiction. Any film, any TV series that was remotely sci-fi was always playing in the background. It didn't matter how bad it was." She smiled. "We watched it anyway."

She was aware of the gentle movements of his finger. She knew he was trying to distract her. Trying to keep her calm. But somehow, in the midst of all this, talking about Jason felt good.

"He'd left the navy and had just got a job as a commercial pilot. We were trying to make plans. Get our lives on track for the future." Her voice drifted off.

Matteo didn't jump in. He didn't push her for more. He just kept doing what he was doing, watching her with those dark green eyes with tiny flecks of gold. "He sounds like a great guy."

She nodded. "He was. And he was big." She shook her head. "We looked like the odd couple." She held up one hand. "I'm not exactly in the tall department and Jason was six foot six." She raised her eyebrows. "It certainly came in handy when I had any clients I felt uncomfortable around. One look from Jason was enough."

The air hostess bumped past them with the drinks trolley. It seemed the turbulence had ended and the "fasten seat belt" sign was off now.

It was nice. It was nice to talk about Jason and remember him. Remember how much she loved him and the part he'd played in her life. "Thank you," she whispered.

"What for?"

She stared down at their hands. "For this. For distracting me. For letting me talk. For letting me remember."

"Don't you talk about Jason?"

She gave him a sad smile. "Sometimes with my mom. But I think she worries it makes me sad. What I worry about is forgetting. I feel guilty."

Matteo pressed his lips together for a second. His voice was husky. "Remembering is good. We'll never be able to remember every detail." He put one hand on his heart, while using the other to intertwine his fingers with hers, "But what we hold in here is really important. Anyone we lose, we carry them with us every day. In our hearts and in our minds. That's what's important."

There was something about the way he said the words that made her heart give a little flip. He understood. He got it.

And all of a sudden so did she. She'd loved Jason for so long. She always would. She shouldn't be scared of forgetting him—that wouldn't happen. But that didn't mean that once she was ready, she wouldn't be able to open her heart to someone else.

She shouldn't feel guilt. Jason would have hated that. She nodded at Matteo as her heart gave another little pitter-patter against her chest.

"You're right," she said quietly. "That's exactly what's important."

The heat levels in Rome were mild. But compared to the chill of New York, it was practically balmy.

After their connection on the plane, Matteo seemed more relaxed in Rome; he spoke his native language fluently and she almost laughed out loud at the gestures he used when chatting to others. In New York, he was so much more reserved.

She was tired. She'd only managed a few hours' sleep on the flight over the Atlantic and the bright morning light of Rome felt harsh on her eyes. But Matteo had assured her that the family home in Rome was much more habitable than the one in the Hamptons, and the interior design work would be much less intense.

The car passed through Rome, giving Phoebe a few glimpses of some of the wonders. She couldn't help but smile. "First time in Rome?" asked Matteo.

"First time in Italy," she breathed. "I've always wanted to come here."

Matteo gave a small nod. "We'll need to try and see if we can fit in some sightseeing."

"Really?" She hadn't expected that from him, and when he gave another nod she settled back into the soft leather seats and took a deep breath. Rome. Wonderful.

The car pulled onto a long winding road set on a hill. After a few minutes a sixteenth-century-style house appeared in front of her with panoramic views over Rome, the sea and Tivoli.

"How beautiful," sighed Phoebe as the driver stopped the car and came around to open the door for her.

Matteo opened the front door to the house and gave her a smile as they stepped onto the red-tiled floor. He waited a few seconds as she let out a gasp.

He gave a nod of acknowledgement. "The villa contains within its walls works of art by masters of the sixteenth and seventeenth centuries. The galleries and lounges all have late baroque and rococo frescoed ceilings. I think you'll like all the features—the oval staircase, the *trompe-l'oeil*, the wood paneling and the parquet."

Even though she was tired from the flight the sight of the magnificent villa was enough to kick-start her again. Matteo did a walk through, showing her the five elegant state rooms and thirteen bedrooms. "This place is wonderful," she said as she clasped her hands to her chest. "Why on earth would your family want to sell it?"

Matteo shrugged and held out his hands. "Because we never use it. You're right. It is a great property, but when anyone from the family is in Italy we are generally down at the villa in Tuscany where the vineyards are. In the last year I think someone from the family had used this villa for less than two weeks. We only stay here for the odd day on business. It doesn't make sense to keep the house any longer."

Phoebe gave a nod. "It just seems such a shame."

Matteo turned back to her. "So, what do you think? Can you can dress this place to sell?"

Phoebe nodded. "Without a doubt. And you're right. It won't take much." She gave a little smile. "Because this has been a family home, it really just needs a little..." she tried to find the right word "...streamlining."

Matteo raised his eyebrows. "You mean decluttering?"

She smiled. "I might. The selling point for this house is actually the frescos. Everything else just needs tailing back to let them shine. And I need to help with the flow of the house. That can be done easily by having one color palette throughout the house. I think cream would work best with a few little splashes of red. That will complement the tiled floor and the frescos."

Matteo nodded. "I think that could work." He slipped his jacket off. "Which room would you like?"

"Excuse me?"

"Which room? You can pick any one you like."

"We're staying here?"

He looked surprised. "I'm sorry. I thought I'd told you that. I imagine you want to get some sleep. Even for a few hours? Then perhaps I can take you to one of the warehouses in Rome. I had my PA search out places similar to the one in New York. I thought it would save some time. Then, we can have a late dinner." He gave a soft smile. "I'm sure we'll be able to find somewhere in Rome no matter what time it is. I know you think New York is the city that never sleeps, but give Rome a chance, I think you'll like it."

She wasn't quite sure what to say. "You seem to have everything planned."

He nodded. "I feel at home here. So, pick a room. Which one did you like best?"

She tilted her head. "Isn't one of these rooms yours?"

He waved his hand. "That doesn't matter. I'm happy to sleep in any of the rooms."

She gave a smile and a small nod. "In that case, I'll take the room at the back that looks out over the garden."

"The one that can give you a glimpse of the Coliseum?" He smiled knowingly.

"And the one with the huge canopy over the bed and the ceiling fan."

He laughed. "It's all yours."

She glanced at her watch. "What time should we get up?"

There was a pause as Matteo met her gaze with an amused expression. Blood rushed to her face. What time should *we* get up? She hadn't meant it like that, but sheer exhaustion was obviously taking its toll.

She shook her head as Matteo put a hand on her shoulder. "I'll get someone to wake you around one p.m. If *we* sleep too late," he emphasized the word with a glint in his eye, "it will knock off our body clocks."

"I guess you're right." She looked around for her bag, but Matteo shook his head. "Don't worry. Carlo, the driver, has taken it up to your room." He paused for a second. "And, Phoebe?"

"Yes?"

He bent down to her ear. His voice was quiet. "Today I think you were exceptionally brave. You should be proud of yourself." He brushed a kiss to the side of her cheek, "Sleep well," he said before disappearing down the corridor.

Phoebe stood in the perfect silence. Outside she could hear the rustle of trees and the chirping of birds. The citrus smell of lemon and orange was drifting through the house.

Maybe it was fatigue, or maybe it was the setting, but Matteo seemed different here. More relaxed. More… accessible.

She put her hands up to her face. The kiss was nothing. A gesture of sympathy. Or maybe of friendship.

She walked up the stairs slowly and crossed into the airy bedroom. The shutters were wide open, allowing her a tiny glimpse of the Coliseum. She smiled. Dressing this house would be a joy and a pleasure.

And maybe something else…

He'd wanted to kiss her. First, on the plane when she'd been so upset. But that had hardly seemed appropriate when she'd mentioned the loss of her fiancé. Then second, when her eyes had lit up with pure pleasure at the house.

Her excitement was palpable. And it felt infectious. No matter how worried he was, no matter how many other things he had on his mind, being around Phoebe just seemed to make the world feel a little more right.

She'd been in the villa five minutes before she'd been able to visualize what she could do to make some improvements. And she'd been right. He'd known that instantly.

A few hours later he was showered, changed and only slightly jet-lagged. Phoebe appeared a little more tired. Dressed in a bright pink dress with a light cardigan, her bag on her arm and a notepad in her hand, she seemed ready to go.

"Would you like to have some brunch?" he asked.

She shook her head and put her hand on her stomach. "I'm feeling a little queasy to be honest. Give my body time to realize what zone it's in." She pulled a bottle of water from her bag. "I'll just stick to this for now." Then she glanced around. "Oh, I'm sorry, you're much more used to traveling than I am. Do you want to have brunch?"

Her openness was so refreshing and his heart gave a little twist. Brave. That was what else Phoebe was. But it wasn't her most obvious trait until you got to know her. Was that what had happened to him? He'd got to know her?

Phoebe had shared probably the worst thing that had ever happened to her. She'd also showed him that fears could be conquered if you really faced up to them.

He could learn a lot from Ms. Gates. He still hadn't had that conversation with Brianna. Every day, time grew shorter. His sister had experienced enough during this pregnancy; at the end she was hoping and praying for a healthy baby—and so was he. But he was also hoping for a happy, healthy sister.

Brianna had no idea what had happened to their mother. She couldn't possibly understand that the happy, well-balanced woman had acted strangely after the delivery of her third child. Matteo hadn't understood it himself. He just remembered her shouting and acting irrationally. But those memories were fuzzy. Because his father had tried to shield him from the worst of it.

As an adult he understood a lot more. Postpartum psychosis had been a little-known diagnosis thirty years ago. His mother had no history of mental health problems. So, her disintegrating mental capacity had bewildered those around her. The sudden paranoia, delusions, severe confusion and manic behavior had been confusing for her friends and family. The ultimate tragic outcome, overdosing on medication and leaving a suicide note, telling her husband how she couldn't bear the thoughts she was having—thoughts of harming her new baby—was quietly hushed up. It was years before Matteo finally put the fragments of his memories together in his brain, and when he had, his father had begged him not to tell anyone else.

But he should tell someone else. He should tell Brianna. Because Brianna was more at risk. Postpartum psychosis could run in families. And from the day and hour his sister had told him she was pregnant, he'd thought about nothing else.

"Matteo?" Phoebe was standing directly underneath him, her hand touching his wrist and her light floral scent floating up around him. Her dark eyes were fixed on his. "Matteo, are you okay?"

He nodded and gave himself a shake. Focus. That

was what he needed to do. "Sure. Everything's fine. Are you ready to see Italian-style warehouses?" He crooked his elbow toward her and she gave a smile as she slid her hand into place.

"Lead the way. I can't wait."

It seemed that Italian warehouses were very like the ones in New York. A few hours of serious shopping seemed to get her most of the things she would need to dress the gorgeous home. By the time they'd finished, the sun was a little lower in the sky and the air a little closer. Matteo made arrangements to get all the goods shipped directly to the villa.

Rome was a bustling, vibrant city. She was here to do a job, but part of her wanted to steal away on one of the open-topped buses to see the sights of the city. What chance would she ever have to come back here?

Phoebe licked her lips and looked around. She'd got on a plane. She'd actually *got* on a plane. And in a few days, she'd have to do it all again. Part of that made her stomach flip-flop. And part of that made her proud. Jason would have been proud of her. Her mother was proud of her. And, she was proud of herself. Even if she was still a little terrified.

It seemed that in the last few weeks she'd made more progress than she had in the last three years. Her first kiss. Her first connection. Her first plane ride. And the one constant thing was Matteo Bianchi.

He turned toward her. "I know you're probably tired, but it's best if we try and stay up late, to try and get into the time zone. How about some dinner and some sightseeing?"

Phoebe raised her eyebrows. "You're actually going to let me see a little of Rome?"

He leaned down and whispered in her ear. "Only the most important parts."

A little tremble snuck down her spine. "Am I dressed appropriately?"

His smile reached from ear to ear. "Oh, don't worry. You're perfect."

When the car pulled up outside the Coliseum bathed in the oranges and reds of the setting sun, Phoebe almost couldn't breathe. She twisted in her chair in excitement. "Is it still open? Can we still go in?"

Matteo gave a nod as the car door opened. "Oh, we can do more than that."

The ancient monument towered above her. Matteo walked around the car and held his hand out toward her. She couldn't help but stare up in wonder as she slid her hand into his. Tingles shot up her arm as Matteo pulled her toward him and slipped his arm around her waist. He held his other hand up to the magnificent structure. "Some of the outer wall has crumbled, due to earthquakes and stone robbers. What you see now is mainly the old interior wall."

Phoebe held her hands in front of her chest. "It's just huge. You can't really understand the size until you're standing right here."

Matteo was still smiling at her. "Can you imagine what this was like? Eighty thousand people crammed in here, shouting, watching the main event—watching the gladiators?"

His words sent a thrill down her spine. There were other people around, late tourists who looked as if they were heading home for the night.

"Can we really go inside?"

Matteo's gaze connected with hers. "Let me give you a special tour. Then we can have dinner."

She stared at him for a few seconds then nodded with excitement. Matteo led her to a special entrance and she held her breath as she walked inside.

There were only a few people left inside the structure. The illumination from the setting sun was a perfect backdrop of orange with streaks of lilac. Phoebe took a few tentative steps forward.

Matteo held out his hands. "Most of the arena floor is gone now—as is a lot of the seating. It was arranged strictly by social status." He raised his eyebrows, "Boxes at the North and South ends for the Emperor and the Vestal Virgins, podiums at the same level for the senatorial class." He gave a little wink. "They could bring their own chairs, you know."

Phoebe let out a laugh. "Really?"

"Really." He pointed to the next row up, "This was for the non-senators or knights, the one above that was for ordinary Roman citizens, split into two parts, one for the rich and one for the poor."

Phoebe gave a nod as she glanced around in wonder. "Hundreds of years on, and we're still obsessed with social class. You'd think we'd be past all that now."

Matteo looked at her thoughtfully. "I know. We should be." They moved a little further into the amphitheater. He pointed out some other parts. "There were specific sections for other people. Boys with their tutors, scribes, priests, soldiers on leave and foreign dignitaries."

"Where did the women get to sit, then?" asked Phoebe. "The ones who *weren't* vestal virgins."

Matteo shook his head. "You might guess. The other

women were allowed to stand with the slaves or the common poor."

Phoebe gave a nod and kept looking around. "Well, I love the wonder of the place. I love the structure. The architecture." She spun around, holding her hands out. "But I'm not sure that I agree with the history of the place."

Matteo held out his hand again. "Come on, I'll show you some more history."

His hand held hers firmly as he led her down some steps. It was darker down here, with some dim lights that only added to the mysterious atmosphere. He gave her a knowing smile over his shoulder. It was colder down here. Threatening. But the warmth from his hand was reaching up all the way to her heart. This was a wonderful surprise. Something she could only have dreamed of. Matteo had done this for her?

He lowered his voice as they walked slowly. "This is the hypogeum. It literally means underground. Two levels with a subterranean network of tunnels and cages underneath the arena where the animals and gladiators were held."

Phoebe stopped walking. "That makes the gladiators sounds like prisoners. I thought the Romans treated them like heroes?"

Matteo pulled a face. "It was complicated. There was a gladiator training school, *ludus magnus,* just outside the Coliseum. The gladiators could come straight through the tunnels to get here. They didn't need to walk with the crowds. Some were volunteers, and some were slaves. Stories about them fighting for their freedom are greatly exaggerated."

Phoebe looked around and rubbed one hand over her arm. All of a sudden this beautiful place gave her chills.

"You okay?"

She gave a small smile. "Maybe just a little overwhelmed. People died here. For sport. I know it's glorified, but suddenly it all seems so real."

Matteo nodded and slipped his arm around her shoulders. "Let's go back upstairs." His arm felt entirely natural there. More than comfortable. It certainly wasn't comfort that was flooding through her veins right now.

He took her up a few flights of stone stairs and walked her out to one of the upper levels. There, sitting in front of her, was a table covered in a white linen cloth with candles flickering on top of it.

It was as if the world stopped.

"What…?"

Matteo walked over and pulled out a chair. "Have a seat, Phoebe. We can look over the rest of Rome as we dine."

She blinked, wondering if any second she was actually going to wake up. "Wh…when you said we were going for dinner I imagined we were going to a restaurant somewhere." She looked around again, not quite believing what she was seeing. The sky had darkened around them, and yellow lights were illuminating the arches of the Coliseum. "I didn't think we would be eating dinner…" she waved her hands "…here."

For a second Matteo looked worried. "You want to eat somewhere else?"

She shook her head as she strode over. "No. Of course I don't." She sat down quickly and a few seconds later her glass was filled with wine and an entrée salad appeared in front of her.

She looked around once again. There was a waiter. But she couldn't see another single person.

"Where is everyone?" she whispered.

"Oh," said Matteo easily, "we have the place to ourselves. The evening tours have just finished and the Coliseum has closed its door to the public."

Phoebe lifted her fork and took a breath. "Matteo, just how rich are you?"

He winked at her. "Not rich at all. Haven't you heard? I'm selling two houses."

She let out a laugh and tried her food. "Did you get them to build a whole kitchen for you too?"

He held up his hands. "You got me. I sweet-talked a local chef at my favorite restaurant."

Now she put down her fork. "You sweet-talked someone? You? Matteo Bianchi? You actually know how to sweet-talk?"

He gave an embarrassed shrug. "Sometimes, I can be nice."

She kept a hint of teasing in her voice. "Just not to me."

He looked at her warily. "I might have been…short with you. But that's all. You think I haven't been nice to you?"

She could see the hint of worry in his eyes. She held out her hands. "Matteo, we're sitting in the Coliseum, in Rome, having a private dinner." She picked up her wine glass and gave an appreciative nod. "I think we can put this one in the nice column."

He sighed as he picked up his wine glass too. "Well, thank goodness. I don't know if we could have made it to the Leaning Tower in time for dessert."

She smiled and leaned across the table toward him, clinking her glass against his. "Hmm… Pisa, now there's a thought."

"You want to visit Pisa too?"

She shook her head. "Not right now. In my lifetime?

Yes, I'd love to. But right now, I'm just getting over the shock of finally getting back on a plane and completing a journey." She picked a little at her salad. "You know, it wasn't quite as bad as I thought."

"No?"

She leaned back in her chair as she studied the beautiful surroundings. "No, it wasn't. It was more just the *thought* of it. All the fears. The expectations. I knew they were irrational. The sensible part of my brain could tell me that." She met his dark gaze and gave him a smile. "I just had problems listening to it." She tilted her head to the side. "I'm not promising I won't be terrified on the way home."

He held her gaze. The candles flickered on the table between them, his dark hair falling across his brow. Her hand itched to reach over and brush it away. To touch him, to feel his skin under the palm of her hand. For a few seconds it really felt as if no one else were there but them.

His voice broke through the silence. It gave the slightest waver. "Sometimes the thought of something is always worse." He bowed his head a little. "And don't be afraid, Phoebe. I'll be with you on the way home."

She could hear the emotion in his voice. His shoulders had tensed, as had his jaw.

"What are you afraid of, Matteo?" The words came out before she could think them through. From the moment she'd met him there had been glimpses of the man struggling to fight his way out from the dark looming cloud that seemed to hang above his head. He was someone in pain—and she could recognize that. She just didn't know if she could help.

She reached across the table and gently interlinked his fingers with hers.

His gaze was dark, intense, but she held it, not letting herself flicker for a second.

"I'm afraid of what might happen to my sister."

"Your sister?"

There was a flash of regret on his face and she could sense his fingers pull away a little. But she held them firmly.

"She's pregnant, isn't she? Why could something happen to her?"

His eyes fixed on the table. He sucked in a deep breath. "Because it happened to my mother."

It was as if the almost mild air in Rome vanished and a chill swept over her body. Every tiny little hair on Phoebe's arms stood on end. Her stomach clenched.

She reached over and put her other hand over their intertwined ones. "What happened to your mother, Matteo?"

He pulled his hand back sharply, throwing it in the air in exasperation as he shook his head. "It's...it's too complicated."

Phoebe nodded her head slowly. "Okay, but..." she glanced around the virtually empty Coliseum "...I think we have time."

She was right at the edge. Dangling. Just waiting to find out what it was that caused Matteo to have that permanent frown marring his complexion. The thing that meant he wasn't quite living life the way he wanted to.

But the moment was broken as the waiter came to lift their plates, and deliver their main course. The rich aroma of ravioli drifted up around her. She stared down at the plate and licked her lips. "Well, it looks delicious. But we're not starting until we finish this conversation."

"It's maybe a good time to have a break," Matteo said quickly as he picked up his fork.

"Stop it," she said sharply, annoyed by how instantly dismissive he could be. She could almost see him putting all his shutters back into place.

"What are you afraid of, Matteo?" She let her voice soften. "Tell me what happened to your mother."

Silence. She didn't fill it. She let him take his time and think. After a few minutes he put his fork down and sighed.

"My mother...my mother committed suicide."

"Oh." Phoebe couldn't help it, her hand had instantly gone to her mouth. "I am so sorry, Matteo, for you and for your brother and sister."

She could see his tongue digging into the side of his cheek. It was clear there was more.

He shook his head again. "My mother...was sick. But the condition she had wasn't well known. Nowadays they would call it postpartum psychosis."

Phoebe wrinkled her nose. She'd heard the expression somewhere but she wasn't quite sure what it was.

Matteo pressed his hands on the table. "My mother didn't have existing mental health problems. But after the birth of my sister—only a few days really—she became confused and a bit manic. I was the oldest, but I was only five. I couldn't really understand what was going on. To be honest, my father didn't understand either. Apparently, it's really rare. It causes depression, paranoia and can cause suicidal thoughts." He took another deep breath. "It can happen in a few days, or a few weeks after delivery of the baby and the onset is really sudden. My mother...she became unwell really quickly. One minute she was walking about the house, talking constantly. Next, she was lying in her bed sobbing. Some nights she didn't sleep, but spent all night pacing the house. My father thought she was just overwrought. But she knew it was more. She knew she was unwell." He wrinkled the fine linen tablecloth in his hands. "Apparently she started to have thoughts about harming my sister. She couldn't make sense of them. She was worried she was going to do something awful. She panicked. She felt as if no one was listening to her—no one really understood how sick she felt. She became absolutely sure she was going to do something to Brianna. She didn't even want to be in the same room as her. So she overdosed."

Phoebe had been leaning back in her chair, trying to comprehend the words that Matteo was saying to her. But as soon as he got to the end of the last sentence she was on her feet instantly, walking around the table and putting her arms around his neck. She didn't hesitate. She sat in his lap and put her forehead against his as the tears welled in her eyes.

"Oh, your poor mother. I can't even imagine how frightened she was." She put her hand on Matteo's chest. His shirt was open at the neck and she could feel his warm skin beneath her fingertips. "And you, as a little boy, must have been terrified by it all."

He gulped. His eyelids were heavy as he lifted his dark eyes to meet hers. She didn't think she'd ever seen such sorrow before. "I found her," he croaked. "She was lying on her bed, with a few of the tablets scattered on the floor. I just thought she was sleeping and I... I was happy, because she'd been so upset before and she looked peaceful. The note was lying on the bedside table but I couldn't read it. It wasn't until I told the housekeeper that she was sleeping, but hadn't woken up for Brianna, that everything seemed to go mad." A single tear slid down his cheek. "I should have told them sooner. I should have known something was wrong."

"No," she said quickly. "You were five. You were a child. You couldn't possibly know or understand." She pressed her head against his. "Oh, Matteo," she breathed as she put a hand at either side of his face. "And you've had this on your shoulders ever since?"

He blinked, with the briefest nod of his head.

"Your brother and sister, they don't know?"

His breathing was a little stuttered. "They know my mother committed suicide." He shook his head. "They don't know the circumstances. My father was never able to talk about it. I found out the real truth much later. I tracked down the housekeeper when I was an adult. She told me exactly how my mother had been in the few days before. She'd ranted to Rosa about wanting to hurt the baby—Brianna. She'd told Rosa to take the baby away from her. She'd been sobbing—breaking her heart. Years on, it's easier to see what happened. But at the time? Any mental health condition was virtually not discussed."

Phoebe wiped the tear away with her finger. "What about Brianna? Why are you worried for her?"

He closed his eyes for a second. She could feel his whole body tremble. "Because it can run in families. If someone else in the family has had it…" His voice tailed off.

Phoebe felt her heart twist in her chest. "You have to tell her. You have to speak to her. You've been carrying this for too long. Your brother and sister are adults. They have a right to know what really happened."

He shook his head fiercely. "I can't tell her. Her pregnancy has been difficult. I can't tell her anything that would put her under stress. This baby means the world to her. They've had problems controlling her blood pressure. They've already told her they might need to deliver her in a few weeks. I can't do anything that would put her blood pressure up and put her, and her baby, at risk."

Phoebe pressed her lips together for a second. "How long? How long have you kept this secret? You're adults, Matteo. You, your brother and sister are all adults. You should have sat down and discussed this a long time ago." She knew it seemed harsh when he'd just bared his soul to her, but she was struggling to get her head around all this. Struggling to understand why the man she'd grown to care about—the man who'd made her start to *feel* again—would have let himself get in this position.

"It's family," he said without hesitation. "You'd do anything for family."

Something started to unfurl deep inside her. She got it. She did. More than he knew.

She kept her voice steady. "Yes. Yes, you would. I understand—probably better than you know."

His expression changed. "What do you mean?"

She licked her lips. "I mean that, for the last six months I've been supporting my mother go through cancer treatment. She's had surgery, radiotherapy and chemotherapy. Part of the reason I took this job was the pay scale. We have huge medical bills to cover. This money…it will make things easier for us. I don't want my mom to have to worry about covering the bills the insurance company won't. She's spent her life, and particularly the last few years, looking after me. It's time for me to return the favor." She met his gaze steadily. "That's why I got on the plane."

"For your mom?" All of a sudden his accent seemed so much thicker.

She nodded. Her insides were twisting. Part of her could tell he might have hoped she'd got on the plane for him. Not for the job. Or for the prestige of working on the house. Or for the chance to visit Rome.

She lifted her hand and paused it for the briefest of seconds before running it through his hair. "I get why you did this, Matteo. But things have changed. You're not a little boy anymore. The world has changed. Diagnosis and mental health services are so much better now. Isn't the way to protect your sister to tell her the truth?"

He held her gaze for the longest of times, as if he was contemplating her words. "It's just never been the right time. Vittore was getting married—then he wasn't. My father got sick. Then we had the funeral. Then there was all the family business to sort out. The houses were the last thing, but then Brianna announced she was pregnant and started having problems—what kind of brother would I be to sit her down and tell her something devastating now?" His hand reached up and closed over hers. He tilted his head to the side and gave her a sorrowful expression. "Why didn't you tell me your mother was sick? Is she okay now? Is she feeling better?"

Phoebe gave a nod. "She's well on the road to recovery with a big support system. I would never have left her if I wasn't sure she was okay." His hand reached up and stroked her cheek.

"But you did," he whispered.

"I did," she replied.

She felt it. The flicker low, deep down in her belly. The tiny pulses emanating out throughout her body. His lips touching hers confirmed everything she needed to know.

Her breath caught in her throat and her eyes filled with tears. Finally, she could acknowledge how she was feeling.

She was ready. She was ready to let go and move on. And she'd found the person she wanted to move on with.

She didn't care that he was her boss. She didn't care they had a million other things to talk about. He needed her just as much as she needed him. There was a reason they'd met.

Matteo Bianchi was her reason to move on. Her reason to let her heart be exposed to the world again.

As that thought crowded her brain she pulled her lips back from his to catch her breath.

She let out a gentle laugh as the scent of the spicy ravioli drifted around them. "I'm sorry," she whispered. "You've gone to such a fabulous effort, and it might smell wonderful, but all of a sudden I'm not so sure I want dinner."

His dark green eyes met hers. This time they were different. There wasn't so much sorrow. This time there was a glimmer of something else. His fingers brushed over her cheek. "I ordered my favorite, but I'm happy to leave it behind."

His hands went to her waist as he eased her from his lap, stood up, then pulled her against him. "How about we go someplace else?" He gave her a sexy smile. "They say the world is your oyster. But tonight—Rome is your oyster. Where would you like to go?"

She slid her arms up around his neck. She was delighting in feeling his body against hers. The angled planes, wide chest and taut muscles. It was easy. It was so easy. And she'd never wanted it more. She put her lips to his ear. "How about we just go home?"

CHAPTER SEVEN

HE WOKE UP to caramel-colored limbs tangled around his own, and tight springy curls just under his nose. Their breathing was synched. Phoebe's chest rose and fell with his own. The remnants of last night's passion was evident throughout the room. Her shoes were near the doorway. Her pink dress on the wooden floor, close to his pale blue shirt. His trousers were crumpled near the bottom of the bed. As for their underwear? He had no idea what had happened to it.

For the first time in thirty-five years Matteo finally felt a true connection to someone outside his family. He'd had no idea about Phoebe's mom. A tiny selfish part of him had been initially disappointed that she hadn't braved the plane journey for him—but that was ridiculous. Phoebe Gates was the bravest woman he'd ever met. She'd lost her fiancé, helped her mother fight cancer, then faced her biggest fear to complete a job. And the job wouldn't be completed for over a week. Somehow he knew that in that space of time Phoebe could work her magic and sprinkle her fairy dust on this villa. Right now, he was contemplating how many excuses he could make for work that would allow him to stay here this week in Rome with Phoebe.

He hadn't had a vacation in…how long? Plus, he

could fly up and down to some of the vineyards in Tuscany in one day. He could have breakfast with Phoebe in Rome, leave her to do her work while he completed his, then meet her for dinner at night back in Rome. And then...

Something squeezed inside him. Today felt different. Today was the morning after the night before.

The first time he'd shared the secret he'd kept since he was five years old.

For years he'd been haunted by the sight of his beautiful sleeping mother. Thankful she looked so peaceful after a strange few days. Except she hadn't been sleeping. As a child, he would never have known that. Should never have known that. And he'd actually sat on the floor of her room for a while, playing with his trains while Brianna gurgled in the cradle.

It was only when Brianna had started to get noisier and his mother hadn't roused that he'd gone to find someone else. At five, he wasn't quite sure he wanted to pick up the squirming bundle. But he certainly hadn't been ready for the reaction that had followed.

Those days all blurred into one. Police cars. A quietly spoken doctor. People dressed in black around his father. A funeral that he'd never been told about and certainly not been part of. The invasion of a million Italian relatives who all squeezed him tight and whispered to his father. As for the house at the Hamptons? It had more or less been left exactly as they'd found it. They'd been whisked away to the apartment near Central Park where two female relatives of his father had helped settle him and his brother and sister, before hiring help for the new apartment.

But that horrible feeling of something being really wrong had never left him. As a child he'd learned quickly not to ask his father anything about his mother—it just seemed to leave him eternally sad.

As an adult, he'd made a few enquiries. It hadn't been easy. But even when he knew the truth his father had still been pained to talk about it. He'd told Matteo to remember his mother as before, not in her last few days, and not to mention it to his brother or sister.

And Matteo, being the good Italian son that he was, respected his father's wishes.

Suicide. The one subject most people didn't want to discuss. Phoebe's face had crumpled last night. But the one thing that had struck him completely was her empathy. Empathy for the confusion his mother must have been feeling.

But that didn't surprise him. Not at all. On every occasion, Phoebe had proved to him what a good person she was.

But was he as good a person as Phoebe was? Something was unsettling him. Phoebe had been brilliant last night. But there was more. She was blossoming. Phoebe had always had an internal glow—but when he'd first met her it had been tempered.

Yet ever since they'd touched down in Rome, the sparkle in her eyes and passionate nature had been brimming over.

Something twisted inside. Should he really be doing this? He'd never felt a connection like this. He'd never let himself. What if he wasn't enough for Phoebe? The last thing he'd ever want to do was dim the light in the vibrant, happy person she'd become. He was so used to keeping secrets. So used to keeping his emotions in check. Could he ever behave any differently?

And while he was comfortable here, lying with her in his arms, she'd made him face up to his next reality. At some point, he would have to speak to Vittore and Brianna. Just not right now. When Brianna had the baby he would make sure he was around her constantly. He would watch. He would monitor. He'd made a few casual enquiries about what to do if he needed to find some professional help. He was confident, in this day and age, things would be fine. And once that stage had passed, once Brianna had her healthy baby and was settled, he could wait and tell them both at a later date. Things would be fine.

"Hey…" came a murmur.

He glanced down. Phoebe was rubbing her brown eyes; she gave him a sleep-filled smile. "Hey," he replied.

Her stomach gave an involuntary grumble and she let out a deep laugh as she pulled her body back from his and flopped back next to him. Her eyes were twinkling as she turned to him. "I guess this is what happens when you cheat me out of my Italian ravioli."

"*I* cheated you out of your Italian ravioli?" He leaned his head on one hand so he could get closer to her.

Her smile spread from ear to ear. She looked relaxed. She looked *happy*. Something struck him. This was the first time he'd seen her like this. It was almost as if a weight had been lifted off her shoulders. It was something about her eyes. A different kind of shine.

He was getting to see the true heart of Phoebe.

She winked at him. "I also missed dessert." Her hand snaked up around his neck again as she leaned in. "I kind of think that's your fault too. How do you plan on making it up to me?"

He laughed as his hand slid along her silky skin. This felt perfect. It felt so right. If only he could stay just here. If only he could freeze time and let things stay like this. Not have to think about anything else.

Planet Phoebe. No worrying about family. No worrying about business. No selling houses. Just spending the rest of his time with a warm, beautiful, good-spirited woman.

Her stomach growled again. She flipped him onto his back and swung her leg over his body, leaning above him. "Enough, Mr Bianchi. I think it's time you introduced me to what Italians have for breakfast."

He raised his eyebrows. "Well...when you put it like that..."

She lifted her finger to wag it at him but he spun her onto her back so quickly the breath left her body.

He winked at her. "Let me show you."

The day couldn't be better. Last night had been beautiful, surprising, and then emotional, tense and unbelievably hot.

Every time she closed her eyes she could still feel Matteo's breath on her skin, feel his lips trailing across hers and feel his beating heart next to hers.

The connection was so strong. It was as if now she'd finally decided she was ready to move on, her body and brain had decided to catch up on three years and move at breakneck speed. And although she had the odd thought of caution, Matteo seemed to be matching her every step of the way.

Today had been magical. Matteo had shown her the sights in Rome. He'd taken her to the Sistine Chapel, the Vatican and St Peter's Basilica. Instead of going by chauffeur-driven car, they'd joined the tourists and Phoebe had loved it.

She'd got to see the excitement and wonder on everyone else's faces—just like her own—all the while having Matteo's rich Italian voice in her ear giving her insight and information like her own personal tour guide.

As they lunched at a little restaurant near the Vatican Matteo's phone rang. He finished the call quickly with a huge smile on his face.

She leaned across the table toward him. "What? What is it?"

He shrugged and held up his hands. "It seems that word has got out. The villa isn't even on the market, and yet, my solicitor has just had a very substantial offer on the property subject to a viewing next week."

"Really?" Phoebe could hardly believe it.

"Do you think you can have the house ready for next week?"

She nodded her head. "Of course I can. No problem at all." She raised her glass of wine toward him. "It just goes to show you, someone has probably had their eye on your family villa for years, and has just been waiting for word that you were ready to sell."

Matteo nodded. "It seems likely, and, to be honest, I'm glad. I want the house to be lived in, to be enjoyed the way it should be. I've always hated the fact that the villa has virtually been unused for the last ten years. It should be brought back to life." He lifted his wine glass to Phoebe. "It seems you might just be my good luck charm."

Her heart gave a little flutter. She clinked her glass against his. "Maybe I am. I guess we just need to find out."

The smile he gave her in return sent little shivers of expectation down her spine and they spent the rest of the afternoon drinking wine and coffee, then finishing with the most wonderful tiramisu. Matteo held her hand across the table the whole time, listening to her ideas for the villa with interest. But when he started talking about plans for them going home her expression must have changed.

"Phoebe, are you okay?"

She nodded nervously. One mention of going home made her mouth go dry. She'd made it on the plane out here. Of course she knew she'd have to make the same journey as before. But last time around, there wasn't so much time to think about it. Matteo had booked the flights, she'd visited her doctor and felt as if there was a push to come here. The whole chance of not being paid had huge implications for her; it was the biggest motivator for getting on that plane.

But for the journey home?

Matteo now knew about her mother. He wouldn't withhold payment. Yes, she would complete the job in Rome, but right now the thought of getting on another plane was making her want to be sick.

She gave Matteo a weak smile. "I'm just trying not to think about the flight home. I know it's more than a few days away. But I guess one flight isn't enough to cure my fear. I'm worried I'll be like this forever. Spending my whole life wanting to be sick all over my shoes and having palpitations at the mere thought of a flight."

Matteo put his other hand over the top of hers and squeezed. "But I'll be with you. I'll be with you every step of the way. Don't worry. And this time, you'll have my full attention. You don't need to worry." He gave her a wicked smile. "I have lots of ways to distract you— if you'll let me. Or, I can just hold your hand. And you can squeeze mine until there's no blood flow and it's a strange shade of purple. Whatever you like."

She took a deep breath and smiled. She would always

be nervous. She didn't imagine those feelings would ever go away. But having someone who would support her would make things a little easier. Someone she could rely on. Someone she could trust.

It swept over her. Like a warm, soothing breeze. Someone she might love.

For the tiniest second she couldn't breathe. It felt as if a little flower were blooming and opening in her chest. She'd had her heart sealed off and protected for so long—she'd just never thought she would get here again.

And now, when she least expected it, Matteo had just bolted into her life. With his brisk, businesslike manner she hadn't expected to be attracted to him. But somehow or other, this man with so many barriers in place, yet with a rich sexy accent and the occasional cheeky twinkle in his eye, had made her feel a whole lot of something.

Sometimes love caught you unawares.

She reached her other hand over Matteo's. "I think I might like that." She smiled. They stayed like that for a few minutes, their gazes meshed, just touching, against the backdrop of St Peter's Basilica—one of the most beautiful places in the world. Life really couldn't be more perfect.

She'd told him her biggest secrets, and he'd told her his. But together they could do this. He would support her. And she would support him with what he needed to do when he got home.

Matteo reached over and gently stroked the side of her face. "Thank you for being here," he whispered. "I can't imagine being here with anyone else. Just you, Phoebe. You make Rome perfect for me."

Her heart swelled in her chest. He felt the same as she did. So she did what felt entirely natural. She leaned forward and met his lips with hers. "You do the same for me."

Nothing felt so sweet. Nothing felt so right. She would remember this moment forever.

When they finally pulled apart, Matteo laughed and straightened his clothes. "I guess we should take a walk. I think I might need to cool off a little."

Strolling through Rome with Matteo's arm over her shoulders couldn't have been sweeter.

She should have really spent all day working at the villa in Rome—after all, that was why she was there—but she was confident she would be able to do the task over the next week.

Since they'd arrived back at the villa she'd spent the last hour writing notes for work tomorrow, and then dressed for dinner. Apparently, tonight she would get to taste the best ravioli in Italy.

She tugged at the red dress she was wearing. It was a little longer than she normally wore, but the light floaty fabric skimmed her curves in a way she liked and it would be perfect for dinner.

Matteo was waiting for her downstairs. He met her with a kiss that made her knees tremble and sent little sparks flying around her body.

But as they went to leave Matteo's phone rang.

"I'll switch it off," he said quickly as he pulled it from his pocket. But his brow dipped sharply once he glanced at the screen.

He didn't hesitate to answer. "Brianna?"

Phoebe felt her heart squeeze in her chest. She walked straight over and put her hands on his other arm. "What is it?"

He changed from English and started speaking rapidly in Italian. She could see him trying to stay calm, even though his words were coming out more frantically and more sternly.

She hated the fact she couldn't understand almost as much as she hated the fact she couldn't hear what was being said at the other side. "Is she okay?"

Matteo blanched. His tone of voice changed. She heard his brother's name. Vittore. At that point, he launched into a tirade, before walking over to the house phone and starting to dial another number.

"What can I do? What can I do to help you?"

But Matteo didn't seem to hear her. He moved between phone calls. Hanging up on the mobile and giving rapid instructions—still in Italian—into the house phone.

When he finally hung up he looked as if he'd aged ten years in a few minutes. "What is it?" she persisted.

"Brianna. She went into hospital yesterday and didn't let Vittore tell me. Things are bad. They have to deliver the baby in the next few hours. I have to go home."

Phoebe blinked then nodded. "Absolutely. Of course you do. I'll pack."

"No."

His voice was sharp. It was almost as if he'd switched off and gone into automatic pilot. "You stay here. You finish the house. Make it ready for the viewing next week that will complete the sale. That's what I need you to do right now."

"But your family?" Phoebe took a deep breath. "Maybe you should speak to Vittore before you take off. Let him know you're worried. Tell him why. He'll be with Brianna for the next few hours."

He drew back and looked at her as if she were crazy. "I can't tell Vittore something like that on the phone.

That's ridiculous. I need to be with my family right now. I can't stay here with you."

It was like a chill washing over her body. It wasn't the words. It was the way that he said them. In the last twenty-four hours she'd never felt as connected to someone as she did to Matteo. But he was acting as if the last twenty-four hours hadn't happened—as if they meant nothing at all. Had she been stupid? Had she imagined something that wasn't actually real? Her automatic reaction was to self-protect. To withdraw. "I'm not asking you to. I absolutely understand you going to your sister. I would never ask you not to do that."

She turned around, trying to ignore the pain washing over her body.

She put her hand on the metallic rail of the staircase and held her breath, squeezing her eyes closed for a second, and praying that he might reconsider—praying that he might say something else. Anything to acknowledge the connection between them. Anything that might make her realize this wasn't all one-sided. That he might love her as much as she loved him.

But there was nothing. Matteo completely ignored her. He shouted a few commands in Italian to some of the staff at the villa then stalked off into his study to grab a few items.

A few minutes later the car pulled up in front of the villa, ready to take him straight to the airport. Phoebe hadn't moved much. She'd only made it to the top of the stairs.

There was a fist clenching around her heart. She knew how upset he was. And she got it. She did.

But she also knew that no matter how worried or upset she was about her mother, she wouldn't treat Matteo so dismissively. She would at the very least try and take a few minutes to explain—to let him understand.

But it seemed that Italian men were different. She knew Italians were famous for family loyalty. But she couldn't imagine that Matteo could love his family any more than she did hers.

But, it appeared, it didn't matter. Matteo appeared a few moments later with a bag in hand.

"Matteo?"

He glanced up at her. But the look he gave her was so detached—a world away from the connection of earlier. Her insides felt as though she were on a roller coaster.

His shutters were back in place. The ones he continually hid behind. The ones she'd thought she'd broken through.

He let out a sigh. But it seemed almost dismissive. He shook his head. "It's better this way, Phoebe." He paused then added, "Better for us both." He turned and swept out of the door into the dark night.

It appeared that her plane ride home would be taken alone—the thing that she'd always dreaded.

She couldn't depend on Matteo after all. And why should she?

She was just an employee.

CHAPTER EIGHT

PHOEBE WORKED ON automatic pilot. It was easy. She'd already made the plans for the house and just saw them through to perfection.

The staff in the villa looked after her well. All of them could speak English and translated anything for her that she required and dealt with any orders or deliveries she needed.

By the end of the week the villa was immaculate and ready for viewing.

And Matteo hadn't called. Not once.

Nor did he call when she contacted the family solicitor to arrange the viewing.

Nor did he call when she arranged her flight home.

Curiosity was killing her. Her fingers found the Hampton house listed for sale on the Internet. The photographs were gorgeous, capturing the true beauty of the surroundings and the stunning views.

And it seemed that word had spread. Her phone hadn't stopped ringing with offers of new jobs. The solicitor in Italy sent her photographs to use from the villa for her portfolio. She updated her website adding the Italian villa and the Hampton house.

She never discussed the flight home with anyone. The first flight she'd actually refused to board, frozen to her seat in the departure lounge, trying to remember all her breathing exercises.

Thankfully for her, one of the airline staff had taken pity on her. Marsha had experienced many nervous flyers and had been due to fly home herself. She'd distracted Phoebe before the next flight, and held her hand through the take-off and the landing. Laughing off the fact that Phoebe must have practically crushed every bone in her hand.

And after she'd returned, nothing. Not a word. Not a single word from Matteo.

"You tell us this now?"

Vittore was furious, and didn't care who knew about it.

Brianna seemed calmer. She walked over to the bassinet and laid Jay down with barely a flicker of emotion. It was only as she moved back over toward Matteo, taking his arm and steering him sharply out of the room, did he see the little flicker at her jaw. She gestured with her head for Vittore to follow, before closing the doors firmly behind her.

"What?" was her only response.

Matteo licked his dry lips. "I'm sorry," he said simply. "I wanted to tell you both before. But...it didn't seem appropriate."

Vittore was in his face in an instant. "In thirty years—you couldn't find an appropriate time? We've spent our whole lives together, Matt. This was the first time you thought to tell us?" His face was scarlet and his hands were in fists at the sides of his body.

"Of course it wasn't! But I haven't known since I was five. I figured it out. Papa would never discuss it. Never. On the few occasions I tried to ask him about it, it was clear I was upsetting him. He always told me to leave it."

"You found her. You never told us that before." Brianna's voice was quiet, but packed with emotion. Vittore turned to their sister, his face wracked with confusion; it was clear he expected her to be angry too.

Matteo sucked in another breath. "Yes." His voice shook. He couldn't help it. "I thought she was sleeping."

Once he'd started telling his brother and sister, things had just spilled out, often in the wrong order. But he couldn't keep it together any longer. He'd spent the last month practically on Brianna's shoulder and it was clear she was suspicious of his overly protective behavior. At first, she'd thought he was just a smitten uncle. But after a few weeks, she'd become more in tune to his observations and questions.

Ever since he'd taken that panicked flight home from Rome he'd felt as if he'd been living on a knife edge. Phoebe's words had constantly echoed in his brain. The last look on her face haunted him.

He tried to persuade himself it was for the best. He'd never be enough for the bright shining star that was Phoebe Gates. Things would cool, fade and be a disappointment for her. Walking away at this point was actually protecting her—saving her from any future pain he might cause.

But the truth was he'd been so focused on his family he hadn't left any room for her. It was a mistake. A massive mistake. And the only person he'd been trying to protect was himself. Protecting himself from actually sharing the love and emotional commitment that came from being in a loving relationship with someone who could potentially hurt him. Just as his mother had.

He'd felt abandoned by his mother. Let down.

Surely if she'd loved him more she wouldn't have committed suicide—wouldn't have left him, Vittore and Brianna?

He'd also felt responsible. If he'd sounded the alarm sooner—maybe something could have been done—maybe his mother's life could have been saved and he wouldn't have grown up with his heart locked away. Scared to let anyone hurt it again.

All thoughts and feelings that any psychologist in the world could pick apart and dissect, and reconstruct in a more healthy, rational manner.

But never had it been clear to him until this moment.

He'd spent the last month tiptoeing around Brianna, watching for any sign of postpartum psychosis. Any sign that might alert him, as an adult, to what he'd missed as a child.

But Brianna was just Brianna. Initially elated and overwhelmed with parenthood like any new mom. Then tired, over-emotional and occasionally irrational. Entirely just Brianna.

But there was something else too. A side he'd never seen of his sister. He was obviously imagining it, but sometimes he could swear Brianna just seemed to glow. Jay had put the biggest smile on his sister's face that he'd ever seen. In fact, Jay had put the biggest smile on the whole family's face. The little guy just had to make one squeak and there were ten adults around the crib, palms itching to pick him up.

Brianna walked across the room and wrapped her arms around her brother. "How long have you felt like this? Have you always felt like this? You thought she was sleeping?" Brianna shook her head as a single tear fell down her cheek. "That's so much for a kid to shoulder. Didn't you have anyone to talk to about it?"

Matteo shook his head. Vittore sat down on the chair next to him. "So...how did you find out? You said you figured it out."

Matteo nodded slowly. "Do you remember Rosa, our housekeeper?"

Both shook their heads.

"Of course you don't. You were both too young. Never mind. I tracked Rosa down. She could fill in all the details. She told me about the note and what was in it. She told me exactly how Mom had been acting—what she'd been saying. Rosa had been so upset about what happened. It turns out in later life she'd been diagnosed herself with depression. Her own psychiatrist and counsellor told her what Mom's likely diagnosis was. Thing were different thirty years ago and it wasn't well recognized or diagnosed. They helped her come to terms with the fact that she hadn't done anything wrong. And she...helped me understand that my mother had committed suicide out of complete desperation. She didn't want to harm her baby. She couldn't stop the way she was feeling, and she couldn't bear feeling like that. She didn't feel as if she could be responsible for her own actions."

Matteo's words hung in the air as Vittore put his head in his hands, and Brianna stared wordlessly at the doors behind which her baby lay.

She put her hand to her chest. "So, the risks, the worry. Why were you worried about me?"

Matteo reached over and clasped her hand. "Because women who have a close relative who've suffered from postpartum psychosis are slightly at higher risk."

"That's why you've spent the last month looking over my shoulder?"

Matteo cringed and nodded.

"You couldn't just tell me?" She held her hands out. "Tell us? Then I could have spoken to my physician. Asked him about the risks. Don't you think that would have made more sense?"

He shook his head slowly. "It might seem that way. But how could I tell you? Your blood pressure was up, you'd had that scare...what kind of brother would I be if I'd told you something like that, at a time when the last thing you needed was stress?"

Brianna gave him a sad smile. "I understand. I do." She looked around and put her hands on his shoulders. "Now I get it. Now I understand why you wanted to sell the Hamptons so quickly. Why you wanted to get rid of the place."

Something washed over him. A realization.

He looked at them both. "You don't?"

Brianna and Vittore exchanged glances. Vittore frowned a little. "Well, obviously it's worth millions of dollars. But I don't have bad memories of the house— to be honest, I don't have any memories at all. I've always thought of it as a bit of a forgotten beauty. I've always been sorry it's been neglected and left empty."

"Do you want it?" Somehow that made Matteo's skin prickle.

Vittore shook his head. "I spend most of my life in California. What would I do with a house in the Hamptons?"

Matteo turned to his sister. "Brianna?"

She shook her head. "I love my place here in the city. I don't want to move to the Hamptons. But I don't care about selling. I never really have. I just went along with it because you seemed so insistent." She waved her hand. "I understand about the villa in Rome. It seemed ridiculous to keep it when we are never there. And your interior designer? Oh, my goodness. What a great job she's done. The photographs are amazing. As for the selling price for the house..."

As Brianna's voice tailed off Matteo sagged in the chair. Every time he'd thought about Phoebe in the last few weeks he'd felt instantly sick. He'd let her down. He'd left her.

He'd known exactly how worried she was about the flight, but he'd been so worried about Brianna he couldn't even think straight. He'd convinced himself he was protecting Phoebe by leaving the way he did. Someone as closed off as him could never offer her the love and life she deserved. As soon as he was back, he'd arranged the transfer of her fee for doing all the work on both houses. The offer for the villa in Rome had been more than expected. It seemed that someone had their eye on the place and was waiting to snap it up.

But who was he kidding? Phoebe might need the money to pay her mother's medical bills but, somehow, he knew that the transfer of the money was a cold, hard way to complete the end of their business.

As for the house in the Hamptons? He'd had three offers already. But something had stopped him discussing them with his brother and sister, and until this minute he hadn't really understood why.

He lifted his head.

Now he was seeing the house through new eyes—eyes like Phoebe's. Because now when he thought of the house at the Hamptons, his first thought wasn't a sad, horrible one of his mother dying. Now his first thought was bright, and featured Phoebe dancing on the stairs in her yellow dress. When he closed his eyes he could see the brilliant light shining through all the windows in the house, leaving it clean and airy. When his mind drifted, it went straight to the red library with a fire burning, a comfortable rug and fireworks going off in the background.

Phoebe had done this. He'd made these memories with Phoebe.

All of a sudden he realized that the heart he'd been guarding so fiercely had a mind of its own.

"Matteo, what's wrong?" Vittore was looking at him curiously.

Matteo ran his fingers through his hair. "I might have done something I shouldn't."

"Again?" Vittore raised his eyebrows.

Matteo stood up and started to pace. "I might have treated someone...not as well as I could have." There was a hideous sinking feeling in his stomach. "I might have made a big mistake."

Brianna's eyes locked onto his. "What did you do?"

The sinking feeling changed to more like a plummet to the bottom of the Marianas Trench. This time there was no "thinking."

"I've made the biggest mistake of my life."

Vittore looked at him in complete confusion. He turned to Brianna. "Do you have any idea what he's talking about?"

Brianna nodded. "Unfortunately, I think I do." She gave a little smile. "And I think her name is Phoebe."

CHAPTER NINE

IT WAS DARK. She hadn't meant to stay out so late. But she'd been on a date.

A date.

It was a month since she'd seen or heard from Matteo. She hoped and prayed that his sister was well. But after that? She refused to allow him anymore space in her brain.

She'd checked yesterday and the house in the Hamptons still wasn't sold. That surprised her. She was sure it would have sold quicker than this. It made her stomach flip-flop a little. Maybe she hadn't done as good a job as she thought?

Nonetheless, it was time for some changes. Work was flooding in. There had been a sizeable bank transfer into her account and she'd wasted no time in paying her mother's bills. There was no doubt. It was a weight off her mind.

Last week a casual acquaintance had asked her out for dinner. For the last three years her default position had been to automatically refuse. But this time, she hadn't. This time she'd agreed—which had resulted in dinner tonight.

He'd booked an Italian restaurant and it would have been rude to insist on going someplace else. So Phoebe had smiled and tried not to baulk when John, her date, had ordered ravioli. It was almost as if everything about this date was trying to stir up memories of Matteo.

Two glasses of wine later it was clear there was no spark, no electricity—at least on Phoebe's side. And John had been gentlemanly enough to accept her thanks for dinner graciously before she'd made her excuses and left.

Trouble was...the date had stirred up a lot of emotions and as she'd walked home she'd ducked into a little jazz club and sipped a cocktail for an hour, soaking up the music and trying to shake off her melancholy feelings.

She climbed the stairs to her apartment on automatic pilot but when she turned the corner she stopped dead.

Flowers. Lots of them. All lined up outside her apartment door.

Her neighbor, Latisha, must have heard her footsteps because she opened her door and folded her arms across her chest. "Well, Phoebe Gates. What have you been up to?"

Phoebe shook her head as she walked up and down the line.

"These are for me?"

"Do you think I would have left them in the hall if they were for me?"

Phoebe shook her head and bent down and plucked the card from the first beautiful display of yellow roses.

Can we talk please?
Matteo.

She pulled a face and stopped herself from throwing the card on the floor.

Latisha raised her eyebrows. "Oh, don't worry, honey, I've read all the cards."

Phoebe looked at the line and counted along, "Six, seven, eight, nine."

Latisha smiled. "He gets kind of desperate at the end. Apparently there'll be a car outside for you at nine tomorrow morning."

Phoebe shook her head as she stomped past the coral-colored roses, the white lilies and the purple lisianthus. "I'm not getting in any car."

"Well, honey, if you don't, *I will*."

Phoebe spun around and glared at Latisha. "You would not."

Latisha looked along the line of flowers on the floor. "I wouldn't? Whatever it is he's done, I guess he's sorry."

"Not sorry enough!" Phoebe slammed her door closed and squeezed her eyes closed for a second, willing the tears away.

He'd left her. He'd left her to fly home alone when he'd known how scared she was. He'd waited more than a month to contact her. Why now?

She was angry with herself. Even though she'd spent all night telling herself she wouldn't, by nine a.m. she'd found herself washed, dressed and sitting in her brand-new green coat at her kitchen table.

When the knock at the door came she gulped as a wave of anger swept over her again. She swung the door open and started as she saw Matteo's driver, Carlo.

He gave her a smile. "Morning, Ms. Gates. Are you ready?"

He held out a caramel latte and a strawberry frosted donut. She blinked. It was a little unexpected. Carlo nodded his head toward the line of flowers along the floor.

"You didn't like them?"

Phoebe pressed her lips together. "Flowers aren't an apology," she muttered.

Carlo nodded in agreement. He waved out his hand. "Are you ready?"

She bit her bottom lip. What was she doing? Was she crazy?

She grabbed her bag and pulled the door closed behind her. "Let's go."

The route was familiar. It didn't take her long to realize where they were going. For a few minutes she had a mild panic. Were they returning to the home in the Hamptons because Matteo's family were unhappy with her work? Surely, if they were unhappy they wouldn't have paid her?

She took a deep breath and settled back against the comfortable leather seat. New York City disappeared behind them making way to the cute streets of the villages and to the wide open spaces of the Hamptons.

By the time they turned into the driveway of the house her stomach was churning.

Carlo pulled up outside and opened the door for her. She waited a few seconds, sucking in a few steadying breaths before she grabbed her bag and stepped out.

She hated it. The way she loved this place. The way just being here made her skin tingle. She knew this place was blackened and tinged with bad memories for Matteo, and maybe now she should have a few bad memories herself. But she couldn't. She just couldn't. Every part of her loved this place. Every room. Every piece of furniture. Every scent. And every thought.

Because most of them were filled with Matteo.

She tried to clear her head. She tried to focus. Flowers, coffee and donuts were not an apology. Not in this lifetime.

She might have decided she was ready to move on. But she would ultimately decide when, and with whom.

Her heels clicked across the marble floor, the steps echoing up the spiral staircase she loved so much. She stopped.

There was a different kind of scent in the house. A mixture of lemon and fresh linen with a hint of something else. Was it lavender?

"Hello?" she shouted. There was no response, so she started to walk. It wasn't as if she didn't know this place.

Flowers. That was the extra scent. Flowers in every room. A different display, sometimes shades of white, yellow and pale blue to match the surroundings. Sometimes something completely different to add a splash of color. As she walked through to the back sitting room, a tall vase of orange gerberas adorned every table.

She walked over and touched one of the petals. Bright orange and green. It was an interesting combination.

There were footsteps behind her. She turned around as Matteo walked in, holding a tray with coffee and a china plate filled with desserts. He gave her a tentative smile. "I visited our favorite bakery and bought you one of everything."

She didn't respond. Just watched as he walked over and slid the tray onto one of the tables.

She was tempted. Tempted by the smells. Tempted by the sight of him again after a month. That strong jaw, his floppy hair and broad shoulders. But she wouldn't waver.

"What is this, Matteo? What do you want?"

It was the first time in her life she'd seen him look a little uncertain.

"I want to talk," he said quietly.

She moved across the floor quickly. "Is something wrong with the house? With my work?"

He shook his head. A familiar furrow creased his brow. "Why would you think that?"

She glanced around. "The house—it's been a month. Why hasn't it sold yet? I know it's the wrong time of year. But a place like this? I expected it to be snapped up in a second."

Matteo licked his lips and nodded. "I've had three offers."

Now it was her turn to wrinkle her brow. "And they didn't offer enough?"

He shook his head and glanced out the window at Mecox Bay. "They offered more than enough. We... I mean... I decided I didn't want to sell."

"You don't?" She couldn't hide the surprise from her voice.

She moved over beside Matteo and hesitated for only a second before sitting down.

He turned to face her. "You made me think about things. You made me think differently—" he held up his hands "—about this place."

She shifted on the seat. "What do you mean?"

He sighed and looked around. "You didn't have the same cloud hanging over your head when it came to this place. You saw it through different eyes, and you helped me see it through different eyes too."

Her heart rate started to quicken. "But you have reasons for how you feel. I don't want you to hang onto something that you'll always associate with something bad from your childhood. You need to move on. You need to let go."

"Like you did?"

It was like a dozen little caterpillars crawling gently up her spine. "What do you mean?"

He reached for her hand. "You're the bravest woman I've ever met, Phoebe. And the one with the biggest heart. I'm sorry I left you in Rome. I'm sorry I left you to travel home alone."

She pulled her hand back. "I'm not." She couldn't help how blunt the words were.

"What do you mean?"

She turned away from him and looked at the array of desserts in front of her. She didn't want him touching her. She didn't want little electrical sparks shooting up her arms and heading straight to her heart. She picked up a slice of pie and a fork. She stabbed at the pie. "I mean, it was good for me. It was probably what I needed. Life is about looking after yourself. The first time I got on the plane it was for you—and for my mom. I could tell myself there was a reason to do it. I *needed* that money. I needed to complete the job. But the second time? It was for me. It was to tell myself I could do it. I didn't need anyone else. I could do this on my own—on my own terms. It was more important than you could ever imagine."

Matteo shifted uncomfortably in the seat next to her, eyeing the way her fork continued to stab at the pie.

"And what did you learn?"

She licked her lips. "I learned I could trust myself. I learned I could do anything." Her voice wavered a little. "I learned I could live this life on my own."

He reached over; the hand holding the fork was trembling and she hadn't even noticed. He put his warm hand over hers. "And do you want to? Because I believe, Phoebe, that you can do anything you want to do."

She swallowed and gulped, letting the plate rest down on her coat.

He kept talking. "You're beautiful and you're talented. I'm so lucky that I met you. Every day I regret leaving you behind. I was so focused on my sister and my family that I didn't realize my family reached further than my blood. I didn't realize my heart had already decided that you were family too."

Her hand froze. "What do you mean?"

He gave her a half-smile. "I mean, that this house, you, taught me to look ahead, to look to the future. The memories I have about this house are now about you, Phoebe. You even helped me remember some happy memories as a child here too. And you were right. Right about my sister and brother."

"How is your sister?"

"Brianna's good. She can't wait to meet you. Jay—and I might be biased—is possibly the most beautiful baby on the entire planet. And Brianna's well. Apart from being mad at me, and using a few choice words." He paused for a second. "But she understands. She understands why I didn't tell her. Not that she's happy." He shook his head and lowered it slightly. "She was particularly unhappy when she heard I'd left you in Rome when I got the news about her labor."

Phoebe pushed herself back in the chair. She was trying to take in what he was saying. But she'd been left in Rome feeling as if she'd misinterpreted everything. She couldn't feel like that again. She *wouldn't* feel like that again.

She glanced down at the pie on the plate on her lap. It had been well and truly desecrated.

Phoebe looked up into Matteo's eyes. They seemed sincere, but all she could think about right now was the ache in her heart.

"Why did you leave me in Rome, Matteo?"

He opened his mouth. The easiest thing for him to say was to repeat that it was all for Brianna.

"I was afraid."

She blinked. "You were afraid?"

He nodded. "I told myself I was protecting you—leaving you like that."

She gulped. "Well, it certainly didn't feel like that."

"I know. I thought I could never be enough for you. You're so open and honest, Phoebe. You're so full of life. You grab life. You want it. And you love with your whole heart."

She nodded and bit her lip. "And what about you, Matteo?" She understood more than he'd already said.

He shook his head. "I didn't think I could do that. I've never done it before. I've never been able to."

"Why?" She pushed him. She knew she had to.

He lifted his eyes to meet hers. "Because I don't want to open myself up. I don't want to open myself to the same kind of hurt I felt before."

Pain was written all over his face. Her fingers ached to reach out and touch him. But Matteo wasn't quite ready for that. She needed everything. She needed to know that he could love her just as much as she loved him.

"When your mother died? But you already have. Don't you see that? You opened yourself when you told me about your mother. You did it again when you told your brother and sister."

He nodded slowly. But her insides twisted. She

needed more. He was almost there. But he had to get there on his own. She couldn't do it for him.

She set the plate down on the table with a bang. "What do you want, Matteo? Why am I here?"

"You're here so I can say sorry." The words came out quickly—almost automatically.

She blinked. "Well, you've said it. I've heard it."

He tried to reach for her hands again but she brushed him off. "Please, Phoebe…"

"Please, Phoebe, what? What is this? What do you want me to say? I'm glad your sister is well, Matteo. I'm glad she has a healthy baby. I know you sold the house in Rome, great. And, as for why you don't want to sell this place?" The anger was starting to dissipate from her voice. She looked around the room. "That's entirely up to you. Maybe this place just needed a face lift." She shook her head, "Maybe you just needed to open the shutters." She couldn't help the metaphor.

Matteo shook his head. "What I needed, Phoebe, was you."

She stood up and walked over to the glass doors looking out over Mecox Bay. Matteo was right behind her and he gently laid his hand on her shoulder. "And maybe, what you needed was me."

She spun around to face him, tears brimming in her eyes. She pressed her hands up against her heart. "How can you say that? How can you? You were the first person I kissed since Jason died. The first person I actually *felt* something for. I didn't expect it. I wasn't looking for it. But it just happened. And I thought you were right there alongside me. But I was imagining it. I made a fool of myself. And now this? You ask me here?" Her voice was getting louder and louder. "Is this just to remind me about the time we spent here? Is this just to rub my face in it? Because you've still not told me why I'm here. You've still not told me what you want."

Matteo reached up and touched her cheek. "Because what I want is you, Phoebe. I want you to give me a chance. I'm sorry, for leaving you behind. I'm sorry for not being there on the flight with you. I want to make this work. Ever since I've met you, I've felt differently. You're like no one I've ever met before. You see the good in people. You walk into a room and just bring the light with you." He was smiling at her again. "I love being around you, Phoebe. I've always been a worka-holic and I'm not like that with you. When I'm around you, all I can think about is you." He pressed his hand against his heart. "I love you, Phoebe. I'll say it. I'll say it out loud for the world to hear. I don't care I've only known you for a couple of months. Every day for the last month, all I've thought about is you. Every day I've wanted to speak to you—to message you."

"Then why didn't you?"

He met her gaze with his bright green eyes. "Because I hadn't done what I should have. You challenged me before I left Rome. You told me I had to be honest with my sister and brother. I couldn't make excuses any-more for not telling them the truth. It didn't feel right, to come back and ask you to be part of my life when I hadn't taken the journey you'd challenged me to take. You'd faced your fears, Phoebe." His voice dropped. "I hadn't."

She sucked in a deep breath. "You thought I wouldn't want to be with you until you'd told your family?"

He closed his eyes for a second. "I thought I prob-ably didn't deserve you if I hadn't. I was still so wor-ried. I was watching Brianna the whole time. What if she had become ill? How fair would it be to ask you to be part of a family that could potentially be dealing with health problems for a long time?"

She tilted her head to one side. "And how fair would it be to ask you to be part of my life when my mother has just finished her cancer treatment? It could come back, then I'll spend all my time taking her for treatments and worrying about taking care of her. Do you see how ridiculous that sounds, Matteo? Family is family. What if you're ill? What if I'm ill? None of this should matter. The only thing that should matter is how two people feel about each other."

He nodded. "You're right. You're always right, Phoebe. It seems that even when I plan to tell a woman how much I love her I get that wrong too."

She was frozen to the spot. She wasn't sure how to respond. Her heart was swelling in her chest. Partly because of his response, and partly because she was still cautious.

Matteo stepped in front of her. "I did plan something else." He held out his hand toward her. "Will you come with me?"

As she lifted her hand toward his, he paused. "Wait a minute—do you want to slip off your coat?"

She glanced down. She was a little embarrassed to admit she was wearing the yellow dress underneath— the one he'd caught her dancing in. But she tilted her chin toward him as she undid the buttons on her bright green raincoat and handed it to him. Matteo left her coat over one of the leather chairs then held out his hand toward her again. There was a flicker in his eyes and the corners of his mouth turned upwards as his eyes took in her yellow dress.

He led her down the corridor to the atrium with the

curved staircase, pulling his phone from his pocket and pressing some buttons.

There was a gleam in his eyes. "I added a little extra to the house in the last few days."

She frowned and looked around. She couldn't see anything different. "What?"

Gentle music filled the air around them. The music from Phoebe's favorite musical. She couldn't help but smile.

"May I have this dance?" Matteo asked.

"Do you know what you're doing?" she asked.

He raised his eyebrows. "Around you? Apparently not. But I'm willing to spend a lifetime finding out."

She was holding her breath as she slid her hand into his. "I believe you need to start on the stairs," he said as he led her up the curved staircase, then stood a little underneath her.

It was silly. It was ridiculous. But it was exactly what she'd dreamed of. Matteo was just underneath her. He wasn't in a suit—just a simple pair of dress trousers and white shirt.

This time when he looked up at her there were no shadows in his eyes—only sincerity. His gaze was fixed entirely on her.

Her heart was playing a pitter-patter kind of tune in her chest. It had taken three years to kiss someone again. It had taken three years for her to find the courage to step onto a plane again—and whether he believed it or not, Matteo had given her the boost to do that. But was she really ready to give her heart away again?

The music was infectious. Her body started to sway in time to the tune, her feet soon following. Matteo was watching her the whole time. She moved up and down the staircase but as she reached the last few steps Matteo held out his arms to lift her down onto the main floor. One hand fitted snugly at her waist, the other held her hand tightly as he started to move around the room. Matteo could dance. He held her tightly to him as he swept her around the atrium. "How do you feel about doing this, every day, for the rest of your life?"

Her footsteps slowed. "How can I trust you, Matteo? What do you have to give me?"

He didn't hesitate. "My heart. It's yours. Forever. I hadn't realized that I needed to learn to trust. To open the shutters. To put myself out there. So, I'm here now. My heart. From this point on, we're family. You and me. For always."

Phoebe snaked her hands around his neck. "I might have some conditions."

He picked her up and swirled her around. "Name them."

She was smiling as her feet touched the ground again. "I might want you to dance me around every room in the house."

"Done."

"I might want the same amount of flowers in every room. I love them. The orange gerberas were particularly ingenious." She raised her eyebrows. "You might have a good eye."

"Done. Anything else?"

She stood on tiptoes and whispered in his ear. "We might need to reach a more formal agreement."

For a second, his brow furrowed. "How?"

This time it was her turn for there to be a twinkle in her eye. "It might involve a certain book, in my favorite room in the house."

Matteo gave her a wide smile as he slipped her hand

into his and led her down the corridor. "I'm not quite sure what you mean," he said as he winked at her. "I think you'll have to show me…"

EPILOGUE

New Year's Eve

THERE WERE A million little butterflies currently beating their wings in her stomach. Phoebe's mother smoothed down her veil. "You look beautiful, darling. I've never felt so proud." Phoebe's heart swelled in her chest as she bent forward and kissed her mother on the cheek.

"Neither have I. Love you, Mom. I'm so glad we're doing this together."

There was a sweep of royal blue satin as Brianna appeared at the entrance of the door with three champagne glasses on a tray. "A toast," she declared. "To my new sister-in-law, and my son's honorary nanna." Phoebe's hands were shaking as she took a tiny sip.

"I'm too nervous. I can't drink."

Brianna and her mother laughed as her mother handed over her bouquet of yellow roses and green leaves. "Then, let's not keep the groom waiting."

Phoebe sucked in a deep breath and placed her hand on the smooth satin of her bodice. Brianna nodded and picked up her own bouquet. "Maid of honor first." She smiled as she disappeared out the door.

Phoebe's mother crooked her elbow. "Come on, then.

Let me make Matteo Bianchi the happiest man on the planet."

Phoebe slid her arm into her mother's and walked down the long corridor of the Hampton house. The whole house was buzzing with excitement; it was filled with their family and friends—just the way it should be. It seemed as if half of Italy were here to celebrate their wedding.

This was the way the house had always felt for Phoebe, as if it should be full of people, full of life, and finally Matteo had agreed.

She reached the top of the curved staircase and paused for a second. The whole wedding party was gathered in the huge hall, underneath the glass atrium. Outside the night sky was black, but just as she reached the top of the stairs fireworks started going off outside, sending streaks of pink, blue and red across the sky.

Matteo was waiting. His eyes only on her.

The dark suit with yellow tie to match her roses showed off his sallow skin and dark green eyes. His hair was flopping around his forehead—just the way she loved it—and, as she and her mother walked down the last few steps, his hand was waiting for hers.

"You look stunning," he whispered.

"You're not too bad yourself."

When he'd proposed a few months ago and asked her where she wanted to marry she didn't have a single doubt. It had to be here. It had to be in the family home. And it had to be on New Year's Eve, when they'd shared their first kiss.

The library was too small to fit all their guests, so the ceremony was taking place in the sitting room overlooking the gardens and Mecox Bay.

As they walked through to where the celebrant was

waiting, the glass doors were open to the garden and the white marquee outside fluttered in the wind.

Vittore stood proudly as his brother's best man, and Brianna served as her maid of honor as almost one-year-old Jay slept in his cradle in the corner of the room.

Phoebe turned to face Matteo. The celebrant looked at them as he checked his watch. "Are we ready to begin?"

More fireworks lit up the dark night sky outside as Phoebe slid her hands into Matteo's. And instead of sticking with tradition, they recited their vows together.

"To have and to hold, from this day forward, for better for worse, for richer for poorer, in sickness and in health, to love and to cherish, till death do us part."

And Mrs. Bianchi kissed her new husband as the ball dropped in Times Square and the world welcomed in the New Year.

* * * * *

*If you enjoyed this story, check out
these other great reads from Scarlet Wilson*

*THE MYSTERIOUS ITALIAN HOUSEGUEST
CHRISTMAS IN THE BOSS'S CASTLE
A BABY TO SAVE THEIR MARRIAGE
HIS LOST-AND-FOUND BRIDE*

All available now!

MEET THE FORTUNES!

Fortune of the Month: Nathan "Nate" Fortune

Age: 37

Vital Statistics: Tall, dark and muscle-y; a military man with a cowboy's heart.

Claim to Fame: The former navy SEAL is one of the Fortune triplets. But not one of "those" Fortunes—and he wants nothing to do with his notorious relatives.

Romantic Prospects: We're pretty sure there is something brewing between him and single mom Bianca Shaw. But it's…complicated.

"When I came back to Paseo, I thought I was putting the past behind me. But then Bianca showed up on my doorstep. Eddie's little sister is not so little anymore, and if she was anybody else, well, I might just sweep her up in my arms and never let her go.

"But she *is* Eddie's little sister, which makes her the very last person I should be interested in. There is so much she doesn't know about what happened to her brother overseas. And I'm determined that she never find out. Even if it means I have to push her and her little boy, EJ, away…"

* * *

The Fortunes of Texas: The Rulebreakers—
Making their own rules for love in the Wild West!

HER SOLDIER
OF FORTUNE

BY
MICHELLE MAJOR

First Published in Great Britain 2018
By Mills & Boon, an imprint of HarperCollins*Publishers*
1 London Bridge Street, London, SE1 9GF

© 2017 Harlequin Books S.A.

Special thanks and acknowledgement to Michelle Major for her contribution to the Fortunes of Texas: The Rulebreakers continuity.

ISBN: 978-0-263-93633-9

23-0118

MIX
Paper from
responsible sources
FSC™ C007454

Printed and bound in Spain
by CPI, Barcelona

Michelle Major grew up in Ohio but dreamed of living in the mountains. Soon after graduating with a degree in journalism, she pointed her car west and settled in Colorado. Her life and house are filled with one great husband, two beautiful kids, a few furry pets and several well-behaved reptiles. She's grateful to have found her passion writing stories with happy endings. Michelle loves to hear from her readers at www.michellemajor.com.

To the Fortunes of Texas readers—
thanks for making me a part of your reading life
with these books.

Chapter One

Nathan Fortune heard car wheels crunching up the driveway through the open kitchen window at his family's ranch outside the tiny town of Paseo, Texas. It was almost noon, but he'd just made his second pot of coffee for the day.

Ignoring whoever was stopping by for an unannounced visit, he poured a steaming stream of coffee into a mug, took a big gulp, then promptly spit it into the sink. Grimacing, he grabbed a container of vanilla creamer from the refrigerator and dumped a generous amount into his cup. While it wasn't up to the standards of his brother's wife, at least it was palatable.

He'd never realized he made coffee that tasted like tar until late last spring when Ariana Lamonte arrived on the ranch. Hope sparked inside him that maybe Jayden and Ariana had returned to the ranch from their research trip down to Corpus Christi. They weren't scheduled to be back until next week, but if they were here now he could definitely convince Ariana to make him a cup of coffee in that fancy espresso maker he and the third triplet, Grayson, had gotten for her last Christmas.

During his time as a navy SEAL, he'd come to master over a dozen different types of guns, but that shiny machine remained a mystery to him. Ariana loved coffee, and Nate needed caffeine like he needed air when memories of that final mission in Afghanistan kept him up at night. Sometimes he slept like the dead, and even managed to convince himself that he was getting over that last tragic mission. But then he'd wake in a cold sweat, nightmares prodding at him like an insistent finger, making sure he knew he could never move past the way he'd failed the man who had been his best friend.

The doorbell rang, and he sighed. Definitely not his brother and Ariana. He took another swig of coffee and wiped a sleeve across his mouth, approaching the front door slowly. Most people in Paseo knew Nate well enough to simply call out a greeting and let themselves in. Actually, most people would assume he was out working the land at this time of day. Normally they'd be right, except he'd been up half the night and needed coffee to keep him going—even the kind that tasted like burnt tar.

He opened the front door almost warily, not sure what to expect. Ever since he and his brothers had discovered that the father they thought had died during their mom's pregnancy was not only alive, but was tech mogul Gerald Robinson, and more specifically Jerome Fortune, there was no telling who might show up on Nate's doorstep. Jerome Fortune had faked his own death over thirty years ago, shortly after a fight with Nate's mom, to make a break with his own controlling father, but as Gerald Robinson, he not only had eight legitimate children with his wife, Charlotte, but a host of illegitimate offspring.

Nothing could have prepared Nate for his body's reaction to the woman who stood on his front porch, glancing around like she was more than a little lost. He didn't recognize her, although there was something familiar in the big brown eyes that looked into his. What was wholly unfamiliar was the sharp prick of desire that stabbed him as he took in her delicate features—those molten chocolate eyes, a pert nose and lips that looked almost bee-stung in fullness despite being pressed into a tight line.

Her hair was thick and dark like her eyes, tumbling around her shoulders. She wore a plain white T-shirt over faded jeans, and Nate swallowed as his gaze took in the perfect curve of her breasts and hips. He promptly cursed himself for his line of thought. Here was a stranger at his front door, and he was ogling her like some sort of randy teenager instead of a grown man of thirty-seven.

"Can I help you?" he asked, hoping he sounded more polite than lecherous.

"Hi, Nate," she said softly. "How are you?"

"Um…fine." He took off his Stetson, slapping it against his thigh, and ran a hand through his hair with his other hand. "Do I know you?"

The woman flashed a shy smile. "I'm Bianca Shaw. Eddie's sister. Don't you remember me?"

Nate lifted one hand to grip the doorframe, whether to steady himself or to keep himself from reaching for

Bianca, he couldn't say. The beautiful woman in front of him was Eddie's little sister?

"Busy Bee," he murmured, repeating the nickname Eddie'd used for his younger sister.

She gave a short laugh. "I haven't had someone call me that since..." Her voice trailed off as her hands clenched in tight fists at her side.

"I'm sorry about Eddie," he offered, the words tasting like dust in his mouth. "He died a hero." Nate cleared his throat. "If it helps."

"Thank you," she whispered, and swiped her fingers across her cheek.

The familiar regret and blame churned through his stomach, turning the coffee he'd drunk to acid in his belly. Eddie Shaw had been like a brother to him. They'd met their first day of Basic Underwater Demolition/ SEAL training—more routinely known as BUD/S. Although as a triplet, Nate had always been close to his brothers, he'd formed an immediate bond with the stocky, wisecracking soldier that was just as strong.

From the few times he'd been to Eddie's mom's cramped apartment in San Antonio, he remembered Eddie's sister as a gangly teenager who giggled at everything and constantly tried to tag along with the brother who was nine years older than her. Eddie had been infinitely patient with Bianca, and even when they were stationed overseas or on a ship, he'd always taken the time to answer her overly perfumed letters and all the silly questions she asked about life as a navy SEAL.

"You're here in Paseo," he said, stating the obvious because his brain felt about five steps behind the reality of whatever was happening right now.

"I'm here," she echoed and bit down on her bottom

lip, her gaze skittering away from his like she was nervous about something. "I hope I'm not bothering you."

Nate had met people from all over the world and all different walks of life during his stint in the US Navy. He'd become something of an expert on reading body language, and from the splotches of color blooming on Bianca's cheeks to the rigid set of her thin shoulders to the tiny breath she blew out as if her lungs couldn't handle Paseo's clean air, Nate would have sworn on everything he had that the woman standing in front of him was in trouble.

Eddie's sister was in trouble. The brother-in-arms whom Nate had failed to save during their last mission wouldn't have let that happen. Neither would Nate. All he had left of Eddie were memories and the guilt that burned his gut. But he could honor Eddie by taking care of Bianca. It was the only thing he had left to offer.

He pushed aside his reaction to her, pretended he didn't feel attraction pulsing through him like a drum beat and tried to see her as the girl she'd once been. Eddie's baby sister. That was all she could ever be to Nate.

"What do you need, Bianca?" he asked, wishing suddenly he was a different kind of man. One who could give her everything she wanted and more.

Bianca's breath whooshed out in a shuddery rush at Nathan Fortune's simple question.

The summer she was five years old, new renters had moved into the tiny apartment next door to the cramped space where Bianca lived with her mom and Eddie. The walls in the run-down complex were paper-thin, and the young couple stayed up late with friends, music thumping so loud it would make the pictures on the wall vibrate.

Bianca's mom had quickly become a regular at the all-night parties, and Bianca would often wake in the middle of the night to laughter or voices yelling out or other strange noises she didn't understand at the time.

She'd tiptoe from her tiny bedroom across the hall to where Eddie slept and listen to his regular breathing. When Bianca complained about the noise, her mom told her to plug her ears with toilet paper, but that never worked. She'd creep closer to the mattress Eddie slept on. Bianca had a real headboard for her twin bed, but Eddie only had a mattress pushed up against one wall.

Her brother always seemed to know when she was coming because by the time her knobby knees hit the threadbare covers, he'd sigh and ask, "What do you need, Bianca?" at the same time he'd lift one corner of the sheet so she could crawl in next to him.

She never had to answer the question out loud because Eddie always knew what she needed without her even saying it. There in the dark, with her big brother next to her, Bianca would fall back asleep. With Eddie at her side, it didn't matter what was happening in the apartment next door. Eddie would keep her safe.

She was a big girl now and had been taking care of herself for enough time to know she didn't need to rely on anyone. Everyone except Eddie had disappointed or abandoned her, so she'd quickly learned to stand on her own two feet. But recently she'd lost her footing as the angry hurricane of her life pummeled her from all sides. Now when she laid awake in the wee hours of the night, the only thing she wished was not to be so alone.

It was as if the universe had heard her silent plea and answered her need with Nathan Fortune. He stood in front of her, strong and sure, exactly the opposite of how Bianca felt. He was muscled and clearly in shape, his shoulders broad beneath the fabric of the chambray shirt he wore. His skin was tanned from the sun, despite the wide brim of his hat, and she could see a faint patchwork of lines fanning out from his light brown eyes when he smiled.

He was a few inches taller than Eddie had been but not so much that he towered over her. In fact, it looked as though she'd fit perfectly tucked underneath his shoulder. She locked her knees to keep from stepping into him, wrapping her arms around his lean waist and burying her face in his shirtfront.

"Now that you mention it," she said with an awkward little laugh, "I was hoping I might stay with you for a few days." She swallowed and added, "A week or two at the longest." She glanced to either side of the farmhouse's wraparound porch, as though the house itself might offer up an answer.

The ranch was just as Eddie had described it, with huge fields and rolling hills in the distance. The house was a charming, if modest, two-story stone structure with picture windows and faded trim that gave it a settled-in, well-loved look. "If you have room and it's not too much of an inconvenience."

"Are you in trouble?"

His gaze was unreadable as he studied her.

Yes, she was in big trouble because she'd sought out Nate in place of her brother, but her reaction to him was both unexpected and dangerous, as it threatened to overwhelm her at a time when she was already holding on to her composure by a thin thread.

"No," she answered immediately, which she figured they both knew was a lie. "I just need a break from my life—a fresh start. Eddie thought of you as family, so I came to, as well. Even though you're practically a stranger. He talked a lot about coming to visit Paseo between deployments. He really enjoyed his time on the ranch. So I thought—"

She sucked in a breath when Nate reached out and placed his fingertip against her lips. "You can stay here as long as you want, Bianca. Eddie was my family in every way that counts. In some weird way, that makes you my little sister."

Bianca opened her mouth to argue. There were a hundred things she wanted from Nate, but for him to think of her as his little sister darn sure wasn't one of them. But she needed a place to stay more than she cared to admit, so she simply leaned forward and gave him a small hug, the way she'd done with Eddie all the time. It was a test, she told herself, to see if she could ignore the way he made butterflies dance across her stomach. To see if she could pretend she didn't notice his rock-hard abs when her fingers brushed his shirtfront or how good he smelled—like soap and the outdoors.

She managed it pretty well and didn't even let the soft whimper that bubbled up in her throat escape into the charged air between them.

Instead she gave him one last pat on the back and stepped away, surprised to find him staring down at her like she'd just grabbed his butt.

"I'm alone here," he blurted. "At the ranch."

"Okay," she answered with a shrug.

"My brother Grayson is touring with the rodeo and Mom manages his career, so she's with him. Jayden and his wife won't be back until next week." He crossed his arms over his chest. "Whenever Eddie was here, we had a full house."

She nodded. "I think he was jealous that you were a triplet. He always wanted a brother or two. I look forward to meeting your family."

"You might not be comfortable being out here with only me," he suggested. "It's a haul to town and Paseo is a postage stamp compared to San Antonio."

"San Antonio is too crowded these days," she countered, wondering why Nate suddenly looked so uncomfortable. He hadn't shown a moment's hesitation in offering her a place to stay, but now he seemed to be almost warning her away.

"I'm not great company," he continued, glancing over his shoulder into the entry as if he might find a reason for her to venture inside the cozy farmhouse. "I make terrible coffee."

"I can make my own coffee."

"I'm grumpy in the morning. You might not like me when I'm grumpy."

"As long as you don't turn green and bust out of your clothes, I think I'll manage."

"I can be mean as a grizzly coming out of hibernation."

"If you've changed your mind," she said, crossing her arms over her chest to mimic his stance, "just tell me, Nate. Otherwise, you're not going to scare me away. Remember, I grew up with a navy SEAL. Talk all you want about grizzlies, but I know you guys are big teddy bears at heart."

"A teddy bear?" He shook his head, looking as offended as her late granny had when Bianca's mom cursed in the middle of the Christmas church service.

"I'm not a teddy bear and neither was your brother. In fact—"

"Want to see my teddy bear?" a voice called from Bianca's car. The back door opened and a pair of scuffed sneakers hit the dust, the heels lighting up as they did. "His name is Roscoe, and he's my best friend."

"EJ," Bianca called as the boy ran forward, swinging a battered stuffed animal above his head. "I told you to wait—"

"You talked too long, Mommy. Roscoe got bored. He wants to see everything." Her beautiful, energetic, precocious four-year-old son climbed the front porch steps, and she automatically held out a hand. As was typical, EJ ignored it.

"Are you Uncle Eddie's friend?" he asked Nate, who had taken a step back, staring at her boy like EJ was a snake in the grass. Or maybe it was shock over EJ's resemblance to Eddie, with his dark hair, olive-colored skin and deep brown eyes that always seemed to be full of mischief. Mischief and EJ were bosom pals. "Are you a cowboy? Are we staying with you? Can I have a glass of water?"

EJ didn't wait for an answer to any of his questions. He ducked away from Bianca when she reached for him and barreled past Nate, disappearing into the house.

Bianca started to follow but Nate filled the doorway, blocking her way. "Is there something—or someone— you forgot to mention?"

She flashed what she hoped was an innocent smile and managed to only cringe a little when there was a crash from inside the house. "That's my son, EJ," she said quickly. "And we'd better go after him unless all the other breakables in your house are nailed down."

Chapter Two

"I'm sorry, Mommy. It was an accident." EJ clutched the raggedy teddy bear tight to his chest. "Roscoe bumped the lamp when I was looking at the game. He didn't mean it."

"You owe Mr. Nate an apology," Bianca scolded gently. "This is his home and we're guests here." She glanced up at Nate from below her impossibly long lashes. "At least I think we're staying for a bit. But after this—"

"Of course you're staying," Nate told her. "Accidents happen, and I never liked that lamp, anyway."

Bianca offered the hint of a grateful smile. She ruffled her son's dark hair. "EJ."

In that way that mothers of boys had, Bianca seemed to be able to communicate an entire sentence simply by speaking her son's name.

"I'm sorry about your ugly lamp," EJ said solemnly. "Roscoe is sorry, too."

"How old are you, EJ?" Nate asked.

The boy held up four dirt-smudged fingers. "Four."

"How about Roscoe?"

That question earned Nate a smile so like Eddie's it made his chest ache.

"Roscoe is two," EJ explained. "So he's still kinda clumsy."

"Is there a broom in the kitchen?" Bianca asked as she bent to pick up the top half of the lamp, which hadn't cracked. "I'll sweep—"

"I can get it," Nate told her, still shocked that Eddie's little sister had shown up on his doorstep all grown up and with a child of her own. "Did you drive all the way from San Antonio today?"

She placed the broken lamp gently on the table next to the sofa. "It's only six hours. We got an early start."

"Did you stop for lunch?"

"Nope," EJ answered before Bianca could. "I had cheese crackers and a banana."

"I'll make you both lunch."

"You don't have to," Bianca protested at the same time EJ offered, "I like peanut butter and honey with the crusts cut off."

"I can make him a sandwich," Bianca offered, her cheeks flaming bright pink. "He's a picky eater."

"I'm not picky." The boy shook his head, still clinging to the bear. "I just eat what I eat."

"You sound like your uncle," Nate said, a ball of emotion lodging in the back of his throat. "Do you know he put hot sauce on everything?"

Bianca chuckled softly. Nate's gaze tracked to her

and they shared a smile, clearly both remembering the man they had in common. "I once saw him shake hot sauce on a brownie."

"Yuck." EJ made a face. "I like ketchup."

"Me, too," Nate agreed. "But not on a peanut butter and honey sandwich."

"Do you own horses?" EJ asked.

"Yes."

"Cows?"

"Yep."

"Pigs?"

Nate shook his head. "No pigs, but we have a chicken coop."

"Do you make nuggets out of them?"

"They lay eggs," Nate explained, grinning at the boy. "I'll make you an omelet in the morning."

"I like cereal," the boy told him. "Where's my room? Do I have a place to put my clothes? Can Roscoe have his own pillow?"

"Let's eat lunch and then I'll give you a tour of the house."

"EJ," Bianca said, putting a hand on the boy's thin shoulder. "Can you thank Mr. Nate for letting us stay with him?"

"Thank you," EJ said, then added, "I need to pee."

"Bathroom's right around the corner," Nate said, pointing toward the hall.

As the boy skipped out of the room, Bianca let out an audible breath. "I'm sorry I didn't mention him at the start."

"It's fine."

"I wasn't sure—"

"Bianca." Nate stepped forward and tucked a strand

of hair behind her ear. "I'm happy to have both you and EJ here. He reminds me so much of Eddie. I bet your brother loved having a little mini-me running around. I can't believe he never mentioned a nephew."

"EJ's a great kid," she said, not directly addressing his comments. "He has a lot of energy, just like Eddie."

"It should serve him later in life. Eddie had more stamina in his little finger than the rest of our squadron combined."

"I hope it does," she said, almost wistfully. "He's the light of my life. I'd do anything for him."

She blinked several times and turned to look out the family room's picture window to the fields south of the house. Nate had a million questions, but suddenly she seemed so fragile, and he was afraid she might cry if he pushed her for details on how she'd ended up at his house. He couldn't stand to see a woman cry, especially not one who was clearly trying to hold it together.

As he looked at her more closely, he noticed faint circles under her big eyes, like she hadn't had a decent night's sleep in ages. Where was EJ's father? Nate knew if he had a son, he'd be a part of his life.

Was EJ's father dead or had he deserted Bianca? Nate thought about his newly discovered extended family of Fortunes. He and his brothers had grown up simply, unlike Gerald and Charlotte Robinson's children. But they'd had a mother who loved them and the ranching couple who'd taken Deborah in, pregnant and alone, when she'd had nowhere else to turn. Did his mom ever feel as weary and desperate as Bianca looked right now? His heart clenched at the thought.

"Ham or turkey?" he shouted suddenly, then forced a

calming breath when Bianca whirled to him, her brown eyes wide.

"Excuse me?"

"Didn't mean to startle you," he told her. "I'm going to make sandwiches. Would you like ham or turkey?"

"You really don't—"

"I'll choose if you don't."

Her delicate brows furrowed as she stared at him. "Turkey," she said finally, and with that one word Nate felt like he'd won some sort of battle. He liked winning.

"Great. Lunch will be ready in ten minutes." He paused on his way to the kitchen. "Unless you need help unloading your bags from the car."

"No," she said, almost too quickly. "We don't have much. Just a weekend bag. We're not staying that long. I don't want to impose. It won't—"

"You can stay as long as you like," he told her. "Eddie was family, Busy Bee. That makes you family, too. If you want to tell me what's going on, I'll listen. If not, I won't intrude. But know that you have a place here."

He saw the sharp rise of her chest as his words seemed to hit their mark. "Thank you," she whispered, and then hurried out of the room.

"It's quiet here."

EJ flipped onto his side to face Bianca on the double bed in Grayson's room later that night.

"We're in the country," she said, gently pushing back the lock of hair that had flopped into his eyes. It was dark in the room, other than the faint glow from the night-light she'd plugged into the wall near the door. She'd told Nate that she and EJ could share a bedroom, but he'd insisted EJ could take Grayson's room and she could use his mom's since they'd be on the rodeo circuit until spring.

Her son loved claiming the space as his own, and Bianca wondered if she might actually get a decent night's sleep without the noise from the freeway across the street from their run-down apartment building in San Antonio. "There are country sounds here."

"Like the horses and cows," EJ said in wonder, inching closer until his leg pressed against hers and she could smell his toothpaste-scented breath. She'd be sad when her boy got old enough that he didn't want to snuggle any longer.

"Don't forget the chickens," she told him.

"The rooster is my favorite."

She dropped a quick kiss on the tip of his nose. "The rooster might even wake up earlier than you, buddy."

"No one wakes up earlier than me, Mommy."

Bianca sighed. "Think of this as vacation. You can sleep late."

He yawned, then smiled. "I don't like to sleep late."

"I know, bud."

"I like it here," he said sleepily.

"Me, too," she whispered, almost afraid to say the words out loud for fear she'd jinx her new bit of luck. She rolled her shoulders against the mattress, amazed at how light she felt. Strange that the weight she'd been carrying for so long it felt a part of her had already started to lift.

She needed to find a way to earn her keep on the ranch, but not having the pressure of a dead-end job and the stress of worrying about childcare for EJ was a gift. She'd been running on all cylinders for so long with no time to catch her breath or figure out a plan for making a better life. Nate Fortune, with his matter-of-fact demeanor and quiet intensity, seemed to have no issue with giving her space. True to his word, he hadn't pushed her for details about her circumstances. Not during the simple but satisfying lunch he'd made or on the brief tour of the house he'd led them on after they ate.

He seemed to be almost more comfortable with EJ than he was with her, patiently answering EJ's litany of questions while barely making eye contact with her.

She had a healthy dose of curiosity where the former navy SEAL was concerned.

Why did he leave the service and return to Paseo in the first place? She knew he'd been with Eddie on the mission that had killed her brother. Could he give her any more information about how and why her brother had died?

She'd practically memorized the reports and brief news stories she'd found online, but nothing in the official paperwork told her what she wanted to know. Did Eddie suffer? Was it quick? How had things gone so wrong for the brother who'd always seemed invincible?

She hadn't asked any of those questions. If she wasn't willing to share the specifics of her life, could she really expect Nate to open up his past for inspection? But he must have read something in her eyes because in the middle of the tour, his shoulders had stiffened and he'd made some excuse about needing to get back to work and all but bolted out of the house.

Other than a distant trail of dust on the horizon, she hadn't seen him again. He hadn't returned to the house at dinnertime, and she'd eventually heated EJ a meal of chicken nuggets and macaroni and cheese. She'd placed the leftover macaroni in a bowl on the counter in case

Nate wanted dinner when he came in. It was a meager offering, and she planned to drive into town for groceries the following morning. The least she could do while she was here was to cook Nate a few decent meals.

She'd learned to cook as a teenager so Eddie would have home-cooked meals when he was on leave, and sitting around the small table listening to her brother tell tales of his adventures in the navy were still some of her happiest memories.

EJ made a tiny whimpering sound and shifted away from her on the bed. She listened to his steady breathing for a few more minutes, then climbed out of the bed and crossed the hall to Deborah's room, which Nate had offered her without reservation. She heard a noise from downstairs, alerting her that Nate had returned to the house. It was past nine and she wondered what he'd been doing to keep him away for so long. The thought that he might have a girlfriend in town both intrigued and frustrated her. She laughed inwardly as she realized EJ came by his curiosity honestly.

The urge to see Nate again was almost overwhelming, but Bianca walked into her room and closed the door, leaning against it as if that would keep her inside. She was lucky Nate had agreed to let her stay so easily, and didn't want him to regret the decision because she couldn't help but make a pest of herself.

His mother's room was simple, with one chest of drawers and a faded quilt covering the bed. Bianca appreciated the framed photos scattered around the room, all featuring the triplets at various ages. Bianca's photos of EJ and his preschool artwork that she'd framed were among her prized possessions, all of them currently stuffed in the trunk of her car.

She dressed for bed, leaving the window cracked slightly so the night breeze cooled the air. She'd mostly kept her apartment windows shut, even in the blistering heat of a Texas summer, both for security reasons and to limit the outside noise. But the ranch was quiet and peaceful, and she took a deep breath as she slipped between the sheets.

Bianca had gotten used to being tired, but that didn't mean sleep came easily to her. She expected to toss and turn as she normally did into the wee hours, but the next thing she knew she was blinking awake as pale gray light began to creep through the curtains that covered the window.

"It's morning, Mommy."

EJ's face was only inches from hers, and she turned her head to glance at the clock on the nightstand.

"It's six o'clock," she said with a groan and then sat up, yawning widely. "I let you stay up a whole hour past your bedtime last night so you'd sleep later this morning."

"Didn't work," EJ reported with a wide grin. "I haven't even heard the rooster yet. I beat him."

"You sure did," she agreed. She'd slept through the night without waking but somehow felt more exhausted than she had in ages. She struggled to sit up against the pillow, letting the sheet and quilt slip down to her waist. "But it's too early, sweetie. I bet Mr. Nate isn't even—"

"Good morning," a deep voice called from the doorway. "I'm impressed that you two keep ranch hours."

Maybe it was her fuzzy brain, but Bianca felt her mouth drop open as she took in Nate Fortune leaning against the doorjamb, sipping from an oversize mug. He looked even more handsome than he had yesterday, wearing a red-checked flannel shirt and faded jeans molded to his lean hips and muscled thighs. Bianca must have been more desperate than she'd even realized because she was jealous of a pair of pants. His hair was damp at the ends and curled over his collar like he was a couple of weeks past needing a haircut.

"I beat the rooster," EJ repeated, grinning widely.

"Nice work," Nate said with an answering smile.

Bianca stifled a yawn. "This is an unholy hour for people to be awake and chipper."

"Mommy's grumpy in the morning," EJ announced helpfully.

She made a face. "It's practically still the middle of the night."

Nate chuckled, the sound reverberating through her. "At least you're not turning green and busting out of your clothes."

At the mention of clothes, Bianca glanced down to the thin tank top she wore for sleeping. The words *You Can't Make Everyone Happy. You're Not Pizza.* were printed across the front, and she'd taken off her bra before she went to bed last night. She looked up again and Nate's gaze slammed into hers. She automatically crossed her arms over her chest, but at the way his brown eyes sparked, it was obvious he'd already noticed her lack of a bra. Goose bumps rose on her skin in response to the intensity of his stare. Maybe Nate's thoughts where she was concerned weren't so brotherly, after all.

Bianca's heart hammered a frantic beat in her chest. She definitely didn't need coffee to wake her up when Nate looked at her like that.

"Come on, Mommy," EJ urged, tugging at the covers. "You should get out of bed."

She pulled him into her lap, keeping the covers tucked around her. She'd put on a pair of short boxers and wasn't quite ready to expose her legs for Nate's inspection. When was the last time she'd shaved them, anyway?

Nate cleared his throat. "Hey, EJ, maybe we can let your mom catch up on sleep this morning while you help me with chores in the barn. What do you think?"

The boy squirmed out of her grasp, his bare feet hitting the carpet with a soft thud. "Can I go, Mommy?"

"Sure," she mumbled, swallowing to wet her throat when the word came out on a croak. "You need to get dressed, brush your teeth and eat breakfast first."

"We'll handle that," Nate told her as EJ ran past him, heading across the hall. "You go back to sleep. You obviously need it."

Ouch. Bianca raised a hand to her cheek. She could feel her face flooding with color as she let out a half laugh, half sigh. "I guess it's been rougher recently than I realized. Plus the drive from San Antonio took a lot out of me. I'm not normally this much of a mess."

"You're not a mess." Nate took one step toward the bed then stopped, his fingers gripping the mug so tight his knuckles turned white. He stared at her for several long moments, a muscle ticking in his jaw. "You're beautiful, Bianca. But it's obvious you've been taking on too much. If Eddie were alive, he would have never let that happen. You're here now…with me. I only want to help."

Her toes curled as relief and gratitude whirled through her like a tornado. She hated what her life had come to in the past few months but was so happy to have this chance at a literal do-over. She could make things right for herself and EJ because Nate was in her corner.

"Thank you," she whispered. "I'm going to make this up to you someday. I promise."

"You don't have to do anything. I owe Eddie more than you can ever know. Helping you is the least I can do." His voice was tight with tension as he spoke, as if there were more he wanted to say. Then EJ ran back in wearing his favorite dump truck T-shirt, a pair of baggy jeans and his light-up sneakers.

"I'm ready for breakfast," he said, tugging on Nate's free hand. "I got dressed by myself. My sneakers have Velcro so Mommy doesn't have to tie them."

"Clever," Nate murmured, smiling at her son.

"Do you always wear cowboy boots?" EJ asked, pointing to the toe of Nate's leather boot.

"Almost always."

EJ turned his attention to Bianca. "Mommy, can I get a pair of boots?"

She wondered how much youth-sized cowboy boots would run. "We'll see."

"Get some rest," Nate told her, ruffling EJ's hair as he turned for the door, then quickly added, "Not because you look like you need it. Because you deserve it."

She flashed a smile. "Good save, cowboy."

He nodded then led EJ from the room. Bianca re-adjusted the pillow, then laid back and stared up at the ceiling. She wasn't sure she'd be able to fall asleep again, but within seconds her eyes drifted shut. Maybe just a few minutes more, she told herself. Just a few.

Chapter Three

"Like this, Mr. Nate?"

"Exactly. Hold the nail steady with one hand and the hammer with the other. Careful of your fingers."

Later that morning, Nate stood next to EJ at the workbench on the far side of the barn, watching as the little boy hammered together two boards to be used as a ramp for the chicken coop. It was a mundane chore Nate had been putting off for weeks, but it was the perfect job for an eager four-year-old.

Nate never would have guessed how much he'd enjoy having a kid shadow him all morning as he fed and watered the livestock and then drove out to check the perimeter fences. EJ's enthusiastic stream of questions and excitement over every new task made the time fly by. EJ wanted to be involved in every piece of the action, reminding Nate of himself and his brothers when they were kids.

Earl and Cynthia Thompson, who'd owned the ranch, had been like grandparents to the triplets. Had his mother been as exhausted as Bianca seemed?

Probably.

He and his brothers were more than a handful.

Earl had been a quiet man with a surly countenance that hid a gentle heart. From the time Nate could remember, the craggy rancher had worked the Fortune boys, teaching them to manage the land and livestock and giving them a purpose when they might have turned wild with a less steady hand guiding them.

Nate wanted to do that for EJ, the way Eddie would have if he'd survived that last mission. As guilt exploded in Nate's chest, he had to force himself not to step away from the boy. What right did he have to insert himself into this child's life and try to offer direction?

When push had come to shove, he hadn't been able to save his best friend. His brothers and mother had done fine for decades on their own while he was traveling the world with the navy. And shortly after he'd come home, all hell had broken loose with the discovery that Gerald Robinson was their father. Not that Nate could blame himself for that bombshell, but he hated that he hadn't been able to protect his mom from revisiting that old heartbreak.

At the end of the day, he couldn't trust himself to offer support to anyone. Bianca and EJ were far too precious to risk.

But they'd sought him out, and Nate had to believe that meant something. He *needed* to mean something to Eddie's sister and her boy. He placed a hand on EJ's arm to steady him and gave a few quiet instructions about how to position the next nail. The pink tip of EJ's tongue poked out from the corner of his mouth, a sure sign the boy was deep in concentration.

"I thought I might find you two out here."

At the sound of his mother's voice, EJ stopped hammering and jumped off the stool Nate had pushed to the front of the workbench.

"Mommy," he shouted, running toward her and launching himself against her legs. "I petted a cow and scooped horse poop and fed the chickens and now I'm fixing part of the coop. That's what you call the chicken's house—a coop. There are fifteen but only one rooster on account of he doesn't like to share his girlfriends."

"Whoa," Bianca said with a laugh, lifting EJ into her arms. "Slow down, buddy. Take a breath. It sounds like you had a busy morning."

"I got boots, too," EJ said, kicking out his feet. "They used to be Mr. Nate's."

Her grin faltered as she looked to Nate. Damn, she was beautiful. She wore a simple white T-shirt and a pair of snug jeans with a tiny rip above one knee. That small strip of skin was the sexiest thing he'd ever seen because it held the promise of so much more.

Nate had never been one for flash and dazzle in his women, so Bianca's natural beauty hit him hard. Her hair was pulled back into a loose bun at the nape of her neck, exposing the graceful line of her throat. More than anything, he wanted to know if her skin was as soft as it looked.

He was so damn close to making a fool of himself and embarrassing them both.

"Or one of my brother's pairs." He shrugged, feeling suddenly self-conscious that he'd dug through the shed out back to track down the bins of clothes and shoes his mom had kept from his childhood. "It's hard to know, but my mom saved anything we didn't wear out and Earl insisted on good boots, even when we were young. We all had the same style."

"Thank you for sharing them with EJ," she said after a moment.

"He needed a decent pair of shoes for the ranch." The words came out more gruffly than he meant them because he didn't want her to think that after one day he was trying to step in as the boy's father or something. "It's not a big deal."

"Mommy, I got so many things to show you." EJ wriggled to the ground and skipped in a circle around Bianca. "You want to see the poop I scooped or the fence I helped Mr. Nate fix?" He waved his hands in a windmill motion as he moved, a bundle of boy energy even after working for hours. Temperatures in January usually hovered in the low fifties, but today the thermostat had climbed nearly ten degrees above normal. Nothing appeared to dim EJ's enthusiasm.

"Right now," Bianca said gently, pulling a cell phone from the back pocket of her jeans, "I need to talk to Mr. Nate. Why don't you check out your favorite YouTube channel for a few minutes?"

Nate frowned as EJ took the phone and hit a button, the blue light from the screen illuminating his small face. "It's not working, Mommy," EJ said almost immediately, handing the phone back to Bianca.

"No service," Bianca muttered. "I guess it's because we're so far out of town. Do you have a Wi-Fi password?" She glanced from the phone to Nate.

"Nope," he said, massaging a hand over the back of his neck.

"Maybe the signal is bad in the barn," she told her son. "If you take it to the house's front porch—"

"You still won't have any luck." Nate stepped forward. "Cell service out here is spotty, and the ranch doesn't have Wi-Fi."

Bianca and EJ stared at him with mutual horror in their dark gazes.

"You can get internet in town at the library," he added quickly. "Normally it's open on Wednesdays."

EJ's mouth dropped open.

"Once a *week*?" Bianca asked, her tone incredulous.

"I haven't been there for a few months. It might have different hours now."

"I want to watch a show," EJ complained.

"We have a satellite dish," Nate said. "My mom likes to watch the Rodeo Live channel when she's not on the road with Grayson."

"Do you have *Elmer the Elephant*?" the boy asked.

"I'm not sure about that," Nate admitted. He'd heard of a puppet named Elmo but never an elephant called Elmer. "What channel is Elmer on?"

"YouTube," Bianca and EJ answered at the same time, then Bianca crouched down at EJ's side.

"It's okay, buddy. We'll figure out something to watch when you need a break. Besides, there's so much to keep you busy on the ranch, you'll hardly have time to miss Elmer."

"I miss him already, Mommy."

Nate watched Bianca's shoulders deflate as she sighed.

"EJ, would you put extra hay in each of the horse stalls while your mom and I talk?"

For all the boy's earlier enthusiasm, EJ looked like he wanted to refuse. Nate understood the sentiment. As much fun as a ranch could be for a boy, there was always the moment when a kid realized work was work. It was a lesson Nate and his brothers had learned early on, and it had served each of them as they grew to be men. He wanted to make sure he instilled the same work ethic in Bianca's son. He knew Eddie would have done the same thing.

"Remember how we talked about chores," he said gently.

EJ scrunched up his face and nodded. "Taking care of the animals is most important."

"Right," Nate agreed.

EJ looked up at Bianca. "I'll be back after I finish my chore, Mommy."

"I'll be here, sweetie."

Nate gave EJ a few more instructions about how much hay to give each horse, then watched as the boy made his way to the first stall.

"I can't believe how well he listens to you," Bianca murmured. "No access to Elmer would have ended in a full-blown temper tantrum with me."

"Sometimes a boy just needs a man in his life."

He was thinking of how much Eddie would have loved being a part of EJ's world but cringed as Bianca sucked in what looked to be a strained breath.

"You probably think it's terrible that I rely on an animated elephant to help me parent my kid. I do limit his screen time, but sometimes—"

Nate shook his head. "No. I'm sorry. That isn't what I meant. I'm not judging you, Bianca. A single mom raised me, and I know how much trouble we gave her. I don't know how she handled the three of us most days. It's clear you do a wonderful job with EJ, but it kills me that Eddie is missing this."

"Me, too," she said softly. "Sometimes I still can't believe he's gone. And EJ reminds me of him in so many ways."

"He's a great kid."

"Thanks. He clearly loves being with you. My feelings of inadequacy aside," she said with a small laugh, "it's good for him to spend time with a man who can be a role model. But I don't want you to feel like he's a burden."

"That would never happen." He couldn't put into words how much he enjoyed the young boy.

"He's also a handful and his energy is nonstop. Sometimes it gets to be too much for people."

"People like his father?" Nate asked, unable to tamp down his curiosity. EJ talked a mile a minute but all he would say about his dad was that he'd liked when EJ was quiet. Nate couldn't imagine EJ not talking a mile a minute other than when he was sleeping.

"My ex-husband isn't involved in our lives anymore. I've gone back to my maiden name, and I'm working to have EJ's legally changed to Shaw." She bit down on her bottom lip. "Brett walked away two years ago and never looked back."

"He's an idiot," Nate offered automatically.

One side of her mouth kicked up. "You sound like Eddie. He never liked Brett, even when we were first dating. He said he wasn't good enough for me."

"Obviously that's true." Nate took a step closer but stopped himself before he reached for her. Bianca didn't belong to him, and he had no claim on her. But one morning with EJ and he already felt a connection to the boy. A connection he also wanted to explore with the beautiful woman in front of him. "Any man who would walk away from you needs to have his—" He paused, feeling the unfamiliar sensation of color rising to his face. His mother had certainly raised him better than to swear in front of a lady, yet the thought of Bianca being hurt by her ex made his blood boil. "He needs a swift kick in the pants."

"Agreed," she said with a bright smile. A smile that made him weak in the knees. He wanted to give her a reason to smile like that every day. "I'm better off without him, but it still makes me sad for EJ. I do my best, but it's hard with only the two of us. There are so many things we've had to sacrifice." She wrapped her arms around her waist and turned to gaze out of the barn, as if she couldn't bear to make eye contact with Nate any longer. "Sometimes I wish I could give him more."

"You're enough," he said, reaching out a hand to brush away the lone tear that tracked down her cheek. "Don't doubt for one second that you're enough."

As he'd imagined, her skin felt like velvet under his callused fingertip. Her eyes drifted shut and she tipped up her face, as if she craved his touch as much as he wanted to give it to her.

He wanted more from this woman—this moment— than he'd dreamed possible. She'd fit perfectly in his arms and he could show her exactly how it felt to be with a man who appreciated what a gift she was. He let his finger trail over her cheek and trace the line of her jaw, edging down to her throat. He leaned in, so close he could smell her shampoo, something fruity and utterly feminine. A loose strand of hair brushed the back of his hand, sending shivers across his skin.

She glanced at him from beneath her lashes, but there was no hesitation in her gaze. Her liquid brown eyes held only invitation, and his entire world narrowed to the thought of kissing Bianca.

"I finished with the hay, Mommy," EJ called from behind him.

Bianca jumped away like she'd been scalded.

"Nice work, buddy," she said, her voice high and tight. "Want to show me that fence you fixed now?"

"Can you come, too, Mr. Nate?" EJ smiled, his face all wide-eyed innocence.

The boy trusted him. Bianca trusted him. Eddie had trusted him.

And Nate didn't deserve any of it.

He had to put the brakes on the careening desire he felt for his best friend's sister. She'd come to him for help. That was all he had to offer.

"Um… I…" He shook his head, trying to clear his muddled brain. "I promised a neighbor I'd help with some damage to his barn." As excuses went, it was totally lame but also true. In this part of rural Texas, neighbors relied on each other. Nate had made the commitment before Bianca and EJ arrived. "I'll see you later."

The boy looked confused at his change in demeanor, but Bianca kept her gaze on the barn's dirt floor. "Thanks for this morning," she said softly, and he noticed her hands were clenched into fists at her sides.

"No problem." He turned and walked out into the bright January sunlight before he changed his mind and found a reason to spend the day with his houseguests.

Keeping Bianca at arm's length was the only way he was going to survive her stay.

The only way.

She and EJ drove into town for lunch and found a surprisingly yummy Mexican restaurant open in the back of the building that housed both the grocery store and gas station. They'd shared a plate of chicken enchiladas and she'd eaten way too many of the crispy chips and tangy salsa the owner, Rosa, had brought to the table.

Lunch at a restaurant might be typical for some people, but it was a real treat for Bianca. She'd cashed the check she received from her crummy apartment deposit in San Antonio before leaving town, so she had an extra five hundred dollars to her name before her finances got precariously tight again.

She and EJ had been equally shocked at how tiny Paseo was compared to their neighborhood in San Antonio. There was something oddly comforting about making her way through a town that only stretched a few short blocks. The pace of life was clearly less rigorous in this part of the state, and everyone she met went out of their way to be welcoming, especially when she mentioned she was a family friend of the Fortunes.

Saying the name out loud almost made her giggle since there were a whole mess of very wealthy and well-known Fortunes living in different parts of Texas. Bianca might not be worldly, but even she'd heard of cosmetics mogul Kate Fortune and her famous youth serum. She'd also read headlines about British Fortunes who had ties to the royal family, and wondered how

Nate and his small-town brothers felt about sharing such an illustrious last name.

But despite—or possibly because of—their humble beginnings, Nate, Jayden and Grayson were the famous Fortunes in Paseo. Particularly Grayson, of course, who was so famous he was mainly known by his first name. But all during lunch, she heard a litany of stories and compliments about the brothers and their mom.

After buying enough food at the grocery store to make several days' worth of meals, Bianca stopped into the RV that housed the town's public library. She logged on to their Wi-Fi to check her email, surprised to find a note from her former boss, asking if she'd be willing to make another batch of personalized gift boxes for the shop she'd gotten fired from a week ago.

"He's got some nerve," she muttered under her breath and promptly deleted the email.

"Man trouble?" the older woman behind the counter asked.

Bianca glanced to where EJ was positioned in front of one of the computer screens, a pair of retro-looking headphones engulfing his small head. She'd allotted twenty minutes for him to have a screen break and watch two episodes of the *Elmer the Elephant* cartoon he loved so dearly. Reassuring herself he was engrossed in the show, she turned to the woman.

"I was working in an upscale retail boutique before we came to Paseo. The woman who'd owned the store for years sold it six months ago, and the new owner wouldn't allow any flexibility in my schedule to take care of my son."

"Big city folks," the woman said, spitting out each word like venom.

"I guess," Bianca agreed, not bothering to mention that she was, in fact, born and raised in San Antonio. "I had a great babysitter for EJ. A woman who lived around the corner from the store ran a small day care out of her home. EJ loves her, but he got a bad case of the flu right before Christmas, so I had to take time off work. I had vacation hours banked, but the owner said I couldn't use them during the holidays. I offered to come in on the weekends and afternoons when I could hire a sitter to be with him at the apartment, but he wouldn't budge."

The librarian rolled her eyes. "So much for 'lean in.'"

Bianca felt a grin split her face that this woman had heard of the popular movement.

"I stayed home and raised my two kids," the woman offered. "They're twenty-eight and thirty now. My daughter works as an attorney in some hoity-toity law firm in Houston. She just had her second baby, and I went down there to stay for a couple weeks. She was answering phone calls from one of the senior partners in the hospital. They barely honored her maternity leave, and that's a law. The stress moms are under these days is crazy. It's not right."

Bianca felt a lump of emotion clog her throat at this stranger's sympathy. Her own mom lived in San Antonio, but when Bianca had swallowed her pride and called to ask for help during EJ's illness, Jennifer Shaw had lectured her about how she shouldn't have taken on more than she could handle in the first place. As if Bianca had had a choice about working since Brett deserted them. She certainly hadn't seen one cent of child support from her ex-husband.

"So does the man want to hire you back?" the librarian asked.

"Not exactly," Bianca admitted. "I like to sew and do crafty stuff, so I spent evenings making specialized gift boxes for the store, celebrating birthdays and other occasions. I knew they sold well, but apparently they were more popular than I realized. He sold out and has customers asking for them. He wants to put in an order."

"Congratulations."

Bianca shrugged. "With what he paid me, I barely covered the money I spent on materials, although he sold them for almost triple the cost. I mainly did it to have something to keep me occupied at night after EJ went to bed."

"Seems like you could use a boyfriend for that," the woman said with a cheeky grin.

"Oh." Bianca pressed a hand to her chest as an image of spending a quiet night at home with Nate popped into her head. "I don't really date."

"You're young," the librarian said, pointing a finger at Bianca. "I tell my daughter she needs to schedule regular date nights with her husband."

Bianca swallowed. "I don't have a husband."

"But that blush tells me you've got someone who's caught your eye. No one would blame you if it was one of Deborah Fortune's boys. Those three are far too handsome for their own good." She tapped a finger against her chin. "Although Jayden got married last year to a lovely girl."

"Ariana," Bianca confirmed. "They're traveling while she researches a book." It felt strange to talk about Nate's brother and sister-in-law as if she knew them.

"Well, that's the great thing about triplets." The

woman laughed. "We still have two of them up for grabs." She pushed away from the counter and reached up to one of the bookshelves behind her. "I've got something that might come in handy for you."

Bianca was half afraid the woman would pull out a book on spicing up a single mom's sex life, but instead she handed Bianca a thin paperback titled *Starting a Business That Stands Out*.

"I ordered this when Steph Renner decided she was going to start selling her jewelry on Etsy. She's got a steady revenue stream going now, and I'm sure she'd be willing to give you some tips if you want."

"But I don't have anything to sell."

"Sure you do," the woman countered. "If those gift boxes can sell in a boutique, they can sell online. You could create a business and still be at home with your boy."

Bianca sucked in a breath. She'd never thought of her boxes as a viable business, but why not? If it would give her more time with EJ, she'd try anything. For the first time since she'd gotten fired, hope bloomed in her chest. Maybe she really could get her life back on track here in Paseo.

She stood and impulsively wrapped her arms around the older woman's shoulders. "Thank you," she whispered, "for listening and for the idea."

"You remind me of my daughter," the woman said, patting Bianca's cheek. "You're a good girl."

"Mommy, Elmer ended." EJ pulled off his headphones. "Can I watch another?"

"Not today, buddy." Bianca tightened her grip on the book in her hands. "But I'm sure we'll be back to the library to visit..."

She glanced at the woman who said, "My name's Susan."

"I'm Bianca. Nice to meet you." She took EJ's hand. "We'll come back and visit Susan because Mommy's going to start making the gift boxes again. I'll need to order supplies online."

Susan smiled. "I've expanded my hours now that my husband's retired. He and I need a little space to keep our marriage happy. I'm open ten to two Monday through Thursday and from nine to four on Saturdays."

"Well, then, I'm grateful for your happy marriage," Bianca said and led EJ out of the RV.

She drove back from town feeling happier than she had in ages and couldn't wait to share with Nate her plan for a new business venture. Not that she wouldn't still pull her weight around the ranch, but the idea of having an actual career was so exciting after all the speed bumps she'd hit in the past two years.

It was nearly six before Nate's big silver truck pulled down the driveway again. Bianca had started to think she'd really scared him away after that scene in the barn.

Had she imagined the desire in his eyes and the way he was leaning in as if to kiss her? The only man she'd been with was her ex-husband and he hadn't been interested in her sexually since she'd gotten pregnant. So maybe she was that out of practice in reading the signs of attraction. Or perhaps she was projecting her own lust onto Nate because every time he looked at her it felt like her skin burst into flames and sparks danced across her stomach.

She'd honestly thought motherhood had sucked all the woman out of her. She hadn't felt a yearning like she did for Nate in—well, she'd never felt anything like it.

But if he truly saw her as only Eddie's little sister, where did that leave her? She wasn't exactly going to throw herself at him and risk losing the second chance she had in Paseo. That didn't stop her heart from racing as she heard the truck door slam shut.

Chapter Four

"Mr. Nate is home," EJ shouted, jumping up from where he sat coloring at the kitchen table. He ran down the hall and a moment later reappeared, holding tight to Nate's hand as he peppered the handsome rancher with questions about his day.

"Something smells great in here," Nate said, his smile making Bianca's heart beat even faster.

"It's dinner," she said. "I hope you like stir-fry."

He chuckled. "I like anything I don't have to cook. Do I have time to take care of a couple things in the barn? The day got away from me."

"I can help," EJ told him, tugging on his hand.

"Sure," Bianca said. "When would you like to eat?"

"Twenty minutes?"

"I'll have it ready."

"Mommy's making fried rice," EJ announced. "Even the vegetables taste good."

"I can't wait to try it."

"It's nothing special," Bianca said quickly. "An easy midweek meal."

Nate studied her for a moment, then said in his deep, rumbling voice, "It's special."

He and EJ headed for the barn. Bianca adjusted the stove's temperature to low, set the small farmhouse table with three place settings, then impulsively ran upstairs and dabbed a light coat of gloss on her lips. She pulled her hair out of its ponytail and ran a brush through it as she studied her reflection in the mirror over the bathroom sink.

Was it too much to leave it down? Did she look like she was trying too hard? Of course she was trying too hard. Any woman in her right mind would try to impress a man like Nate. She grabbed a jeweled clip out of her toiletries bag and fastened it at the back of her head, figuring hair half up and half down was a good compromise. She was trying but not *too hard*, if that was an option.

She hurried back downstairs just as Nate and EJ returned to the house. EJ was still talking a mile a minute, but Nate paused in the doorway to the kitchen, his eyes darkening as he took her in. Clearly he appreciated the small effort she'd made. Feeling like a teenage girl again, she gave her hair a gentle toss over one shoulder, gratified when his lips parted and he simply stared at her.

"Hi," she said, her voice a little breathless.

"Hi," he answered, removing his Stetson and setting it on the kitchen counter.

They stared at each other for several seconds until EJ shouted, "I'm hungry, Mommy."

"Wash your hands," she told him, quickly moving to the stove.

"Would you like something to drink with dinner?" Nate rubbed a hand against the back of his neck. "Not sure there's any wine in the house, but I've got beer."

"A beer would be great. Thank you."

With Nate's big presence in the kitchen, the space felt smaller—more intimate. It felt like a real family dinner, something simple but an activity Bianca had always craved. She loved the normalcy of it.

"This is a real treat," Nate said as he sat down at the table.

"It's the least I can do," she told him and dished out a generous amount of rice and chicken onto his plate.

"EJ told me you went to town today. Paseo must seem like a speck on the map compared to what you're used to in San Antonio."

"It's a nice change," she said, taking a seat across the table from him.

"Really?" He took a long pull on his beer. "Your brother liked to say that Paseo was a half-a-horse town because there wasn't enough room for a full horse."

She smiled. "He made the worst jokes."

"He cracked himself up every time, though." Nate forked up a big bite of chicken. "This is unbelievable," he said after swallowing. "It's like real Chinese food."

"I can't tell if that's actually a compliment," Bianca said with a laugh.

"It's amazing," he clarified. "Best I've ever had."

"Mommy's a good cook," EJ announced. "Even

though she couldn't find the targreron." He stumbled over the last word.

"I'd planned to roast the chicken," she explained when Nate threw her a questioning look. "But they didn't have tarragon at the local market and there's none in your spice cabinet. Stir-fry was my backup plan."

"Hold that thought," Nate said, and pushed back from the table. He walked into the hallway, where Bianca could hear him rummaging through a closet.

"Found it," he announced, and returned with a small camo knapsack rolled tight. "I don't know if the spices are still fresh, but we have tarragon."

"That's the care package I sent to Eddie on his final deployment." She frowned. "No, that's the second one I sent. He wrote and told me he lost the first, but I couldn't find the material I'd used for it so I made that knapsack out of a camo vest I bought at a local thrift store. I forgot that I'd included tarragon along with the basic spices. Eddie loved the licorice flavor."

Nate put the sack down on the kitchen table, looking a little sheepish. "Eddie was the envy of all of us with these little tubes of spices." He unrolled the sack to reveal a row of test tubes, each filled and labeled with a different type of spice. Bianca had gotten the idea for it after Eddie'd complained so bitterly about the bland navy food. "Turns out one of the guys from the squadron had taken the first one you sent. He ended up returning it but not before Eddie had asked you for another. He gave the second package to me for my birthday." He ran his fingers over the labels on the front of each tube. "It was my most prized possession when we were deployed."

"Really?"

Nate nodded. "I'm not a picky eater, but it gets old when every meal starts to taste the same week after week. These spices were a reminder of home, and that somebody cared."

Conflicting emotions unfurled in Bianca's chest, happiness at knowing her gift had meant something to her brother tinged with the familiar ache of missing him.

"You should sell those, too, Mommy." EJ looked at her matter-of-factly. "If Uncle Eddie and Mr. Nate liked them so much, other soldiers would, too."

"That's a heck of an idea, buddy," Bianca murmured, staring at her son in wide-eyed wonder. As they were driving back to the ranch, she'd told EJ about her conversation with Susan the librarian. That was the thing about being a family of two. EJ might be only four, but he was Bianca's constant companion and often her first sounding board. She tried not to burden him with her stresses, but he'd been as excited as she was at the prospect of a business that would allow her to work from home.

"What else are you selling?" Nate looked confused.

"I haven't had a chance to tell you about my visit with Susan at the library," she said.

"I'm done, Mommy," EJ interrupted, shoveling the last bite of food into his mouth. "Can I go out to the pasture and see if the horses are still eating their hay?"

She let out a small laugh. "Mr. Nate and I have barely started eating. How can you be done already?"

"I was chewing while you talked," EJ answered with a shrug. "I chew fast."

"You do everything fast." Bianca used her napkin to wipe a stray piece of rice from EJ's chin. "Are you sure you don't want to sit here and visit with Mr. Nate while he eats?"

"Nope. I want to visit the horses."

She glanced at Nate, who nodded. "Take your plate and glass over to the sink first," she told her son, who scrambled off his seat to obey.

She took another bite as EJ ran from the room.

"He's sure taken to ranch life," Nate said, humor lacing his tone.

"It's okay for him to be out there by himself?" Bianca asked. "I kept him close to me this afternoon. Horses aren't really my thing."

Nate nodded. "He'll be fine, and I'll check on him when we're finished. This truly is the best food I've had in ages."

"I'm glad you like it. I've got meals planned through the weekend."

"You don't have to cook for me."

"I want to," she told him honestly. "I like sharing a meal, and it's the least I can do to thank you for letting us stay here."

"You don't owe me—"

She held up a hand. "I do, Nate. I want to pull my weight around the ranch. EJ's not the only one who can help."

"I appreciate that. Tell me more about your visit to the library."

"It started because I got an email from the man I used to work for." She grimaced, then added, "The one who fired me."

To her surprise, Nate didn't look shocked at the news. "EJ told me you lost your job because of him."

His words were a sharp stab to her chest. "I didn't realize he understood that." She sighed. "I guess I didn't do as good of a job hiding it as I thought. The bottom line is, EJ was sick and the shop owner didn't like that I took time off work to be with him."

"Of course you took time off. You're his mother."

She smiled at his matter-of-fact tone. "You sound a lot like Susan at the library. I'm starting to think I could get used to small-town life."

"It doesn't take a million people living in a place to understand what really matters."

"Sometimes all it takes is one," she agreed. "Especially for a mother. Anyway, the boutique owner is upset because he's sold out of the birthday and special occasion gift boxes I made to sell in the store. Susan suggested I look into starting my own business, maybe something online like Etsy or supplying them to other shops around the state." She tapped a finger against her cheek. "I might even focus on gifts for military families to send overseas. I could add the little spice packs to the mix. They weren't difficult to put together and if they were so popular—"

"You can't understand unless you've lived on a carrier for months at a time." Nate grinned, as if remembering. "What about those shampoo bars? Or the homemade lip balm? Whenever a package came for Eddie, we all hung around to see what he'd gotten. He'd show off whatever you sent, mainly to make the rest of us jealous."

"Really?" Pride bubbled up inside her at the thought. She'd missed her older brother so much when he was away and had taken to creating products she thought he could use to keep from getting lonely. "I figured Eddie and his navy buddies thought I was just a silly girl with too much time on her hands."

"He did get some major grief when you went through your boy band phase."

"Oh, my gosh." Bianca covered her face with her hands. "I forgot about that. I used to cut out pictures of all the celebrities I was crushing on and send collages to Eddie. I'd spray them with perfume."

"A *lot* of it," Nate said with a chuckle. "It amazed me your letters arrived still scented, like they'd been dipped in a vat of perfume."

"The funniest part was Eddie used to write me back like he knew stuff about the guys in the photos."

"That's because he did," Nate explained. "Whenever we were in a place with internet access, he'd troll the gossip sites so he'd have something to add to his letters to you."

Bianca's heart pinged in her chest. She could just imagine her bad-to-the-bone brother, who favored pounding heavy metal music, doing research on the latest boy band craze to make her happy.

"I miss him so much," she whispered.

"I know." Nate reached across the table and took her hand. "He'd be proud of the woman you've become, Busy Bee. You're a great mother, and I'm glad Susan gave you the idea of starting your own business. You're smart and creative and I bet you can make a success of anything you set your mind to."

Tears sprang to her eyes as she pushed away from the table, making a show of clearing plates. Gripping the edge of the counter in front of the sink, she blinked and tried to pull herself together. A few kind words and Nate had all but reduced her to a puddle on the floor. But how long had it been since anyone believed in her?

Even in the best of times during their relationship, Brett had brushed off her creativity as nothing more than a waste of time and money. Her mother, too, complained about Bianca's crafting supplies taking up too much space in their small apartment when she'd still lived at home.

She'd had no idea that Eddie had so much invested in the care packages she'd sent him. Her brother loved her and would have done anything for her, but he'd been a consummate career military man—the strong and silent type. He'd always been the one to take care of her. Bianca had never had a reason to believe she could truly make something of herself.

Until now.

"Did I say something wrong?" Nate asked quietly. His warm hand brushed her shoulder.

She sniffed and turned, pasting on a bright smile. "You said all the right things. I'm simply unaccustomed to hearing them."

"I want to change that, Bianca." His gaze dropped to her mouth. He was going to kiss her now. At least in this moment she had no doubt he wanted her as much as she wanted him.

He leaned in and she closed her eyes, anticipation making her breathless.

Suddenly the sound of frenzied barking blasted through the open window followed by her son's high-pitched shouting.

"EJ!" she screamed and hurried after Nate, who was already rushing through the house toward whatever trouble her son had gotten himself into.

"EJ!"

Nate ran toward the fenced pasture behind the barn as fast as he could.

A small figure was sprawled on the ground near the gate. Nate's heart felt like it was going to beat out of his chest with worry that the young boy was hurt.

As he got closer, EJ lifted his head and then sat up, leaning against the fence post.

"EJ, are you okay?" Nate dropped down next to the boy.

EJ swallowed and nodded, but his face crumpled as Bianca joined them.

"Sweetie, what happened?" She knelt and opened her arms. EJ flung himself into them, his thin shoulders shaking as he sobbed loudly. "Are you hurt?" She let the boy cling to her for several minutes, then set him away from her, running gentle hands over his head and torso as if searching for injuries.

"No. The dog saved me."

"What dog?" Nate straightened and scanned the area, but all he could see were the horses gathered around the feeder, munching on the hay he and EJ had put out before dinner. There was no other sign of life near the barn.

"The black-and-tan one," EJ said, wiping his nose on his sleeve. "One of the horses bit the other. They started fighting so I went over the fence to break it up."

"Cinnamon," Nate muttered. "He's a hay hog and

will give the other horses trouble if they get too close when he's eating."

Bianca lifted EJ into her arms and hugged him close. "We talked earlier about staying on this side of the fence."

"But Cinnamon was being a bully," the boy argued. "You told me when Bryson was being mean to Harper at preschool that I should use my words to stop a bully."

"That's with another child, not a thousand-pound animal."

Nate could see from the residual fear in Bianca's brown eyes that she was imagining EJ being trampled under one of the horses. The thought of what might have happened made cold sweat break out along Nate's shoulders.

"What happened when you got close?" he asked quietly, almost afraid to hear the answer.

"I yelled at Cinnamon," EJ reported. "Him and Jobuck tried to bite each other, but then he went after Daisy." He pointed to the dapple-gray mare standing serenely near the edge of the trough. "He was hurting her, and she's my favorite."

"Remember we talked about the hierarchy of the herd?" Nate smoothed the dark hair away from EJ's face, his elbow brushing Bianca's arm. "Cinnamon isn't going to hurt Daisy. He's just letting her know who's boss."

"He was mean," EJ insisted. "I had to help her. But then I tripped and fell and they were still fighting. Cinnamon came up on his back legs, and I thought he was going to land on me. But I kept yelling at him to leave Daisy alone. I didn't give up, Mommy."

So much like Eddie, Nate thought. He wanted to pull both of them against him until the panic gripping him subsided. He could taste metal in his mouth and the familiar prickling sensation, like ants marching under his skin.

He was overreacting but couldn't stop it. A vision of Eddie's lifeless body tore through his mind, and he jerked away from EJ and Bianca.

How many times had he and his brothers had close calls while ignoring directions their mom or Earl gave them as kids? Hell, Grayson had first broken a bone falling off a horse when he was younger than EJ. There was no threat of punishment that could keep his horse-crazy brother away from the barn when they were kids.

He tried to focus on breathing and the fact that now that EJ had calmed down, the boy didn't seem to have a scratch on him. In fact, when he looked to Bianca and her son again, they were staring at him like he was the one who'd been in jeopardy.

"Tell us about the dog." Bianca shifted EJ in her arms and raised a questioning brow toward Nate.

He nodded and forced one side of his mouth to curve, trying to convince both her and himself that he had things under control.

"I saw him yesterday, too. He was behind the house when I went out back to play but ran off when Mr. Nate came out."

"He's a stray," Nate muttered. "He used to come around when Jayden's dog, Sugar, was here. I don't know why because Sugar's mostly blind so it's not like she's going to go rambling with another dog."

"Is he friendly?" Bianca asked.

Nate shrugged. "Hard to say. He won't let me get close. I haven't seen him since Sugar left with Jayden and Ariana on their trip."

"I think he needs a home," EJ said quietly.

"Not this one," Nate answered without hesitation. "I like Sugar, but she's Jayden's responsibility. I've got enough on my plate without taking on one more thing." He saw Bianca cringe slightly at his words. Of course he didn't mean her and EJ. They were the best things that had happened to him in years. How could he explain what a difference they'd made in his lonely life in such a short time without sounding like a fool?

"The dog saved me, Mommy. He ran up to Cinnamon and was barking so loud. He stood in front of me until the horses backed away."

Bianca placed a soft kiss on the tip of EJ's nose. "Your own personal guard dog."

"Don't read too much into it," Nate told her. "Chances are the dog reacted to the commotion. I doubt he was purposely trying to protect EJ."

"Which doesn't change the fact that he did," she countered. "This stray dog is a hero. We need to help him."

"That isn't how things work in the country. Unfortunately, there are always animals on the loose without a true home."

"That's sad." EJ dropped his head to Bianca's shoulder. "Everybody needs a home." He yawned. "I hope the dog comes back so I can thank him. Do you think he has a name, Mommy?"

"Probably not if he doesn't belong to someone," Bianca said.

"I'm going to call him Otis."

She hugged him closer. "Otis is a good name for a dog."

"You can't name a dog that doesn't belong to you." Nate's tone came out sharper than he'd meant.

EJ yawned again, clearly too tired to notice. "I'm still going to call him Otis."

"Let's go inside so you can take a bath tonight," Bianca told the boy. She seemed wary of Nate's mood, which he could understand. He wanted to assure her he was fine, but how was that possible? He hadn't been anywhere close to fine since the day he watched his best friend die. "You've had a big day."

"Did you bring bubbles?" EJ asked.

"I sure did."

"I'm going to check the horses," Nate said. "EJ, from now on, I want you stay on the far side of the fence unless your mom or I is with you. Okay?"

The boy scrunched up his nose. "But what if—"

"Even if it looks like they're fighting. The horses will take care of themselves, but what's most important to me is keeping you safe."

Bianca's shoulders relaxed, and he was happy he'd finally said the right thing. He wanted to wipe away the past few minutes, the shock of hearing EJ scream and the terror of knowing the boy might have been badly hurt on Nate's watch.

He wanted to return to those moments in the kitchen when he and Bianca had the world to themselves and all that mattered was pressing his mouth to hers. He wanted her to want him again.

But that was dangerous territory, especially when

what he felt for her was already more complicated than physical attraction. She was smart and strong, and he respected how hard she was working to make a better life for herself and EJ. He'd never met a woman quite like Bianca, but to tell her that would give away too much, so he simply nodded and let himself into the pasture. When he looked up again, his hand pressed to Cinnamon's muscled flank, Bianca and EJ were already gone.

Chapter Five

"Mom, it's me. I've been trying to get a hold of you."

"Where are you? Why are you calling from this area code?" Jennifer Shaw let out an exasperated breath. "I've been getting calls from this number all week."

"I just told you that." Bianca paused and counted to ten in her head. It wouldn't do any good to get angry with her mom. "I'm out of town and there isn't decent cell phone service where we're staying. Why haven't you picked up the phone?"

"Because I didn't recognize the number. For all I know you could have been..." Her voice trailed off.

"A creditor?" Bianca guessed. "Are you in financial trouble again?"

"A telemarketer," Jennifer answered. "You know how persistent they can be."

Not as persistent as collection agencies, Bianca thought. She couldn't help the bitterness that lingered over the college education she'd sacrificed to bail her mom out of a rough patch a few years ago. Normally Jennifer kept her gambling habit low-key, but it had gotten out of control, and Bianca had drained her savings account to pay down her mother's debt. "EJ and I left San Antonio. I wanted to tell you myself instead of leaving a message."

"How could you leave?" her mom demanded. "You have no place to go."

Bianca pressed a hand to her stomach. It felt like her mom had just punched her in the gut. "I'm in Paseo."

"Why does that name sound familiar?"

"It's where Nate Fortune lives. You remember Eddie's navy SEAL friend."

"Tall, handsome, cowboy-looking type?" Jennifer whistled softly. "Oh, I remember him all right." She made a growling sound low in her throat then laughed. "Nate Fortune is the kind of man for whom the term *cougar* was named."

"Um…whatever you say, Mom." Bianca rolled her eyes. "I'm just letting you know we're staying with Nate for a bit. I didn't want you to hear that I'd moved and worry."

Her mother sniffed. "You know I've got my own life to deal with, Bianca. I can't get all involved in yours at this late date."

"Or ever," Bianca muttered.

"What was that?"

"Nothing. Never mind."

There was a long, awkward pause before Jennifer asked, "How long will you be there?"

"I'm not sure. I'm working on a plan for a new business. One that will let me work from home so I can be with EJ."

"Why couldn't you do that in San Antonio?"

"I needed a break. After my boss fired me—"

"Your brother got all my work ethic genes."

"Mom, EJ was *sick*. I had to take time off. I asked you to help but—"

"Now you're blaming me? Like I was supposed to jeopardize my career by asking for personal leave?"

Her mother was the receptionist at a used car dealership, and Bianca didn't think her boss would have minded if she'd taken off an extra day or so since he was also her boyfriend. But it was one more thing not worth the trouble of mentioning.

"It's fine," she said instead. "Maybe it was even a blessing. EJ needs me at home more now that he'll be starting kindergarten in the fall. I want to be there for him after school."

"Another thing you've always held against me," her mother said, her voice tight. "The fact that I had to work to support you and your brother."

"I didn't," Bianca argued. "I always had Eddie at home in the afternoon. He took care of me."

"Your brother took care of everything." The sound of Jennifer blowing her nose reverberated through the phone. "I miss him."

"Me, too," Bianca whispered. Grief over Eddie's death was the one thing she and her mother had in common. "It's actually been nice to be with Nate. Somehow he makes me miss Eddie less."

"I can hear it in your voice that you're getting attached the way you do. It's not a good idea, Bianca. Nate Fortune isn't the man for you."

Bianca blinked several times, unsure of how to answer. She couldn't believe her mother had read her so easily just in their short conversation. Her temper pricked at the same time. Of course her mom would assume Bianca didn't deserve someone like Nate.

"He likes me. We're friends, Mom."

"Of course he likes you. I bet you're *real* grateful he's taken you in."

Jennifer said the words like there was something salacious about Bianca's friendship with Nate. "It's not that way," she said through clenched teeth.

"All I'm saying is you don't know the whole story about Nate Fortune. You might think you do but— Shoot, the office phone's ringing. I gotta answer it, Bianca. Don't do anything stupid and tell EJ his mimi said hi."

Before Bianca could answer, Jennifer had ended the call. Bianca replaced the receiver on the old-school phone that hung on the kitchen wall. As usual, the phone call with her mother made the doubts she'd recently held at bay spring to life with renewed energy.

What was she doing in Paseo? Could Nate really be the right man for her? It had all seemed so clear last night when Nate had been about to kiss her. But once again, she wasn't sure of anything except that the enigmatic rancher made her wish for things he might not be willing to give her.

"I can't decide if you work this late every night or if you're just trying to avoid me."

Nate paused as he climbed the porch steps later that evening. It was dark now, the sky a jumble of stars and planets. Growing up near downtown San Antonio, she'd never appreciated the night sky. But here in Paseo, the vast swath of inky blackness dotted with bright lights fascinated her.

She'd come onto the porch after EJ had fallen asleep, wrapping a blanket around her shoulders to ward off the evening chill. She could imagine the summer air in the country must be as sweltering as it felt in the city, but in January the temperature dipped to the midforties each evening, and she was grateful for the coolness.

"A little of both, I suppose," he said, taking off his hat and running a hand through his hair. Bianca had quickly come to realize the gesture meant Nate was uncomfortable, and she wasn't sure how she felt about him doing it so often when she asked him a question.

She was both grateful for his honesty and disappointed at his answer.

"I'm sorry," she said automatically. "This is your home and I don't mean to chase you away. If it's easier—"

"It's because of how much I want to be near you," he interrupted, and her heart thundered in her chest.

What was she supposed to make of that?

"You stay away because you want to be near me?" she asked with a laugh that sounded breathless to her own ears. "Mixed signals much?"

He flashed a self-deprecating smile and leaned a hip against the porch rail. "That pretty much sums it up. You've got me mixed up like a can of soda someone's shaken too hard. I don't even understand it, but I feel like I'm about to explode from wanting you. I'm happy you found me. Hell, until you showed up I would have sworn I liked being on my own. You and EJ came along and changed everything. But you're Eddie's little sister."

"I'm not a baby."

"Trust me, I know that. You said yourself that Eddie told you I'd take care of you. I don't think wanting you was what he had in mind."

She swallowed. "You want me?"

"I can see where EJ gets his penchant for asking a million questions." He sighed. "Of course I want you. Any man in his right mind would want you."

An image of the door slamming behind Brett flashed in her mind.

"Now don't be thinking about your dirtbag ex-husband." Nate pointed a finger at her. "We've already established he's an idiot."

"Staying away because you want me doesn't make sense." She wrapped the blanket tighter around her shoulders.

"It makes all the sense in the world. I'm trying to be a gentleman." Nate threw up his hands. "For once in my dang life, I'm doing the right thing, even though it's just about killing me. You're a beautiful woman, Bianca. But you're also a mother. What kind of role model would I be to EJ if I took advantage of his mom?"

"It's not taking advantage if your feelings are reciprocated."

"If Eddie were here—"

"He's not," she shouted, then pressed her fingers to her mouth. "Eddie isn't here, and EJ's father wants nothing to do with either of us. You're the first decent man my son can remember in his life."

"Which makes it even more important that I treat you with the respect you deserve. I know what it's like to grow up without a father, Bianca. We were lucky to have Earl Thompson, but there was always something missing. My mom never dated that I can remember.

We were her only priority, and I always felt sad that she didn't have someone. That Jayden, Grayson and I didn't have someone."

"Eddie told me your dad died when your mom was pregnant."

Nate's eyes narrowed as he looked out into the night. "That's what we always thought."

"It wasn't true?"

He shook his head. "My mom thought the same thing." He paused, as if weighing how much to share with her.

Whatever he had to say was obviously difficult, so Bianca stood and stepped closer, wanting to offer whatever kind of support she could.

"We found out last year that our father has been living in Austin this whole time," he finally said.

She sucked in a shocked breath, and he turned to look at her. "Have you heard of Gerald Robinson?"

Bianca nodded. "The tech mogul who was revealed to be Jerome…" Her voice trailed off as she thought of the laugh she'd had earlier that Nate and his brothers shared the same last name as a famous Texas family. "You don't mean your dad is Jerome Fortune?"

"He and my mom met in New Orleans. They were in love but argued about something and he stormed out. After he left, he faked his own death to get away from his own controlling father. He created an entirely new identity for himself as Gerald Robinson, married a woman named Charlotte and had eight legitimate children." He gave the approximation of a smile but there was no humor in it. "There are also a bunch of illegitimate offspring. Gerald Robinson was a serial cheater."

"Nate," she whispered. "No."

"We found out when Ariana, Jayden's wife, came to Paseo looking for us. She worked for a magazine in Austin and was profiling several of Gerald's children. She'd heard a rumor of his relationship with my mom and that there was a son from their brief time together. She didn't realize at the time that we were triplets."

"How did your mother react?" she asked without thinking. Bianca couldn't imagine the shock Deborah must have felt.

"She hasn't said much. She and Grayson were on the road when we found out. Jayden told her but by the time they returned to the ranch, she was back to business as usual."

"It has to be hard for her."

"Yeah," he agreed, his voice tight. "I know she loved him. She never talked much about our father, but when she did it was clear her feelings for him hadn't dimmed through the years. To learn that he'd been alive all this time must have been a blow."

"Did he know about the three of you?"

Nate shook his head. "According to Mom, he didn't even realize she was pregnant. She tried to find him— Jerome Fortune—when she found out, but he'd already faked his death and created the Gerald Robinson persona by that time. Jayden met him last year at a grand opening party to celebrate some office complex in Austin designed by one of our half brothers."

"Have you talked to him?"

"No." The word was spoken with so much emptiness, she couldn't help but reach out and put a hand on his arm, encircling his wrist with her fingers. She prayed he wouldn't pull away.

"Do you want to?"

He looked past her shoulder, a muscle working in his jaw, and she wondered if he'd even answer. Finally, he shrugged. "He's nothing to me. I had a father figure in Earl Thompson, and I was never alone thanks to Jayden and Grayson. I don't need more siblings, and I sure don't need a father who doesn't want to be a part of my life."

"What makes you think he doesn't?" she couldn't help but ask.

"He left my mom."

"But it changes things if he didn't know she was pregnant."

"Maybe," he admitted after another long moment. "Ariana believes he really loved her at the time. Jayden seems to think he feels bad about not being a part of our lives."

"It definitely sounds like Gerald Robinson made plenty of mistakes, but family is important. Even new family. Trust me, you don't want to be in a position to have regret plague you."

He jerked back, as if she'd struck a nerve.

"You have nothing to regret, Bianca."

She thought about her son not knowing his uncle. Eddie had been deployed when she'd gotten pregnant with EJ. She knew her brother hadn't approved of Brett, so she hadn't talked to him about her shotgun marriage. She'd planned to, of course, but he'd been under so much pressure as his squadron had endured a series of deadly missions. Then her marriage had started to break down, and she'd been too embarrassed to say anything in the emails and letters she sent.

Eddie had been scheduled for redeployment, but he'd

been killed a month before he was supposed to come home on leave. Before she'd been able to tell him about EJ, the boy she'd named in his honor.

Regret had become her constant companion, yet how could she admit that to Nate?

"Neither do you," she told him instead.

He didn't answer, but raised his hand to her cheek, the pad of his thumb stroking back and forth. Shivers raced along her spine at the delicate touch. "Thank you for saying that." He smiled, and this time his eyes appeared less shadowed than they had minutes earlier. He looked younger, more like the soldier she remembered from his visits to San Antonio with Eddie.

This is how I can repay him, she thought suddenly. She could ease his burden. She could help him remember how it felt to be happy. She knew he'd been injured in the mission that had killed her brother, and between that and his responsibilities running the ranch and the shock of discovering his tie to the Fortune family, Nate had been dealt as much of a blow as she had in the recent past.

Maybe what they both needed was some joy in their lives.

She reached up on tiptoe and pressed her mouth to his. Not a demand, but an invitation. He stilled, and she wondered if her own need had made her misjudge the situation. Nate was a sinfully handsome bachelor. If he wanted a woman—any woman, Bianca imagined—he'd only have to crook his finger.

He'd said he wanted her, but did he want her as much as she did him?

Her answer came a moment later when he reached around her back and pulled her tight against him, angling his head to deepen the kiss. He took control in a way that was both tender and thrilling, as if she was a precious gift he wanted to savor.

Running every day until she dropped into bed, Bianca hadn't had time to savor anything in years. She sank into the kiss, letting the desire swirling through her take over until she was total sensation.

She lost herself in the moment, pressing her breasts against the hard planes of his chest and lifting her hands to grip his biceps. His heat enveloped her, and her body came alive. This was everything she'd ever wanted and more than she'd realized was possible.

And this was just a kiss.

She could so easily lose herself to this man.

The thought had her wrenching away, taking several stumbling steps toward the edge of the porch.

"I'm sorry," she said automatically. "Looks like I'm the one taking advantage now."

He barked out a short laugh. "It's not taking advantage if we both want it."

She glanced over her shoulder. His arms were crossed over his chest like he was having trouble stopping himself from reaching for her again.

"I didn't come here expecting this."

"I know."

"We should—" She paused, not sure how to give voice to the things she knew were right when her body was screaming for so much more.

"Take it slow," Nate finished, rubbing a hand across the back of his neck almost sheepishly.

"Slow," she agreed. "I should…um…go in now."

His brown eyes never left hers. "Good night, Bianca."

"Good night, Nate," she whispered, and hurried past him.

Chapter Six

Nate woke the next morning from a deep sleep.

He blinked and turned to glance at the clock on his nightstand.

Five o'clock.

He'd slept for seven hours.

In a row. Without waking.

It was a damn miracle.

A grin split his face as he sat up. He felt better than he had in months, longer even. Since he could remember.

After Bianca had gone into the house last night, he'd stood on the porch, pulling air in and out of his lungs, as he forced himself not to go after her. He pictured her walking up the stairs, the squeak from the loose floorboard echoing in his brain. She'd undress slowly and slip into the thin tank top she'd worn before—the óne he could easily imagine peeling off her to reveal the pale skin beneath.

A movement had caught his attention out of the corner of his eye, and he'd turned to see a four-legged figure trotting toward the barn in the pale moonlight. The stray dog EJ had named Otis. The dog seemed almost feral the first time Nate had seen it on the ranch, but the animal always lurked about when Sugar was in residence. He thought about shooing it away but couldn't bring himself to after the dog had saved EJ.

Instead, he'd gone into the house and scooped up a cup of Sugar's kibble into a bowl he placed at the bottom of the front porch steps. The small business had been enough of a distraction that the pounding urge to follow Bianca had subsided. He'd gone to bed then, reciting SEAL navigation training exercises in his head to keep his mind from wandering.

He'd expected to toss and turn as he did most nights. He'd closed his eyes knowing that the next time he opened them would be in the middle of the night, his body drenched in a cold sweat as memories pummeled him from the deep recesses of his mind.

Although the sky outside his window was still dark, he knew the light of morning would be coming soon, heralding a new day. A fresh start.

He hadn't shared his feelings about Gerald Robinson with anyone. He'd barely discussed his father with Jayden and Grayson. He figured they understood where each other stood. Being triplets, they could often communicate without speaking. Even when careers in the US Army and Navy had sent Jayden and Nate to farflung locations throughout the world, the bond the three of them shared had never wavered. They might not spend hours talking over their feelings, but Nate never doubted their love for each other or the devotion each had toward their mother.

Maybe he'd thought he was fine after discovering his father hadn't died like his mother believed. He'd always been the fun-loving triplet, leaving the serious stuff for responsible Jayden and intense Grayson. But nearly twenty years in the navy had tempered him, and that last disastrous mission had all but destroyed his ability to see the bright side of anything.

Today he felt a new sense of hope, and he wasn't going to take it for granted. He got dressed, then slipped out of his room and started for the stairs. But as soon as he passed EJ's room, the door opened and the boy popped out.

"Morning," he said in an overloud voice.

Nate lifted a finger to his lips, then pointed to his mother's room across the hall. "I bet your mommy's still asleep," he whispered.

"I'm awake." EJ grinned. "I got dressed and brushed my teeth so I'm ready for morning chores."

"Then let's get going. If we finish quickly enough, we'll have time to make your mom breakfast in bed. I bet she'd like that."

"She likes pancakes," EJ said, following Nate down the stairs.

"I make darn good pancakes," Nate told him.

EJ frowned. "Mommy told me Daddy used to say making food is women's work, and the man's job is watching sports on TV."

Nate resisted the urge to roll his eyes. It didn't surprise him that Brett would have given that advice to his young son. The more he learned about Bianca's ex-husband, the more he disliked the man.

At the bottom of the stairs, he crouched down in front of EJ. "A real man takes care of the women in his life. That's what my brothers and I were taught." Once again, he was grateful for Earl Thompson's presence in his life. He wondered what values Gerald Robinson had instilled in the children he'd raised. And whether his other illegitimate offspring had been lucky enough to have the kind of happy childhood Nate had experienced. "I know you love your mommy, and you understand how hard she works to make sure you have a good life. Right?"

EJ nodded solemnly.

"Then sometimes you want to do special things for her to thank her for that. Trust me, buddy, most women appreciate a man who is willing to help in the kitchen. It's an important lesson for you to learn."

The boy scratched his nose, looking about as interested in lessons on women as Nate had been as a boy. That hadn't stopped Earl from teaching them, and Nate would be forever grateful. "Okay."

He didn't say anything against EJ's father. That wasn't his place. But he figured if he made sure to share with EJ his own values—the values Eddie Shaw would have taught his nephew—hopefully Nate could balance whatever stupid, Neanderthal ideas Brett had put into his son's mind.

"Can I learn to ride a horse today?" EJ asked as Nate held open the front door for him.

"We'll need to ask your mom about that."

EJ sighed loudly. "She'll say no because she's afraid of horses. She won't want me to get hurt."

"You won't get hurt on my watch," Nate promised, even though the boy nearly had been the other day.

"Look," EJ shouted, then skipped to the bottom of the porch steps. "There's a dog bowl and paw prints in the dirt."

Nate lifted a brow. "I saw the stray hanging around last night as I was going to bed. I left out a scoop of food for him."

"His name's Otis," EJ said patiently.

"We're not naming him," Nate countered. "He doesn't belong to us."

"You fed him." EJ held up the metal bowl.

"It was a onetime thing," Nate explained a little sheepishly. "To thank him for coming to your rescue with Cinnamon."

"Can I feed him this morning?" EJ bounced on his toes. "Since I was the one he rescued, I should thank him."

Nate grinned but couldn't fault EJ's logic. "One scoop. There's a bin of dog food next to the washer in the laundry room."

EJ let out a whoop of delight then ran into the house, returning a few minutes later carrying the bowl piled high with kibble.

Nate chuckled. "That's a heck of a lot more than one scoop."

"I want to thank Otis a whole bunch." EJ set the food at the bottom of the porch. "Where do you think he sleeps?"

Nate started walking toward the barn, EJ at his side. "I'm not sure. But that dog can take care of himself."

"Everybody needs somebody," EJ reminded him. "Even Otis."

"Right now the horses need their morning hay. Let's get them and the chickens fed, then we'll make pancakes before your mom wakes up."

EJ seemed to have no trouble believing that a real man worked in the kitchen and was so excited at the prospect of surprising Bianca that he made quick work of morning chores. Within an hour they were back in the house, washing their hands and then mixing the pancake batter.

Nate had loved weekend mornings as a kid when his mom made huge stacks of pancakes. He and his brothers would polish off a half dozen each after their morning chores. They didn't make nearly as many now, but EJ was thrilled to pull up a chair in front of the stove and use the wide spatula to flip the pancakes. Nate washed and plated the blueberries Bianca had bought at the grocery store then poured a glass of juice. He didn't bother with coffee. Her first morning on the ranch Bianca had confirmed that his coffee was unpalatable. She'd quickly mastered Ariana's fancy coffee maker and had made him promise that he'd let her handle their morning caffeine.

It was such a little thing, but it felt like they were on the same team. Nate found that idea strangely appealing.

They put everything for breakfast on a tray then headed upstairs. Nate knocked softly on the bedroom door, but EJ just pushed it open.

"We made breakfast, Mommy," he shouted.

Bianca was already awake, sitting up against the pillows, her hair pulled back in a messy ponytail and a notebook propped in her lap.

She gave her son a brilliant smile. "This is a special treat. What's the occasion?"

"Mr. Nate said real men cook." EJ took the tray from Nate and carried it to the bed.

Nate sucked in a breath as Bianca's gaze lifted to his. She looked so fresh and happy, and an adorable blush colored her cheeks when he winked.

"Mr. Nate is a smart man," she murmured. She put aside the notebook and took the tray from EJ. "I love pancakes. Thank you both."

She was wearing an oversize, shapeless scoop-neck T-shirt that was about the sexiest thing he'd ever seen. Maybe because she looked relaxed and a little bit rumpled, and he could easily imagine a night spent with his body curled around hers.

He stayed in the doorway, afraid all his willpower would disappear if he stepped any closer. She took a bite of the pancakes, closed her eyes and then smiled as she chewed.

"They're perfect," she said, forking up a bite and holding it out to EJ.

"I flipped 'em," the boy reported.

"You did a good job." She brushed the hair away from his face, and Nate's heart clenched. He couldn't get enough of Bianca and the love she had for her son. She was exactly the type of woman he would have never chosen for himself. He usually went for the party girls, the ones who wanted a good time and expected nothing more.

No expectations meant nobody got hurt.

But Bianca made him crave more, a different life than the one he'd grown accustomed to. He wanted to be the kind of man she deserved, but could he trust he wouldn't fail her the way he had Eddie? Despite having Earl Thompson as a role model, Nate was still Gerald

Robinson's son. What if he took after his dad and hurt the people who cared about him the most?

There was no doubt Gerald had broken Deborah's heart, and Bianca had already had one man desert her. She needed someone who could truly commit to her and EJ. As much as Nate wanted to, he wasn't sure if he had it in him to be that guy.

"What are you working on?" he asked when she glanced toward him again. It was a struggle to do anything except stare at her like a googly-eyed teenager, but despite the amazing kiss they'd shared, Bianca wanted to take things slow. She considered him a friend. He needed to act like one to her. He owed it to Eddie.

She bit down on her bottom lip, looking almost embarrassed. "It's nothing."

"I don't believe that for a minute."

"It's the start of a business plan," she said, dropping her gaze to the plate in front of her. "Just an initial inventory list and some ideas for how to market the care packages and gift boxes."

"That's fantastic," he said, and was rewarded by one of her sweet smiles.

"You don't have to say that. It's probably a silly idea in the first place."

"It's a great idea, and good for you for making a plan. You'll be back on your feet in no time, and you won't need me anymore."

Something flashed in her brown eyes that looked like disappointment, but it was gone a second later. She took another quick bite of pancake, then set the tray aside and threw back the covers. "Hopefully we'll be out of your hair sooner than later."

"That's not what I meant." All the warmth he'd felt

from her minutes earlier had disappeared. He wanted
to kick himself for his careless words. The last thing he
wanted was for Bianca and EJ to leave, not when they'd
already made such a difference in his life.

How could he explain that without sounding like a
wuss? He was supposed to be a big, strong navy SEAL,
not a broken man who was no longer sure of his purpose in life.

"Have you already been helping Mr. Nate with
chores?" Bianca asked EJ as she stood.

"Yep," her son confirmed. "We fed the horses and
the chickens. After breakfast we're going to fix the gate
behind the shed. It needs new hinges."

She wore a pair of pajama pants with a pattern of
rubber ducks all over. She was medium height but had
a delicate bone structure that made her seem younger
than twenty-eight. He had to remind himself she was
nine years younger than him. And his best friend's little sister.

Nate sighed. As amazing as their kiss had been, he
needed to keep Bianca at arm's length. He had no reason to ask her to stay once she'd gotten her life back
on track. Despite the setbacks she'd obviously faced, it
was also clear she hadn't lost her sense of hope or her
willingness to work hard and try new things.

"Can I join you?" She reached behind her head and
pulled out the ponytail holder, her dark hair falling over
her shoulders and making his mouth go dry.

He should say no. He should walk away, put some
sort of distance between them. Instead he found himself nodding. "It's not easy work."

"I'm good with that," she assured him.

"Meet me at the barn in twenty minutes." He moved

forward and picked up the tray from the bed. "I'll take this downstairs."

"I can do it," she told him, her fingers brushing his as she reached for the tray.

He ignored the sparks that raced along his skin and gave EJ a pointed look. "A real man also cleans up the dishes."

The boy nodded and picked up the juice cup Bianca had set on her nightstand. "I'm a real man, Mommy."

"My best man," she murmured. She met Nate's gaze again, the tenderness in her brown eyes almost bringing him to his knees. "Thank you," she whispered.

He nodded. "Let's go, little man," he told EJ, and the boy followed him out of the room.

Chapter Seven

The following week Bianca drove into Paseo to pick up the boxes of supplies she'd ordered to start on her stock for military care packages and birthday boxes. The post office was also housed in the general store, so she'd had the packages delivered to town because it seemed quicker than trying to find a delivery driver willing to make the trek out to the Fortune ranch.

Rosa, who owned most of the businesses in town, asked her to open several of the packages then immediately placed an order for two gift boxes for her daughters, who both had birthdays in February.

"They'll feel so special." Rosa clasped her hands in front of her ample chest. She was short with generous curves and a bright smile. "I've gotten into the habit of sending gift cards because it's so easy, but I love giving them something personal."

"I appreciate the business," Bianca told her honestly.

"I can't help but wonder if people will see the point of them. Nothing I offer is extravagant—"

"But you make it look so beautiful," Rosa interrupted. "You have an eye for color and design."

Susan from the library had stopped into the post office while Bianca was still there. Both of the older women oohed and aahed over the photos Bianca had saved on her camera of the gift boxes she'd put together for the store in San Antonio.

"Thanks." Bianca couldn't hide her grin. She was excited to start putting together the boxes. She'd used the internet at the library to go online and set up an Etsy page and a website for her business, which she was calling "Just the Two of Us Designs." She already had a half dozen preorders. It was hard to believe that only a short time ago she'd left San Antonio with no idea what she was going to do with her life. Now she was a small business owner and part-time ranch hand.

She glanced at her watch. "Oh, no. It's almost noon. I told Nate and EJ I'd make lunch and I promised that EJ could start horseback riding lessons this afternoon."

Susan laughed. "Just make sure it's Nate teaching him and not Grayson. Otherwise your son will be bronco riding by the time he starts kindergarten."

Bianca felt her eyes widen. "No way. I'm nervous enough to let him be led around the corral."

"Nate will take care of him," Rosa said matter-of-factly.

"I know," Bianca agreed softly. Rosa gave her a calculated look, but before the women could ask any questions about Bianca's relationship with Nate, she picked up her stack of boxes and walked out into the bright Texas sunshine.

It wasn't exactly a surprise that everyone she'd met on her regular trips to town knew Nate and his family. Paseo was a tiny, close-knit community. Bianca hadn't been in the area long, but already most of the people she encountered greeted her by name. So different from San Antonio, where the barista at the neighborhood coffee shop she'd frequented for almost two years still got her name wrong almost every day.

Brittany. Bethany. Becky. But never Bianca.

Two weeks in Paseo and she was a regular.

She realized people were curious about how she knew Nate and why she and EJ were staying at the ranch while the rest of the family was away. Bianca doggedly continued with the "family friend" line, unwilling to share any more than that when she barely understood her feelings for Nate.

All she knew was she wanted him to kiss her again, but somehow she'd been relegated back to the realm of "Eddie's little sister." Nate was careful to keep his distance, especially at night after EJ had gone to bed. She tried not to let it hurt her feelings, but the longer she spent with Nate, the harder she fell for him.

She'd gotten so desperate for his company, she'd even made herself into a morning person. Waking before sunrise wasn't in her nature, but a person could train themselves to do anything with the right motivation.

Nate Fortune was it for her.

He'd been surprised the first day she'd stumbled down to the kitchen and offered to make breakfast while he and EJ handled the early morning chores. But now it was a routine, and she'd come to enjoy that quiet time in the kitchen with the scent of coffee filling the air.

She enjoyed everything about her time at the ranch,

other than Nate's refusal to admit he felt more for her than physical attraction. Sometimes, though, when they were in the barn or driving down the dirt road that led to the far end of the property, she'd catch him staring at her like she was a hot-fudge sundae and he'd been without dessert for months. It had to be only a matter of time until he kissed her. She'd told herself she would wait for him to make the next move, but it was difficult to be patient.

Still, she was happier in Paseo than she'd been in years. It was more than Nate. There was a sense of community she hadn't realized was missing in her life. The rolling hills and wide pastures gave her a feeling of being grounded to the earth and somehow a better understanding of her place in it. She loved watching the open sky above her as she drove. It was a welcome change from the constant traffic of her San Antonio neighborhood.

Here she could sometimes drive the whole way from town to the ranch without passing another car. And when she did, whoever was driving the approaching vehicle would undoubtedly offer her a friendly wave.

But today, when she pulled into the long driveway, there was an unfamiliar truck parked in front of the barn. EJ burst out the front door and came running toward her car before she'd even turned off the ignition.

"Sugar's here, Mommy!" he shouted as she opened the door. "And Jayden and Ariana. And Mr. Nate bought me a pony."

"He didn't," she whispered.

"I didn't buy the pony," Nate called from the front porch as if he'd read her lips. She heard a deep laugh come from the direction of the barn. A man who was the spitting image of Nate, but somehow totally different, walked toward her.

"You must be Bianca," he said, pulling off a faded leather glove. "I'm Jayden."

"Nice to meet you," she said automatically, relieved her voice didn't falter. She knew Jayden and his wife would be returning to the ranch, but somehow she'd put the thought out of her mind. This place had begun to feel like home, like it belonged to Nate and her and EJ.

But it wasn't hers, and Nate didn't belong to her. She was the outsider here, as she'd been in every other part of her life. What if Ariana resented a woman other than the triplets' mother being at the ranch? What if neither Jayden nor Ariana could deal with EJ's exuberance the way Nate did?

Bianca prided herself on her resilience—on being able to keep a positive attitude no matter what life threw at her. No one other than Eddie had made her feel valued, so she'd learned early on to value herself. But recently, life's disappointments and misfortunes—both big and trivial—had worn her down until it felt like she was made of tissue paper, easily crumpled, torn and tossed aside.

"The pony's name is Twix." EJ tugged on her pant leg. "Mr. Nate says he's the perfect size for me." He looked up at Jayden. "Can I go get Sugar so Mommy can meet her?"

"You bet." Jayden chuckled as EJ took off for the house. "I'm guessing my brother didn't clear the pony with you?"

Bianca pressed her lips together. "No."

"I didn't plan it," Nate said behind her. She turned to find him standing closer than he'd been to her all week. He was giving her an aw-shucks smile she could imagine had gotten him out of all sorts of trouble when he was younger. "I was over at the Caplans' today and they'd gotten Twix when their grandson came to stay for Christmas. The kid won't be back until spring break, so the pony's on loan until then." He lifted his hands, palms out. "I didn't buy EJ a pony."

"Close enough," Jayden said with a smug grin.

"Not helping," a feminine voice called.

They all turned as a woman walked from the barn, looking both completely out of place on this ranch in the middle of nowhere and utterly like she belonged. She had long dark hair that looked Hollywood A-list shiny and wore a printed shirtdress and the cutest pair of red boots Bianca had ever seen.

Bianca smoothed a self-conscious hand over the front of her faded shirt. She didn't own much in the way of clothes. The day before leaving San Antonio, she'd brought everything decent she had to a local resale shop that bought items outright for a pittance of what they were worth. That left her with jeans, yoga pants, a handful of well-worn T-shirts and a couple of floral-patterned blouses she hadn't been willing to part with because they were her favorites.

She felt shabby in comparison to this woman who she assumed was Jayden's wife, Ariana. Why hadn't she at least taken the time to brush out her hair this morning? Instead, she'd pulled it back into a messy bun, her usual nonstylish style. She'd never considered how much she'd stopped caring about her appearance once she became a mom. Maybe that was part of the reason Nate had backed off. He probably preferred women who were beautiful and pulled together. Women like Ariana.

She didn't realize she'd stepped back until she felt the soft pressure of Nate's warm hand against the small of her back.

"You're perfect," he whispered, and she was once again amazed at how easily he was able to read her.

"I'm a mess," she said under her breath.

"Perfect," he repeated and moved his hand to the collar of her shirt. Her neck was exposed because of the bun, and his thumb gently grazed her skin.

Bianca felt a blush heat her cheeks as her stomach dipped and swirled at his touch. She glanced over to see Jayden watching the two of them, his gaze assessing.

She sidestepped Nate and moved forward to greet Ariana. Instead of taking Bianca's outstretched hand, the other woman enveloped her in a tight hug.

"I'm *so* happy to meet you," she said, squeezing Bianca's shoulders. "Nate told us all about you. EJ is adorable. I'm so sorry about your brother."

"Thank you," Bianca said, slightly overwhelmed at Ariana's warmth. "Congratulations on getting married."

"Thanks." Ariana grinned. "I guess we're still officially newlyweds. Our honeymoon was spent traveling around the state for research on my new book, so it kind of feels like we've been married forever."

"You're definitely stuck with me forever," Jayden said, slipping an arm around Ariana's waist and pulling her closer.

"I'm a lucky girl." Ariana tipped up her face and kissed her husband's cheek. She looked at Bianca again. "We're glad your stay coincides with our visit home."

Jayden nodded. "I only met Eddie a couple of times, but he was a good guy. And he had my brother's back for a lot of years, so we'll always be grateful."

"It goes both ways," Bianca answered, glancing over her shoulder. "Nate was the brother Eddie always wanted."

Something shifted in the air as Nate looked past her to Jayden—a silent communication between the brothers Bianca didn't understand. But she knew it had to do with Eddie, and that made her intensely curious.

"Deborah will be sad she didn't get a chance to meet EJ," Ariana said into the uncomfortable silence. "She loves kids."

"Hard to believe," Jayden said with a smile, "after dealing with us for so many years."

"What were you doing in the barn?" Nate asked Ariana, lifting an eyebrow. "You and Jayden making up for the time you spent working on your honeymoon?" His tone was teasing. He was obviously comfortable with his brother's wife. Bianca felt a pang of jealousy. She'd always imagined becoming best friends with the woman her brother married, but Eddie had remained stubbornly single, making excuses about the SEALs not leaving him time for anything else.

Ariana rolled her eyes. "Get your mind out of the gutter, Nathan Fortune. There's a corner in one of the horse stalls where I can sometimes get a few bars of service on my phone."

"What?" Bianca felt her mouth drop open. "You actually have service on the ranch?"

"It comes and goes, but I always try."

"That would be amazing. Can you show me where?"

Jayden groaned. "Why can't we all just be satisfied with the good ol' landline on the kitchen wall?"

"The ranch is perfect," Ariana agreed, "except for that one little thing. It's not like I'm checking Facebook. I need internet for work." She sent a questioning glance toward Bianca. "I'm guessing you need it for your job, too?"

Embarrassment roared through Bianca, making her stomach twist. Ariana was researching a book and was already a talented writer. Bianca had spent almost an hour at the library in town reading the series of articles Ariana had written last year about different members of the Fortune family. Bianca couldn't possibly compare what she was doing to that.

"I don't—"

"She's starting her own business," Nate interrupted. "Personalized gift boxes people order or buy in stores. Plus care packages for soldiers deployed overseas. She used to send stuff to Eddie and we were all jealous. They're going to be popular. Rosa has already ordered a couple for her daughters."

"That's so exciting," Ariana said. "Do you have pictures? Are you selling them online?"

Bianca nodded, darting a glance at Nate. Of course he knew about her gift boxes, but the pride in his voice as he explained her business idea to his brother and Ariana surprised her. She'd sort of assumed he was just being kind in his support of what she was doing, but he really sounded like he believed in her.

It made her tingle all the way down to her toes.

"I set up an Etsy account." She pulled her phone out of her back pocket. "I just went to town to pick up the supplies I ordered, but I have photos of a few of the boxes I made for the gift shop where I worked in San Antonio. I did different colors and themes." She pulled up the photo stream and handed the phone to Ariana. "They're simple, but it's a start."

Ariana swiped a finger across the screen, her face lighting up as she did. "Oh, my gosh. I love them. I'm totally going to set you up with a couple of high-end boutiques from my old neighborhood in Austin. These would be perfect."

"Thanks," Bianca said softly, wondering why she'd been so intimidated by Jayden's wife. Ariana was one of the friendliest people she'd ever met.

"Mommy, this is Sugar." She turned to EJ, who'd returned with an adorable mutt wearing a red bandana at his side. "She's blind," EJ explained, "but she can get from the house to the barn and that's why there are wind chimes all around. They help Sugar know where she's going."

Bianca smiled. "I just thought this family had a thing for wind chimes." She bent to scratch the dog's head. She could tell by the dog's cloudy eyes that she couldn't see, but Sugar sniffed at Bianca's hand, then gave it a gentle lick.

"She likes you," EJ said, his voice breathless. "She likes me, too." He shaded his eyes with one hand and turned in a circle, surveying the property. "I bet Otis will come out now that Sugar's back. He's been eating the food Mr. Nate and I leave out for him every morning."

"You're feeding that stray dog who hangs around?" Jayden asked with a pointed look toward Nate. "The one you said was nothing but a nuisance."

Nate shrugged, rubbing a hand over his jaw.

"I told you owning a dog would do you some good." Jayden nodded. "It can be lonely out here when no one else is around."

"He's not my dog, and I don't get lonely. I like the quiet."

Bianca tried not to flinch. She knew he didn't mean to direct the comment toward her and EJ, but they'd certainly shown up and disturbed Nate's quiet world.

"Well, I'm glad we're all here together now," Ariana said quickly. "We're going to have so much fun." She scrunched up her nose. "Bianca, I hope Nate hasn't been subjecting you to his coffee."

"It's not that bad," Nate protested.

"I'm making coffee every morning," Bianca assured Ariana.

The other woman smiled. "Smart girl."

"Can I take Sugar to the backyard?" EJ asked. "Maybe Otis doesn't realize she's here."

Nate looked like he wanted to say no, but Jayden cleared his throat and gave a small nod to Bianca.

"Since it's okay with Jayden," she told her son. "But don't go any farther than the shed."

Nate let out a long breath and ruffled EJ's dark hair. "Jayden and I need to look at one of the tractors that hasn't been running right. When we're finished, I'll bring Twix out to the corral for you to ride."

EJ pumped his little fist in the air. "Best day ever," he said and called for Sugar to follow him around the house.

Bianca leveled a look at Nate. "Back to the subject of you getting my son a pony."

"I think that's our cue," Jayden said quickly, grabbing his wife's hand.

"Good luck," Ariana called over her shoulder as the pair hurried to the house.

"Was she wishing luck to you or me?" Nate stepped

closer again, and Bianca ignored the effect his nearness had on certain parts of her body.

She narrowed her eyes.

"Me," he said with a grimace. "Definitely me."

She sighed. "Seriously, Nate. A pony?"

"It's on loan," he said, holding up his hands.

"A pony is the stuff of childhood fantasies. Now it's EJ's reality."

"It's not a big deal in Paseo," he countered. "Most families keep at least one horse, and lots of people have ponies when their kids are little."

She couldn't argue that point, but still…

"How am I supposed to compete with a pony when we leave here?"

"It's not a competition," he insisted. "You're a fantastic mom. Besides, there's no reason you have to leave anytime soon."

My heart, she wanted to tell him. Protecting it was a good reason.

"I thought you liked quiet."

He inclined his head. "I do, but I like you and EJ more." He reached out and ran a finger along her collarbone. "A lot more."

"We don't belong here."

His mouth went hard, but his eyes stayed gentle. "You belong here for as long as you want. I thought you'd be happy with the pony. EJ's determined to learn to ride, and this way he can start on a horse that's more his size."

"I guess you're right."

He grinned. "Darlin', I'm always right. Trust me."

She laughed, but the truth was she did trust Nate.

And she cared about him far more than she was willing to admit to either of them.

"What am I going to do with you?"

"I've got so many ideas," he whispered, and she sucked in a breath when he dropped a quick kiss on her lips. "Right now there's a tractor to fix. We'll meet behind the barn in an hour for EJ's first riding lesson if you want to watch."

Bianca blinked, unable to put a sentence together with how blown away she was by his sudden flirtation. "Sure," she whispered and pressed her fingertips to her lips. She had so many ideas of what she wanted to do with him, as well. Each one of them sexier than the last.

His eyes turned dark as if he knew every erotic thought she'd ever had. But he only winked and walked past her toward the barn.

She brushed her hair out of her eyes and turned for the house like she wasn't about to explode from pent-up need. Bianca was used to wanting things she couldn't have. And she wanted Nate more than anything.

Chapter Eight

"You're in deep."

Nate kept the smile plastered to his face as he reached behind his back to give Jayden, standing at the edge of the corral, a one-fingered salute.

"You're doing great, EJ," he called. "Loosen up on the reins a little. Remember you're using them to talk to Twix, not scream at him."

The boy nodded, the tip of his tongue poking out from the corner of his mouth. He gave the reins more slack and the docile pony continued his wide circle in the ring.

Bianca stood on the far side of the corral, leaning against the fence and looking tense as she watched her son. Ariana was at her side, a supportive hand resting on Bianca's shoulder.

"Rude hand gestures don't make it any less true," Jayden said.

"She's Eddie's baby sister." Nate took a few steps back until he was standing next to his brother.

Jayden chuckled. "She's not a baby."

"I'm giving her a helping hand."

"That's not all you want to give her." By his amused tone, Jayden was obviously loving a chance to give Nate grief about a woman.

"Don't make me kick your—"

"Mr. Nate, I want him to go faster." EJ looked over at him hopefully.

Nate saw Bianca stiffen and shook his head. "Next lesson. First you get comfortable, then we'll increase the speed."

"I'm happy for you," Jayden said, nudging his shoulder. "You look better than you have since you left the SEALs. Are you sleeping?"

"Like a rock."

"Like you used to."

Nate sighed. When he'd first gotten back to Paseo, he'd tried to hide the nightmares that plagued him. He didn't want anyone in his family to worry, especially since there was nothing they could do to help him. He hadn't thought anything would help him. Until Bianca.

"What have you told her about Eddie?"

"She hasn't asked many questions," Nate admitted, giving EJ a thumbs-up when the boy tugged on the reins to keep the pony from lowering its head to eat grass. "I haven't offered anything. The official report didn't give details, so why should I?"

"Because you believe you're responsible for her brother's death."

Nate's head jerked back like Jayden had punched him.

"Not that I think that," his brother amended. "No one

does." He leaned closer. "Except you. Which is what counts."

"What good would it do to tell her?"

"It's a secret between you. That isn't the way to start a relationship. Trust me."

"There's no relationship to speak of. She's a friend."

"She's more than that," Jayden insisted. "You deserve to be happy, Nate. Eddie would want that for you."

"No one can say what Eddie would want because he's not here. That's on me."

"It's not."

Nate shook his head, his cheeks aching from continuing to smile through this ridiculous conversation. "Did you make a stop in Austin on your way home?"

"Yeah. Ariana wanted to visit her family."

"Did you see any of the others?"

He didn't need to spell out which others he was referring to.

"We had lunch with Keaton. He was the first person Ariana profiled last year in her *Becoming a Fortune* blog series for *Weird Life Magazine*, so they're still friends. He's a good guy. Every one of them I've met has been."

"What about Gerald?"

Jayden shook his head.

Before Nate could ask more questions, EJ called for him. He jogged out to the boy and took hold of the reins. "Done for today?"

"Can Mommy come out while I'm on Twix and pet him?" EJ bit down on his lip, a nervous habit he'd inherited from his mother and one that made Nate's heart melt just a bit. "I think she'll like him better then."

"I like him fine," Bianca called from the fence. "I like him with some space between us."

"Please, Mommy?" EJ called.

Nate arched a brow in her direction, then smiled as Ariana gave her a gentle nudge. She climbed through the slats of the fence and slowly made her way toward them.

Her chest rose and fell in shallow breaths as if she was approaching a man-eating tiger rather than a slightly paunchy and docile pony.

"He smells like a real horse," EJ informed her.

"He is a real horse."

"He's a pony," Nate and EJ said at the same time.

Bianca reached out a hand, which Nate noticed was trembling slightly.

"Are you okay?" he whispered, moving to stand directly behind her.

"Peachy keen," she said through clenched teeth.

"You saw them out here. Twix's as gentle as they come," Nate assured her.

"Right." She stroked her hand up the pony's nose, yanking it away when the animal let out a soft whicker.

"He likes you, Mommy," EJ said brightly.

Bianca nodded, although to Nate it looked like she was about to lose her lunch. He glanced up but Jayden and Ariana had started toward the house.

"End of your lesson," he told EJ, tugging on the reins he held. "Let's get Twix back to the barn."

"I can do it," EJ said.

Nate helped the boy off the pony and handed him the reins. "Put him in his stall and start brushing him down."

"Yes, sir," EJ answered and made his way into the

barn, the pony happy to follow since the barn meant rest and food.

"I'm such a wimp." Bianca covered her face with her hands when EJ disappeared around the corner. "I don't want my fear to rub off on him."

"What happened with you and a horse?" Nate gently pulled her hands way from her face, lacing his fingers with hers.

"Nothing."

"Your reaction to Twix isn't nothing."

She took a shuddery breath. "I fell off a horse when I was in third grade and got kicked in the back. My mom blamed the accident on me because I kept sliding off the saddle. The horse wasn't tame like your herd. He belonged to one of her boyfriends, and she insisted I learn to ride so she'd have an excuse to be at his house every weekend."

"I'm sorry, Bianca. That must have been terrifying."

She shrugged. "Eddie had just left for boot camp, so it was Mom and me on our own. That was never a good thing. I missed a couple of days of school, but the next Saturday she dragged me back out there. I had a panic attack and puked all over her new boyfriend. It was kind of the end of their relationship."

"I imagine that didn't sit well with her?"

"Not at all. I missed Eddie so much at that moment. I wanted to call and beg him to leave the navy, to come home so I wouldn't be alone with her. It was miserable with the two of us in the apartment. Eddie could always make her laugh or lighten the mood. I couldn't do anything right. I still can't, according to her."

Nate ignored his resolve to keep a safe distance between the two of them and pulled her closer. He wrapped his arms around her waist and she rested her head against his chest with a sigh that made his heart ache. When he'd enlisted, it hadn't seemed like a big deal. Yes, Jayden also left home for a career in the army, but Grayson was still with their mom, and Nate came back to Paseo during every leave to pitch in at the ranch. Between the three boys, they'd always been able to take care of Deborah.

He knew from the little Eddie had talked about his mom that she was the exact opposite of Nate's mother. Based on how Eddie had described Jennifer Shaw, she was an immature, insecure party girl who'd never grown up. There was no doubt Eddie loved his mother, but he'd often seemed relieved to be far away from home. Nate hadn't given much thought to how Eddie's sister would fare being left alone for so much time with a woman who clearly had very few maternal instincts.

It was a wonder Bianca had turned out as sweet and nurturing as she had with Jennifer as a role model.

"You're amazing," he whispered into her hair, loving how the flowery scent of it seemed to envelop him.

She snuggled closer, and Nate realized that if his brother or Ariana was looking out the window in the kitchen, they'd have a perfect view of this embrace. He should care. He should step away from her, but he didn't.

"And you're not alone," he told her. "Not anymore."

She lifted her head. "Maybe you can teach me to ride?" Her voice shook slightly.

"You don't have to do that."

"I want to," she insisted. "I've made a lot of decisions in my life based on fear. That needs to stop. I want to be brave. I figure if I can get back on the proverbial horse, I can do anything, right?"

He could feel her fear like it was a living thing, radiating from her in waves. "You can do anything."

One side of her mouth kicked up. "Even this?" she asked and pressed her mouth to his.

The kiss was over so quickly he didn't even have time to respond. It was a soft promise, and her eyes danced as she pulled away. "The next move is yours."

He wondered how he'd ever thought he'd be able to stay away from her. His need was a palpable force, humming under his skin and making his blood feel like he'd just taken a shot of adrenaline.

He rubbed a hand over the back of his neck. "I've got all kinds of moves," he said, trying to sound romantic or sexy or something.

But he realized how out of practice he was when Bianca laughed. "I just bet you do. I can't wait to see them." She glanced over her shoulder toward the house then back to him. "Are you okay with EJ in the barn? I'd like to get Ariana's opinion on a couple of marketing descriptions I did for the military care packages."

"He's safe with me," Nate told her, then closed his eyes for a moment as images of Eddie's lifeless body pounded into his brain. *Safe.* His most despised four-letter word, since he no longer believed he had the power to keep anyone safe. "I mean—"

"I know he is," she said with a gentle smile. "I'll be out to check on him in a bit."

She walked away before he could answer, and despite Jayden's advice, Nate knew he'd never tell Bianca the details of Eddie's death. He couldn't stand the thought of hurting her and would do anything he could to make sure that didn't happen.

Anything.

"What inspired the idea for your book?" Bianca asked Ariana later that evening as they worked together in the kitchen. Nate and Jayden had taken EJ with them an hour earlier when they left to go check on the irrigation system in one of the fields at the far end of the property.

Ariana had offered to help Bianca make dinner—homemade meatballs and spaghetti. Bianca was shocked to discover how easy and companionable it was to have a friend in the kitchen.

"It was a local couple actually," Ariana answered as she chopped tomatoes for the salad. "Paloma and Hector Ybarra. I got stuck on Jayden's ranch last June when my car conked out just before a tornado touched down nearby. There was some minor damage to this ranch, but the Ybarras' house was completely destroyed."

"That's terrible," Bianca whispered.

"It was, but the community immediately pitched in to rebuild it. I went to their farm with Jayden and was shocked at how calm both of them seemed. Paloma told me how blessed they were to have each other and their friends even when they had nothing but the land beneath their feet. They had so much wisdom to offer, and their words really meant a lot. It was a time of transition in my life, and although I had a great job, I felt strangely at loose ends. I'd just met Jayden, and he changed everything for me. Does that make any sense?"

Bianca sighed. "More than you know."

"Once I realized things were getting serious with Jayden—or at least that I wanted them to—I quit the magazine. The Fortunes were no longer simply a family I was reporting on. I was in love with one of Gerald Robinson's sons. It no longer felt right making the family my business, and I'd always wanted to write a book." She laughed softly. "When I first met Jayden after my car died, I accused him of being an ax murderer."

"I'm sure that went over well," Bianca said with a smile.

"He likes to joke that I should write a story about an ax murderer, but I like interviewing real people and learning their stories. The Ybarras inspired me, and I knew there must be more stories like theirs around the state, so I decided to write a book about people who embody the spirit of Texas."

Bianca dumped a box of dried spaghetti into the pot of boiling water on the stove. "It's a great idea. How do you find your subjects?"

"Articles in local papers, news stories, social media."

"Social media?"

Ariana nodded. "I set up a Facebook page and Instagram account for the book. I posted about what I was doing and asked people to message me if they knew anyone who would be a good fit. The response was unbelievable. Then I sorted through the stories, contacted people for initial interviews and went from there. Jayden and I are visiting the dozen people I'm profiling."

"It's nice of him to travel with you."

"I think he was nervous about letting me go alone, but it's wonderful to have him on the road with me. I've got pages of notes and lots of recorded conversations.

In fact, I only have three more people to interview and I'll be ready to start compiling everything."

"Are any of them famous like the Fortunes?"

Ariana shook her head. "A few are well-known in their communities, but very few people in Texas are as famous as the Fortunes."

"Nate told me the story of their mother and Gerald Robinson. Or I suppose she knew him as Jerome Fortune."

"He did?" Ariana paused with the knife in midair. "Was it a secret?"

"No, of course not. It's just that Nate doesn't talk about his father much. He's like Deborah in that way. Both of them like to pretend that discovering Gerald is alive hasn't changed anything."

"That's impossible."

"I know, but it's a pretty overwhelming discovery. Having interviewed several of the Fortune kids, I've seen a span of different reactions. I'm glad Nate finally talked to someone. I'm glad he has you."

"I happened to be here," Bianca said with a shrug, unwilling to allow herself to believe Nate confiding in her meant what Ariana wanted it to.

"It's more than that," the other woman insisted. "Nate is charming and funny, but Jayden said something changed in him when he returned from his last mission."

"The mission where my brother died."

"Right," Ariana agreed, her gaze sympathetic. "Obviously that was a tragedy you can't truly recover from, but I think it affected Nate more than even he realized. I've only known him a short time, but there's a big difference in how he seems with you and EJ here. He's lighter somehow."

"He takes on too much."

"Each of the Fortune brothers does." Ariana dropped the tomatoes into the wooden salad bowl Bianca had placed on the counter. "I think it comes from being raised by a single mom. They're protective of Deborah and feel responsible for anyone they care about."

"I wonder if that's how EJ will be when he grows up." Bianca stirred the tomato sauce simmering on the stove then turned to Ariana. "Nate told me he doesn't care about a relationship with Gerald Robinson. Does Jayden feel the same way?"

"Not exactly. I think Jayden is wary but curious. He's met some of the Fortunes as well as Gerald. And I'm not sure Grayson has actually processed his feelings on having a father. He's been busy with the rodeo circuit and his sponsorship responsibilities. I doubt Deborah's fully dealt with it, either. She spends so much time with Grayson that it's easy for her to lose herself in his life. She does that with all the boys. They've always been her whole world."

"Did you have a normal family growing up?" Bianca couldn't help but ask.

"I did. What about you?"

Bianca shook her head, the familiar disappointment and regret burning a hole in her stomach. "I never knew my dad. According to Mom, he took off after Eddie was born but came back when he was around seven. He wanted another shot and to finally be a family. I guess life was pretty good until I came along. The baby thing just wasn't our dad's cup of tea so he left again—permanently. Mom blamed me, although Eddie never did. He always told me he didn't remember much about those two years with our dad, but now I think he might have been lying. Eddie was a great big brother. I'm so lucky I had him because our mom didn't have much use for me."

"That can't be true," Ariana said, sounding stunned. "You're obviously a great mother. Where did you learn that if not—"

"Maybe it's natural instinct," Bianca said with a tired laugh. "Or maybe I'm trying to make up for what I never had. Either way, I can appreciate how Nate must feel. It breaks my heart because my jerk of an ex-husband walked away two years ago and hasn't contacted EJ since. I don't care that he was done with me, but a boy needs a father."

"You're doing a great job on your own."

Bianca shook her head. "I appreciate you saying that, but you have to understand what I'm talking about after profiling even a few of the Fortune kids." She leveled a look at Ariana. "How many of them have daddy issues?"

Ariana grimaced before quickly schooling her features. "Point taken, but they're also a group of accomplished, smart, talented and generally fun-to-be-around people. They may have some issues to work through, but show me one person who doesn't. I had a great family, but that doesn't make me perfect." She opened the refrigerator and pulled out a bottle of white wine. "Besides," she said, grabbing a corkscrew from a drawer, "perfect is boring."

Bianca smiled and took down two wineglasses from the cabinet next to the stove. "One thing you can say about the Paseo Fortunes is they are *not* boring."

Ariana filled each of the glasses and handed one to Bianca. "To not perfect."

They clinked glasses. "And not boring," Bianca added and took a long sip.

Nate walked out of an empty horse stall, staring at his cell phone's home screen, and almost plowed into Jayden.

"Ariana and Bianca called us in to dinner," his brother told him. "I sent EJ in to wash his hands and—" Jayden's eyes narrowed. "What's wrong? You look like you've seen a ghost."

"Not a ghost," Nate clarified. "But I did just get off the phone with Ben Fortune Robinson in Austin."

Jayden raised a brow.

"Why is it that I can have no service at the house but somehow I get three bars in the back of that stall?"

"Ariana would tell you it's luck."

"Bad luck," Nate muttered.

"Was Ben giving you trouble?"

Nate shook his head. "On the contrary, he was ten kinds of friendly."

"All of Gerald's kids I've met have been. The Robinson brood—Ben, Wes, Kieran, Graham, Rachel, Zoe, Sophie and Olivia—had just as much of a shock as the rest of us."

"I can't believe you can rattle off their names."

"We now have a lot of family around Texas," Jayden said with a shrug. "But I think there are actually more."

"We know there's more," Nate countered. "Keaton for one." He began to tick names off on his fingers. "Then Chloe and—"

"I'm not talking about the kids from Gerald's affairs.

Ariana uncovered information while she was doing research last year. It seems Gerald got his wandering eye honestly. His father, Julius, had secrets of his own. And quite possibly Fortune offspring that even Charlotte Robinson isn't aware of. I was thinking—"

"Stop thinking." Nate held up a hand. "Stop talking. Whatever you and Ariana believe you know, I don't want to hear about it. Gerald Robinson was a sperm donor as far as I'm concerned. Leave me out of any sort of search for more Fortunes."

"You know Ben was the one who first reached out to his—I guess our—father's illegitimate kids. He believed everyone had a right to know their roots."

"Yeah. He told me as much during our conversation." Nate blew out a breath. "He also invited me to the Mendoza Winery in Austin for some big Valentine's Day bash. According to Ben, it would be a perfect occasion for me to meet some of the other Fortunes."

"And the Mendozas," Jayden added. "The two families are pretty intertwined at this point. There's a lot of history there, and now Rachel and Olivia—"

"Two of Gerald's legitimate daughters, right?"

Jayden nodded. "They're both married to Mendozas."

"Sounds complicated." Nate gave Jayden a pointed look. "I don't do complicated anymore."

Jayden tipped back his head and laughed. "Right. I'm going to ignore the fact that you've got it bad for your best friend's little sister, who happens to be a single mom and also happens to be living under the same roof as you. Hate to break it to you, bro, but that's kind of the definition of complicated."

"It's not the same thing."

"Right," Jayden repeated with a smirk.

"I'm heading to dinner. This conversation is going nowhere." Nate didn't wait for an answer but started walking toward the barn door.

"So are you going to do it?" Jayden asked, catching up to him in a few strides.

Bianca's beautiful face filled Nate's mind but he shook off the image. "Do what?"

"Make an appearance at the Mendoza Winery party?"

Nathan shrugged. "It's a busy time around here."

"It's always busy at the ranch," Jayden countered. "Make time, Nate. I think it would be good for you."

"I'll take that under consideration," Nate answered, unwilling to admit how curious he was becoming about his extended Fortune family.

Chapter Nine

Jayden and Ariana stayed for two more days. The house was crowded in the best way possible with all of them together. When Eddie had joined the navy, Bianca had dreamed of a big family with lots of brothers and sisters instead of the cramped apartment where she could feel the weight of her mother's silence like a boulder balanced on her shoulders. Being on the ranch with the Fortunes was a dream come true.

During the day, she organized her inventory, taking photographs and cataloging everything for her website and Etsy shop. She also spent time with EJ, working with him on letter recognition and writing his name. He'd been in a prekindergarten program at his daycare, and she didn't want him to be behind when they returned to San Antonio.

Although the thought of going back held no appeal. They couldn't stay in Paseo forever, even though watching the love between Jayden and Ariana made her long for her own happily-ever-after. She and Nate had little time alone with his brother in residence, and she supposed that was a good thing.

Or at least an excuse as to why he hadn't tried to touch her again. She knew he wanted her. Sometimes when no one was looking, she'd meet his gaze and the intensity in his eyes made her feel like she might spontaneously combust.

But he'd stayed up with his brother both nights, although it was clear Jayden would have rather gone out to the tiny guest cottage situated to the west of the house he was sharing with his wife. Bianca didn't understand why Nate insisted on the late-night bonding sessions, and she didn't like not knowing.

Now she stood at the front porch rail, a cool breeze whipping between the house and the barn, as Jayden loaded duffel bags into the cargo bed of his truck, then opened the back door so Sugar could hop in.

EJ was next to Nate a few feet from the car, and she watched her son wipe his eyes on the back of his shirtsleeve. He'd miss that sweet dog. The stray he'd named Otis had indeed been more visible with Sugar at the ranch. The dog still wouldn't let anyone near enough to touch him, but if they let Sugar out on her own, Otis would soon enough be hanging out at her side.

Sugar seemed to take the stray dog's devotion as her due. She was like a queen with one of her loyal subjects. EJ remained determined to tame Otis and had convinced Ariana to help him bake dog treats to lure the animal closer.

Bianca worried about his attachment to a dog whose history they didn't know, but both Jayden and Nate assured her that if Sugar was comfortable with Otis, he must have a decent temperament.

Ariana waved from the passenger-side window. They'd said their official goodbyes after lunch, and Bianca was only a little embarrassed that she didn't walk all the way to the car to see them off. She was afraid she might lose it in a far more embarrassing way than EJ. In such a short time, Ariana had come to feel like a true friend, and she appreciated the calming effect Jayden had on Nate, who seemed more relaxed at his brother's side.

Jayden said something to Nate and held up a finger toward Ariana, then jogged toward the house and up the porch steps.

"Forget something?" Bianca asked lightly, relieved her voice didn't crack.

"Take care of him," Jayden said quietly, coming to stand in front of her. "He pretends to be stronger than he is."

"I know," she said with a slight nod. "But Nate can take care of himself. He doesn't need me."

"Yes." Jayden crouched down so they were at eye level. "He does."

She blew out a breath, unsure how to answer. What she wanted most in life at the moment was to be needed by Nate Fortune.

"Losing Eddie was a blow to both of you," he continued, "but it isn't the only thing that holds you together. You make him remember what it's like to feel happy. That's special, Bianca."

"I think he's pretty special," she whispered with a shaky smile.

Jayden frowned slightly. "He also doesn't believe he deserves that happiness."

"What do you mean?"

"It's his story to tell, but I'm asking you not to give up on him. Me, Nate and Grayson aren't the sharpest knives in the drawer when it comes to women."

"You were pretty smart choosing Ariana."

His gaze softened. "I almost messed it up, but I loved her too much to let her go."

"It was so nice to meet you both."

"You, too." He reached forward and gave her a friendly hug. For as much as the two brothers—and she guessed Grayson, as well—looked alike, her body didn't react at all to Jayden. It was as if she'd been specifically calibrated to respond to Nate. All she had to do was feel his gaze on her and she'd start to tremble. "I'm guessing we'll be seeing more of you."

She lifted one shoulder. "I'm not sure how long we'll be staying. I don't want to take advantage of Nate's hospitality."

Jayden laughed at that. "No one takes advantage of Nate. Stay as long as you like. You're good for him. EJ is good for him."

"Are you going to talk all afternoon?" Nate called, impatience clear in his tone.

"He's jealous," Jayden said with an eye roll, and he gave Bianca another hug. "I'll see you next time."

"Bye, Jayden."

She waved as the truck pulled away, then a movement on the side of the house drew her attention. Otis cocked his ears and glanced at her, his black eyes strangely expressive. The dog was a mystery to her, always hanging around like he was tied to the ranch and this family, but never coming close enough to truly belong.

EJ remained convinced he could turn the stray dog into a pet, but Nate repeatedly reminded him the dog would eventually need to be captured and taken to the county shelter. She found it hard to believe Nate could so easily give up the animal that seemed to be devoted to Sugar and had also rescued EJ, but maybe that was wishful thinking.

She felt a little bit like a stray in the world. With Eddie gone, there was no one to claim her. She'd come to the ranch—to Nate—and while she'd never admit to needing rescuing, she definitely wanted a place to belong.

She wanted to belong to Nate.

Yet would he discard her the way he seemed willing to do with the dog?

As Nate and EJ approached, she shook off her ridiculous thoughts. They both knew this arrangement was temporary. It was silly to pretend anything different.

"I miss Sugar." EJ leaned against Nate's leg. Nate immediately bent down and swung the boy up into his arms.

"She'll be back in a couple of weeks, and you have Twix to take care of while she's gone."

"And Otis," EJ said, pointing to where the black-and-tan dog was trotting toward the barn.

"We need to stop feeding him," Nate said, "or call in the humane society to help catch him."

"No," EJ cried. "You can't let them take him away, Mr. Nate. I *need* him."

The ferocity in her son's tone was a shock. "EJ, you know Otis doesn't belong to us. If Nate wants—"

"Never mind," Nate interrupted, as if he couldn't stand to upset the boy. "We'll deal with the dog at another time. I'm in no hurry."

EJ gave a hiccupping sigh. "I need him," he repeated and rested his head on Nate's shoulder.

The sight melted Bianca's heart and she swallowed back the emotion that clogged her throat.

"Aren't we a glum bunch?" Nate asked with a rough laugh. "How about we go into town tonight? We can have dinner at Rosa's then get ice cream at the soda counter in the grocery store."

Bianca smiled. "Convenient that both businesses are in the same building."

"The blessings of small-town life," Nate said with a wink.

EJ lifted his head. "Can I get two scoops?"

"With whipped cream and a cherry," Nate promised then quickly added, "as long as it's okay with your mom."

"It's a two-scoop kind of day." Bianca leaned in and placed a soft kiss on EJ's cheek, trying to ignore how right it felt to be standing here with Nate holding her son. Trying to pretend that this didn't feel like the family she'd always craved.

What made Nate think it would be easier if they went into Paseo for the night? He hadn't anticipated that Bianca was already a part of the community. Yes, she'd made trips into town during her stay to work on her new business venture. But he'd forgotten how welcoming the people who lived here could be, generous in their willingness to wrap their arms around a stranger and make her one of their own.

That's what had saved his mother when she'd come through town, alone and pregnant with triplets. And clearly Bianca had made a place here just as quickly.

Rosa greeted her like an old friend when they moved from the gas station/grocery to the restaurant housed in the back. Just as many people stopped by their table to talk to him as they came to visit with her. She seemed uncomfortable with the attention, but at the same time radiated happiness as she deepened the connections she'd made on her visits to town.

Everyone clearly approved of her, and moreover people seemed thrilled to see him out with a woman, even though it could hardly be called a date with her son in tow. Well, everyone but Tiffany Garcia, who'd moved back to Paseo last year after a difficult divorce. She spent the evening shooting death glares at him from across the tiny restaurant. Nate and Tiffany had gone on a couple of dates, although nothing had come of it. He hadn't thought he wanted anything more than a casual encounter, at least not until Bianca arrived on his doorstep. Tiffany obviously wasn't happy he'd changed his tune.

Had he changed?

Could he change?

The questions and doubts warring in his mind had plagued him through dinner, although between Bianca and EJ they more than kept the conversation going.

The boy reacted with wide-eyed wonder at the size of the ice-cream sundae Rosa made for him, and Nate managed to quiet some of his uncertainty. If only everything in his life could be fixed with a double-scoop ice-cream sundae.

Bianca talked even more on the way home, sharing

stories of her childhood and the exploits she could re-member from Eddie's teen years. Nate's anxiety sub-sided even more, and he matched her anecdotes with tales of his own. Eddie might have been wild, but be-tween the three Fortune brothers, there had been plenty of mischief.

He laughed as he told one particular story of when the boys decided to make an after-school snack of brownies. "None of us was particularly neat, so when chocolate batter got all over the kitchen, we decided to clean it up with dish soap. But Grayson accidentally stepped in it and discovered how slick soap can be on a linoleum floor. Of course we had to make a skating rink and poured the entire bottle onto the floor. It was like Olympic speed skating until Mom walked in."

EJ cracked up from his booster in the back seat of Nate's truck and Bianca had gasped, then shook her head.

"I can't believe it," she whispered in horror. "What did your mom do?"

"As I remember she was about ready to kill all of us just on principle."

"That's funny," EJ shouted.

Bianca choked back a laugh. "I don't think you should share any more stories." She grinned at him then rolled her eyes. "I'm not even sure I should let my son near you."

Nate returned her smile but her words ripped into him like bullets tearing through flesh. She *shouldn't* let EJ near him. Or at least she shouldn't trust him as much as she did. He wanted to be a permanent part of her and EJ's lives so badly he could taste the need like the first bite of a summer strawberry on his tongue. It was sweet and a little tangy, almost unfamiliar even though it felt like he'd been missing the flavor forever.

He listened more than he talked the rest of the way home, then made a stupid excuse about needing to run to a neighbor's place when they stopped in front of the house.

Bianca frowned as she got out of the truck, her mouth pulling down at both corners. Damn, he wanted to kiss the smile back onto her face.

"I'll see you later?" she asked hopefully. "EJ's going to go to bed soon."

"I'm not tired, Mommy," the boy said as he unbuckled his seat belt. "I had too much sugar."

"You're fine," Bianca told him then looked to Nate. "Later?"

He shrugged. "Maybe. But it could take a while. Don't wait up."

She looked like a puppy he'd just scolded. "Okay," she said with a too-bright smile. "Thanks again for dinner."

He cursed himself as ten kinds of a jerk as he watched her walk in the house. Then he drove away, gravel spitting up from his back tires as he plowed his foot into the gas pedal. He drove like he used to when he was a stupid teenager. Too fast. Too reckless.

He peeled out onto the highway, turning away from town and feeling adrenaline spike in his veins. He recognized the sensation, had spent years as a SEAL shaping it, controlling it, learning to use it to his advantage. Now he was going off the rails over nothing more than dinner and an ice cream.

The truck slowed as he took his foot off the accelerator and pulled onto the shoulder. A few deep breaths in and out helped him get things under control again. It was more than their night out. Bianca had made a comment about trusting him with EJ, and while Nate understood she'd meant it as a joke, the truth of her words burned in his gut.

He was no longer a kid who could afford to be reckless. Bianca and EJ needed him. He owed it to Eddie to be there for them. Hell, he wanted the two of them to be able to count on him. He longed to give Bianca the happiness she deserved and to be a father figure to EJ.

But he wouldn't do either of them any good like this. He pulled back out onto the highway and drove at a normal speed this time. For a moment he entertained the thought of heading back to Paseo and texting Tiffany. Maybe if he found an outlet for the need and desire pulsing through him, he could make some sense of everything else in his life. But he dismissed the idea almost as soon as it entered his mind.

He might not have the guts to claim Bianca, but he knew himself well enough to understand that no other woman would be a substitute for her.

He drove for another hour, counting headlights on the highway and listening to country music on the station out of Wichita Falls. A mix of relief and disappointment filled him as he returned home to a darkened house. It was better that way, he'd told himself, even though the lie was harder to stomach with every day that passed.

Instead of entering the house, he headed to the barn, not surprised to see Otis trotting around the edge of the corral. The dog was already waiting for Sugar's return. Nate whistled low, and the animal's ears twitched. He turned and slowly walked into a pale sliver of moonlight, near enough that Nate knew he was responding but not close enough to touch.

"She'll be back in a couple of weeks," Nate said as the dog looked toward the house and let out a pitiful whine. "You've got it bad, don't you?"

The dog cocked his head and met Nate's gaze, as if to say, "Takes one to know one, buddy."

Nate laughed softly and shook his head. What the hell was going on that he was imagining himself having a conversation with a dog? He was worse off than he thought.

He entered the barn and began stacking bales of hay. He didn't look up as Daisy snickered gently. He stayed focused on the physical labor, waiting for the mindless task to clear his head as it had so many other times.

It was nearly midnight, and the world was quiet other than the faint rustling of the wind and the soft sounds of the animals. Nate had always been a night owl, but growing up on a working ranch had conditioned him for early mornings, and nearly twenty years as a soldier had taught him to take sleep wherever he could find it.

He still appreciated the peace of this late hour, although his brain and body didn't get the message that they were supposed to relax. He felt like his insides were an engine revving with no clear destination. He remained stubbornly stopped, unable to move forward or go back. His feelings for Bianca roared through him without pause, and he had no idea how to regain control of his life.

Or even if he wanted to.

"Can't sleep?" a soft voice asked and he whirled around to find Bianca standing in the middle of the row of stalls.

She was so damn beautiful, wearing an oversize sleep shirt with a faded illustration of the Eiffel Tower on the front. Her dark hair was down around her shoulders and her legs were bare. The shirt grazed her knees, and she was wearing her well-worn cowboy boots. At the most there was about six inches of skin showing between the hem of the shirt and the top of her boots. But she might as well have been in a lacy negligee based on the reaction Nate's body had to her.

He almost laughed at the irony of the hours he'd spent working to clear his mind. Because right now he couldn't form even the suggestion of a coherent thought. His brain had gone totally blank.

"Haven't tried yet," he said, pulling off his leather gloves and tossing them onto one of the hay bales. He wiped his hands across his jeans.

"Did you have fun with the neighbor?"

"Didn't make it to the neighbor's."

Her hands clenched into fists at her sides. "That was never the plan, was it?"

He shook his head.

"You just needed to get away from the ranch?"

"Something like that," he answered, inclining his head.

"Was it that woman in the restaurant?" Her dark eyes flared as she asked the question. "The one who was staring at you the whole time."

"Tiffany?"

"I don't know her name, but she was sending you some 'come hither' looks."

"Come hither," he repeated with a soft laugh.

"It's not funny."

There was a catch in her voice, and he realized with

a start she actually thought he'd left the ranch to be with another woman. Maybe it wasn't funny. Hell, he'd entertained the idea for a lightning-fast second. But it would have been an effort in futility because the only woman he wanted was standing right in front of him.

Still, he couldn't quite give himself permission to claim her. She was so damn perfect, and he was terrified of contaminating her with the mess in his head.

"No," he agreed carefully. "And I wasn't with Tiffany. I drove around for a while to clear my head then came back here and started on a few chores to distract myself." He took a step toward her then stopped. He could feel his chest rising and falling like he'd just run a marathon. Like he was using every ounce of strength he had to keep from closing the distance between them. "From you."

She sucked in a breath and bit down on her bottom lip. His knees almost buckled.

"Why?" she whispered.

"Can't you see how broken I am?" he asked, his voice hoarse. "The things I've done, the horrors I've seen." He paused, then added, "The ways I've failed the people I care about."

"We're all broken in some way," she said with a sad smile. "But we keep going. You've kept going. You're helping your family because you're loyal to them."

"It sounds like you're describing a family pet."

Her smile widened. "You're also hot as hell." She pressed her hands to her cheeks, as if saying the words out loud embarrassed her. "You make me want things I can't even name."

"Try."

The word hung between them for a few long moments, and he thought she'd walk away rather than give voice to her desires. But his Bianca was braver.

So much braver than him.

"I want you to kiss me." Her fingers traced her lips then trailed down the graceful column of her neck. "I want to kiss you." She swallowed. "Everywhere."

Nate stifled a groan, but she wasn't finished.

"I want you to touch me and I want to explore your body. I want everything you're willing to give."

He closed his eyes, trying to keep his body from trembling. "You're killing me here, Bianca."

"Look at me, Nate."

Nate had never been one for classic literature, but he felt a sudden affinity for that poor sop Odysseus trying to resist the Sirens. He focused his gaze on Bianca, and she must have read in his eyes the desire he was sick of denying.

Her lips curved into a sultry smile as she grabbed the hem of her shirt and tugged the fabric up and over her head. That left her standing in front of him, shivering slightly from the cold evening air, in a pale pink lace bra, cotton panties with smiley face emojis all over them and her cowboy boots. It was the most erotic moment of his whole damn life.

Chapter Ten

As she tossed the comfy cotton shirt off to one side, Bianca glanced down at herself and almost died of embarrassment.

How could a man take an attempt at seduction seriously when the woman seducing him wore smiley face emoji panties?

Of course, she hadn't come to the barn expecting to seduce Nate. She'd been resolved he needed to make the next move if their relationship—if it could be called that—was going to progress to the next level.

But he looked so alone in the quiet night—like he was purposely keeping his distance as some sort of self-induced punishment she couldn't understand. Somehow she knew deep inside that he needed the connection between them as much as she did.

More even.

So she'd ignored her doubts and thrown caution—and her nightgown—to the wind. But as Nate's gaze met hers, his face was unreadable. The only thing that made her think he was affected by her impromptu strip-tease was the slight tremble of his hand as he lifted it to massage the back of his neck. Another of Nate's tells.

Or was it?

He stared at her for a long time without speaking. Probably only seconds in reality, but the moments felt like hours. Days. Months and years of her being exposed, baring herself for judgment and ultimately rejection.

Oh, God. Bianca couldn't take any more rejection.

"My bad," she whispered with a strangled laugh and bent to retrieve her nightgown from the barn's dirt floor.

"No."

The word was spoken with such intensity, Bianca froze, her arm stretched out like a statue.

He was in front of her a moment later. She could feel the heat radiating off him, seeping under her skin and warming her entire body. She pulled her arms close to her chest, an automatic reaction, and straightened until she was looking up into Nate's brown eyes. In the soft light they looked lighter and were rimmed with gold. Or maybe that was the emotion in his gaze.

"You're beautiful," he whispered.

"Having a baby changes your body forever," she said then mentally kicked herself. Maybe she should grab a tube of lipstick and circle all the flaws on her body in case he hadn't noticed them.

"I wouldn't change a thing about you." He circled her wrists with his long fingers and eased them away from her body. She bit back all the excuses that wanted to tumble off her tongue. For her shabby lace bra with the frayed edges to her silly emoji panties. For wanting to seduce him but not having any idea how to go about it and bungling the whole thing.

The way he was staring at her made her feel like she hadn't spoiled anything. The mix of desire and tenderness in his eyes made her heart sing.

"The next move was supposed to be yours."

"I couldn't make one, even though I wanted to so badly. I'm not good enough for you." He lifted his hands and grazed his fingers over her collarbones. When he got to her bra straps, he gently pushed them to the edges of her shoulders but no farther. A shiver passed through her as the calluses on his fingertips tickled her bare skin.

"You are," she countered.

He shook his head, and his gaze remained focused on the patterns his fingers were tracing. "I'll never be good enough for you. There's too much of the past that's—"

"Stop." She placed her hand against his mouth. "Look at me, Nate."

He pressed his lips together but lifted his gaze to hers.

She cupped both his cheeks in her hands. "I don't want to talk about the past tonight. I don't want to think about the mistakes either of us has made. Trust me, you're not the only one who's done stupid things."

"You have no idea what I've done."

"Are you here with me now in this moment?"

"Yes. I'm here."

"Then this moment is what we have. It's all we need. *You* are all I need, Nathan Fortune."

His nostrils flared and his eyes intensified even

more. He bent his head and claimed her mouth in a kiss that lit her body like a brush fire, fast and all consuming. She was nothing but an empty canvas—a blank landscape for Nate to do with what he would.

He twined his arms around her waist and pulled her tight against him. The soft cotton of his shirt brushed her nipples through her lace bra and she moaned deep in her throat.

"So damn beautiful," he said against her mouth. She gasped as she felt the evidence of his desire press against her stomach, and he took the opportunity to sweep his tongue into her mouth. This was everything she'd imagined, and she gave herself over to the sensations bursting through her.

Suddenly one of the horses gave a loud whinny, and then a cacophony of answering snorts and whickers rang out in the barn.

Nate stilled, which made Bianca giggle. "We've got an audience," she said, trying to muffle her laughter.

"I love hearing you laugh," Nate said, grinning down at her, "but right now I could do without the livestock peanut gallery."

He lifted her into his arms like she weighed nothing, looping one arm behind her knees while he supported her back with the other. She giggled again then settled against him, the warmth of his chest chasing away the evening's chill as he hurried across the driveway to the house.

She kissed the underside of his jaw, loving the taste of salt on his skin. He tilted up his chin, stumbling a step, then chuckled low in his throat. "Save that thought until we're in my bedroom, darlin', or I'm liable to faceplant going up the stairs."

"I like having that effect on you," she admitted.

"You have no idea the effect you have on me." His voice was a low rumble, and it made her tingle from head to toe.

Opening the door to his bedroom, he turned to fit through with her in his arms. The door to Nate's room had always been closed, and as intrigued as she was, she'd never allowed herself to sneak a peek into it. Somehow that had felt too intimate, like she needed to wait until he invited her in before she could satisfy her curiosity.

"I haven't changed much in here since I moved back," Nate said, watching her gaze sweep across the room.

There was a double bed with a colorful patterned quilt, a tall dresser and a simple wood chair pushed against one wall. The walls were painted a soft green and several trophies sat on top of the dresser along with a glass bowl filled with loose change.

"It's nice," she said.

"You're nice," he countered, pulling back the covers and laying her gently on the sheets.

She shook her head, sitting up and kicking off her boots. She wiggled her bare toes and tried not to let nerves get the better of her. "Not tonight. Tonight I'm wild and crazy."

"Really?"

Well, wild and crazy to Bianca was ice cream for dinner. But instead of admitting that, she reached behind her back and unclasped her bra. The straps were already almost off her shoulders and she shrugged them all the way down and tossed the small strip of fabric off the bed.

"Uh-huh," she said, wishing she could think of something cute or sexy to say. Right now she was trying hard not to spontaneously combust. Sexy talk was beyond her capabilities.

"You're seriously going to kill me," Nate whispered, his tone reverent, like she was a fine piece of art or a priceless treasure.

It gave her the confidence to pull her shoulders back and drop her hands to her sides. She'd never put herself on display for a man this way, but she wanted to be someone different with Nate—a woman she barely recognized but enjoyed trying on for size.

The truth was, she'd only been with one man in her life—her ex-husband. She'd been grateful for any attention, but their time together had always been more about his pleasure than hers. Suddenly trying to claim her sexuality felt like skydiving without checking whether her parachute worked. It was exhilarating, but was she in for the mother of all crash landings?

She was already hurtling through the air, so she figured she might as well enjoy as much of the view as she could.

"There's one problem," she told him, arching a brow like she knew what the heck she was doing.

"Not from where I'm standing."

"You have too many clothes on."

"Easily remedied," he answered and unbuttoned his shirt. Bianca had gotten a few glimpses of his toned body, but her breath caught in her throat when he pulled the shirt off and tossed it to the side. His chest was all hard planes and angles; a sprinkling of dark hair covering his bronzed skin.

"More," she whispered, pointing a finger at his jeans.

One side of his mouth kicked up. "Wild, crazy and commanding. I like it."

He toed off his boots then undid his jeans, pushing them and his boxers down over his hips. Bianca couldn't even stop the little whimper that escaped her mouth as he moved toward the bed.

She blew out a breath. "Wow."

Nate grinned. "I'll take wow." He climbed on the bed and stretched out next to her. "I'm feeling a little 'wow' myself right now."

Reaching out a hand, she splayed her fingers across his chest, through the dusting of hair covering his skin. The muscles there twitched at her touch, and her hand looked so small against him. Now that she'd seen him— all of him—she realized he was big everywhere. Big enough that she wondered if he'd actually fit. So much for her minute of confidence in the bedroom. She was back to feeling like she had no idea what to do next. She was back to reality. As usual, reality was not her friend.

"Hey." Nate placed a hand on her hip, squeezing gently. "I lost you there for a minute."

"Sorry. I was just…um…thinking."

He dropped a soft kiss on the tip of her nose. "If you're thinking right now then I'm not doing this right."

"You are," she said quickly. "It's me. I thought I could be someone different tonight but—"

"I don't want you to be anyone but who you are." He kissed her, gently sucking her bottom lip into his mouth.

Bianca moaned once and then again as his fingers moved to graze across her belly, then lower.

"Do you want this?" Nate asked against her skin.

"Yes," she answered without hesitation. "I want everything."

"Then trust me, darlin'. Trust us." His head moved lower, blazing a trail of openmouthed kisses down her throat. Then he was at her breast and she gave a tiny cry when he sucked one sensitive nipple into his mouth.

Her body felt like it was melting into the bed, and she relaxed her legs, opening for him. Letting him in. Trusting. She arched back as his clever fingers found her center, even as he moved his attention to her other breast.

Pressure started to build inside her, and she wanted to chase it, to hunt it down and claim whatever brilliance she could feel shimmering on the other side. But Nate seemed in no hurry. He took his time, wringing every ounce of pleasure from her.

"Now," she whispered when she couldn't bear it any longer. He claimed her mouth, kissing her deeply as his fingers moved against her, inside her. He was everywhere, and she lost herself in the feel of him. Then she was breaking apart and it felt like a million stars raining down over them, bright and hot and more dazzling than she could have ever imagined.

He broke the kiss to reach across her, pulling a condom packet from the nightstand drawer. She was boneless and satisfied, but as he adjusted himself at her entrance, need built low in her body once more.

"I want everything," she repeated, lifting her head off the pillow to kiss him.

He entered her as their mouths melded, his tongue mimicking the rhythm of their bodies. She grazed her fingers over his shoulders and down his back, pressing him closer. They moved together, a tangle of limbs. Nate whispered sweet words against her hair then nipped gently on her earlobe.

It nearly sent her over the edge again, but he cupped

her face in his hands and whispered, "Wait for me, Bianca."

She'd wait forever if that's what it took. If she'd known how easily she'd fall for this man, how tender and sweet he could be…well, she would have gotten in her car and hightailed it to Paseo long before now.

She wrapped her legs around his hips, tilting her own so she could take him even deeper. There was nothing she wouldn't do to give him the same release he'd given her. She felt a tremor pass through him as he kissed her again.

"*You* are my everything," he said, lifting his head to gaze down at her. "You are mine."

"Yes," she breathed and broke apart again. Nate groaned as he came and buried his face in the crook of her neck, and it was hard to tell where she stopped and he began.

All Bianca knew was that this moment changed everything. Nothing between them would ever be the same.

Nate wasn't sure how much time passed before his breathing slowed and he trusted himself to lift his head and look into Bianca's dark eyes again.

It could have been minutes. It was probably minutes, but it felt like an eternity to him. Because that's how long it would take until he regained control of his heart.

Which was stupid because he'd had enough great sex in his life to understand that hearts didn't need to be involved for bodies to fit together perfectly.

Being with Bianca didn't change anything, he told himself, even though he knew it was a lie.

"Is it always like that?" she asked, a sleepy grin on her face.

"Not always," he said.

Never, his brain screamed. *Only with you. Only with us.*

But how could he tell her that without admitting everything he felt? Hell, he barely understood his emotions for this woman. They were unfamiliar, and the unknown scared him half to death. It was like walking through an Afghanistan landscape that could be breathtaking in its peaceful beauty, and the next moment a land mine would explode and he'd be blown into next week.

He rolled onto his back, taking Bianca with him as he did. Her body curled into his as if she was made to fit against him.

"You've got some crazy mad skills," she said, draping an arm over his chest. She turned into him, and her long dark hair cascaded over her shoulder and spilled across his body. She was soft in all the places he was hard, and he wanted to explore every inch of her until he knew what she liked, the kind of touch and kiss that would drive her crazy. He had the undeniable urge to claim her as his for as long as she'd allow it.

As satisfied as he was at the moment, desire began to spark inside him again, his body humming to life at the thought of taking her again.

"I could say the same about you."

She laughed and lifted her head. "You're joking, right? I've got no skills and very little experience."

He shifted so their legs were tangled together and he saw her eyes widen slightly when she felt him against her hip.

"You're the sexiest woman I've ever known," he told

her, sifting his fingers through her hair. "I can't get enough of you."

She arched a brow. "As in can't get enough right now?"

"You probably need to sleep. It's fine. Ignore me."

But she didn't ignore him. Instead, she reached between them and… Oh, hell. She was going to send him over the edge with her featherlight touch.

"Do you know an unexpected bonus to being with a single mom?" she asked, her tone teasing.

Right now he could barely come up with his own name.

Her mouth quirked as if she understood the power she held over him and reveled in it. "I'm used to functioning on a tiny bit of sleep." Her fingers squeezed and he arched off the bed, then reached for the nightstand drawer again.

"Then I'm going to keep you up all night long," he promised and kissed her again.

Chapter Eleven

Bianca blinked awake and drew in a breath that caught in her throat as she became aware of Nate's trembling body next to her.

She hadn't planned on falling asleep in his bed, but after he'd made love to her a second time she'd been so relaxed and happy. He'd wrapped an arm around her waist and pulled her into his chest so they were spooning, and she'd quickly drifted off.

Grabbing his T-shirt from the floor next to the bed, she pulled it over her head then checked the clock on the nightstand—not even five in the morning. The sky outside the bedroom window was still black, and she wasn't sure whether she'd woken on her own or if Nate's restless tossing and turning had prodded her from sleep.

He was sprawled on his back, one hand above his head and the other at his side, fingers clutching the bedsheet. She sat up and her heart ached at his pained features. He looked miserable, his jaw working and his eyes tightly closed as if he was in agony.

"Nate," she whispered, wondering if he was truly asleep. She hated to think he was stuck in some kind of nightmare he couldn't escape.

"No," he muttered. His chest rose and fell and she could hear his breath coming in shallow gasps. "No. Eddie, no."

Bianca stilled at the mention of her brother. Nate had been with Eddie the night he died. She had so many unanswered questions. Why Eddie? Did he suffer? Was there anything that could have been done to save him?

She couldn't believe there had been. Surely Nate would have moved heaven and earth to save Eddie if it had been a possibility. She hadn't asked Nate about that night. It felt intrusive and too personal, like poking her finger in a still-raw wound. She knew he missed her brother as much as she did.

Clearly the night of Eddie's death plagued Nate. She'd heard of soldiers coming home with post-traumatic stress disorder. Men and women who'd given so much to their country but couldn't fit back into their regular lives because of the intense trauma they'd encountered while deployed. Nate had been a SEAL for almost twenty years. PTSD could be a reality for him. He didn't even have a regular life.

Except now they were creating one together.

Bianca wanted that more than anything.

Between what he'd faced as a SEAL and coping with the knowledge that his birth father was Gerald Robinson plus having a passel of instant half siblings strewn across Texas, Nate was dealing with some heavy stuff.

It was up to Bianca to bring light into the darkness he seemed to feel was his due.

She reached out a hand and touched his shoulder. His muscles tensed, and he stilled but didn't open his eyes.

"Nate, wake up." She gently shook him.

"No," he repeated, but she could tell by the movement of his eyes behind the closed lids that he remained imprisoned in the nightmare. "Eddie, no." He let out a desperate cry. "I'm sorry. No."

Emotion clogged her throat, and she swiped at her eyes. When they'd first gotten the news of Eddie's death, there had been weeks when Bianca's dreams were filled with images of Eddie walking in front of her, just out of reach. No matter how fast she ran or how loudly she called to him, she could never catch up. To know Nate had possibly gone through something worse and that his memories continued to hold him in a choking grasp...

It made her feel both closer to him and so sad at how alone he was in the world, despite his extended Fortune family.

If she had her way, neither of them would ever be alone again. She cupped his cheek, leaning over him, letting her hair brush his bare skin. "Nate, come on. Wake up. Come back to me."

A moment later, she yelped, her heart pounding a crazy beat as she found herself flipped onto her back, Nate looming over her. The look on his face was terrifying. His eyes were open but unfocused, totally empty of any sort of recognition or emotion. He was like some sort of cowboy cyborg, unrecognizable as the man who'd held her so tenderly hours earlier.

"Nate." She breathed his name through clenched

teeth, afraid any sort of movement might set him off. Might put her in real danger.

He blinked once…twice. Sweat beaded along his hairline. With a muttered curse, he threw back the covers and scrambled off the bed, stalking to the edge of the bedroom.

She watched as he bent forward, sucking in air like he'd just run a marathon. Slowly she sat forward, swinging her legs over the side of the bed. He put a hand up, palm facing toward her like he feared she might approach him.

"I'm sorry," he said, his voice hoarse.

"It's not a big deal. You were having a bad dream."

He turned but didn't move toward her. He stood in the shadow, light from the window playing across the muscles corded along his arms and chest and the black boxers he wore to sleep. "I could have hurt you, Bianca."

"No." She made her voice firm, ignoring the way the hairs at the back of her neck stood on end. "You'd never hurt me."

"I don't want to," he whispered, and his eyes were so miserable she could feel his suffering like a physical force between them. Keeping her away at the same time it drew her toward him. "But you saw me." He swore again and ran a hand through his hair, the ends sticking up in wild tufts. "I hate that you saw me like that."

"It had something to do with Eddie. You were dreaming about him."

He gave a slight nod.

"I used to dream about him," she said, forcing her shaking legs to stand. "It's normal."

"Nothing about me is normal anymore. I'm broken,

Bianca. I told you I wasn't good for you. You have to believe me. This proves it."

"What does this prove?" He backed up as she approached him, until he was standing against the tall dresser. "You're human. You lost a friend, and you miss him. You saw things—did things—that no man should see or do. You protected our country."

"Don't make me into a hero."

She reached out a hand, pressing her palm over the place where his heart beat a wild rhythm in his chest.

"It's hard not to when you keep acting like one."

"I'm not."

"Fine," she agreed, sliding her other hand up and around the back of his neck.

"You should go before EJ wakes up."

"Not quite yet." She closed her eyes and laid her head on his shoulder, plastering her body to the front of his. He remained rigid, but she paid no attention. She knew what it was like to be alone, unsure if you could overcome all the fears and doubts weighing on your shoulders.

Her fingers splayed over his heart as her other hand gently massaged the back of his neck. She'd seen him do it enough to know it relaxed him. His hands gripped her waist as if he would set her away from him. Instead he held her closer, bending his head until it rested on the top of hers.

Neither of them spoke, but slowly Nate's breathing returned to normal. His hold on her was tentative, as if even now he didn't trust himself with her.

"I'm sorry," he said again.

"Do you want to talk about it?" She tipped up her head to look him in the eyes. "Your dreams?"

"Nightmares," he corrected. Then he shook his head. "Not now." She must not have been able to hide her disappointment because he quickly amended, "Not yet."

"Thank you for last night."

One side of his mouth quirked. "Thank *you*, Bianca. For everything you are."

When a bird chirped outside the window, she pulled away from him. "I do need to go."

He nodded, but his lips pressed into a thin line. He'd tried to run her off minutes earlier but now it felt like she was hurting him by leaving. "You're protecting EJ."

"I'm protecting all of us. This is too new for him to know about. He'd have expectations. He might not understand that sometimes two people are together and it doesn't mean anything."

She waited for him to argue. It's what she longed for—Nate to tell her what was between them meant something to him. She was quickly falling in love with him. With the tough, hardworking rancher and the scarred, troubled ex-SEAL and the sweetheart of a man who'd borrowed a pony so her son could learn to ride.

"I understand," he said tightly, and she wanted to scream as the invisible wall he kept around him snapped into place again. Every time she broke through his defenses, something would happen to rebuild them just as quickly. One step forward and a million miles back.

"Are you busy today?" she asked as she picked up her boots from the floor. She didn't want him to see the disappointment that must be apparent in her eyes. How was she supposed to hide how she felt? She'd always been an open book with her emotions, and it's what had often gotten her in trouble. At least she was learning that if she couldn't hide them, she needed to keep them to herself as best she could.

"The usual work," he said. "Why?"

"I was wondering if this afternoon would be good for a riding lesson?" She held the pile of underwear and boots in front of her stomach like a shield. What if Nate said no? What if after one night she was out of his system? "I'm going to work with EJ on his numbers and letters this morning, and I'd like to finish organizing the garden storage shelves in the shed. But after lunch—"

"How about I pack a lunch and we eat it on the ride?"

"Do you mean in the barn?" Her voice sounded high-pitched to her ears, like she'd just inhaled a giant shot of helium.

Nate's features relaxed fully as he smiled. Good to know her obvious terror helped him regain his equilibrium. "I mean on the trail. You and EJ haven't been out to the windmills yet. It's the spot where Jayden and Ariana got married last year."

"Shouldn't we stay in the corral? You made EJ stay in the corral on his first ride."

"EJ's four."

"But he's way braver than me."

"You can do it, Busy Bee."

"A trail ride." She swallowed and forced an even breath. "Okay. Can Twix handle a trail ride?"

"EJ can ride double with me. Normally I wouldn't do it, but we'll let you get comfortable in the saddle before I put him on his own horse for a trail ride. Trust me, he'll love it."

"I'm sure he will." She wasn't sure about herself. "No running."

"You mean galloping?"

She nodded. "That, too."

"I promise I'll take care of you."

She wanted him to trust her with his demons and doubts, and turnabout was fair play. "I know you will. We'll meet at the barn at eleven?"

"I can't wait. And, Bianca?"

"Yeah?"

"As far as last night…"

She licked her lips, a strange mix of dread and anticipation sifting through her. "Yes?"

"Once with us is not enough." His eyes darkened. "Nowhere near enough. If this thing is happening between us, I'm all in. You good with that?"

"Very good," she answered and hurried out of the room before she did something embarrassing like rip off his shirt and pounce on him.

Nate got to the barn twenty minutes before Bianca and EJ were meeting him. He'd left the house before the boy woke this morning, not sure he could face the four-year-old with the knowledge of the night he and Bianca had shared burning through him like a wildfire that had spread out of control.

How was he supposed to curb his feelings for her when he wanted so much more? Along with his need came an equal amount of fear. He knew the things he was capable of, and even though Bianca thought she understood Nate's life as a soldier, she didn't.

She couldn't.

She was light to his shadow. Goodness to the darkness that dwelled deep inside him. He craved her glow, but at the same time he was terrified of contaminating her with who he was on the inside.

Or worse…hurting her.

The nightmares that plagued him were vivid and real, at least to his unconscious self. The line between waking and sleeping blurred more nights than not. When he'd first left the navy, he'd spent months sleeping with a knife under his pillow, his hand wrapped around the handle. It was the only way he could force his body to relax enough to get any rest.

What if he'd had that knife when Bianca had woken him? Hell, he didn't need a knife to hurt her. He knew a dozen different ways to kill a person. Bianca was beautiful and delicate. The thought of putting his hands on her in anger made the breakfast he'd eaten hours earlier churn in his stomach.

So what was he doing here cinching the old Western saddle he'd loved riding on as a kid with Earl Thompson? He and his brothers had fought over who would get to accompany the rancher on the trail ride he took every Sunday afternoon after church. It hadn't been long until they'd gotten good enough in the saddle to warrant their own horses. He thought of EJ, who was showing a natural gift for animals of every kind. Even now, Nate glanced up to see Otis sitting calmly in the corner of the barn.

He'd stopped pretending he wasn't going to continue to feed the stray dog and secretly loved EJ's attempts to tame the animal.

Nate loved everything about having Bianca and EJ in his life, which made him the most selfish bastard in the world. They deserved a man who could give them unconditional love and devotion. Not the person who'd failed to save Bianca's brother. Not the man who had so many demons he didn't know where to begin fighting them.

Yet he couldn't let them go. Not yet.

"Mr. Nate, I'm ready," EJ shouted as he ran into the barn. He climbed up onto the bench Nate had set in front of Cinnamon's stall so the boy could watch him groom the big horse. "I wrote my whole name and spelled it right." He held up his hands like he was a preacher calling down the Holy Spirit. "Edward James Shaw. That's me."

"Edward James Shaw," Nate repeated, wondering at how he hadn't realized the connection before. "Like your uncle."

Bianca came to stand next to her son, a shy smile on her face. "He will be a Shaw. I've applied to have EJ's last name legally changed. He was named after Eddie, so I want him to fully be a Shaw."

"I bet your brother loved that he was named after him."

A shadow crossed her face. "Are we ready to go?"

He studied her for a moment but chalked up her sudden change in mood to nerves.

"You're riding Daisy today."

She swallowed. "What about you and EJ?"

"We're on Cinnamon, Mommy. I told you."

"Is that a good idea?" Bianca asked. "That's the horse that almost came down on EJ."

"I've been riding him for years," Nate assured her. "He's spirited but with the right rider, he's an angel."

"He's so tall."

"You trust me, right?" Nate asked.

"Yes," she said without hesitation, and his heart soared.

"Let's go, then."

He led Cinnamon out into the corral and dropped the reins.

"Won't he run off?" Bianca asked as she followed.

"Nope. He's used to being ground-tied so he's not going anywhere. EJ, I want you to help me get your mommy settled on Daisy. Can you do that?"

The boy nodded. "Come on, Mommy. I'll teach you how to hold the reins."

EJ took Bianca's hand and led her toward the stall that held the dappled mare. Nate followed, giving Bianca an encouraging nod when she glanced over her shoulder.

"Are you sure this is a good idea?"

"The best." Nate grabbed the horse's bridle from its peg on the wall and opened the stall. He led Daisy out into the aisle and attached her to cross ties. "The first thing you'd normally do is make sure she's been groomed so there's nothing under the pad and saddle to irritate her. I've taken care of that part so why don't you grab Daisy's pad and put it on her?"

"Always walk up to a horse on the left, Mommy," EJ told her when she took a step forward.

"Thanks, buddy. I'll remember that." She picked up the pad and approached the horse, then frowned as her gaze flicked to Nate. "Why are you smiling?"

"The look on your face makes it seem like you're approaching a fire-breathing dragon."

As if she'd heard him, Daisy gave an indignant snort. Bianca tightened her hold on the saddle pad but kept moving. "Not at all," she said, her voice dramatically gentle. "Daisy is a sweet girl. She's calm and docile and she'd never buck or kick." She lifted the pad onto the horse's back and adjusted it so the sides were even.

Daisy turned her head, her eyes focusing on the new person at her side. "We're going to a have an easy day together. Right, girl?"

Nate watched as Daisy shifted position so she could sniff at Bianca. "Take a breath. She can sense your fear."

"Horses as far away as Mexico can sense my fear," Bianca shot back but reached out a hand and stroked the velvety tip of Daisy's nose.

The horse snuffled and rubbed her head against the front of Bianca.

"She's a cuddler," Nate told her, earning a small smile from Bianca.

"Mommy likes to cuddle, too," EJ announced. "When I used to have night terrors, I'd sleep in her bed. She snuggled me too much."

Bianca threw a tender look toward her son. "There's no such thing as too much snuggling."

When her gaze met Nate's, pink rose to her cheeks.

"I agree," he said quietly. "Let's get Daisy's saddle on her then you can lead her out."

"Or we could just call our little visiting session good for the day."

"Mommy," EJ said with the type of exasperation only known to young boys. "I'm starving. I want to ride so we can eat lunch."

Nate pulled the saddle from its rack and hefted it onto the horse. Daisy sniffed but didn't move as he tightened the front and flank cinches around her. "We'll adjust the stirrups after you're on. Ariana was the last one to ride her, so they should be close in length."

He put the bridle over the horse's head and showed Bianca how to fit the bit in her mouth.

Her eyes widened. "I'm never going to do that."

"Never say never," he told her with a laugh then handed her the lead rope. "We might make a horse-woman out of you yet."

They walked together into the afternoon sun. The day was clear and crisp, a gentle breeze blowing from the south. Winter was one of his favorite times in Paseo. After years spent sweltering in deserts across the Middle East, he enjoyed the mild Texas winters, when temperatures could dip below freezing at night but warmed to near perfect during the day. This was one of those perfect days, and he thanked his lucky stars to be able to spend it with Bianca.

He could hear her murmuring to Daisy but couldn't make out what she was saying. The horse's ears twitched, as if she were hanging on to Bianca's every word. Nate could relate to that.

Bianca stopped a few feet from where Cinnamon stood. The big horse gave a foot stomp and Daisy seemed to answer with several twitches of her ears. "They're friends now, right? Cinnamon isn't going to mess with Daisy?"

"Mommy, you can see them talking with their bodies. It's like when Reed Parker pushed me so he could cut in line on the first day of school." EJ held up his hands as if he was a teacher explaining a concept to one of his students. "He was just nervous and didn't know how to use his words. Then he learned and now we're best friends." The boy frowned. "Well, we were when I went to school. Maybe he won't remember when we go back."

"He'll remember," Bianca said gently.

Nate wanted to argue—not that EJ's friend wouldn't want to be his friend but that the two of them weren't going back to San Antonio anytime soon. It had only been a few weeks, but Nate couldn't imagine life on the ranch without Bianca and her son.

"Time to saddle up," he said to Bianca instead. "Do you want a block to stand on?"

She shook her head. "I can handle this part."

Nate came to her side anyway, holding Daisy's bridle with one hand and turning out the stirrup so it was easier for Bianca to manage with the other.

She swallowed, fit her boot into the stirrup then grabbed the horn and lifted herself up and over the saddle like a pro.

"You did it, Mommy," EJ called.

"I sure did," she agreed with a too-bright smile, her voice breathless.

Nate handed her the reins and squeezed her leg. "You're doing great."

"Liar," she breathed, her smile not wavering.

"Keep Daisy a few lengths back from Cinnamon. We'll go slow to start."

"We'll go slow the whole time," she corrected.

"Do you have the food, Mr. Nate?" EJ asked.

"I have a ton of food." He pointed to the saddlebag positioned behind Daisy's saddle. "We've got sandwiches and chips and fruit—"

"And cookies?" EJ asked hopefully.

"You bet. Ready?"

EJ nodded and Nate swung him up on the thick pillow at the front of the saddle. He mounted Cinnamon behind EJ, being sure to give the boy enough room. "Once we get on the trail, I'm going to let you take the reins."

"Mommy," the boy called, "I'm going to drive the horse just like you."

"Uh-huh," came the choked answer from behind them.

Nate kissed the air and pressed a thigh to Cinnamon's flank, giving the horse direction. Cinnamon loved trail riding, so he didn't need much prodding. With a shake of his head and mane that made EJ giggle, the horse turned and started for the field leading to the path that wound its way through the entire property.

"Give her a little nudge," he instructed, glancing over his shoulder to Bianca.

"Don't leave me," she called.

He gave Cinnamon's reins a gentle tug. "Whoa, boy."

"Mommy, come *on*." EJ didn't bother to turn around as he shouted the command.

Nate patted the boy's shoulder. "Be patient with her. Remember, a man's job is to take care of the women he loves. You love your mommy very much." He turned perpendicular with the trail so he could watch Bianca's progress. "You're doing great. Daisy can be kind of lazy when she sets her mind to it. Give her a kick with your heels."

"I'll hurt her."

"She's a thousand pounds. You won't hurt her. Do it gently—just like I showed you back in the ring. You're telling her she can't have her own way."

Bianca popped her heels into the horse's sides then yelped when Daisy trotted forward a few steps. The horse quickly slowed to a walk, and Nate gave Bianca a thumbs-up.

The horses fell into a rhythm, and Nate played the part of tour guide, pointing out landmarks on the ranch and explaining the history of the area to Bianca and EJ.

The boy settled back against his chest, making Nate's heart twist. Even Bianca seemed to relax, becoming somewhat of an expert on tugging Daisy's reins when the horse tried to stop and eat grass.

"How much farther?" EJ asked when his stomach rumbled loudly.

Nate chuckled and pointed to the west of the trail. "The pond and windmill are just over that rise. Only about ten minutes longer until we break for lunch. Maybe we should have had a snack before we started."

"I can wait ten minutes," EJ told him. "Come on, Mommy."

Those words had become the boy's refrain during the ride. He continually turned and looked around Nate's arm to ensure Bianca and Daisy were keeping up with them.

"I'm with you," she called back. Nate saw her press her thighs against Daisy's side when the horse slowed.

"If we teach her to shoot a gun, your mom could be a regular Annie Oakley on that horse," he said to EJ when Cinnamon started down the trail again.

"I don't know Annie Oakley," EJ told him.

Nate chuckled. "I'll introduce you."

"Do you love her?"

"Annie Oakley?" Nate flexed his fingers against the fabric of his jeans. "She's dead now and I only knew her through her reputation, of course. Grayson was a bigger fan when we were younger. She was a famous sharp-shooter but an excellent horsewoman, as well. Annie Oakley could—"

"I mean Mommy," EJ interrupted.

Nate sucked in a breath, jerking back on the reins enough to make Cinnamon pin his ears for a moment. He glanced behind him, but Bianca only smiled and waved, looking almost relaxed in the saddle.

Clearly she hadn't heard EJ's question.

"What do you mean, buddy?" he asked, keeping his voice light. Were his feelings for Bianca that obvious?

"You said a man takes care of the women he loves. Since we came to visit, you've been taking care of Mommy." EJ tipped up his head to look at Nate. "Is it because you love her?"

Oh, hell. That question was as loaded as one of Annie Oakley's Wild West Show pistols. Of course he didn't love Bianca. Not like EJ was talking about. Nate didn't even know if he was capable of that kind of love. The situation was...

"It's complicated."

EJ blinked, his gaze remaining focused on Nate's face. "What's comp-ki-lated?"

"Well, your mom and I are friends. I care about her and about you. Your uncle Eddie was my best friend. So we've all got some shared history. We're like family."

"Uncle Eddie was family," EJ countered, "but you're not really."

"True," Nate admitted, wondering how the hell he was going to get himself out of this conversation. "Let's put it this way—the way I was raised, a man looks out for women, especially those he's friends with—"

"And loves," EJ interrupted.

"Or that he considers a friend," Nate clarified, feeling sweat bead between his shoulder blades. "But all women really... You have to be a gentleman with all women. Does that make sense?"

"Kind of."

That was a start since Nate felt like he was babbling nonsense at the moment.

"So you don't love Mommy, but you'll take care of her because she's a girl?"

"Well, I'm not sure I'd put it that way."

"How *would* you put it?"

Nate shifted in the saddle. Lord save him from boys with a one-track mind. "I guess I'd say—"

Bianca's high-pitched scream cut off his words. He yanked on the reins, turning Cinnamon just in time to see Daisy veer off the well-worn path. The horse galloped across the field like she was being chased by the devil himself, Bianca bouncing precariously in the saddle as she screamed Nate's name.

Cinnamon jerked hard just as EJ yelled, "Snake!"

The boy lurched to one side, and Nate pulled him in tight at the same time he dug his heels into the horse's flank.

Cinnamon came up on his hind legs again as a Western diamondback curled in a defensive coil on the trail in front of them and the telltale rattling sound reverberated through the air. After a quick glance to where Bianca and Daisy hurtled across the field, Nate backed Cinnamon off the trail and out of danger. As soon as they were clear of the snake, Nate readjusted EJ in front of him.

The boy let out a hiccupping breath. "Mommy," he whispered, his tone clearly terrified.

"We're going to get her, buddy. Are you ready?"

"Yes," EJ answered, his voice shaky.

"Then hold on tight."

Chapter Twelve

Bianca did her best to hold tight to the reins, as Nate had instructed, even though it felt like her teeth were going to rattle right out of her head.

"Whoa, Daisy," she shouted, doubtful the horse could even hear over the pounding of hooves. She wanted to turn around and see how close Nate was. Every moment she expected to see him gaining on her, but it felt like Daisy could outrun even a Triple Crown winner at the pace she was going.

She tried to remember the exact instructions Nate had given her for stopping a horse. She'd dropped one of the reins, which was flapping wildly next to Daisy's head, probably only adding to the horse's panic. The snake had come out of nowhere, or at least that's how it had felt to Bianca.

Daisy lost her footing for a second, and Bianca grabbed

hold of the saddle horn, squeezing her eyes tightly shut, expecting to end up thrown or crushed under the animal's massive weight. But the horse righted herself again and kept running.

Pull back on the reins and down, she remembered what Nate had told her. Not up because that will make the horse rear. Bianca yanked on the rein, and Daisy changed direction but didn't seem to slow.

"Whoa," Bianca shouted, trying to make her voice deep and commanding instead of terrified. Terrified wasn't going to help her in this situation. She leaned forward and reached for the loose rein, then yelped as she almost lost her balance and toppled off Daisy's back.

Where was Nate? Why wasn't he coming to rescue her?

Maybe something had happened with EJ. Maybe the snake had spooked Cinnamon, too. The thought gave her a burst of adrenaline that had nothing to do with her own fear and everything to do with worry over her son. She was going to have to rescue herself.

She leaned forward again, wrapping her right hand around Daisy's sweaty neck as she stretched out her left. Her fingers grazed the rein but couldn't quite grab hold, so she reached farther and…

Nate's big hand closed around the rein.

"Hand me the other one," he shouted, and she quickly straightened and passed it over Daisy's neck. Her breath caught in her throat at the sight of EJ tucked against Nate's chest, his big eyes wide and his cheeks wet with tears as he stared at her.

"Whoa," Nate repeated the command over and over as he galloped next to the horse.

Immediately she felt a shift in Daisy, a slowing in

the pounding of hooves and the merciless jostling. She held tight to the horn until the two horses had come to a stop in the middle of the grassy field.

"Mommy," EJ cried.

Nate dismounted then pulled EJ off Cinnamon's back and into his arms.

"I'm fine," she said, her voice trembling.

As soon as EJ was safely on the ground, Nate reached for Bianca. She accepted the help because her body was shaking so badly she would have ended up in a puddle on the ground otherwise.

"We didn't talk about snakes," she whispered as his arm tightened around her shoulder and he pulled her close.

EJ launched himself at her, wrapping his arms around her legs. Nate bent and picked him up, and they stood in a group hug without speaking for several minutes. Nate's breathing was ragged, and EJ whimpered softly, but eventually she could feel them each begin to calm. It was as if they silently pulled strength from holding each other.

Bianca's brain felt jumbled in her head, but she knew she had to pull it together for her son's sake. That's what moms did, after all.

"What an adventure," she said softly and kissed the top of EJ's head, using the pads of her thumbs to wipe the tears from his cheeks. "Did you even know Daisy could run so fast?"

The boy gave a soft laugh. "I didn't think Cinnamon was going to catch her."

"I knew you and Nate would manage," she said, then took him from Nate. The boy wrapped his arms tightly around her neck. His skinny legs clamped her waist.

"It's not because he loves you," EJ said against her ear. "He takes care of all of his friends."

Bianca forced her knees not to buckle at the strange and oddly prescient comment. "But you love me," she told him, "and we're in this together. No silly snake is going to hurt me."

"Snakes are scary, Mommy. Not silly."

"You did good staying in the saddle." Nate's voice was hoarse and she saw his Adam's apple bob as he swallowed. "We usually don't see rattlers on the trail this time of year, or you hear them with enough distance to change direction. I'm sorry, Bianca. I was paying attention to EJ and not—"

"I'm fine, Nate." She reached for his arm, ignoring his slight flinch as she touched him.

He took off his hat and wiped a sleeve across his forehead. "I'm not. I was scared out of my mind watching Daisy tear across the field with you on her back."

"So much for our beginner trail ride."

Nate's mouth thinned.

"This wasn't your fault," she told him. "If I had more experience riding, I could have handled Daisy's reaction better."

"I should have seen the snake."

"You did." EJ lifted his head from Bianca's shoulder. "The snake scared Cinnamon, too, Mommy. He went up on his back legs. But Mr. Nate held on to me so I wouldn't fall and then we came after you."

"You two rescued me," she said, pressing her forehead to EJ's.

"It looked like you were doing a decent job taking care of yourself," Nate told her.

She found it easy to smile at him. "Was that before

or after the part where I was holding on to a runaway horse for dear life?"

His eyes were guarded and she couldn't understand why he looked so miserable. Yes, Daisy getting spooked had been scary and could have ended badly, but it hadn't. She was fine. EJ was fine.

"I'm still hungry," her son said, rubbing his stomach.

Nate moved forward and pointed over her shoulder. "You took a shortcut."

She turned to see a metal-framed structure situated on a slight rise above the trees about a hundred yards away. The windmill's fan turned in the breeze and the pond in front of it was surrounded by high grass. "We're almost there." She brushed EJ's hair out of his eyes. "Do you want to walk or ride the rest of the way?"

He thought about it for a moment, then said, "Ride. Will you ride, too, Mommy?"

Her chest tightened as panic seeped under her skin, but she nodded. "Of course."

Nate lifted EJ out of her arms and up onto Cinnamon's saddle. "Are you sure?" he asked.

"I have a way better understanding for the term 'get back on that horse,'" she told him.

He tucked a strand of stray hair behind her ear. "So damn brave," he murmured.

Bianca had never felt brave, but maybe she needed to change her definition of bravery. She'd always thought of courage as reserved for people like her brother, who purposely put themselves in harm's way to save others. Not someone like her, who spent far too much time scrambling for purchase on the endless mountain of life. Fear often motivated her. Truly it was her constant companion. Fear that she wouldn't be able to provide for EJ. Fear that she'd turn into the screwup her mom had always made her believe she was. Fear that, in the end, she wasn't lovable. She'd never be chosen.

But every moment with Nate felt like he was making a choice and it was her. When she'd first arrived at the ranch, she'd thought his attention was a gift, but what if it was actually her due?

Maybe she needed to start believing she deserved to be the one chosen. Maybe she had to start choosing herself.

"You're right," she told him, earning a smile. "But I think I've depleted my stores of bravery for the morning." She held up a trembling hand. "I'll take calm and uneventful for the rest of the day."

He slid his hand into hers and kissed each one of her knuckles. "We can walk the horses over to the windmill."

She shook her head and turned to Daisy. Running a hand along the horse's damp neck, she moved forward until she was directly in front of the animal. "No more freaking out," she said gently, and gave Daisy a scratch between the eyes. The horse snuffled as if her breakneck run across the field was already forgotten.

"Mommy, she's a horse. She can't understand you."

Bianca moved to Daisy's side, placed her boot in the left stirrup and hoisted herself up and into the saddle. "She senses that I mean business." She pointed at EJ and wiggled her eyebrows. "Just like you do when I tell you to take a bath."

The boy giggled, and Nate mounted Cinnamon behind EJ, smiling as he settled EJ against his chest.

"Let's go find our lunch spot," he said, "We all need a break after that."

* * *

"He's so happy here," Bianca said as she watched EJ chase a grasshopper from the copse of trees where they'd had lunch all the way to the water's edge.

"It's a good place for a boy to grow up." Nate broke a cookie in half and handed her the larger piece.

"Does terror burn off calories?" She plucked it out of his fingers, moaning softly as she took a bite. "Because I can't get enough to eat right now." She waved at EJ, then flopped onto her back on the wool blanket Nate had packed. "Thanks for bringing everything for lunch. This has been a wonderful afternoon."

Nate shook his head. "How can you say that after your scare with Daisy? I'm really sorry. I told you to trust me and then—"

She placed a hand on his back. "Don't you dare blame yourself, Nate Fortune. You didn't put that snake on the trail."

"But if I'd been paying more attention, I would have seen it first. Just like with—" He placed his elbows on his knees and hung his head between his hands. "I would have protected you. I failed."

She sat upright again, scooting closer so her arm and leg brushed his. "Take off your shirt."

"What?" He darted a glance toward EJ before turning to her. "You want me to undress right now?"

"Not really." She gave him a playful nudge. "I mean, I wouldn't complain, but I was really just trying to figure out if you were wearing your superhero cape underneath that denim shirt."

He snorted. "Not funny, Busy Bee."

"Neither is you making the situation today into something more. Yes, I was scared. Yes, something bad could have happened. But it didn't. I'm fine." She poked his rock-hard bicep. "Do you know why?"

"Because you're amazing," he said softly.

"Hardly," she said with an eye roll. "But when Daisy was out of control, and I thought for sure I was going to be thrown or trampled, I heard your voice in my head. All those instructions you gave me as we started out on the ride."

"You had a few minutes of riding tips. I should have never let you—"

"I'm a grown woman," she interrupted. "I wouldn't have climbed on that horse if I didn't want to."

He blew out a long breath. "I was so damn scared you were going to be hurt." He draped an arm around her shoulder and pulled her close.

"That makes two of us." She turned her face into his shirt and breathed him in, the scent of mint gum and the earth and laundry detergent. "Thank you for taking care of EJ. I was most worried about him."

"I had him," Nate whispered.

"I know." Somehow the knowledge of that soothed her soul in a way she barely understood. She'd come so far from the morning she'd hightailed it out of San Antonio. She was stronger now. Strong enough to ask—

"Did Eddie suffer?"

Nate stiffened next to her, and suddenly it felt like she was snuggling up to a glacier. He was silent for so long, she didn't think he would answer. Finally he said, "No. It was fast."

"Do you think he was scared?" She couldn't imagine her strong, brave brother scared of anything, but she had enough distance and experience now to understand that

Eddie hadn't only been the bigger-than-life hero she'd worshipped as a girl. He'd been human.

"We were all scared." He hung his head again. "Hell, Bianca. Fear and adrenaline were our bread and butter over there. Eddie was one of the bravest men I knew. He saved at least a dozen men on that last mission." He paused, then added, "He saved me. But don't think for a minute he wasn't soil-his-pants scared when it was going down."

"I associate being scared with weakness," she admitted. "That's how it always seemed to me. Eddie was strong. You're strong."

"Not like your brother."

She shook her head then covered his hand, which was resting on his thigh, with hers. "Think of all you've been through."

"I can't," he said on a ragged breath. "When I think about it, I feel like I'm going to lose my mind. I don't want to think. I don't want to remember."

"But the nightmares… Talking about it might help."

A shudder passed through him and she squeezed his hand, leaning in closer. "You're not alone," she whispered.

"I've been alone so damn long." He said the words more to himself than her, but they broke her heart just the same.

She was torn between pushing him, wanting to know more about Eddie's death and the demons that made Nate suffer so much, and simply soothing him. Was it fair to force him to relive the traumas or atrocities he'd seen in the line of duty?

"Not anymore," she said finally. "I'm here for you as long as you need me."

He pulled away, got up off the blanket, paced a few steps and then turned back to her. "There are things you don't know about Eddie—about that last mission."

"Do you want to tell me?"

He closed his eyes. "Yes. No. I'm so messed up, Bianca."

She drew her knees to her chest, as if they could protect her heart from whatever pain she was sure to endure in learning the details of her brother's death. "Whatever it is, I can handle it."

"Mommy, I caught a grasshopper."

She sucked in a breath, her focus switching to EJ in a split second. "Bring him here," she called, shielding her eyes from the Texas sun. "Let me see."

As EJ ran forward, Nate backed away. It felt like more than just a physical distance between them. Somehow the connection they'd shared moments earlier had been severed. His mask was in place again, and she wanted to rip it from his face. Until Nate was truly honest with her and himself about how Eddie's death had affected him, could they really have a chance at making this work?

"Look at his big eyes." EJ came to stand at the edge of the blanket, his small, dirt-smudged hands cupped in front of him. "He's green."

"So cool," she whispered.

EJ smiled. "He tickles my hand with his legs. Can I keep him?"

"No, sweetie. His home is out here on the grass. He probably has a grasshopper family waiting for him."

"What if he's alone?" EJ asked.

She could feel Nate's gaze on her and glanced up,

but his eyes were unreadable under the wide brim of his Stetson.

"I doubt he is," she answered.

EJ scrunched up his face into a frown but then opened his hands. The grasshopper rested on his palm for several moments, probably stunned by being captured. Then the bug hopped into the grass and disappeared in the high stalks.

"There are a thousand more you can catch," Nate told EJ. "Grayson, Jayden and I used to chase those things all over the place."

He smiled at her boy, and Bianca's heart stuttered. She had to convince him to face his demons because she needed a future with Nate Fortune like she needed her next breath. She'd fallen hopelessly in love with him.

Not the start of something that felt like love. Not a little bit. Full force with everything she had. It was difficult to fathom how that was possible given the brief amount of time she'd truly known him, but it was her reality just the same.

She wasn't going to give him up without a fight.

"We should go." When both Nate and EJ turned to stare, she realized she'd shouted the comment. She was willing to fight but didn't quite know how to start. That made her nervous, and when she was nervous she talked too much…or blurted out random commands.

She'd never had the nerve to fight for anything she wanted. Everything in life had simply happened to her and she'd made the best of it. This was different. She was different in Paseo, and as much as she yearned to embrace it, the thought also made fear pound through her. She took a breath and thought of what Nate had told her about Eddie. Her brother had been scared, but he'd kept going. She could keep going. Or at least try to keep going without making a fool of herself.

"I mean…" She tapped a finger on her watch. "It's probably time to head back to the ranch."

"Sure," Nate said, giving her a questioning glance. "Are you feeling okay?"

She grinned, wondering if her smile looked as fake as it felt. "Fine."

"Then let's pack everything up." Nate placed a hand on EJ's shoulder. "You ready, buddy?"

"Fifteen more minutes, Mommy?" EJ asked, his eyes darting toward the windmill on the hill. "I'm not done exploring."

Bianca sighed. "Fifteen more minutes."

EJ pumped a fist in the air and ran toward the windmill.

"Would you like to see it, too?" Nate approached her slowly, as if not sure how she might respond.

Perfect. He thought she was a crazy person. What a great start to her plan to fight for him.

"I can show you the spot where Jayden and Ariana said their vows." His voice was gentle. "Are you sure everything's okay?"

I'm in love with you.

"Yep," she said quickly, pressing a hand to her stomach.

"I don't think so." Nate slipped his hand into hers. They began walking toward the windmill, where she could see EJ bobbing up and down in the tall grass, clearly still on the hunt for grasshoppers.

"Does this have something to do with what we were talking about?" His voice was hollow. "About me being messed up?"

"No," she answered immediately, hating that her own tumbling emotions had made him think she was judging him.

"Because I wouldn't blame you. You and EJ are important to me. Getting to know you is one of the best things that's happened in my life in forever."

"Me, too."

"But I don't know if I can give you what you want."

"Then give me what you can," she blurted.

"Bianca." He shifted so he was in front of her, blocking the path. "You can't mean that."

"It's not forever," she told him, forcing her gaze to remain on his. A spark flared in his coffee-colored eyes, like her words disappointed him somehow.

Was it possible Nate wanted forever with her?

"What I'm trying to say is I can be patient. You've been through a lot. I get that. We can go slowly. It doesn't have to be a rush. You and I have all the time in the world, but I'm not going to give up because I'm scared and you believe you're messed up." She bit down on her lip, took a breath. "I'm going to fight for us. I believe this is something special, and I refuse to let it go."

He lifted his hands to cup her cheeks and leaned in to brush a kiss across her lips. The touch was feather-light, but she felt it to her toes. There were things he couldn't say yet, secrets he wasn't willing to share. But the kiss was a promise of more. It felt like a pledge, as if he was giving her an answer to a question she hadn't even known to ask. But the "yes" in his kiss meant everything.

"How did you get to be so amazing?" He pressed his forehead to hers, their breaths mingling so that it felt like they were connected even by the air around them.

She tipped back her head and laughed. "I was born that way."

"Mommy, I got another one!" EJ's voice rang out across the meadow.

Nate looped an arm around Bianca's shoulder and they walked toward her son. Suddenly the fear that had become Bianca's constant companion dissolved, hope blooming in its place. Hope for a real future with the man she loved.

Chapter Thirteen

It was a week later that Nate got the call he'd been expecting since Jayden left the ranch. He driven into town to pick up materials to replace a section of fence that had been damaged by a windstorm just after Christmas. His phone rang as he loaded the back of the truck, and he sent the call to voicemail.

Almost immediately, the device buzzed with an incoming text.

Don't you dare screen my call, Nathan.

He finished sliding a piece of timber into the cargo bed and punched a button to return the call.

His mother answered on the first ring.

"It wasn't on purpose," he lied. "I'm in the middle of fixing the south pasture fence. It's not a great time to talk."

The familiar sound of one of Deborah's patented sighs came through the phone. "Talk to me, anyway," she told him. "I've been trying you for days."

"I've been too busy to get to town."

"You're not answering the house phone, either. Did you get my messages?"

"I meant to call you back earlier."

"Lucky for both of us, you made the right choice today."

He shut the back of the truck and leaned a hip against the tailgate, resigned to get this inevitable conversation out of the way. His mother wasn't going to let him off the hook. The truth was, he'd been secretly waiting for her call. He was a grown damn man, but sometimes he wanted his mom to help smooth the rough edges of his life. Of him. The way she had when he was a boy. Even though Deborah had been busy raising triplets and working, she'd always made time for each of them as individuals.

"Hi, Mom. How are you? How's Grayson? I hear you're heading to Tulsa."

"Fine. Fine. Yes," she said in rapid succession. "Are you going to explain why I have to hear about your new girlfriend from Jayden?"

"She's not my girlfriend," he said, which was both true and not. He'd never taken Bianca out on an official date but he felt closer to her than any other woman in his life. "She's Eddie Shaw's little sister."

"Jayden explained that part. He told me she has a son."

"EJ," Nate explained. "Edward James." Guilt twisted in his chest as he added, "Named after Eddie."

"He also said you're different with her."

"Different how?"

"Happy," Deborah said, her voice a caress across the miles that separated them.

"I was happy before," he argued but couldn't manage to put any conviction in the words.

"No, you weren't. Not for a while, Nathan. I've been worried about you." His mom had a knack for ignoring the nonsense her three sons tried to feed her and cutting through to the truth. "I'd like to meet Bianca and her son."

He took off his hat and swiped an arm across his forehead, sweat beading along his hairline despite the cooler January day. "I don't know how long she's staying. She hit a rough patch and is trying to get her life back on track."

Deborah let out a soft laugh. "I can relate to that."

"You'd like her. She's smart and funny and she loves her son more than anything. She'd do anything for EJ."

"I can relate to that, too," his mom answered. "It's how I feel about all three of you, even though you're grown men now."

"What about you?" he asked. "How are you, Mom?"

"I told you I was fine."

"Fine doesn't mean anything to me. Or to you. We both know that. Did Jayden tell you he had lunch with one of Gerald's kids when he and Ariana stopped in Austin?"

There was a charged silence on the other end of the line. "He mentioned it," Deborah said finally.

"How are you dealing with the fact that our father is still alive now that we've all had some time for it to sink in?"

Another pause. "The same as you, I'd imagine."

He laughed. "Well, that doesn't reassure me you're okay."

"Oh, Nathan."

"We'll make it through."

"We always do," she agreed. "One thing I've been thinking about is what I might have done differently back then. The regrets I have about letting Jerome—or Gerald now, I suppose—walk away."

"Mom, he made that choice."

"I didn't stop him. We had a stupid argument, and I let fear and pride dictate my actions. I didn't fight."

Nate sucked in a breath. Bianca had told him she was willing to fight. Hell, she was so much braver than he imagined. Than she gave herself credit for.

"You couldn't have known," he insisted, "what he would do to break ties with his family."

"You're right, of course. It's the past now, anyway. It doesn't do anyone any good to let regret take over and dictate how you live your life."

Nate didn't answer. What could he say to that?

But his mom knew. Even though he hadn't talked about Eddie's death to her—to anyone except the tiny snippets he'd shared with Bianca—Deborah didn't need words. She had that spooky maternal sixth sense, where she understood what he and his brothers were going through without them uttering a word.

"You know this, right?" she asked, her voice still gentle. "Regret is not a way to live your life, Nathan. You can't change what happened in the past." He heard her draw in a breath. "You can't blame yourself for Eddie's death."

Of course he could. He did.

"I want to talk about Eddie Shaw," he told her, "about as much as you want to discuss Gerald Robinson."

Deborah chuckled. "You're like him, you know."

"Eddie?"

"Your father," she corrected. "You're strong like he was. And so darn stubborn."

"I thought I got that from you," he said, letting humor lace his tone.

"From both of us," she admitted. "Don't let it change the course of your life. If you care about this Bianca, tell her."

"She knows how I feel." But doubt niggled the back of his mind as he said the words. What did Bianca really know? That he'd opened his house but not truly his heart. That he wouldn't share the details of his past. That he was willing to make love to her every night but would sneak away after she fell asleep, afraid of what she might witness when he was in the middle of one of his nightmares.

"Take it from the voice of experience," his mom said, as if reading his thoughts. "A single mom who's built a life around her son needs to know a man is committed to her and her son. The stakes are too high any other way."

"There are things about me she doesn't know," he admitted. "The night Eddie died…" His voice cracked and he swallowed.

"Tell her," his mother urged. "If she's the kind of woman I think she is, the two of you will find a way to get through it, Nathan." She let out a delicate sniff. "You deserve happiness."

"Mom, I don't want to upset you."

"You're not. Sometimes I just wish things had been

different for our family. That I'd been able to give you boys more."

"You gave us everything."

"You were always sweet," she said. "A teddy bear heart in a tough navy SEAL body."

He smiled. "Bianca called me a teddy bear the first day she showed up in Paseo."

"I like her already. Remember, no regrets," she said. "I love you, Nathan."

"You, too, Mom. Say hi to Grayson for me."

They disconnected and he got in the truck and headed for home, surveying the land that he'd grown up working on as he drove. The ranch had been a kind of salvation to him when he'd left the navy. A place to escape and hide out, where he could lose himself in the backbreaking labor and honest sweat of a hard day's work. He'd needed a reprieve from life and from the hell his existence had become the moment Eddie died, but he was quickly realizing there was no way to outrun what he'd gone through.

He thought he could escape the bad memories by ignoring them, but in doing that, he'd allowed the past to dictate his future. He didn't want that. He wanted Bianca and EJ.

He wanted to be the man they both deserved.

As he approached the ranch, he noticed a car he didn't recognize parked in front of the house. Not that he knew every vehicle in Paseo, but the cherry red sports car seemed out of place in this part of Texas.

In front of the old farmhouse, the Miata gave the impression of nail polish on a pig. The car wasn't new. It had several small dents in the back bumper and the paint's shine was worn down on the hood. He did a mental eye roll at the car's bumper sticker, which read My Other Ride Is…Your Mama.

Nate didn't know who was visiting the ranch today, but he could guarantee they were no friend of his.

He parked the truck and took the steps two at a time, not sure why his heart was hammering in his chest. As he burst through the door, Bianca, EJ and a man Nate didn't recognize all turned to him.

"Mr. Nate," EJ shouted, his voice shaky. He let go of his mother's leg and ran toward Nate.

Nate scooped him up in his arms, holding a protective arm on the boy's back.

Who the hell was the guy glaring at him from across the room?

"Nate, you're here." Bianca pressed two fingers to her temple.

"Yep," he agreed. "I live here."

The stranger's eyes narrowed and Bianca took a step forward, as if she was breaking up a potential fight on the playground. "This is Brett Pierson. He just arrived." She swallowed. "My—"

"Husband," the man supplied.

"Ex," she corrected.

Brett raised a brow in Nate's direction. "For now," he muttered.

"Don't do that," Bianca whispered, and Nate hated the panicked look in her warm cocoa-colored eyes. She shook her head. "Not in front of EJ."

Brett gave the barest hint of a nod, as if agreeing only to humor her.

"This is Nate Fortune." She gestured toward Nate. "He was a friend of Eddie's."

Brett curled his lip in what could have been a smile but looked more like a sneer. "Right."

Bianca seemed shocked at Brett's reaction. "Really, Brett. I'm sure I mentioned Nate to you. He and Eddie did BUD/S training together. They were SEALs in the same squadron."

"Yeah. I've heard all about him." Brett focused his gaze on EJ. "Come here, *son*." He held out his arms and motioned for the boy.

EJ buried his face against Nate's shirtfront.

"I mean it, EJ. I drove all this way to see you." His gaze flicked to Bianca. "You and your mama. *My* family."

Nate had never wanted to punch a man so much in his life.

"He doesn't know you, Brett," Bianca said. "He was two when you left. It's been a long time."

"He needs to get to know me, and he isn't going to do that with another man holding him. That ridiculous business about changing his name doesn't help, either."

"My name is Edward James Shaw." EJ took a deep, shuddery breath and burrowed farther into Nate's shirt.

"I've got you, buddy," Nate whispered, ruffling his hair.

"Nate?" Bianca turned to him. "Would you take EJ to the barn for a few minutes?"

Nate shook his head. "I'm not leaving you alone with him."

"Are you joking?" Brett held out his hands, palms up. "I'm her husband."

"Ex," Bianca and Nate said at the same time.

Then she turned back to Nate. "I need a few minutes to talk to Brett. We have some things to work out."

"What kind of things?" Nate asked.

"Things that are none of your business," Brett told him, his jaw set. The same kind of firm line he'd seen on EJ's face when the boy was digging in his heels about convincing his mother to give him five more minutes before bedtime. And as much as EJ looked like Bianca and Eddie, suddenly Nate could see Brett in him.

EJ's father.

The man who'd walked away, leaving Bianca on her own with a toddler. The man who hadn't offered one bit of support in the past two years, emotional or financial. But still the boy's father. Nate knew what it would have meant to him and his brothers if Gerald Robinson had come into their lives when they were kids. How that would have changed everything.

What right did he have to deny EJ the chance he'd secretly dreamed of as a boy? Despite the fact that Brett looked like a tool and drove a ridiculous car for a trip across half of Texas, this couldn't be an easy situation to walk into. Was Nate helping anyone by making it more difficult?

Bianca walked toward him, only stopping when they stood toe-to-toe. She put a hand on Nate's arm. She looked miserable and strangely hopeful at the same time. "Please," she whispered, and of course Nate nodded. How could he say no?

"We'll be in the barn if you need anything."

"Thank you."

EJ swiped a hand across his cheek. "You should come, too, Mommy. I bet Otis is out there. He might let me pet him today, and you'll want to see that."

"I do," she agreed. "But I need to talk to your daddy for a few minutes."

"You can give Daisy a carrot."

"Maybe I'll bring Daddy to the barn when we're finished with the grown-up stuff. He can meet Twix."

"He might not like ponies."

"I like ponies," Brett called, and acid burned in Nate's gut. For all he knew, Brett had finally realized what an amazing woman and son he'd left behind. He could be ready to make Bianca and EJ his future.

Just like Nate was ready.

"See?" Bianca asked, smoothing a hand over EJ's back.

"I guess you can bring him," the boy muttered.

She lifted onto her toes and kissed EJ's cheek. As she did, her fingers curled around Nate's bicep and she squeezed, as if communicating something with him she didn't want Brett to know about.

He sure as hell hoped it meant she wasn't interested in reuniting with her ex-husband. That might send Nate over the edge.

And he'd just gotten comfortable on solid ground.

Bianca shut the door behind Nate and EJ, then turned to face Brett again. He gave her one of his stock smiles, a jaunty half curve of his mouth. It was the smile that had melted her heart when she'd first met him.

The girl she was back then seemed like a stranger to her now. How had she been fool enough to fall for Brett, with his slick moves and pretty lines? At the time, she'd been grateful for his attention.

She'd been so starved for anything that felt remotely like love. She'd been coming off a bad breakup after the guy she'd thought she was in love with had cheated on her. Her mother had gambled away her meager savings—

literally—so Bianca left school and drained her own bank accounts to pay Jennifer's debts and bills so she wouldn't lose her apartment lease and have one more thing to add to her list of problems. Eddie was in the field, stationed a half a world away on a mission so covert that Bianca couldn't even reach him.

She'd been alone and reeling. Brett had seemed like a fairy-tale prince to her, and she'd desperately wanted to believe the things he'd told her—she was special and beautiful and he wanted to take care of her.

Now she knew better. She wasn't a princess, and her life wasn't a fairy tale. It was real and sometimes a struggle, but it belonged to her. She was in control. No one else.

A part of her wanted to kick him off the Fortune ranch and out of her life for good. But he was EJ's father, and Bianca understood how hard it could be on a child growing up without a dad. She knew Nate did, as well, which was probably why he'd been willing to let her have this time with Brett.

It was clear he hadn't wanted to, and she appreciated his protective streak toward her, but more importantly toward EJ.

"What do you want, Brett?" she asked, crossing her arms over her chest.

"I told you. I'm here to take you home. That stupid business about you filing to have EJ's name legally changed was a wake-up call. I've missed you, babe."

"Missed me? It's been over two years since you walked out the door. You left our *home*, knowing very well I couldn't afford rent on a house like that on my own. I'm changing EJ's name because he belongs to *me*. He's a

Shaw. You don't even know where your son and I have been living because you haven't bothered to check."

"Not true." He shook his head, a lock of hair flopping into his eyes much like EJ's did. It was cute on a four-year-old, but Bianca wanted to tell Brett to get a haircut. "I kept tabs on you. When I received notification of the name change hearing, I went looking for you. But you'd moved out of that crappy apartment, so I talked to your mom. She told me you'd left San Antonio, and something in me snapped. It was one thing when I knew you and EJ were close, but to have you out of my reach…"

"That sounds unbelievable creepy," she muttered, "even from you."

Brett flashed another smile. "I hoped you'd think it was romantic."

She couldn't believe she'd married a guy who was so delusional. It was a bigger blow to realize her mother had helped Brett to find her after all this time. The conversation with her mom hadn't gone well, but she thought Jennifer understood that Bianca wanted a fresh start.

"How is it romantic?" she asked, pointing a finger at him. "Or even the least bit acceptable that you've kept tabs on us but haven't wanted to be a part of your son's life?"

Brett shrugged. "I had some things to work out. You know I hadn't planned to get married and become a dad when I did."

"Me, neither," she countered, "but that doesn't change reality. EJ is an amazing kid. You've missed a lot."

"I want to make it up to you. I've gone back to

school, and I've got a great job in sales at a medical device company. They're even paying for my classes."

Her own broken dreams of a college degree and a great career felt like glass shards in her throat. "Good for you. What does that have to do with EJ and me?"

"I'm doing all of this for you." He moved forward and reached for her, but she shifted away. "For us. For our future."

Bianca had never been the violent type. But the urge to punch her ex-husband in the throat was so overwhelming she could barely ignore it.

"We have no future," she said through clenched teeth. "If you want to see EJ, we can work out an arrangement. You'll also need to start sending child support checks You've been dodging payments for way too long. It's going to stop."

Brett scoffed. "He's my son. I don't have to pay to see him."

"Raising a child means responsibility. You can live up to yours if you want to be a part of his life." Bianca pressed her fingers to her lips, shocked at the words coming out of her mouth...at the conviction burning deep in her soul. She was done letting anyone take advantage of her, accepting scraps for herself or for EJ because she'd been taught to believe she wasn't worth anything more.

"Now that you've latched onto one of the Fortunes, you think you've got it made." Brett's blue eyes narrowed. "Is that it?"

She shook her head. "This has nothing to do with Nate," she said, which was both true and not. The conviction that she and EJ deserved to be valued resonated through her, but being with Nate had helped open her eyes to recognize it as a fact. "You and I are over, Brett. I'm willing to let you into EJ's life. But not if you're going to hurt him. He needs his dad to be a dependable presence in his life. This isn't about the money, but I know you. If you have to invest in something, it means more to you." She flashed a small smile. "Maybe that's why we were never meant to be. Neither of us believed you had to try to make our relationship work."

"You're not being fair," he muttered.

"I don't blame you," she told him without emotion. "Not entirely. I let it happen, but I was different then. I've changed, and I'm not going back to who I was before. That's the woman you married. Not me."

"And you think Nate Fortune is that man?" He practically spit the words. "You don't even know him."

"I know he's been generous and patient with me. He cares about EJ." She chuckled. "He cooks."

Brett threw up his hands. "What the hell does that have to do with anything?"

"You wouldn't understand. He's a good man. Eddie trusted him, and I do—"

"He killed your brother."

She took a step back as if he'd struck her. "Shut your mouth," she said, the words hissing out on a painful breath.

"I'm sorry. I know you don't want to hear this but—"

"You're right." She turned, stalked the few paces to the front door and yanked it open. "You need to leave, Brett. You can say goodbye to EJ in the barn, and I'll call you next week about arrangements to see him."

"It's a shock, Bianca, but at least let me explain. I'm not trying to throw the guy under the bus."

She rolled her eyes, anger coursing through her. "Right."

"Has he told you the details of Eddie's death?"

She wasn't about to admit that he hadn't. "I read the report," she answered instead.

"It's not the same thing. You don't know the whole story."

"And how do *you* know it?" she demanded.

"From talk I've heard in the old neighborhood. Your mom confirmed everything."

"She didn't," Bianca whispered, then pressed her lips together, thinking of the veiled hints her mom had made during their last awkward phone conversation. Jennifer had intimated that Nate wasn't the man he pretended to be, but Bianca assumed she was talking about his ties to the Fortune family. Nate had been Eddie's best friend. He'd loved her brother as much as she had. Missed him just as badly. There was nothing Brett could say to change that.

She swung the door shut gently and crossed her arms over her chest. "Fine. Tell me if it makes you happy. It won't change anything."

He walked forward until he was only an arm's length from her. "It makes me unhappy to see you fooled by a man who doesn't have your best interests at heart. He's lying to you."

"Go ahead with what you think you know about Eddie's death," she told him. "But stop trash-talking Nate. I won't have it, Brett."

He blew out a harsh breath. "I don't need to trash-talk him. The truth is damning enough. He deserted Eddie over in Afghanistan. Saved himself but let your brother take the brunt of enemy fire during their last mission. He left Eddie alone, Bianca. What kind of a soldier saves his own neck that way at the expense of another man's life—let alone when that man is supposed to be his best friend?"

"Stop."

"You can't depend on him. You can't trust him. He's in it for himself, and as soon as you're not useful to him, he'll walk away."

"I don't believe any of that."

"Come on," Brett urged. "I can tell by the look in your eyes that you know I'm telling the truth. I also know by the way you look at him that you're sleeping together."

She narrowed her eyes. "That's none of your business."

He barked out a laugh. "Knowing you, you're half in love with him already. But he's not the man you believe he is."

"Neither were you," she muttered.

"I made mistakes," he admitted. "I let you down, and I'm sorry for that. But I would have never left your brother for dead. Even I'm not that awful." He leaned in, brushed his thumb across her cheek. She flinched, like his touch was electric. "I've changed, Bianca. I'm trying to be honest with you. Even if you won't give us another chance, cut ties with Nate Fortune. He's going to hurt you way worse than I ever did."

"It's time for you to go," she whispered, unable to argue any longer. There was no way what he was saying about Nate was true. It couldn't be. Nate would have told her if he'd had some direct involvement in Eddie's death. She would have known. Eddie thought of Nate as a brother. He'd practically sent Bianca to Paseo, after all. This had to be a ploy by Brett to ruin her new life just as it started.

But she couldn't stop doubt from easing its way in through the shadows of her mind. Despite what she knew about their friendship, she also recognized there were things about Eddie's death that Nate hadn't shared. Then there were his nightmares and the way he insisted he didn't deserve her. She assumed that was the result of his time as a SEAL, the things he'd seen and done over the past two decades, but what if there was something more?

"Say goodbye to EJ for me," Brett told her. He scrubbed a hand over his face. "I'm not going to take the chance of upsetting him more. I have so many memories of him as a baby, but now I'm a stranger to him. None of this went the way I'd planned it, Bianca."

"Maybe you should have made a better plan," she said, hating how snippy she sounded. She sighed and opened the door more gently this time, feeling exhausted and overwhelmed, the way she had so many times in San Antonio. "If you're serious, Brett, we'll make it work."

He nodded. "I'll call next week and we'll come up with a plan for him to spend time with me."

"Call first, then I'll talk to him about spending time with you."

He grinned, only this time it was genuine. "You're going to make me work for this, aren't you?"

"I sure am, and I should have done it a long time ago."

He leaned and kissed her cheek. "You're a better woman than I deserve. Thank you for being such a fantastic mother to our son."

My son, she wanted to scream. EJ belonged to her.

But she only held open the door with a smile. "He's the best part of me," she whispered. "Always."

With a last wave, Brett walked toward his red Miata. It was the same car he'd driven when they first met. At the time it seemed exciting and fun, but then she'd had EJ and Brett had refused to part with it. It was a two-seater, so they couldn't fit a car seat in it and she should have seen it for what it was—a sign that he wasn't willing to change anything in his life to accommodate EJ. She hoped he'd changed now, but she still didn't trust it.

Up until a few minutes ago, she'd started to believe it hadn't mattered. Nate had stepped into EJ's life and fulfilled all the hopes she'd had for a father figure for her son. Now she couldn't help but wonder if it had all been a lie.

Chapter Fourteen

"You can't avoid me forever. We live in the same house."

"*You* live here." Bianca looked up from where she was clearing weeds in the overgrown vegetable garden situated behind the kitchen windows in the backyard. "I'm only visiting."

The words were spoken casually, but they cut across Nate's chest like a blade. Something had changed between them since her ex-husband's unexpected visit to the ranch yesterday. He knew Bianca wasn't interested in reuniting with Brett. She'd patiently explained to EJ that his daddy wanted to be a part of his life again, but that they weren't going to be a family in the traditional sense of the word.

EJ had peppered her with questions about his father and why he was returning to their lives now. No matter how she felt on the inside, Bianca had done an amazing job of keeping the focus on EJ and how she'd always protect him and make sure he remained her number one priority. It reminded Nate of his own mom.

Deborah had never once spoken an ill word against the triplets' father or how she'd been left as a single mother. Of course, she'd thought Gerald dead for all these years, but even after they'd discovered that his current wife, Charlotte, had kept a dossier on all of Gerald's illegitimate children, Deborah hadn't made any disparaging comments about what they'd all lost.

"What's going on, Bianca?"

"Nothing. I'm working."

He crouched down next to her. "You're going after those weeds like you have a personal vendetta against them."

She paused in the act of digging out a dry tangle of vines. "I want to make sure the garden has a good start when your mom gets back to the ranch this spring."

"She's going to love it." Nate had made an offhanded remark last week about how much Deborah had loved tending her kitchen garden when the boys had been younger. Since she'd started traveling more with Grayson in the past few years, her herbs and vegetables had been left largely ignored. Neither Jayden nor Nate had the inclination to commit to bringing it back to life. His mom lamented her heavily weeded garden whenever she came home but rarely had enough time to clear it out in the way it needed.

Bianca had decided that this was going to be her gift to Deborah—preparing the garden to thrive again. She'd enlisted EJ's help and between other chores, his lessons and work on her business, the two of them spent time each day in the backyard. She attacked it with such vehemence, it seemed she was determined to finish the task today.

At the moment, EJ was on the far side of the yard with Otis, trying to teach the dog to play fetch. Despite Nate's protests, the dog was quickly going from a stray to a family pet. Or at least EJ's pet. Although Otis seemed amenable to chowing down on the kibble Nate put out for him every morning, the dog wouldn't allow anyone but EJ to pet him. Nate liked to argue against believing the dog belonged to them, but it made the boy happy and Bianca didn't seem to mind.

"Bianca." He placed a hand on her arm, hating that she not only stilled but stiffened under his touch. "Talk to me."

She stood and paced to the garden's border, placing her handheld shovel in his mom's gardening bucket. It was strange how much it meant to Nate to see her using the set of tools he'd watched his mom use when he and his brothers were boys. "I think *you* should talk to *me*," she countered. "About the night Eddie died."

He straightened, kicking a ball of dirt with one booted toe. "You know what happened. Your brother died a hero."

She moved toward him slowly, crossing her arms over her chest. Even standing directly in front of him, the scent of her shampoo mingling with the smell of fresh dirt on the morning breeze, he could feel the distance between them. It was more than physical, and Nate had no idea how to close the divide.

"Yes," she agreed quietly, "but is there more?"

More. What an understatement. He tipped his head up to the robin's-egg-blue sky. His heart pounded in his chest and a shiver raced along his spine as panic rushed through him. Memories came swift and severe. So many damn sounds. Rounds coming in...rounds going out. Mortars...grenades. He fisted his hands and forced himself to keep breathing, afraid he might drop to his knees from the weight of guilt and regret.

He licked his lips, swallowed back the bitterness in his throat. "What more do you want to know?"

She studied him as if she was searching for something in his gaze. Some explanation or promise that things were going to be okay. That the chasm that separated them, quickly filling with his poisonous shame, could be navigated. He couldn't give her that. He realized he couldn't give her anything she needed. Now or ever. But he remained still under her scrutiny, hoping that whatever she saw would be enough.

She drew in a shuddery breath. "Brett told me..." She paused, unclasped and clasped her hands in front of her stomach. "He told me you were responsible for Eddie's death," she said on a rush of air. "He said you killed him."

He would have expected her words to hurt, but somehow hearing them spoken out loud was a relief. His shame and guilt had been a silent, secret companion since that last mission. One that stayed with him always but gained strength in the dark of night.

Now the beast yawned and opened its eyes, blinking against the light of day. Instead of being chased away by the spotlight shining on it, the darkness reveled in the notice, as if being acknowledged made it more legitimate. But to Nate, the demons had always been real, and they let out a long breath at someone speaking the truth out loud.

"I know it has to be a lie," she continued when he

didn't answer. "He's only trying to tear us apart. He doesn't want me to move on, but Brett and I have no future. You're my future." She pushed her hair out of her face. "I'm babbling again," she said with a shaky laugh. "But it's been weighing on me. I shouldn't have believed him in the first place. He was trying to warn me away from you, which is crazy." Her mouth curved up at one end, her smile wobbly but sincere, like his silence confirmed what she thought she knew about him instead of the opposite.

It had always been the opposite. As much as he wanted to, he could never be the man she wanted because...

"It's true," he said at the same time Bianca whispered, "I love you."

It felt like his heart was shattering into a million pieces as he watched the hope in her eyes cloud to confusion. "What did you say?" she asked.

He shook his head. He couldn't stand to repeat it, not when all he wanted to hear was her telling him she loved him over and over. Somehow he understood that Bianca's love was the only thing that could mend all the splintered pieces of his soul and patch him back together. She was the only thing that could make him whole again.

"Nate." She raised a hand to her throat, clutching at it like she was having trouble gathering air into her lungs. "You can't be serious. There must be an explanation. You wouldn't have—"

"I killed Eddie," he interrupted, surprised at how calm his voice sounded.

"Mommy," EJ shouted, "Otis brought me the ball."

Bianca held Nate's gaze, tears shining in her eyes.

"Mommy!"

"Go to him," Nate said, wanting to reach for her. To somehow convince her he could make everything right. But he knew nothing had been right in his world since that last terrible mission. Now there was a good chance it never would.

She swiped at her eyes but pasted a bright smile on her face. The mom smile—the one that made it clear that no matter what fresh hell was exploding in her life, she would make things okay for her son.

It was one of the things he loved most about her.

"Let me see," she called, turning and walking toward EJ and the dog.

Love.

The word ricocheted through Nate's brain, wreaking havoc on the parts of his heart that were still intact until his insides were nothing but a sad, pulpy mess.

She'd said she loved him at the exact moment he'd ruined her.

Wasn't that just his way?

He let his gaze soak in the sight of EJ laughing as Otis ran to retrieve another ball, the dog moving so fast he skidded as he tried to grab the ball in his mouth. EJ laughed harder, and Bianca's smile relaxed.

It was suddenly too much. Despite the open space around him, Nate had the sensation that his world was closing in on him. His lungs were in a vise and he could hardly breathe. He needed to get away…to move…to clear his head of the tumult of thoughts pounding him.

One foot in front of the other, striding toward the barn. He moved as if on autopilot, grateful that his body knew what to do since his brain was in the middle of a major meltdown.

Cinnamon's ears twitched when Nate approached his stall, as if he could sense Nate's mood. He saddled the horse, focusing on the scent of the barn and the sound of Cinnamon's rhythmic breathing to keep him grounded. Then he climbed on and took off out of the barn, riding like he used to as a kid, hell-bent for leather across the open fields. He used to race his brothers, but now he sped away from his own demons, hoping that the pounding of hooves and the feeling of being one with the huge animal would calm him.

He needed to clear his mind so he could figure out how to clean up the mess he'd just made of all their lives.

What's wrong, honey?"

Bianca shook her head and smiled, her cheeks aching from the movement. "Nothing, Susan. I just need to return these books I borrowed." She placed her stack of paperbacks on the counter.

"You can keep them as long as you need," Susan told her gently.

"EJ and I are leaving Paseo today. I don't think we'll be back so…" She broke off when tears clogged her throat. She glanced behind her to where EJ sat in front of the computer screen. He had on headphones and was already engrossed in a show, so she had a moment to let her happy-mom mask slip. "I know it sounds strange because I haven't been here long, but I'll miss seeing you."

"Honey, no." Susan stood, moving around the makeshift checkout counter to envelop Bianca in a baby-powder-scented hug. "You can't leave. You're too good an addition to our little town." She pulled back enough to look into Bianca's eyes. "You're good for Nathan Fortune."

Bianca sniffed, embarrassed that she could feel her chin trembling. "I can't," she whispered, then broke down completely, crying into Susan's brightly patterned sweater while the older woman hugged her, swaying back and forth the way Bianca used to when EJ was fussy as a baby.

After a few minutes she took a shaky breath and stepped out of Susan's embrace. She darted a glance at EJ, but he was still focused on Elmer the Elephant's latest adventure.

"Let me get you a tissue." Susan reached over the counter then handed Bianca a wad of them.

"I'm so embarrassed," Bianca muttered. "You don't need me blubbering all over you. I'll pull it together."

"Don't be silly." Susan patted her arm. "Sometimes a woman needs a good cry." She arched a heavily lined brow. "Especially when a man is involved. If your mama were here, she'd give you a big ol' hug and tell you the same thing."

"My mom would tell me that I was a fool to come to Paseo in the first place," Bianca said with a small, sad laugh, "and I'm getting just what I deserve."

Susan made a soft tsking sound. "Because I'm sure she's never made a mistake in her life."

"She's made plenty." Bianca dabbed at her eyes. "I have a feeling she might count me as the biggest."

"Don't say that." Susan wrapped an arm around Bianca's shoulder. "You're a good person and an amazing mother. Look at how hard you're working to get your business started. I heard from Rosa that Nathan Fortune couldn't keep his eyes off you when he brought you and EJ into town for dinner the other night. She said he looked positively smitten."

"I thought he was more than smitten," Bianca admitted. "Or at least I hoped."

"Because you feel more for him?"

"Way more. I'm in love with him."

Susan leaned in and gave Bianca's cheek a smacking kiss. "How wonderful. That boy needs some happiness in his life. I've kept up with him over the years, and he always had such a big smile and easy way about him. But he's been different since he came home this last time. Like he can't quite find his footing away from the life of a soldier. It happens to some of them, you know. Makes me sad that the men and women who give up so much to keep us safe have to deal with that. A fresh start with you and your son is just what Nate needs."

She took a step away and frowned. "Wait. Did you say you're leaving and not coming back?"

"That's the plan."

"But what about Nate?"

Bianca shrugged. "One of the few worthwhile pieces of advice my mom gave me was that loving a man doesn't guarantee a happily-ever-after in the end."

"I wouldn't call those words worthwhile," Susan said, her tone disapproving. "No offense, hon, but your mama sounds like a real piece of work."

"Yeah," Bianca agreed. "But she was right in this instance. Nate and my brother, Eddie, were SEALs together—best friends. Eddie died on their last mission, and there were circumstances Nate didn't share with me."

"It's difficult for soldiers to revisit those bad times. Some of them need to leave the past in the past."

Bianca drew in a breath. How much could she share with the sweet librarian? She didn't want anyone to judge Nate. He took care of that quite thoroughly on his own. Heck, she still didn't understand why he blamed himself for Eddie's death. Yet he hadn't denied Brett's claims.

None of it made sense, but if he wasn't willing to talk about it with her, how could they move forward? She understood letting go of the past, but whatever happened on that last mission still had a choke hold on Nate.

She wanted to fight for their relationship, but not if it was a losing battle. She'd dealt with too many of those in her life already.

"It feels like he's throwing away our future because he can't let go of the past."

"And there's nothing you can do?"

"I need some time to figure it out," Bianca said. "I only just realized that I'm someone worth fighting for. If Nate isn't willing to, then I'm not going to beg." She straightened her shoulders. "I spent too long letting people make me feel less than. I won't do it anymore. If nothing else, I owe it to EJ to be strong and believe in myself."

"You owe it to both of you," Susan agreed. "Honey, I'm awfully sorry to see you go, but I guess I understand. Maybe Nate will come to his senses."

The idea of working things out with Nate had hope blooming in Bianca's heart, followed quickly by a wave of sorrow so strong it almost knocked her off balance.

She'd watched him gallop out of the barn like he couldn't get away fast enough. If that wasn't a clear message, she didn't know what would be.

"I'm going to be fine either way," she said, even though she wasn't sure she believed it.

"You never know how things will work out." Susan walked back around the counter. "Look at Deborah Fortune raising the triplets on her own, thinking all this time that the man she'd loved—the father of her boys—had died." She threw up her hands, her shimmery pink manicure sparkling in the light. "Then suddenly he's back from the grave with a new identity, family and kids crawling out from the woodwork. That had to be a huge shock for all of them."

"But they're getting through," Bianca said. "They have each other."

Susan nodded. "Plus Jayden has that pretty new wife of his from Austin. And Nathan has—"

"It's time to go, EJ," Bianca called, forcing one more feigned smile on her face. She couldn't talk any longer about Nate. Not when she was determined to leave Paseo. If she thought too long about everything Nate had been through and what he meant to her, she'd never find the strength to drive away.

But it wasn't just Nate. The ranch had started to feel like home, and she had one thing to finish before she left Paseo for good.

Because as much as she'd come to love this place, she would never again settle for scraps of a life. Not when she deserved so much more.

Chapter Fifteen

Nate arrived back at the ranch four hours later, hungry and tired but with his head clearer than it had been in weeks. He had to explain to Bianca the full circumstances of Eddie's death. Maybe she'd look at him like the whole tragic incident was his fault, but he had to take the chance. The truth was burning a hole right into his soul, and he couldn't move forward without having everything in the open.

But her car wasn't parked in front of the house. In its place sat Jayden's truck. His brother walked out from the front door as Nate dismounted.

"I've got a problem," Jayden called as he moved to the top of the porch steps. "And I'm hoping you can make it right."

"What's up?" Nate led Cinnamon forward, wondering where Bianca was at the moment. The quicker he got through this conversation with Jayden, the quicker he'd be free to find her.

"It's Sugar."

Nate felt his mouth drop open. "What's wrong? Where is she?"

"In the backyard," Jayden said, crossing his arms over his chest and raising a brow. "With her desolate dog boyfriend."

"What the hell are you talking about?" Nate lifted the Stetson off his head, wiped his brow across the sleeve of his canvas jacket then dropped the hat back into place. "Dogs don't have boyfriends."

"Sugar does," Jayden countered. "EJ's stray, Otis. Since we arrived, that dog has been laying in the backyard, head on his paws, whining. Sugar is beside herself. She can't get him to play or follow her. Apparently she likes being the center of Otis's world, and it's currently killing her. When Sugar is upset, I'm upset. You need to fix it."

"Did you examine Otis?" Nate took a step forward, then remembered Cinnamon was still with him. "Let me put Cinnamon away then I'll come take a look. Maybe he's sick or injured."

"Or heartbroken," Jayden suggested quietly.

"That's ridiculous," Nate said, not bothering to hide his snappish tone. There were times when he was totally in sync with his brothers, and others when it felt like they were speaking another language. "You just said Sugar is with him. EJ is going to freak if something's wrong with that dog." He held out the reins. "You take Cinnamon and I'll try—"

"Where is EJ?" Jayden interrupted, his tone a little too innocent for Nate's taste. "And Bianca?"

"I'm guessing they ran into town. Stop messing around, Jayden. This is serious."

"Is that so?" Jayden tapped a finger against his chin, slowly walking down the steps. "Ran into town or ran away from town? On the drive in, Ariana and I saw a little hatchback with a woman that looked a lot like Bianca on the highway outside Paseo. She was driving like the devil himself was chasing her."

Nate swallowed as his throat went dry. "Take the reins," he commanded.

Jayden kept moving until they were standing boot to boot. "Did you two have a fight?"

"Take the damn reins, Jayden."

His brother closed his fingers around the leather straps, and Nate immediately bounded up the porch steps, through the front door and up the stairs, taking them two at a time. His breath came out in ragged puffs, like he'd just run a marathon by the time he got to the top, more from the panic gripping him than from any kind of physical exertion. He pushed open the door to his mother's bedroom, his heart dropping when he found it empty of Bianca's things.

Grayson's bedroom—the one where EJ was staying—was also back to how it had been before the Shaws had arrived. The perfectly made beds mocked him, as if these past few weeks had been nothing but a dream and he was back to the lonely reality of his regular life.

There was no note from Bianca or clue as to where she'd gone. She'd simply disappeared.

She'd found out the truth about him, and she'd left.

He rubbed at his chest, willing the walls guarding his heart to rebuild themselves. This was an inevitable outcome. Maybe he'd thought they'd have more time, but there was no doubt Nate was supposed to end up alone.

Except he didn't believe that anymore. Bianca had changed everything, and most of all she'd changed him.

He walked back down the stairs only to find Ariana waiting for him at the bottom.

"I'm sorry, Nate," she said gently. "Do you want to—"

"It's fine." He held up a hand. "I'm fine. I've got some work to do in the yard." His voice sounded distant in his own ears. "Good to have you and Jayden back. I'll see you later, okay?"

She nodded. "Okay."

He went out the back of the house, unwilling to have another confrontation with his brother so soon. Nate needed time to readjust his mask into place. To convince himself it didn't matter that she'd left him, so he could go about convincing everyone else.

Otis lifted his head as Nate moved off the back porch, his ears twitching like Nate might help him find EJ.

"He's gone," Nate said as if the dog could understand him. He scratched Sugar behind the ears when she trotted up to him. "You can stay or go, but EJ isn't coming back."

Otis whined softly, then stood and started following Nate as he made his way toward the shed. Sugar barked once but remained in the backyard, trained not to wander far.

"I mean it." Nate glanced over his shoulder at the dog. "You're going to have to deal with the fact that he left you. They left both of us."

He blew out a breath. Hell, he was having a breakup talk with a dog. How pathetic could his life get?

He set his hat on the woodpile near the shed out back and pulled the ax out of a block of wood. A windstorm just before Christmas had felled several large bur oak trees, so he'd quartered them and left the wood by the shed to chop into manageable pieces of firewood. But other jobs had taken priority, and he hadn't made it to the stack of wood yet. Now he welcomed the mindless task.

Physical exertion was the one thing that had kept him sane during his years as a SEAL. When things got to be too much to deal with, he could rely on grueling exercise to work out all the emotions he didn't want to face. So he swung the ax like he had a vendetta against it, welcoming the first twinges of pain in his muscles.

Otis stayed with him, watching his movements from a patch of shade near the front of the shed. By the time he finished chopping, his shirt was drenched and sweat rolled down between his shoulder blades. His arms quivered and he knew by tonight he wouldn't be able to lift his hands above his head. The pain in his body dulled the ache in his heart, although it still remained, an undercurrent of emptiness that seemed to form the base of who he was.

"You know this isn't Alaska?"

Nate drove the ax into a thick piece of oak then turned to his brother. "I'm aware."

Jayden inclined his head toward the shoulder-high pile of wood to Nate's side. "We've got enough firewood there to take us through half a dozen Texas winters."

"Good to be prepared." Nate wiped his brow then began stacking the oak against the side of the shed.

"Are we going to talk about it now?" Jayden asked, pulling a pair of leather work gloves out of his pocket.

"Or do you want me to find some tires for you to throw around?"

"No tires," Nate mumbled.

"Fence posts to dig?" Jayden suggested, walking to the other side of the woodpile and grabbing a piece to stack. "You could run to the county line with a hay bale balanced on your shoulders. I don't know if there's anything else that would beat you down enough to make you happy. CrossFit is all the rage in Ariana's old neighborhood in Austin. Want to try some box jumps? That might make you feel better."

"How about I beat the crap out of you?" Nate asked conversationally. "That would definitely help."

"Ariana wouldn't approve. She likes my face just the way it is."

"And here I thought she had better taste than that," Nate said, ignoring the fact that he and Jayden looked exactly the same.

They worked in silence for several minutes, but finally Nate couldn't stand it any longer.

"She left me," he said, pulling off his gloves and slapping them against his thigh. "I told her I was all in and she left me."

Jayden wiped an arm across his brow. "What exactly does 'all in' mean?"

"You know."

"I don't."

"I was committed."

"As in you love her?"

"As in 'all in,'" Nate repeated.

"Somehow you think that scared her away?"

Nate shook his head. "She found out about Eddie. That scared her. Or disgusted her. I don't know."

"Did you tell her your version or the truth?"

"They're the same thing," Nate answered, glaring at his brother. "Besides, I didn't tell her anything. Her ex-husband showed up here yesterday. He wants her back and was more than happy to explain everything to Bianca so she'd see what bad news I am in her life."

"What exactly did he explain?"

He took a breath, licked his lips then said, "That I killed Eddie."

The string of curses that flowed from Jayden's mouth was so explicit and creative, Nate almost blushed. Nearly twenty years as a SEAL and he was actually learning a few new phrases thanks to his brother.

"Whoa, there." He held up his hands, palms out. "I might not like how the guy treated Bianca, but she was going to find out eventually. I should have been the one to tell her in the first place."

"Birth order," Jayden muttered through clenched teeth, stalking away a few paces then turning back to Nate. "That's the only thing that explains it."

"What are you talking about?" Nate scrubbed a hand over his jaw.

"Your stupidity. It must be a result of our birth order." Jayden pointed an angry finger at Nate. "I was first and Grayson next. You came last, so it stands to reason you got cheated on brain cells. As in—" he leaned closer "—you have none."

Nate scoffed. "Who took your physics final senior year? I did. Don't talk to me about which one of us got the brains. There's no question I did."

"Then give me another excuse for acting like such an idiot. You did *not* kill Eddie Shaw. You tried to save him and could have died in the process."

Nate shut his eyes as images from that last mission assaulted him. "If I'd gotten there sooner, he'd still be alive, Jayden. If I'd taken him out first—"

"You saved four men that night, Nate. Eddie chose to be the last one extracted from the ridge."

"I couldn't even recover his body," Nate whispered, shame making his voice crack. "I had to leave him there."

"He would have understood," Jayden said quietly.

Nate met his brother's gaze. It was like looking in a mirror, a reflection of himself, only stronger and more sure. Nate couldn't be sure of anything at the moment. Since he'd returned from Afghanistan he'd been like a boat in the middle of the ocean being buffeted by waves from every side and unable to get his bearings. He'd thought he'd started righting the ship with Bianca and EJ in his life, but now he was lost again.

"How do you know?" he asked, unable to stop hoping for something that might make the world make sense.

"Because he was a soldier. He knew the risks."

"I was supposed to have his back. We took care of each other for almost twenty years. He was ready to get out—to have a real life—and I took that from him."

"The men who fired the guns and launched that final grenade took that from him." Jayden stepped closer. "What if things had been reversed? If you'd been the one injured, would you have wanted Eddie to save you first?"

"Of course not." Nate felt simmering anger rising inside him, hot and sharp. "But I never would have gotten myself into that position." He shook his head. "I told him we needed to wait for backup. He insisted on going in with just our squadron. He was so damn stubborn. Then it all went to hell."

"Which was *not* your fault," Jayden insisted.

"You don't understand. Someone has to take the blame. I should never have agreed to it. I had a gut feeling. And I told Eddie—" He broke off, regret choking him.

"What did you tell him?"

"I said 'you got us into this, you better get us out.' The way he did that was by sacrificing himself."

"He made the choice, Nate. He knew the risks."

"I'm sick of the anger and guilt. It's like Gerald Robinson, you know? All our lives we thought our dad was dead. Only to find out he was in Texas all along and had his own family. It makes me so damn mad, Jayden. It makes me feel guilty that I didn't push Mom for more information on him when we were teenagers and I got curious."

"You remember what happened when we were younger and I wouldn't stop asking her about our dad."

Nate gave a sharp nod. "She cried."

"It was awful. She didn't want to talk about him."

"But what if I'd demanded to know his identity and I'd tracked him down and figured out that Jerome Fortune had faked his own death? That would have changed so much for all of us."

"You had no way of knowing," Jayden said quietly. "Just like you had no way of knowing what was going to happen in Afghanistan. I get your need to take care of people, Nate, and I admire it. I do. But you're not some sort of all-seeing, all-knowing superhero. You're a man who makes mistakes, but you try your best." He paused, then added, "I think you have that in common with Gerald Robinson."

Nate shook his head. "I don't have anything in common with our father."

"You do if you let Bianca walk away. The same way Gerald let Mom go. I think he really loved her. There's a good chance he still might. But a lot of water has passed under that bridge. You've got time on your side." Jayden made a show of checking his watch. "About three hours based on when we saw her."

Nate threw up his hands. "What am I supposed to do?"

"You could start by calling and apologizing for being the biggest ass on the planet."

"She left."

"Or you pushed her away."

"I've got work to do." Nate grabbed another piece of wood. "No more talking."

"You're not meant to be alone. You deserve way more happiness than you're allowing yourself to have." Jayden shoved his gloves into his back pocket. "It's scary as hell to put yourself out there, but trust me when I tell you it's worth it in the end. Think about it."

Otis perked up his ears and watched Jayden walk away.

"Feel free to go after him," Nate told the dog. "He's heading back to the house. You know Sugar will be waiting. No sense in both of us being miserable."

The dog inclined his head then gave a soft whimper and lowered his body to the ground once more.

Nathan stacked the wood then moved on to shoring up a few loose pieces of siding on the back of the shed. At the rate he was going, he'd be caught up with projects around the ranch by the end of the week. He couldn't allow himself to stop. If he didn't keep moving, the heartache of losing Bianca would overwhelm him.

Ariana brought him a plate of food to the barn when he missed dinner.

He mumbled, "Thank you," but didn't slow his pace.

"It's not too late," she said gently before she left him alone again.

Alone.

He'd been alone for so damn long. It felt right when he'd first come back from Afghanistan. He needed the time by himself to readjust to regular life. But he'd used his guilt over the last mission as an excuse for staying isolated.

Until Bianca had broken through all of his walls.

Around midnight he returned to the darkened house. He knew Jayden and Ariana were worried about him, and while Nate appreciated the concern, he didn't know how to assure them he'd be fine. It felt like he'd never be fine again.

He'd gone into town for supplies and gotten a text from Bianca saying she'd stopped for the night near Stallworth, a small town about four hours from Paseo. She wasn't ready to talk but didn't want him to worry.

As angry as she might be, his Bianca couldn't help her caring nature. It was one of things he lov—

No. He couldn't go there right now.

He showered and put on clean clothes, but instead of making his way to his own room, he sat on the bed where EJ had slept. It was impossible to imagine waking up tomorrow without the boy's enthusiasm and energy setting the tone for the day.

He smoothed his hand over the quilt, stilling when

it hit a lump under the covers. He reached under and pulled out Roscoe, EJ's beloved stuffed animal. The boy cuddled the raggedy bear to his chest all night as he slept. How would Bianca ever get him to settle without it?

Nate ran down to the kitchen, grabbing the phone from the wall and punched in her number, the teddy bear finally giving him an excuse to reach out to her. The call went straight to voicemail.

She and EJ were out there someplace, and Nate had to find them.

Chapter Sixteen

Bianca was half asleep on the chair outside her room when the bright lights of a familiar silver truck pulled into the motel's parking lot.

It was almost four in the morning, and the world was quiet around her other than the sound of the diesel engine. She'd come out of her room when she couldn't sleep, afraid her tossing and turning would wake EJ, who'd taken hours to finally settle without his teddy bear. The cool air and the slight breeze scented with impending rain had settled her enough to where she didn't feel like she was going to break down and begin sobbing.

Emotion gripped her again and she clutched at her throat, feeling like a deer in headlights as the truck turned into the empty parking spot next to her small car. The engine died a moment later, and Nate emerged, wearing a white T-shirt and jeans, his hair sticking up around his head like he'd been compulsively running his fingers through it.

Bianca gripped the edges of the chair to keep from launching herself at him. What was the point of trying to become an independent woman if she melted into a puddle the minute a man came after her?

He'd come for her. That had to mean something, right?

But as he walked toward her, his eyes were unreadable in the faint glow from the motel's neon sign.

"Fancy meeting you here," she said, trying for a jaunty tone.

"You forgot this."

Bianca gave a choked sigh when Nate brought his hand from behind his back to reveal EJ's beloved teddy bear. She stood and reached for the bear, her skin tingling when her fingers grazed Nate's.

"Thank you," she whispered. "You wouldn't believe what a challenge bedtime was without Roscoe."

"I found him under the covers of EJ's bed."

She brushed her fingers over the stuffed animal's worn fur. "I can't believe he forgot to pack him or that I didn't check before we got in the car. Eddie gave him to me the first time he deployed. He said the bear would keep me safe when he couldn't. It's been the only stuffed animal EJ ever cared about, and I always believed that meant something. Roscoe was our connection to Eddie and—" She drew in a deep breath as she looked up at him. "It's the middle of the night, Nate."

"Technically, it's very early morning," he replied.

"Okay," she agreed. "But you drove all this way to deliver Roscoe?"

"You left him." He paused, then added, "You left me."

She felt her mouth drop open. "I couldn't stay. Not after our conversation. How did you find me?"

"Stallworth is a metropolis compared to Paseo, but it's still a small town. You texted that you'd stopped here for the night. As much of an early bird as EJ is, I didn't think you'd get on the road again until daylight, which meant I had a few hours. I checked all the hotels and motels until I saw your car in the parking lot."

"You came all this way to bring EJ his stuffed animal?"

Something flared in Nate's eyes. It was a mix of regret and hope that lanced Bianca's heart. "I came to apologize for how I handled our last conversation and for not telling you the truth about Eddie when you first arrived. You had a right to know."

"I need to know *everything*," she said, unable to stop herself from reaching for him. He flinched when her hand gripped his arm, like her touch was charged, but he didn't pull away. She wouldn't have been able to stand it if he'd pulled away. She inclined her head toward the closed door behind her. "I'd invite you in but EJ's a light sleeper." She gestured to the concrete step that led from the walkway in front of the row of hotel rooms to the parking lot. "Would you like to have a seat on my makeshift porch?"

Nate studied her for a moment then nodded.

She let go of his arm as they sat. Somehow she knew whatever Nate was going to tell her would be easier if they weren't touching.

But the urge was strong to climb into his lap and bury her face in the crook of his neck. She'd only been away from the ranch for half a day, but she missed Nate like they'd been separated for months.

She could feel the tension pouring off him and knew the next few minutes would determine her future and whether she'd be moving forward with or without Nate Fortune.

"Tell me," she whispered.

He closed his eyes as a quiver passed through him. "Eddie was my brother in every way that matters. I never imagined a world without him, and we'd been through some pretty serious stuff over the years. But there was something that felt off to me on our last mission. Our commanding officer wanted action, but the intel wasn't clear and it felt like we were rushing it." He looked at her, his dark eyes filled with regret. "From the start I knew things were going to go bad."

"But you continued, anyway?"

"We were behind enemy lines but so close to finding one of the terrorist cell leaders. Our unit wanted to send a message. Eddie was adamant we move forward. He was worried we were going to let the bad guy slip through our fingers again. It's hard to understand, but there's so much time on a mission spent waiting. So many close calls when you almost get the enemy but you're too late. Guys get antsy. We were SEALs because we could produce, Bianca. We were good at what we were trained to do. Eddie wanted a last chance at making something happen before he got out for good. Whether it was another feather in his cap or to prove to himself he still had what it took…" He shook his head. "We'll never know, but all hell broke loose when we came over that ridge."

"Oh, Nate."

"It was an ambush. We managed to hold them off for several hours, waiting for a rescue force, but a few of our guys got injured." He shrugged. "There was a lot of gunfire. My shoulder. Eddie's leg. He insisted I move everyone down into a ravine where there was more shelter in the rocks. He was going to cover us."

"That sounds like Eddie," she said with a small smile. "He wanted to have everyone's back."

"He had mine that night," Nate told her without hesitation. "Most of us were okay, but there several who were injured. I got three of them out then went back for the one who lost his right leg from the knee down, Dave. I had to carry him out. I got him up to the extraction point and planned to go back for Eddie. The explosion happened as I got to the bottom of the ridge." He pressed his palms to the sides of his head, like it was pounding and he couldn't make it stop. "The hillside had been blown apart. He was gone. I didn't get to him in time."

"You tried," she whispered, wiping at the tears streaming down her face. She couldn't stand the distance between them any longer and scooted closer, gripping Nate's biceps. Needing to connect herself to him. He immediately lifted his arm and wrapped it around her shoulder, pulling her closer.

"The extraction happened so fast." Bianca could hear the tears in his voice. "There was nothing I could do except leave." He took a shaky breath. "I couldn't even bring him home."

"What happened to the other SEAL?" she asked. "You said his name was Dave, right?"

Nate nodded. "He's back in Michigan with his family. He's got a wife and two young girls. I've talked to him a couple of times. It's been an adjustment, but he was fitted for an artificial leg about a year ago and now he's coaching football at the local high school."

"And his daughters have their dad with them."

"Yeah."

Bianca tipped up her head and kissed the underside of Nate's jaw. "Eddie would have wanted that."

"But I failed," Nate insisted.

"Don't say that." Bianca put a finger over his lips when he would have argued. "Don't say that to me ever again. You were a hero, Nate. If Eddie were here he'd tell you the same thing. I don't blame you for what happened to him, and it's past time you stop blaming yourself."

"Then why did you leave?"

She sighed. "I was scared. Not by what Brett told me or listening to you trying to take responsibility for Eddie's death. I know you, Nathan Fortune." She lowered her hand and placed it over his heart. "I know you in here. But I was afraid you didn't care the same way I did."

"I told you I was all in," he said, as if that explained everything.

She rolled her eyes. "Which sounds like you're playing poker or something. I asked you to talk to me about something difficult and you walked away. You wouldn't let me in. It felt like you weren't willing to fight for us. One thing I've realized in the past few weeks—something being on the ranch and in Paseo helped me realize—is that I'm worth fighting for. I needed a little space to figure out what was going to happen next." She felt one side of her mouth curve up as hope, buoyant and light, bloomed in her chest. "And what happened is you came after me."

"Always," he told her.

Her heart stilled. "Always?"

He shifted so they were facing each other and cupped

her cheeks in his hands. "I came back to Paseo because I needed a home to make me whole again. *You* are my home, Bianca Shaw. I felt it the moment I opened the door to find you on the other side. It was like the universe sent you to me so I'd have a reason to deal with all the crap I couldn't stand to face on my own." He pressed his mouth to hers, the touch gentle but firm. "I love you. And I'm all in with you. Forever if you'll have me."

"Mr. Nate?"

Bianca turned to see EJ in the motel doorway, sleepily rubbing his eyes.

"Hey, buddy, look what Mr. Nate brought to you." She held up the ragged teddy bear, and EJ ran forward.

"Roscoe!"

EJ took the bear then wrapped his arms around Nate's neck. Nate pulled him onto his lap so the boy was balanced between the two of them. Bianca thought her heart might burst from the happiness of the moment.

She met Nate's eyes and couldn't wait any longer. "I love you, too," she whispered over EJ's head. "I want—"

"I told Mommy not to leave," EJ interrupted matter-of-factly.

"It's okay," Nate assured him. "Your mommy needed a little time-out, but I'm hoping you both will come back to the ranch real soon."

"Like now?" EJ asked hopefully, his brown eyes wide as he looked at Bianca.

"Now seems like a good time to me," she said with a smile.

EJ jumped up and bounded toward the motel room. "I'll pack," he called over his shoulder, then stopped in his tracks when a dog bark sounded.

"I forgot I had a copilot with me," Nate said, standing

then pulling Bianca up with him. He opened the passenger door of the truck, and Otis hopped out, trotting over to give EJ a sloppy lick on the cheek.

"I missed you, boy," EJ whispered then looked from Bianca to Nate. "We can keep him, right?"

Nate chuckled. "I don't think Otis would have it any other way."

EJ grinned before disappearing into the room.

"I told you SEALs are big teddy bears at heart," Bianca said.

"Will you come back to the ranch for good?" Nate asked, lacing his fingers with hers. "I love you and I want to spend the rest of my life showing you how much. I want you and EJ and I to be a family."

She leaned in and brushed her lips across his. "We already are, Nate. We're yours. Forever."

Epilogue

"I still owe you a honeymoon, Mrs. Fortune."

Bianca rested her head on Nate's shoulder as he wrapped an arm around her waist. "I can't imagine any place I'd rather be than right here."

It was almost two weeks since she'd returned to the ranch, and Bianca knew she'd come home for good. They'd gotten married three days after applying for a license in the county courthouse. Bianca and Nate both understood how precious life could be and neither of them wanted to wait to join their lives together. As she'd told him at the motel, they were already a family.

The wedding might have been short and simple, but nothing had made Bianca happier than becoming Nate's wife.

They'd celebrated with Jayden and Ariana, who'd left soon after for a research trip to Fort Worth. Now they sat on the porch swing Nate had crafted for Bianca—

with EJ's help—as a wedding present, gently rocking as EJ and Otis played fetch in the backyard.

"I'm glad to hear it, sweetheart." Nate dropped a tender kiss on the top of her head. "I'll be counting my lucky stars for the rest of my life that you found me."

"I think we have Eddie to thank. He always said you'd take care of me if he couldn't."

"Did he also mention that I was going to end up needing you like I need the heart beating in my chest?"

She smiled. "I don't think he understood that part."

"Well, it's more than true." Nate's arm tightened around her waist. "I wish I could promise you things will be perfect, Busy Bee. I'm working on it."

"*We're* working on it," she corrected. "And I don't need perfect. I want you, Nate, and everything that comes along with loving you."

"Everything? Are you sure?"

She held up her left hand. "Sure as this ring on my finger." The diamond sparkled, set in a delicate band of gold with a subtle filigree design on either side. It had been Cynthia Thompson's wedding ring, and Bianca was beyond proud to wear something that had belonged to the woman who'd taken in Deborah Fortune when she'd most needed help.

Deborah had been the one to suggest Nate give Bianca the ring when the two of them had called to tell her about their whirlwind engagement. Nate's mom had been sweet and gracious and Bianca was looking forward to meeting her new mother-in-law when Grayson was on his next break from the rodeo circuit and his sponsorship commitments.

"I need to show you something," Nate said, his tone

suddenly serious. He shifted, pulling a folded envelope from his back pocket. "This came today in the mail."

Bianca slipped the one-page letter from the envelope, felt her jaw drop open as she read it. "Do you think it's a scam?"

Nate shook his head. "Jayden already told me about his suspicions that Gerald's father, Julius Fortune, held just as many secrets as his son. Ariana uncovered something while working on the *Becoming a Fortune* series last year. I don't know who this Schuyler woman is, but if she is some kind of a con artist, there are Fortunes with a lot more money and power than me she could have gone after."

"But she contacted you," Bianca said with a nod. "In the letter she said she's looking for an honest opinion."

"Why didn't she just call?"

Bianca laughed at that. "You're not exactly the easiest person to reach out here, Nate Fortune."

"I like it that way," he said and took the letter from her, refolding it and putting it back in the envelope. "All I want is a simple life…"

"But complications just keep showing up on your doorstep." Bianca smiled and tipped up her head to kiss him. "EJ and I were a complication."

"You two are the greatest blessings of my life."

EJ let out a whoop of delight at that moment as Otis caught the tennis ball in midair. "Did you see that, Mommy?"

"He's getting to be a heck of a ball catcher," she called.

"Because you've got a heck of an arm," Nate added. "Hey, EJ, what do you think about looking into a T-ball team come spring? There's a community center in the next town over that runs a rec league for kids."

"Awesome," the boy shouted, and the happiness on his small face made Bianca's heart melt.

"Complicated or not," she told Nate, "we'll get through it together."

"I can handle anything." Nate chuckled. "Even a whole new batch of Fortunes, as long as you're with me."

She closed her eyes as he kissed her again, then rested his forehead against hers. "Forever and always," she whispered.

* * * * *

Don't miss the next installment of
THE FORTUNES OF TEXAS:
THE RULEBREAKERS

Carlo Mendoza always thought he had the market cornered on charm, something that comes in very handy in his job at the family winery. But when he meets the alluring Schuyler Fortunado, he learns quickly that she's a force to be reckoned with—and yes, she's also a Fortune!
One with sexy powers of persuasion . . .

Look for
NO ORDINARY FORTUNE
by USA TODAY *Bestselling Author Judy Duarte*
On sale February 2018,
wherever Mills & Boon books and ebooks are sold.

MILLS & BOON®

A sneak peek at next month's titles...

In stores from 11th January 2018:

- **The Spanish Millionaire's Runaway Bride** – Susan Meier *and* **No Ordinary Fortune** – Judy Duarte
- **Stranded with Her Greek Tycoon** – Kandy Shepherd *and* **An Engagement for Two** – Marie Ferrarella

In stores from 25th January 2018:

- **Reunited with Her Italian Billionaire** – Nina Singh *and* **A Bride for Liam Brand** – Joanna Sims
- **Falling for His Convenient Queen** – Therese Beharrie *and* **A Soldier in Conard County** – Rachel Lee

Just can't wait?
Buy our books online before they hit the shops!
www.millsandboon.co.uk

Also available as eBooks.

MILLS & BOON®

Coming next month

THE SPANISH MILLIONAIRE'S RUNAWAY BRIDE
Susan Meier

She laughed again. "I can't even figure out how to explain running from my wedding. It's not as if I was such a great prize myself."

"You are a great prize." The words came out soft and filled with regret that her dad had skewed the way she saw herself.

She stopped at her door, but she didn't use her key card to open it. She glanced at Riccardo, her pale pink face illuminated by the light beside her door. "I'm a twenty-five-year-old woman who doesn't know who she is."

"You have to know you're beautiful."

She caught his gaze. Her long black lashes blinked over sad blue eyes. "Physical things fade."

"You're pretty in here," he countered, touching her chest just above the soft swell of her breasts. "When you're sixty, eighty, a hundred, you'll still be compassionate."

She shook her head. "You don't know that. We just met. Aside from the fact that I ran from my wedding and my dad's a bit of a control freak, you don't know much of anything about me."

Silence hung between them as they stared into each other's eyes. The warmth in her big blue orbs touched his heart, but the lift of her lips sparked a small fire in his belly. Everything male inside him awoke. The urge to kiss her tumbled through him.

He should have turned, walked the few steps to his own room and gone inside. Gotten away from her. Instead, he stayed right where he was.

Continue reading
THE SPANISH MILLIONARE'S
RUNAWAY BRIDE
Susan Meier

Available next month
www.millsandboon.co.uk

LET'S TALK
Romance

For exclusive extracts, competitions
and special offers, find us online:

Or get in touch on 0844 844 1351*

For all the latest titles coming soon, visit
millsandboon.co.uk/nextmonth

Want even more
ROMANCE?

Join our bookclub today!

'Mills & Boon books, the perfect way to escape for an hour or so.'

Miss W. Dyer

'Excellent service, promptly delivered and very good subscription choices.'

Miss A. Pearson

'You get fantastic special offer and the chance to get books before they hit the shops'

Mrs V Hall

**Visit millsandbook.co.uk/Bookclub
and save on brand new books.**

MILLS & BOON